RALLEN—

planet of legend, hidden deep within the galactic starways. Few knew where Rallen was located but Skeen was determined to become one of those select few because she was almost certain that on Rallen she would find what she sought—the last surviving members of the Ykx.

But to find Rallen, Skeen first had to find a low-down con artist called Rostico Burn, a man whose trail led right to the heart of Pillory, the Empire's top security, inescapable prison world.

Skeen didn't know or care what had landed Burn on Pillory, for time to find the Ykx was running out fast. And that meant there wasn't even a second to waste talking Burn free of the planet. She'd have to break him free instead—even if it brought every star cruiser in the region rocketing down on her trail!

SKEEN'S SEARCH

JO CLAYTON

DAW BOOKS, INC.
DONALD A. WOLLHEIM, PUBLISHER

1633 Broadway, New York, NY 10019

DAW Book Collectors No. 728.

First Printing, December 1987

1 2 3 4 5 6 7 8 9

PRINTED IN THE U.S.A.

Abandoned on Kildun Aalda in the city Chukunsa (she doesn't know why but suspects her companion Tibo ran off with her ship), running low on credit, Skeen sneaks out of the city looking for a hidden ruin she can plunder and thus buy her way off Aalda so she can go after Tibo and roast him over a slow fire. The Honjiukum who control access to such ruins set a saayungka pack after her and chase her into a dry-bones valley. She is captured by a force that draws her into a doorway that turns out to be a Gate into another Universe.

While exploring the new world she lands on (Mistommerk), Skeen is drawn into a conflict between two shapeshifting Min (natives of Mistommerk), twin sisters called Telka and Timka, then discovers that the Gate has closed on her and she can't get back to Kildun Aalda with the loot she has gathered. Timka suggests she seek out the Ykx who were the original makers of the Gate and presumably knew how to work it.

Pursued by Telka and later by vengeful Chalarosh assassins, collecting an assortment of companions (a Balayar Scholar, four Aggitj exiles, a Skirrik youth intent on winning his wedding jet, a Chalarosh boy who's the last of his clan, the others have been wiped out in a feud), Skeen and Timka search for the last Gather of Ykx on Mistommerk. During the journey Skeen discovers a connection between the Ykx of Mistommerk and Rallen, a world populated by Ykx in her own universe. The Ykx are dying out on Mistommerk. They need new blood to keep existing here. Skeen uses this knowledge to buy their help opening the Stranger's Gate.

Down to a handful of silver, Skeen and company (a new member in it, an Ykx called Lipitero), leave Lake Sydo and go downriver to a city called Cida Fennakin. While they wait there for a ship's Captain (and owner), Maggí Solitaire, they earn their living in various ways while Skeen hunts for someone local and unloved to burgle for traveling funds. The owner of the Inn (the Funor Ashon outcast Angelsin Yagan) where they were staying got ambitious and tries to sell them to a number of groups (Telka and her fanatics, Chalarosh assassins, Fennakin Funor slavers) interested in them, drugs them, throws them into dungeon cells while she negotiates for the price she wants. They escape, hold Angelsin prisoner until Maggí Solitaire arrives. Everyone but Skeen, Timka and one of the Aggitj exiles, Domi, sails with Maggí; they stay behind to get the coin to pay passage for the company.

In the house of Nochsyon Tod thē slaver, Skeen is attacked by guard dogs, one hand badly torn; she manages to put darts in them and gets away with the loot. After some more difficulties she and Timka reach the small boat Domi has acquired with them and take off downriver after Maggí. The bitewound throws Skeen into a deep fever; even after they reach Maggí's ship she does not respond to care and what medicines Maggí has. Skeen sinks deeper and deeper and comes close to dying. Pegwai the Balayar Scholar and Timka get together and agree they have to cut the hand off. They use Skeen's laser cutter, sear the wound; that works well enough to bring Skeen back to consciousness and she uses her own antibiotics to suppress the infections, recovers quickly and begins the process of learning to live one-handed.

They run across Chalarosh seeking to kill the Boy, Sea Min after their hides, especially that of Timka, angry Nagamar in coastal swamps, members of the Company peeling off to tend their own affairs until only Skeen, Timka and Lipitero are left. They continue moving toward the Gate, finally coming against Telka and her small army of followers who are waiting in ambush for them as they reach the Mountains and near the Stranger's Gate. Lipitero the Ykx looses the Ever-Hunger on the Min army, opens the Gate. They elude the Min, the

Ever-Hunger and jump the Gate. Telka is waiting there, attacks Timka (both are in the shapes of big cats, nearly identical big cats), Skeen darts both of them. When she looks closer, she knows Timka; with Lipitero's help she tosses the other cat back through the Gate and Lipitero closes it down. Tibo is waiting there; he took Skeen's ship off to protect it from Abel Cidder who was nosing around, came back to Kildun Aalda to pick up Skeen and has been hunting for her since. The four of them (Skeen, Tibo, Timka and Lipitero) slip back into Chukunsa and off the world, on their way to find Rallen and persuade Rallen Ykx to follow Lipitero back through the Gate.

SO. WHERE ARE WE NOW?
BETWEEN THIS BOOK AND THE LAST, SKEEN
HAS SPENT A MONTH AT A TANK FARM
REGROWING HER HAND AND HAVING THE
LAST OF HER CREDIT REMOVED WITH SURGICAL
PRECISION. TIBO HAS BEEN BORROWING
AGAINST FUTURE PROFITS AND OLD FAVORS,
SCOOTING ABOUT HERE AND THERE CHECKING
WITH HIS SOURCES FOR INFORMATION ABOUT
RALLEN AND ABEL CIDDER. TIMKA HAS NESTED
INTO ONE OF PICAREFY'S SLEEP TEACHING
PODS AND HAS BEEN PLOWING THROUGH
INFORMATION SUMMARIES ABOUT THIS
UNIVERSE SHE'S LANDED IN HALF-UNWILLING,
TRYING TO CONVINCE HERSELF SHE CAN
LEARN TO LIKE IT. LIPITERO AND PICAREFY
HAVE BEEN ENGAGED IN INTENSE DIALOG, THE
YKX HAS JUST ABOUT MOVED INTO THE
SHIP'S WORKSHOP AND HAS BEEN CREATING
ITEMS FOR PICAREFY'S PLEASURE AND HER
OWN, SOMETHING TO PASS THE TIME WHILE
THEY WAIT FOR SKEEN. IF YOU NEED
REMINDING ABOUT EVENTS IN PREVIOUS
BOOKS, WELL, TURN BACK A FEW PAGES
AND READ THE UPDATE, THE REST OF YOU
FEEL FREE TO DIVE RIGHT IN.

PART I: THE SEARCH

SCENE: THE BUZZARD'S ROOST, SUNDARI PIT.
A long oval room filled with tables, glass cases, crates, bales, alcoves with viewscreens and reasonably comfortable chairs (several not made for bipeds' behinds); shelves cover most wallspace, gaps where things have been taken away, otherwise a chaotic collection of small items. The room is cluttered, dusty to a reasonable degree, but gives an overall impression of richness, variety, the excitement of maybe-treasures. It is a very good room to be in.

SKEEN ENTERS.
She is followed by a small stubby 'bot carrying the things she is here to sell or put out on consignment.

Skeen picked her way through the clutter on the floor to the small cleared space tucked into one end of the oval, shielded from view by some ceiling high shelves, the 'bot whirring frustration behind her as it rose on extensible braces and drew its wheels into a tighter configuration, balancing precariously as it turned and twisted along the narrow paths between boxes, bales, and piles of miscellaneous debris. She rounded a set of rickety shelves, stopped and stood, hands clasped behind her, watching the solid old man probing at a crusted object with an antique steel tooth scraper. He was a big man with broad, blunt-fingered hands that should have been clumsy but weren't. "Ta, Buzzard," she said.

He looked up, made a sucking sound, tongue against teeth. "So so," he said, a wheeze in his voice. An instant decrepitude slicked over him as he got ready for hard bargaining. "Back already?"

"Dropping by. Got a few things you might find interesting."

He set the conglomerate aside, tucked the scraper into his shirt pocket. "So so, what you got?"

Skeen snapped her fingers. The 'bot whirred past her, stopped beside the desk, opened and extended his top-knot pack into a long thin display shelf, with the contents tucked into transparent boxes, visible but temporarily untouchable. "Nothing very old, but interesting, that you'll give me once you see this collection." She clicked open a box, took out a heavy gold chain, solid links alternating with open circles set with odd dull gems; spreading it on the desk before him, she said, "Take a close look at the chasing. Hasn't been any work like that since the Nagamar worlds were ashed. You know I prefer to provide onsite fots and anecdotal background, but that's not possible this time; you can name me as source for whatever that's worth, but my name's the only documentation you'll get . . . um . . . I can say this, I've found a tiny remnant of Nagamar still alive." She grinned at him. "And a couple other remnants. Pallah and Skirrik." After running a soft cloth over them, she set the Poet's swords down beside the chain. "These items are for sale outright." 'She began setting out the bijouterie and bric-a-brac she'd picked up with the swords and slid smoothly into the cross talk of bargaining.

Skeen settled into the chair the Buzzard summoned for her and sighed. "You're a hard man, Buzzard."

He looked up from the film he was wrapping about a sword, grunted and went back to twisting the film tight. "Hot air and foolishness," he said. "You screwed your price out of me, no pity for a poor old man trying to make a meager living." Eyes the color of dried blood laughed at her. "What else you got?"

Skeen brought out the lumpy objects from Coraish Gather, set them on the desk.

"So so. Rallen work. Now where did you get that, shtoshi-mi?" He took up the lump, let it warm in his hands. The dun blob changed; opaline colors glowed and flowed along the mutating forms, primarily green and gold with flickers and sudden flares of purple and crimson, no configuration of shape and color ever exactly repeated the whole time he held the blob. He clicked tongue against teeth. "Consignment, percentage for me?"

When she nodded, he relaxed. "A wonder," he said, "much better than its mates you saw here a while back."

"Not Rallen work."

His eyes narrowed to slits. "Another remnant? Rumor says you went to Kildun Aalda, looking for a way to take on the Junks." He set the change work down; it began to fade and after a few minutes was once more imitating a squashed dun turd. "You have a source?"

"Buzzard, now I ask you, am I going to tell you or anyone?"

"Hmm. Are you?"

"Hard. Hard. Adamantine man. Look at this first." She began spreading the Min jewelry across the desk, putting the sweetamber pieces together in one corner. "You've never seen any work exactly like these or heard of it." She lifted one of the larger pieces of sweetamber. "Warm this in your hand, no, it's not going to shift shape, hold it awhile then take a sniff." She watched his face, laughed when his eyes snapped open and his breathing turned ragged. "Doesn't matter the species, as long as they have a minimum body warmth and live in an oxygen atmosphere, you get an effect. I've been told it's different for different species." She shrugged. "I wouldn't know about that. Where I got it everyone seemed to prize the stuff."

"Where you got it?"

"I can just about guarantee these items are uniques. Nothing like them coming in from anywhere anyone can get to, nothing about to pop up either, in any market, not for the current century anyway. You can offer them as uniques and be ninety-nine point nine percent et cetera sure that assertion won't come back to haunt you."

"Playing games, Skeen."

"Sure. Why not. It's all a game, isn't it, one you enjoy more than most."

"This collection, anything to do with Rallen?"

"Nothing."

He raised scraggly brows, the freckles on his forehead diving into heavy wrinkles. "Hot?"

"Cold as Winter on the Far Side. Mostly a fee for honest labor. Don't be like that, it's true enough. The rest, well, the previous owners hadn't a hope in hell of coming after it."

He began gathering up the jewelry and replacing it in its boxes. "Uniques. Hmmm. Going to take some doing, getting the word out. I don't know if I want to tie myself up like that. No, not for less than a quarter. Years, Skeen, going to take years out of my life and that's the truth. This kind of thing isn't bargain counter, you know. Can't possibly take it on for less than a quarter share. My overhead is something fierce, keeps me running in place just to have a roof over my head. Got other business you know, the only way it's worthwhile for me to handle these, I'll have to arrange an auction. You got any idea what it's going to take to get folk together who can afford to bid on these?" He went on with the gentle flow of words as he worked to extract the largest commission he could tease out of her. His hands caressed the delicate pieces, his eyes flickered from the amber to the change sculpture to the polished woods set in filigree of gold, silver and translucent opalescent shell, moving over them as lovingly as his stubby fingers, though he tried to control his appreciation since his desire for them gave Skeen an edge in the game. Skeen settled finally at eight percent of purchase price. Buzzard sat back and sighed with satisfaction. "I know five who'll bid against each other till they drop."

Skeen snapped her fingers. The 'bot folded itself together, hiked itself up and rolled away. She got to her feet, watched until it reached the Roost's exit and squatted there to wait for her. In her chair again, she stroked a forefinger along the crease beside her mouth. "Like to earn another percent?"

"So so. That's quite a fee. For what?"

"Rallen. Tell me who sold you that Rallen ware."

"Aaah." He rocked in his chair, fingers tapping a shapeless tune on the arms. Then he nodded. "Fair enough. Tall, skinny, dark boy. If he swallowed a raisin, it'd show. Hadn't seen him before, but he was no novice. He knew pretty well what the stuff was worth and kept chipping at me until he got something near his price. He gave in a hair too soon, he was still that raw then, wouldn't do it these days." He stared at the stained ceiling a moment, brought his head up. "Rostico Burn," he said. "Rumor runs he came out of the Cluster with Imperials on his tail. Not unlike another skinny kid I knew some half a hundred years ago."

"Any idea where I can find him?"

"I can ask around. You want me to do that?"

"Be quiet about it."

"Skeen, you know the low road. Word is already out you're interested in Rallen. Tibo was busy while you were getting that hand regrown. Been half a hundred rumors zipping about since he asked the first question."

"Cidder?"

"I don't talk to the man. None of my folk are on his payroll, I make sure of that. But he's got noses everywhere else. The minute I move on Rostico Burn, he'll know it. Tie it up with Rallen and go after the boy himself. He's really hot to get his hands on you, haul you back to the Cluster. You've rubbed his nose in it a time or two too often, Skeen. One of these days he might even risk going after you inside a Pit. Why do you keep fishing in the Cluster? Plenty of other places for Roon raids. I tell you, when you scooped out the Imperial Museum and got off with the Undying's favorite bits, shtoshi-mi, for a while there I was sure we were going to have Imperial marines scraping us down to bedrock. There were a lot of folk who stopped breathing until you let the Empire ransom its artifacts. There was even some talk of shunning you, but that went away when the fuss died down and the Pits could look back from peace and enjoy your twisting the Empire's tail. I doubt you know how close you came. Hunh, I doubt you give a fist full a shit. You ought to, old girl. Next time you do something like that, you could find yourself without any friends left."

Skeen shook her head. "I know. I know. But don't you forget, I'm Cluster born and Empire bred. Every time I hit them and raise a welt, it's like ice on a burn."

"Ice . . . hmm . . . you can't afford. Give it a rest."

"I'll think about it."

**SHOOTOUT ON STARLONG WAY.
TAKE ONE LIBIDINOUS MALE PIMP WITH
DELUSIONS OF GRANDEUR AND A LONG
RECORD OF KILLS, PUT TOGETHER WITH
ONE DELICATE LOVELY SHAPESHIFTER WHO
DOESN'T KNOW WHAT'S HAPPENING BUT
ISN'T ABOUT TO GO BACK TO DEPENDING
ON ANYONE. NOW. IS THAT EXCITEMENT?
DON'T BLINK. YOU MIGHT MISS THE ACTION.
or
WELCOME TO THE PITS.**

Timka strolled along a street that continually astonished
her, linked tiles springy underfoot, matte black rectan-
gles on a metal web, clean and sweet-smelling (that astonished her until she saw the tiny 'bots that scurried
about like mice sucking up trash almost before it fluttered down, and the larger 'bots that trotted off with
drunken sleepers, dead bodies and anything else too big
for the mice), a black sky overhead with occasional flickers of the forcefield that kept the air in and a glittering
spray of stars. Moving around her on the street and
gliding past her on the slidewalk in the middle of the
street was a noisy eclectic mix of folk who seemed to
share nothing but the air they breathed and sometimes
not even that; she saw half a dozen tanks and atmosphere suits. She felt like a caged bird let out for the first
time; some of her old fearfulness revived. It was a world
where she didn't know the rules beyond the little she got
from Skeen and Tibo, and there was a lot they never
thought to tell her because they were too immersed in
living the life to be aware of what they were leaving out.
She was uneasy, nervous, exhilarated and thrilling at the
tumble of wonders about her.

On the trip from the Tank Farm, Skeen said: You'll be cheated. Expect it till you learn the ropes. Don't feel hurt or stupid, you're just ignorant, a thing that's easily cured. Unlike stupidity. It's a game. You'll see. Believe me, you've got advantages that will knock them out once you start playing. That crazy body of yours throws off drugs and poisons every time you shift, and I'd wager a tangler wouldn't have a prayer at holding you. The only reason the darter got you was I could put them in you faster than you could shift. Don't let anyone know that. It's a weakness. Put your head to it and work out a way of compensating if you can. Um . . . lot of different weapons out there. Look, will you let me do some testing? We can set Tibo's stunner on low and see what it does to you. And Timka said: I caught the edge of the stunner Petro used on Angelsin and nothing drastic happened. And Skeen said: Better you know for sure than be sorry and dead on a guess. Tibo's stunner did nothing but slow her a little, even on its highest setting, her nerve arrangements were too different, though after a full minute at that setting she felt the interior tremble which warned of Chorinya, the uncontrolled shifting that could exhaust and kill a Min. And Skeen said: You're fairly safe in a Pit Stop. The trouble is when you're Pallah, you're pretty much standard female mammalian biped and you look like a breath could blow you away. Too tempting. Other than working girls, the spread in the Pits is weighted to the male and some of those males have the idea that they've got the right to grab what they want when it's got two legs and a cunt. And Timka said: Let them try, they'll pull back a stump. And Skeen said: Well, a Pit's a funny place, different ones have different rules. Make sure you know what the rules are before you do anything drastic. There are protection guilds in every Pit, you pay their fee, they give you a badge and if anyone bothers you, you yell for help and it comes. If it comes too late for your life, too bad for you and too bad for whoever attacked you; the badge transmits the stats of the attacker to the Guild computer and they go after him, eye for eye, tooth for tooth tenfold. If you're robbed, they take ten times the amount out of the robber's hide. If you're raped and knocked about, they sell the man to

the Tank Farms where he's kept alive and used to provide spare parts to the Flesh Welders. If you're dead, it's
an even exchange, his life for yours. That kind of thing.
The only caveat is be sure you're not the aggressor; in
that case they return the fee and take their badge back,
they're not about to let some bloody-minded fool pull
them into a feud. And Skeen said: When you want fast
answers on rules and customs, find the nearest computer
outlet, a one perc chip will get you a rundown.

Timka wandered around the roads and slideways that
wound through this bubble that was one in a necklace of
bubbles about a greenish sun, gawking at what seemed
an endlessly varying assortment of species; before she
stopped counting she'd tallied more than a hundred.
Slightly over half could be called bipedal and tended to
have sensory organs at the apex of their forms, the rest
went from chitinous multipedes to soft and all too often
oozy gastropods. She ambled into and out of dozens of
establishments and gawked some more at the kaleido-
scopic confusion of things for sale and lists of services
offered, cautiously avoided other structures that looked
interesting but too dangerous at the moment. She walked
until her feet were sore and her body yelled for food,
then worked back to Starlong Way and the eating place
called Xochimiyl. Skeen said: You'll like it or you won't,
the food is good and the view is something else.

The portal was delicately carved openwork, the wood
a rich brown with dark streaks running through it. It
swung open as she approached, wafting a subtle, pleas-
antly acrid perfume her way; she stepped into a cavernous atrium that smelled just enough of cool green and
damp earth to wake in her a yearning to be back in the
Mountains working in Aunt Carema's herb garden. As
she hesitated, uncertain what to do next, a small blonde
woman came from behind one of the larger plants, an
elfin creature dressed in layered gossamer robes that
shifted like leaf shadows about a slim childlike body.
"Welcome to Xochimiyl," she said. "My name is Briony.
How may we serve you?"

They must choose them as much for their voices as
their looks, Timka thought, that one makes synspeech
sound like flute music. Serve me? Is this one of Skeen's

questionable jokes? If this is a funny whorehouse, I
swear I'll shave her head so she matches Tibo knob for
knob. Aloud she said, "I'd like food and something
interesting to drink."

"Of course. We have several nodes open now. Have
you any preferences?"

"A friend of mind said something about a view. . . ?"

"You will want the Island room then. One small precaution, despina, do you suffer from motion sickness or
vertigo?"

"No." Timka blinked. Vertigo?

"And do you have objections to any particular food
categories or allergies that would discommode either you
or us?"

"None."

"I must tell you your answers have been recorded,
despina, a needless precaution I'm sure. Follow me,
please."

Timka sat in a malleable chair that tucked itself around
her, supporting her in unobtrusive comfort at a free-form
table that curved about her so she wouldn't have to
stretch for anything, chair and table on short silky realgrass,
a small rose arbor behind her, a graceful willow tree
beside it whose limber branches flickered about her,
pointed leaves painting elegant shadows that drifted across
and around her in ever-new configurations, all of this on
an oval island that wandered about among many similar
islands in a room that seemed open to the nothingness
beyond the Pit Stop, a nothingness with stars that glittered above and below her, that made the triteness *sea of
stars* a reality with nothing trite about it. She drank cold
green wine, ate strange green vegetables and an odd flat
fish with fungus dressing that melted on her tongue like
nothing she'd tasted before. She ate slowly and watched
the other patrons of Xochimiyl float past, a slightly less
astonishing mix than that on the streets outside. Twice
strange males and once a strange female rode the driftways to her table, but she shook her head, not wanting
company or any of the complications it might bring, and
they went away again. She finished the meal with a pot
of hot tea.

When the dishes had been cleared away except for the tea things and she was on her second bowl of tea, feeling warmly replete and happy with the world, a third man came up to her, a big man, dressed in black, head to toe, a shouting extravagant black, he was young, with a chiseled, handsome face, but something wrong with it, something bothersome, something not quite sane. He tapped at the table, sat in the chair that unfolded from the grass and smiled at her.

She sighed and set the bowl down, annoyed that he was spoiling her mood, annoyed that she had to return to alertness and be ready to defend herself. "Go away," she said. "I don't want company and you block my view."

His smile broadened and still didn't reach staring green-brown eyes. Animal eyes with nothing behind them. "I am Hested Vanker."

"So? You're not transparent. Go away."

"I want you. Name your price."

She looked over, thinking: yes, I have changed, I'll never sell myself again; she felt a rush of pleasure at the thought.

He caught the flash of it and misread it; he leaned toward her. "Well?"

She thought about insult, decided that anything she could bring herself to say would be so feeble as to be an insult to herself. "Your pardon, despois, you have made a mistake. I have no price. I am not interested in your offer. Have the courtesy to leave."

"I will have you at the price you quoted. Nothing."

She laughed, still annoyed, but amused a little in spite of her irritation. He was so sure of himself, so placidly arrogant, he was a joke, a not-so-funny clown. Her laughter died to a soft chuckle at the sudden rage it brought to his face. That rage was swiftly smoothed away. He sat silent, waiting. "I'll tell you what you get for nothing," she said. "Nothing. A fair trade, wouldn't you say? Win a little more by leaving me; take my gratitude with you."

"I declare challenge," he said, his voice blaring loud enough to draw eyes to the table. "Your body or my life. The game begins beyond the door." He stood and stalked off, his dignity a bit impaired by the eccentricities of the driftways.

Ah, Timka thought. My education begins. Find out the rules, Skeen said. Find a computer and buy the answers. She signaled for Briony and asked for the check, then began thumbing credit chips from the moneybelt Lipitero had made for her. The cost of the meal astonished her, but Skeen had been generous. She might be nearly broke, but she wasn't about to let that worry her. Timka was looking forward to the time when she'd share some of that insouciance; she could counterfeit it in situations like this, but she had a knot in her stomach as she looked at the chips piled on the shell tray, a small mountain of them needed to pay for the relatively simple meal she'd just enjoyed plus the tip that Skeen told her to add on. Briony was saying something about hoping she'd enjoyed the meal and the ambiance of Xochimiyl's Islands; Timka looked up, interrupted her. "Can you sit with me a moment?"

"Certainly." She slid gracefully into the chair Vanker had left extruded, rested her hands on the table, waited with friendly, alert but impersonal interest.

"You heard the man Vanker?"

"Yes." Briony permitted herself a touch of sympathy, a delicate sigh.

"What is this challenge thing? What is required of me?"

Briony smiled vaguely, looked down at the pile of chips in the tray, then lifted her pale green eyes to Timka. She waited.

Timka thought a minute, then thumbed out more chips and piled them in front of her. "What can you tell me that I couldn't get for one of these," she picked up a chip, held it between thumb and forefinger, "at the nearest computer outlet?"

"Nuances," Briony said softly, "things the Brain can't tell you. Background on Vanker and his habits. Like that."

Timka nodded and pushed the chips across the table. "Enough?"

Fingers moving quickly, neatly, Briony transferred the chips to the tray. "Generous," she murmured, gave Timka a gamin's grin, "but I don't make refunds."

Timka clicked her nails on the table top. "Why me?"

she said, the words exploding out of her. "Why me?" she said more quietly, "From what he could see, I'm nothing special."

"You're new in the Pits?"

"Very."

"Don't think I'm prying, but you have friends here? The folk who brought you?"

"Yes."

"Why did they let you wander about alone? Didn't they warn you something like this might happen?"

"Skeen didn't say anything about challenges." Timka gazed past Briony at a spectacular spray of stars. She sighed. "Probably no one's ever challenged her and she just forgot. She has other things on her mind. Besides she knows me, she knows I can take care of myself."

"Skeen? The Rooner? Ship Picarefy?" Briony leaned forward, a desperate eagerness breaking through her professional mask. "That's your friend?"

"Yes."

"He doesn't know that." There was no question in her voice. "Call her."

"In a while. Why me?"

"Because you're new, you're young, you're attractive, he saw you and decided he wanted you. Because that's the way he is. He sees something he wants, then he takes it. If someone tries to stop him, he cries challenge, and that's the end of it. I'd best tell you, he never loses. Not in the five years standard he's been here. Not in the more than hundred challenges he's fought."

"There's always a first time. What happens to me when I kill him?"

"When?" Briony bit her lips, her eyes shining with emotions Timka couldn't sort out. "If you kill him," she said softly, paused lips twitching into a tight nervous smile as Timka made a gesture of protest, "when you kill him, nothing happens to you. The Challenge is recorded. A life challenge. No, he can't know who your friend is."

"He doesn't know me. If by some wild chance he happened to defeat me, what happens?"

"He keeps you till he's tired of you, then he sells you where he can get the most for what's left of you."

"I've no recourse but fighting him?"

"Skeen. Call her."

"No. I don't think so. If I stomp him, but don't kill him?"

"He'll get you. I don't know how, but he will."

"Then I'd better make sure he's dead." She waggled a finger at the pile of chips. "It's not that, is it. You hate the man."

Briony chewed her lip, looked around like something timid and trapped, then shrugged. "What does it matter, everyone knows. And you paid the price for whatever I can tell you." She closed her eyes, clasped her hands so tightly the tips went pink. "A friend of mine," she breathed, "a sister, by love if not by blood. He took a fancy to her, but she loved me." Her eyes opened, she flushed, paled. "She had a quick tongue, too quick. She told him to go play with himself, if he was lucky maybe he'd enjoy it more than his women had. She was wise enough to have a stunner pointed at him when she said it. She bought me a badge from the Shtrazi but couldn't afford two. When he called challenge on her, she fought him and tried to make him kill her. He didn't. He used her and humiliated her, he broke her, then threw her out when he was finished with her. She killed herself." Briony shook herself, with visible effort she put off the grief that twisted her face and recaptured the image that greeted the patrons of Xochimiyl. She slid her hand under a fine gold chain she wore about her neck, lifted a black metal triangle from under the gauzes of her dress. "I still have the badge, I renew the fees every year, I will do that until he is dead."

Timka rubbed her thumb across her fingertips, flattened her hand on the table. "Thank you."

Briony slid the badge under her gauzes. "Why?"

"Don't be silly, you know the answer to that. Um . . . you implied I could call Skeen to help me."

"To fight in your place. Not beside you."

"Anything to complicate matters. Games, tchah!" She heard herself and laughed. "I . . . no, I can't explain, not without telling you the story of my life. So. Hested Vanker. How does he fight?"

Briony folded her hands, looked inward, spoke with soft non-emphasis. "A challenge lasts three days standard, starting for you the moment you walk out the door. While it's on, you'll not be permitted to leave Sundari. Skeen can't help you that way, not if she wants to keep her welcome here and in the other Pits. He knows Sundari, every bubble of it. He has vermin who'll make sure he knows where you are every minute. When he's ready, *he* chooses the time, *he* chooses the place. You can't hide and you can't run. He favors his right side just a little, will swing right more often than left, but he knows that and compensates. I've seen him sucker at least two men with that weakness. He is very very good, despina. Strong. Fast. Don't judge him by what you saw here. He might be a stupid clown most of the time, but he's brilliant when he fights."

"The thing to do, then, is shake him loose from his patterns. Make him come at me before he's ready."

"Despina, believe me, that's been tried. Over and over."

"My name's Timka. Call me Ti. Tell me his favorite weapons."

"His hands. Anything. For women like you that he doesn't want to damage before he's ready, a tangler."

"Good." Timka giggled. "Be somewhere you can see his face when he tries that on me. If he gets a chance to." She touched the pot. "Cold. I'd like another pot, please. Um . . . could you make a call for me? Without getting yourself in trouble?"

"Of course, despina. Xochimiyl's pleasure. If you prefer it, I can have a com brought to the table."

"Oh." Timka shook her head. "I am not accustomed to this . . . this sort of life. How much is it going to cost me?"

"Nothing, despina. This is Xochimiyl's lagniappe. If you wish, you can tip the person who brings the com, a one perc is sufficient, but a tip is not necessary."

"Um . . . how private are these coms?"

Again Briony chewed on her lip, her face wrinkled as she weighed her priorities. She fixed her eyes intently on Timka, brushed her forefinger lightly across her mouth. "Xochimiyl provides nothing but the best, despina," she said in her lovely liquid business voice.

"I see. Skeen should still be at the Buzzard's Roost

and even if she isn't, they'll probably know where to find
her." She stopped talking as the boy approached with the
com and connected it for them, she gave him a chip and
watched him flow off with the driftway. "Would you
work this thing for me? Where I come from, a needle's
complicated technology."

"Skeen?"
"What is it, Ti?" The tiny face in the image looked
impatient.
Timka went hastily through the events of the past half
hour, finished, "I thought you ought to know. In case of
complications."
"You've got it worked out?"
"Yes. I think so. Shouldn't take long. Briony says it's
probably a tangler."
A chopped-off laugh, then the head turned to someone
off screen, then Skeen was speaking again. "There's no
hurry, Ti. Wait where you are say five, six minutes more.
I'm still tied up here a while, but I'd like Tibo there. As
you said, in case of complications, showing a friend's
face, that sort of thing. Um, Buzzard says be careful,
Vanker's tricky. But he doesn't know you, does he."
Another laugh. "Don't make a fool of me, hmm? . . .
and get yourself killed."
"I'll try not."

Timka sipped at the tea, savoring the taste of it and the
warmth that spread through her body; the gentle drift of
the island was like a cradle, rocking her to sleep. Briony
fidgeted; she maintained her professional smile, but it
was beginning to look strained. "Weapons," she said
suddenly. "Ti, how are you armed?"
Timka poured herself more tea. "I'm not," she said,
"I'm going with what I was . . . born with." She closed
her eyes, consulted her internal timeclock. "Time is."
She got to her feet. "Do me a favor," she said, "take
care of my clothes, please." She unlatched the moneybelt
and laid it on the table, then proceeded to strip to her
skin, folding everything neatly, piling shirt and trousers
beside the belt, laying her boots across them. "Maybe
you could bring them to the atrium in a bit?"

Briony surged to her feet, knocking with atypical clumsiness against the table. "Ti!"

Timka ran her fingers through her black curls, fluffing them out from her head. "I parade out in front like this, yelling for Vanker to come get me, you think he can ignore that? Little naked woman calling him names, making a fool of him. *My* time, *my* place, Briony." With a wave of her hand she stepped onto the driftway and let it carry her toward the exit.

No one spoke though eyes followed her and after a short interval there was a building mutter of voices and the Islands began emptying onto the driftways. Timka ignored her followers; she felt good, alive. She laughed aloud, laughed again as the Islands echoed her joy, broke off, suddenly disconcerted by her reaction to the prospect of killing a man. Tchah, she told herself, this isn't your doing, besides he owes the Lifefire more than one death according to what Briony said. Calmly, Ti-cat, you're getting above yourself. Remember the other thing she said, he's brilliant when it comes to a fight. Idiot-savant. Uh-huh. Definitely not brilliant otherwise. No no, forget that, my girl, don't you be stupid too, borrow some of Skeen's caution. What are you going to do if he ignores you? He can't. Not him. What if he does? I'll think about that when it happens.

Timka strolled into the street, senses alert. She'd been busy practicing the mind-skills she'd neglected. Perhaps because she'd been living with Nemin so long, maybe because she was just better than most at the Min outreach, she'd found she could keep track of Nemin almost as well as Min—if she knew the Nemin and he (or she) was less than a kilometer off. Tibo was somewhere around, interested but not apprehensive. He wasn't all that fond of her anyway and only cared what happened to her because Skeen would. She strained harder, caught whiffs of Vanker. He was close, inside one of the buildings that looked onto Starlong Way. She cupped her hands around her mouth. "Eh, Vanker, where you hiding?" she yelled, and went on to describe in defamatory terms his person, character and probable failings in the sack. The street emptied rapidly before her. She heard gasps then laughter as the growing crowd of watchers understood she'd come to meet Hested Vanker not only unarmed but naked.

He stepped into the street before her. "What do you think you're doing?"

She measured the distance between them, smiled with satisfaction. He thought he was far enough off to be out of her reach and close enough for his tangler to take her when he was ready to use it. "What? You were the one who called challenge on me. I've come to answer you, what else?"

"You're surrendering?"

"Certainly not. If you want me, see if you can take me."

He looked around, moved farther out into the empty street, stopping where he could keep an eye on the gathering crowd. "You're forfeit if someone helps you."

"If you don't want to fight me, I'll understand," she said, loud enough so several watchers heard it and sniggered softly. "I don't need help, pretty man. Is there anything special you want done with your body?"

He forced a grin. "I'll tell you that when I've got you in my bed."

"I won't be hearing you then, I don't believe in ghosts."

More laughter, louder laughter.

He reddened, but didn't let it prod him into hurrying. His body seemed to grow denser, increase its energy tenfold, as he shifted his balance.

She waited, arms hanging loosely at her sides, watching him warily, beginning to understand a little of what Briony had meant.

His hand moved to his belt, his arm snapped out, the sticky net of the tangler came at her driven by the power of his arm and the whiplash of the stock.

And passed through her as she shifted, the net too coarse to trap her S'yer. Timka cat-weasel leaped at him, catching him a fraction off-balance, though he was almost too fast for her, turning the stumble when the net didn't catch into a push to his right that would have avoided her claws if Briony hadn't warned her about his tendency. Ignoring the knife that slapped into his hand, she took out his belly with her hind claws, his throat with her foreclaws and fell off him, the knife sunk to the hilt in her side. Someone ran from the crowd, pulled the knife away, she shifted back to Pallah, the wound closing over as she completed the change.

Tibo was crouching beside Vanker, wiping the blade on his shirt. With an elegant bow, he presented it to her, hilt first.

She laughed, sketched a naked curtsy, took the knife. "Thanks," she said. "Anything I should do about that?" She waved at the corpse.

"Garbage 'bots will clear it away." He touched the body with the toe of his boot. "Time that happened. Too bad, though, that you had to blow your edge on Hested Vanker." He looked her over, raised a brow. "Going to stay like that?"

All around them credit chips were changing hands. The hush during the two breaths the fight lasted was broken by a rising murmur of comment as the watchers began to disperse. They left a large clear space about her and Tibo, went back to work and play as if what had happened was so common an occurrence it didn't warrant any excessive excitement. Briony came hesitantly toward them, carrying Timka's clothing. "I thought you might want these. . . ."

"Oh, yes. Thanks. Tibo, Briony, Briony, Tibo." She took the shirt, put it on, smoothed the closures together, chuckled. "See what I told you, he didn't know what he was taking on." She stepped into the trousers, pulled them up.

Briony handed her the money belt. "They know you now," she murmured. "Be careful, Ti."

"I'm always careful." Timka patted her arm. "That bit about going to his right, that was very useful. Thanks."

"I have my pride," Briony said softly, "what I sell should be worth the price." She knelt, took the left boot. "Raise your foot."

TIBO AND HIS MUM.
or
PROSPECTING FOR GOSSIP, PAST AND FUTURE.

The old woman looked up. Bright blue eyes held a sky-wide life in them. The ananiles had lost their kick for her and age sat on her body like a pleating iron, but nothing age could do touched the spirit inside the shriveling flesh. "Tibo."

"Ta, Mum." He kicked an ottoman across the silky rug (twenty years ago it would have brought a small fortune, now it was so worn from the old woman's broad bare feet and the few privileged others she let visit her here no one would pay a ten perc chip for it). Some while back when Tibo was beginning to learn the tumbler's trade and she was one of his several mums, she divorced the family to marry one of the passengers on the Worldship the extended family was hired to. It was a fairly amicable divorce and she'd never lost her fondness for the children she had co-mothered, especially Tibo who was born the same time as the daughter the family talked her into having though she was old for it, Tibo who suckled at her breast when his body-mother was busy reading the cards for the passengers.

"I hear you and Skeen have got yourselves a new mouser. A herd of folk in the Bubbles owes that cat a blessing and I won't say I'm not one of them."

"Her name is Timka, Mum."

"Hmm. Pretty thing. Is it your branching out or Skeen or maybe the both of you?"

"None of your business, Mum."

"When you're old as I am, Tib, everything's your business."

"Enjoy yourself, then. We're too tame for you."

"So you are, Tib. So you are." She touched a delicate china bell with the tip of her forefinger, producing a small ting. Her companion and nurse, a squat furry Abrushin named Henrietta came padding in and without a word set out a lush tea on the table beside Mamarana's chair, then went padding out again, never a sign she saw Tibo sitting there.

"That's new, isn't it?" He nodded at the porcelain tea pot and the two bowls, pale blue with a darker blue pattern, thin as paper and as translucent. "Nice."

"Your brother Katsif stopped by a few months back. He gave it to me."

"From the look of that, he's doing well."

"Well enough. Though he hasn't got your flare, Tib, he'll never have Great Hounds like Abel Cidder sniffing after him."

"It's a distinction we can do without, Skeen and me."

"Skeen." She sniffed. "So pour the tea and tell me what you've come for, Tib."

"To delight in your blue eyes, Mamarana, and to drink your fine tea."

"Hah! About the tea I don't know, as for eyes, you obviously prefer them yellow. Cat-eyes. Though I hear your pet's eyes are green."

"No pet of mine, no pet at all."

"I suppose that answers my question. Far too tame, my Tib. How's Skeen?"

"Thriving."

"You going to tell me the story behind this?"

"Next time I come through Sundari. Can't now, not mine."

"Ga'houbal came sniffing round here a while back. One of Cidder's noses. I hear the Undying has cut Cidder loose from all duties but chasing Skeen. One of these days he's going to catch up with her."

"Maybe, maybe not. Me, I'll back Skeen. The only way he'll catch her is she wants him to. He might have more men and ships, but she's trickier."

"Sometimes. And sometimes she's moon-foolish and you know it. Forget Skeen. Out with it, Tib. Do I have to call Henrietta to squeeze what you're after out of you?"

"Rostico Burn."

"What about Rostico Burn?"

"Need to find him."

"You?"

"Me. Skeen. What difference does it make. It's business."

"Hers."

"Mum, you're stubborn as a . . . Ours. Hers and mine."

"Your cat friend involved?"

"Some."

"Rostico Burn. Hmm. He's not on Sundari. Been gone a little more than two years."

"Rooning, smuggling, thieving, what?"

"Mostly what, I suppose. He's a various sort. Turns his hand to what comes up."

"Two years. That's a long job. You hear of him touching down at another Pit?"

"Who's to say I asked."

"Well?"

"So I was interested. Coming out of nowhere like that. A boy like that. So I like to keep track of crazy kids."

"Mamarana spins her web and nothing nothing nothing escapes her." He touched her knee, grinned affectionately at her.

"Idiot. No more brains than your father, lovely man that he was. Rostico Burn. Clever boy. Talked a lot but never said much."

"So the Buzzard said. There's always Mala Fortuna. Maybe he had to do some fast dancing and his foot slipped."

"Like someone here who I could name but won't. This urgent?"

"So so. No hurry, but there's a deadline out there waiting for us."

"So give me five days. If I don't know by then, no one can find out. And next time you come, bring that little cat with you. Tiny thing. She sure surprised Vanker. Smoosher Pete had his imager flaking and it's been on the com half a dozen times since. Trust that man to get the fots, it has to be a Talent, no man has that much luck come honestly. That cat suckered Vanker. Look out she don't sucker you. You're not going to tell me where you found her?"

"Ask Skeen, her story."

"You're getting bad as her, Tib. Zipper mouth. I'll ask that cat. Maybe she'll know how to treat a poor old woman."

"Old? Mamarana, you'll still be younger than me when you're dead ten years."

"Five days, you hear? And bring your harem or you'll hear nothing from me. Not a word. Listen how terrible I sound. Your loving Mum and I have to bribe you to bring your women to see me. Ay ay, oh, Tib." She giggled. "Go away, Tib. My secrets are mine and so they stay. Five days. And bring Skeen too so we can bicker some. Clears out my sinuses. And that cat so I can tease out of her where she comes from. Five days. No sooner and not a heartbeat longer."

He got to his feet, kissed her wrinkled cheek. It seemed to birth more wrinkles as he watched. She was close to three hundred now, already long past the two-fifty promised by the ananile drugs. Praise whatever ruled this universe, she kept a mind as sharp as her spirit was young. She would not last much longer, though, he knew that at the pit of his stomach. And the hole she'd leave in his life was too big for anyone else to fill, even Skeen. But he knew too, she looked forward to that approaching end with a serenity he couldn't understand. The last time he visited her she tried to explain it to him, but her explanation was just a string of words, he couldn't make sense out of them. I've enjoyed my life, she said, there's a lot of things I haven't seen or done, but most of them I've run through my dreams so I don't need to do them. That isn't it, though. This is. I'm ready. When fruit is ready, it falls. I'm ready. Not pushing for, not pushing against, just waiting.

Tibo found Skeen in the Junker's Bar talking now and then with the cyborg bartender who'd added another bit of hardware to his body, a finger laser on his left hand, just hot enough to heat up a drink if that was what the customer wanted, or boil an egg inside its shell, or char letters into wet paper napkins, which was what he was showing Skeen at that moment. Skeen was drinking tonic water; she liked the bitter bite of it when she didn't want

anything stronger. He settled on the stool beside her.
"Ta, Flake," he said. "Stir me up a tod."

"Eh, Tib. Coming up."

"How's the mum, Tib?" Skeen sipped at the tonic, the
ice shifting in a tumble of clicks.

"Older." He gloomed at the bar. "You can watch
wrinkles adding on, Skeen, I swear she turned up a
dozen more while I was there."

Skeen patted his hand. "She's a tough old bird, Tib.
She'll last longer than you think."

"She wants to meet Timka."

"Who doesn't these days." Skeen chuckled. "Ti is
having herself a grand time going round with Briony
after the girl gets off work."

"Mamarana wants to see you too, says bickering with
you cleans out her sinuses."

"Sounds like she's mellowing some. When do we go?"

"Five days."

Flake Factry came back with the steaming tod, gave
the drink another pass with his laser finger before setting
it down by Tibo. "I was telling Skeen about Ga'houbal.
He was in here 'bout five six days after you left last time.
Swert the Mouth was sucking his fissatit and in two other
worlds. Ga'hou got him off in a corner and spent half the
night muttering at him. Mala Fortuna solo knows what
he managed to get out of him before Neep and Cleep
pushed in beside them and shut the dribble down. And
you know what, you know what that festered pimple did?
He bugged my bar. He left a trail of lice behind like a
tink shedding his winter coat. I wouldn't a known a thing
about it either, except that clothead had them set so they
started a feedback in my kneejoints. I had a Sweep in
and he rousted a pile big enough to fill a shot glass. He
come in here again, Junker says throw him out so hard
he bounces. Junker says he can't afford to sweep the
place every fuckin' time that maggotmeat walks in. Cidder's
got his hooks in him, Skeen. The Hound's hot after you,
Skeen the Lean. You hear me, you call a Sweep for
Picarefy every Pit you hit." Flake wandered off, picked
up a polish cloth and began working on his beautifully
articulated metal hand, rubbing and smoothing it until
the metal gleamed a rich blued-silver.

The ice rattled again as Skeen drained the last drops of diluted tonic water. "The Buzzard's got a party tonight, Tib. Henry O came in yesterday with a load of totems and godfaces. The Virgin and Hopeless followed him in, still living on the gelt from their Helix finds. I forget who else he said would be there. He said bring Timka and I think Petro might like it, she's been working too hard."

Flake Factry looked up from his polishing. "Virgin and Hopeless, they starting their second round?"

"That's what Hopeless said. I ran into her when I went to check on Picarefy. She said they hit every Pit anyone's ever heard of and still came back with enough credit to stuff a grinch. She said they're going to have to give up and do something sensible with it like endow a home for pregnant fish. She said she and the Virgin 're getting so bored with doing nothing, they've made twin axes to chop each other up into bloody gobbets of quivering flesh while they send the Abode into the nearest sun. You know Hopeless and how she gets. She said they wanted to get to work again, but it's bloody immoral making more money while they still had that much sitting around." Skeen poked Tibo with her elbow, woke him from his morose contemplation of the dregs of the tod. "I had an idea," she said. He grunted, pushed her elbow away. "Virgin and Hopeless, they're looking for something grand and noble and horribly expensive. I thought I'd have them buy and outfit a colony transport and keep it handy till we needed it."

Tibo gloomed at his glass. "If we need it."

Skeen pinched the tight skin on the back of his wrist. "Funerary ware. Lighten up." She glanced at her ringchron. "Time to pretty up for the party." She smoothed her hand over Tibo's gleaming head, stroked the nape of his neck, then got to her feet and moved her hands over the tense muscles of his shoulders. "You can't stop time, love. Come on. Picarefy has negotiated for water and meat, we've got hot showers and bloody steaks waiting for us."

Skeen talked Lipitero into forgetting her trepidations and venturing away from the workshop, telling her that her brain would fry and fall out her ears if she didn't take a break. Lipitero was skeptical but willing.

SCENE: *Lipitero talking with Picarefy through a comlink
ornamented with dancing lights that are extraordi-
narily successful at conveying the emotions of a
supposed-to-be emotionless machine entity, doing
this with varying levels of energy, varying patterns
of the lights, varying colors. The workroom curves
about her, the lathes and the other machine tools
clean but well used, the bins and cabinets full of
metals and other materials, one could build any
smallish instrument here, construct the most intri-
cate memory systems. She is brushing her fur,
burnishing her nails and the skin pads over knees
and elbows, the dark gray skin over the arch of her
ribs, the wide springing ribs that flatten and spread
when she soars, skin that takes a polish like marble, hard as marble with some of the deep glow
when it was properly cared for. Though she bore
her children alive, she is not a mammal and secretly glad of it. Skeen is sleek enough but to
Lipitero even she looks awkward and badly designed. She is talking to Picarefy about what to
expect at the party; she has never been at a gathering such as this outside a Gather. When she thinks
of it, it is absurd to be talking about social occa-
sions with a shipbrain who'd never come close to
being there. Like two cubs helping each other walk
only knowing how to fall. Picarefy searches through
her files, shows Lipitero scenes from flake plays
Skeen had added to the ship's library more for
Picarefy's gratification than her own. When those
have been run through, they talk quietly, Lipitero
giving a little more about herself and her people to
the insatiable curiosity of the ship.*

READER'S ALERT: EXPOSITORY LUMPS AHEAD. SKIP OVER IF DISTRESSED BY SUCH.

Lipitero looked round at the workshop and sighed. "I hate to leave," she said. She looked at the harness hanging on a hook by the iris, smiled with pleasure at the chain mail and ornaments she'd made here in the cracks between her more serious work.

Chuckle from Picarefy. "But how interesting to show off one's work."

"How difficult to escape one's vanity."

More than vanity. From the moment Lipitero stepped into Picarefy, she lost herself in the delights of the Ship's workshop; ornaments and instruments flowed from mind and fingers. Whatever she made, no matter how utilitarian, had the brush of beauty, the simplicity of a child that had nothing to do with childishness, the simplicity that was on the far side of elaboration, the single stroke that took the master to achieve. And Lipitero was a Master. Before the death of her children she had been good, now she was great, a difference in intensity of focus. She could have no more children, but she could MAKE. This long drop into chance that took her into Skeen's orbit had solidified the Sydo Ykx in their role of her surrogate children but only increased her need to MAKE. During the waiting time at the Tank Farm, she divided her days into three parts: sleep learning and talking to Picarefy; learning the possibilities of the workshop, making things she thought useful in the hunt for Rallen and after; talking with Tibo and Timka, she needed to know them to sense their limitations and how far they might be willing to transcend those limitations. She talked with them and with Picarefy for another reason: she needed the warmth of other lives to hoard her own warmth until she could rejoin her own kind. So alone, so far from them, she could die of that loneliness. Her kind did.

They sickened and died kept from their own. The desert Charlarosh discovered this early on and took pleasure in capturing and penning an Ykx then watching the Ykx pine and die. They used that weakness to fortify their own sense of worth because they were envious of Ykx flight and terrified of Ykx technology. Watching Ykx soar out over the desert, riding the thermals, dancing in the air, seeing what the Ykx MADE in their caverns, they felt diminished, dirtied. But in the end an occasional sacrifice was not enough, they had to wipe away the insult; that meant destroying all the Ykx they knew of and they did it with a viciousness and cunning beyond Ykx comprehension. Lipitero escaped death because they thought she was dead. She was alive now because she'd made a leap most Ykx could not. A leap across a world, a leap across old ways of thinking and being. But she was still Ykx; she didn't have the comfort of a rage for vengeance.

"It's a physical difference," she said to Picarefy, "a different assortment of chemicals. We found we couldn't understand the reactions of many of the species we encountered when we first left Ysterai. What they did didn't make sense, reason didn't help us deal with it, didn't tell us why, so we investigated and found certain chemicals that triggered responses that had nothing to do with reason, aggressive responses, responses we lacked and were glad of the lack."

"In a very real sense," Lipitero said to Picarefy, "we share the fault for our destruction, the Ykx of Coraish Gather."

"You blame yourself for being slaughtered?" Picarefy's indignation sounded in her voice and danced in the jagged patterns of the lights, the harsh colors.

"You sound like Skeen," Lipitero said. "I suppose that's understandable. No, I'm not talking about blame. I'm talking about our failure to understand and prevent. I'm talking about how we were absorbed by our own troubles, how we were perhaps affected by the subtle distortions of Mistommerk, how we changed from what we were. No, we don't fight, we have other means of protecting ourselves, more effective means. We aren't a prolific race, each female produces three cubs, only three, during her breeding time. Often less than three. We couldn't afford wars that wiped out any great portion of our breeding population. So we manipulated our dangers away by using our WATCHER skills. Our WATCHERS watched for signs among anyone who could threaten us and when they found them we abstracted bodies and manipulated events to erase the danger."

"I hesitate to moralize, Petro, but I have to tell you I find that appalling."

"Better than war."

'No." Picarefy's lights were pale and agitated, her voice uncertain. "Not for the folk you interfered with."

"They were alive. But I won't argue with you about the benefit to them. We didn't ignore their good entirely, but what meant most was our survival. It didn't always work, you know. Sometimes wars that had nothing to do with us spilled over on us. Sometimes we made mistakes in our manipulations and situations exploded on us. Mostly though, we managed to maintain our neutrality, making our mediation skills valuable enough that the bellicose around us generally let us alone. There's so little need to kill when you cool angers the right way, when you prevent those angers from fruiting by listening to the hurts behind the words. Words aren't so important, no, it's the anger and hurt which is left unexpressed that fester into death. It takes study and time and the ability to WATCH and SEE, the ability to HEAR-BEHIND. We had those in the beginning, we used them. But Mistommerk worked on us like it worked on all the Waves. Our WATCHERS dwindled and died and no more were born. Our genetic base was too small and in the strangeness of that world, we suppressed randomness because we feared losing what made us Ykx. We were too fearful. I see that now. Our last WATCHER saw it then and advised us what would happen, but who listened? It was easier not to listen. We let the irritations build between us and the Chalarosh, we let them manipulate us into becoming more like them, rigid and fiercely inturned. It's simpler to be like that, you slash away tangling nuance, you don't have to do the hard work of understanding alien psyches and alien cultures, you can proclaim right and wrong and if the world doesn't conform, you can ignore the jars or stamp them into shape. Hmm. If this bores you, Pic, it's your fault, you wanted to know."

"Yes, yes, go on. Did I say stop?"

"Your lights are dozing."

"I was thinking, that's all."

"Oh. Hmm. Last time I talked to anyone that dim, I got the same answer, but he was starting to snore."

"If there's one thing I can't do, Petro, it's snore."

"Oh, I'm sure there's an analog if I looked hard enough."

"Now, now, don't be snippy. Go on with your musing, I find it very interesting."

"Where's Skeen?"

"In the shower-room with Tibo."

"Oh. How soon will we be leaving?"

"I'd say about an hour."

"Oh."

"You've time; finish what you were saying."

"Hmm. I'm finished. Except to wonder how Rallen has shaped the Ykx, keeping in mind what Mistommerk did to us." She got to her feet and began strapping the harness about her. "I'm afraid of that, you know. I'm afraid Rallen Ykx and Mistommerk Ykx have become so different that we can't talk to each other. I hope it isn't so, but it's been a long time, hasn't it. A terribly long time." She began brushing her fur again.

A moment's silence. "Petro . . ."

"Mmmh?"

"Flake the party for me."

Lipitero inspected her claws, moved her feet uneasily. "I can't do that, Pic. I'm a guest there, I have obligations. I'll watch everything and tell you about it, but flake it? No. I can't."

The lights seemed to droop. "I didn't think of that. I wanted so much to see . . ."

"I know." She brooded a minute, smiled. "Pic, why don't you call the Buzzard, see if you can send a remote with us, that'll be almost like you're there yourself."

"Oh. Um . . ." The lights and colors were agitated. "Skeen never suggested that."

"She got you the spyeyes. Did you ever tell her you

wanted to talk to people, not just other ships, other brains?"

"I never thought of it before."

"See?"

"I see. Hmm. Skeen's out of the shower, I'll ask what she thinks, tact you know, Petro, then I'll do it."

Buzzard's Roost II where the Buzzard lived his private life was a long loft sparsely furnished with objects he'd grown too fond of to sell. Lipitero walked in feeling shy and uncertain, keeping close behind Skeen and Tibo, the little remote rolling beside her, fizzing with excitement and an interest so intense it seemed on the verge of exploding out of its gleaming metal skin.

The Buzzard's eyes flicked over her; his face didn't change, but she knew he had recognized her from the representations in the work he'd handled and the ornamentations on her harness. She gave him a small tight smile, a murmured greeting, then slipped away, leaving him chatting with the remote. She found a quiet corner and sat watching what was happening. She felt more comfortable like that, her back against a wall, another wall close by in a symbolic replication of a Gather niche.

After a while the Buzzard drifted over to her, sweat in tiny dots, one on each of his freckles or so it seemed, clinging to the polished brown skin on his knobby hairless skull. "You like a sweet-tart taste?"

"Well enough." She took the glass he handed her, touched her tongue lightly to the liquid. Fermented organic, rather mild. She sipped at the pale blue wine and smiled. "Thank you."

He settled beside her on the long bolster, sat with skinny legs stretched out before him. "Friendly warning. I'm going to try my best to get you drunk and babbling."

"Mala Fortuna for you, Sirke, I wouldn't babble, merely settle back and go to sleep."

"I hear and bow my head to my evil fate."

"Why don't you merely ask me what you want to know? I'll answer or not as I choose."

"That's the trouble. I prefer it when I'm the one who chooses."

"Doesn't everyone?"

"No, Sirkiyn. One of my ex-wives, she couldn't make
up her mind to come out of a closet unless you told her
to."

"How boring."

"True. She had other talents. Who are you and where
are you from and why is Skeen hunting what she's already got?"

She sipped at the wine and thought over the questions.
"My name is Lipitero. Where I'm from is not something
I'm prepared to discuss except to say you'd get no use
from the knowledge. Skeen is hunting . . ." she stopped
talking, frowned, "I don't think I should talk about Skeen."
She drank more of the wine, taking it slowly, cherishing
the gentle warmth that spread through her; she liked
having this strange, inquisitive man beside her; he was a
center of warmth which washed over her and mingled
with the wine-warmth.

"Hmm. The gods are practical jokers with deplorably
low taste in humor." His long upper lip curved down at
both ends, giving him a clownish melancholy.

"Why?"

"They made man and gave him speech and right away
he turned words into enigma and oracle. What a joke on
us."

"Words are for playing with, you mustn't take them
seriously, never, never take them seriously." She giggled
suddenly as fumes from the wine tickled her nose.

"Who made your ornaments?

"Me."

He took her hand, turned it palm up to examine it,
then brushed his fingertips across it, a quick almost tender gesture. "If you get tired of flitting about with Skeen,"
he murmured, "I'll stake you to a workshop for a percentage on whatever you make."

She cuddled the glass against her cheek. "Generous
man."

"I'd let you keep that illusion if I thought I could get
away with it—sadly, no. There's a demand, if you aren't
too confined as to the specifics of age and provenance.
Hi-ho, Lipitero, you are a grand Maker, as any fool
could see, but fools buy ugly old and pass by wonders
unknowing if the newness shows. A hint or two, a lie or

three makes it all right." He settled himself more comfortably, his back against the wall. "Now, Skeen's a
wonder herself; ask Picarefy about the Hus someday
when she's feeling talkative. Or the Tangle Stars. What
I'm saying is you won't be bored with her, but she's got
liabilities and picking up more. It's getting so she can't
slide out of a Pit without a dozen sundoggies sneaking
after her to see where she's going. Then there's Abel
Cidder and the other Hounds. The bigger she gets, the
worse they hurt when she foxes them. Let me tell you,
Lipitero, if ever you get anywhere near the Cluster, you
find a place to sit that one out. She goes a little crazy
when she punches into the Empire."

She hunched forward, twisted around to grin at him.
"Oh, Buzzard, oh, dear, you're so not-subtle."

"Oh, Lipitero, oh, dear, what's the point? Tell me you
wouldn't see through me whatever I tried."

She gave him her glass. "Fill this up a few times and
maybe you're right, I'll babble."

He laughed, waved over one of his guests, a squat little
centaur with blue skin and elaborately plaited mane and
tail. "Henry," he held up his glass with a centimeter of
wine in the bottom, "bring round the bottle, will you."

Henry O slapped out a knotty tentacle, caught the
glass, sniffed at it. "Hiding out on us, B'sss." He winked
at Lipitero, fanning his long curly lashes at her. "Bribe
me. A glass o' me own and an introduction."

Buzzard raised his brows. When Lipitero nodded, he
said, "Consider yourself bribed."

The Virgin and Hopeless looked like identical twins
except that the Virgin was a hair over one meter tall and
Hopeless was two meters and then some. They had polished glowing skin the color of bitter chocolate, elegant
chiseled features, high cheekbones, long oval faces, knife-
blade noses with small tight nostrils, generous mouths,
large black eyes (true black, not just a very dark brown),
nubbly black hair a little over a centimeter long. They
had dressed themselves for the party in festoons of gold
chains about neck, arms, legs, some of them set with
large emeralds, but were otherwise quite bare, not even

body hair. Skeen took Timka over to them and introduced her.

Hopeless bowed with regal grace, but the Virgin's eyes passed over Timka as if she were empty air, eyes that were as shallow as a beast's with no awareness in them, either of self or other; abruptly her face lit up. She smiled and nodded at the emptiness beside Timka; she angled her head slightly as if listening with care to something she found fascinating. After a moment of this, she turned away to twitter incomprehensible syllables at another invisibility. She finished that as suddenly, turned to Hopeless and spoke at length in a liquid language that seemed more like vocalized music than words. Hopeless listened, nodded. Then the Virgin swung away again and began murmuring quietly to a third of her unseen companions.

Hopeless smiled lazily. "Virgin says it's a wild and wonderful story. She says they say we should do it. She says do it. I say do it. We're in. We should talk over details some place secure."

"Picarefy or the Abode?"

"The Abode. Virgin's Eye has a clearer focus there, more to talk to. Fifteen thirty tomorrow."

A while later.

Timka drifted over to Lipitero, the Buzzard and Henry O. She nodded at the Virgin who was curled up on the floor asleep. "Is she crazy?"

"There's a couple of ways of looking at that," Henry said. He rocked onto his hooves, awkward as a new-born colt with something of the same felicity, making room for her to sit beside Lipitero. "Now there's no denying the Virgin talks to lots of things that aren't there. On the other hand, they tell her things she couldn't find out any other way." He folded his tentacles across his broad chest and grinned at her. "Crazy, not-crazy, who cares. She makes out just fine. Fact, some say she's a luck pole. There's not a casino in Sundari that'll let her in the door."

Across the room, Hopeless flung her head back and let out a crack of laughter that drowned for the moment the muted roar of conversation. Skeen had her flute out and a lacertilian named Wolfman Leonard was beating a hard fast rhythm on the bottom of an icebucket. Chains flying, Hopeless began a stamping, whirling dance.

Timka patted Henry's nearside tentacle (he'd collapsed beside her as soon as she was down). "Hopeless," she said. "I never heard a name less fitting. What's the story?"

"Hopeless is what she said to call her, so that's what we call her."

"No one ever asked?"

"Didn't seem like a good idea."

"Ah."

I DON'T LIKE YOUR GIRLFRIEND, SHE'S A TROUBLEMAKER, SHE'S GOING TO GET YOU KILLED IF YOU DON'T BACK OFF.
or
TEAPARTY WITH MUM WITH REPORT ON ROSTICO BURN, WITH SIDEBAR ON CAUTION.

Henrietta shadow-silent moved among them filling bowls, passing around tea cakes, faded out through a curtained doorway.

Mamarana sipped at her tea, bright blue eyes moving slowly from face to face. Skeen, lean and sharp and amused. Lipitero, hieratic serenity and scarred, austere alien beauty. Timka, fragile, deceptive, green eyes, long black hair, exuberantly curly, small pointed face. Knowing her cat shape, Mamarana sought and found a kitten look in her face. She gazed at Timka longest, trying to find in her the lethal steel that dispatched a tried and proven fighter like Hested Vanker in something like thirty seconds. She cupped her tea bowl in both hands, relishing the gentle warmth that flowed up her arms. "Thirty seconds?"

Timka wrinkled her nose. "I should try playing with him? He was a fool. I'm not."

"And I shouldn't make the same mistake?"

"Why fuss over me? You've nothing riding on my head."

"Might have."

"Only if you're more fool than you look."

Skeen chuckled. "Ware the claws, Mamarana."

The blue gaze switched to her, cooled several degrees. "I could say the same to you, I hear you're tying up with the Virgin and Hopeless."

"The Virgin said Yes before I asked. Tell me how to cross that."

"The Virgin's Eye works for her and Hopeless. What's good for them could be lousy for you."

"True. But the Eye SAW."

Mamarana made a sucking sound, tongue against teeth, but she didn't push on with an argument she couldn't win. She turned instead to Tibo. "You have worms in your head, my Tib. You should wiggle loose while you have your skin." When Tibo shook his head, she sighed, eyes gone bitter with defeat. She rocked in her chair a moment, saying nothing; when she spoke again she ignored Skeen and focused on Tibo. "Rostico Burn. He came out of the Cluster. Rumor says somewhere around the Veil."

Tibo glanced at Skeen but said nothing.

Mamarana ignored that also. "He arrive to Sundari Pit seven year standard ago working by himself a Empire cruiser which he didn't say how he got that had a bellyful of uniques he sold Buzzard which credit he use mostly to have the ship worked over in Luo's shipyards into something a singleton could handle with more than hope and luck. He shut his mouth about where he got his cargo though there was pressure put. Zald and Zabeeda 'bushed him when he nosed over to Riddle in the Lop. He turned up half a year later in Stridor's Whistle. He sold the cruiser and registered Zald/Zabeeda in his own name. Had Zald's name on a quitclaim. Haven't seen Zald and Zabeeda since. People backed off some. Next thing he went in with Roman the Fly on a Rooning, did pretty well on that. Got involved with a woman in Whistle Pit, hung around there for some months. Disappeared for a year. Not many know this, but he spent that time on University studying and poking about in the Library. One of the things he spent some time on was that study Scholar Kettel did on the Rooners. You're in there, Skeen, the Rooning of Kyapol, though I wouldn't be one to scratch that vanity of yours. Came back to Stridor's Whistle, but the woman had moved on by then. Took up with Seraph and his Pets, went over to the Herren worlds and got off with a load of technies that he peddled through Pincher in the Whistle. Came back to Sundari a couple months after you went for Kildun Aalda, Tib." She raised her brows, lifted a corner of her generous mouth, shifting the map of wrinkles her face had fallen into, velvety curtains of pale flesh, as she looked from one carefully blank face to the next. "He played around a bit, took off again. Alone this time. Which was a bad idea because the Herren had snagships waiting for him. As soon as he cleared Pit Space, they fished him up from the insplit and went off with him. Either he hadn't covered himself enough or Seraph got high and breathed into the wrong ear. Bad judgment picking on Seraph and the Herren worlds at the same time. Young. Time would cure that if he could find some. The Herren bought him space on Pillory."

Tibo slapped his hand against his thigh, clamped his mouth on what he wanted to say but would not in his mum's presence.

Skeen rubbed at her nose. "The woman?"

"Word is Cidder got her."

"The Buzzard's fairly sure Rallen is somewhere around the Veil because that's where Rostico Burn came out of the Cluster." Skeen set her tea bowl down, brushed crumbs off her thighs. "Maybe so, maybe not. If it was me with the load, I'd have backed and filled a lot before I popped loose, used the Veil as a last trap to suck the snagships off me. I'd say a lot depended on how hard he was being pressed."

"Hmm." Mamarana's hands twitched, but she made no direct comment on Skeen's musings. "Smart boy, kept his mouth shut. Chanidi Bli, that's the woman, she probably did some prying, but I doubt she learned anything important. I happen to know Waygoz the Nose went to University for a few days, trying for cross-matches on Rallen. Got nothing, came back more than half convinced Burn made up the name." Again she scanned the faces, grunted as they told her nothing. "Cream took his slider into the Cluster and poked about the Veil, one of the working girls from the Nymph's Navel got that much out of him, you know Cream, he's slipp'rier than a ghost's shadow, but he beat it out of there, his tail on fire. Old Bones the Undying has tightened his grip some more. He's got the Cluster divided into sectors and any traffic between them has cruiser escort; legit trade's down to a trickle, the other kind's been near squeezed out, but the

Cluster's a big place and there's more sliding around the rules than you'd expect. Especially near the Veil. Cream said it did peculiar things to his instruments and he couldn't stay in the Insplit very long, he was popping his head up like a dog running through high grass. He come out of the Cluster with two snagships on his tail and a mauler pooting along behind them; he said it was Bona Fortuna and vortex that broke him loose. And he come out empty. Lot of stars in the Veil, he said, he sampled a few of them hoping he'd stumble across Rallen, but when he got low on fuel he had to give up."

Skeen sighed. "That means we have to get Burn off Pillory." She tried to look rueful but wasn't very convincing; she was excited, aching to try it.

"No!" Mamarana slapped her hand down on the chair arm, knocking her tea bowl onto the carpet. "I forbid it, no!" She scowled at Tibo, but got no help from him; the wildness in him had leaped to meet the fire in Skeen. He was gazing at her, holding in laughter. Mamarana couldn't be sure he even heard her protest; she felt her strength flaking away and for the first time in a long time regretted her dying and felt the helplessness of great age. She gathered herself, put force in her voice. "Redeem him," she said. "Pay Pillory's price."

Skeen relaxed, stretched out her long legs. "I'll think about it, supposing I can come up with the sum and can work a way of doing it without calling Cidder down on me. Provided the Kliu Berej don't have him on a no ransom contract. Provided it doesn't take too long to arrange, we've got a deadline that can't be shifted."

Tension slipped out of Mamarana. She closed her eyes. "Pour me some tea, Tib," she said and let a quaver into her voice. When he tapped her hand to tell her the bowl was there, she smiled fondly up at him, then began working at Timka and Lipitero, trying to tease their histories out of them.

"Djabo's toes!" Skeen burst out. "We'll be hanging round here forever if we don't start moving. If I knew where Cidder was, I'd drop-kick him into the nearest sun. Mamarana, would you find out how much it'll take to ransom Burn and how long? Do it through about three other mouths, ah! what am I doing telling you your business?"

"Finally come to you, eh?" Mamarana said dryly. "I'll have it say two days, Tib. Come see me."

It was a dismissal. With murmured polite insincerities Skeen and the other women left. Tibo stayed behind. He went to her, stroked her cheek. "Don't worry about me, Mum."

She caught his hand. "That Skeen. Crazy, skinny, not even pretty, but you spend your stash pulling her out of a mess she made herself. Let me give you a ship, Tib. I want you loose from her. She'll get you killed."

He hesitated, felt his face get hot and tight. He was glib, a word or phrase for anything, he could tell a story, bare bits of his soul when he was high enough, but cold sober in the cool white light of day, it was hard. And she was losing her edge, the wrinkles were getting to her brain. He could see Death eating her little by little, stripping slowly away what made her the woman he loved and admired. Mum was somewhere inside Mamarana, he thought, then changed his mind. A caricature of Mum with most of her subleties worn away. He could say to her: I love Skeen. I like Skeen. I could have left her long ago if all I wanted was a ship. Skeen and I fit together. I know she isn't easy, I know she's a little crazy, maybe a lot crazy, but so am I, Mum, and these two crazinesses, they fit together comfortably. Aloud, all he said was, "She suits me, Mum." He freed his hand gently but firmly, patted her cheek. "Find out about Pillory for us, Mum. I'll be by."

Skeen was waiting for him outside, she looked at him closely, said nothing for several turns of the walkway. When they reached Starlong Way, she touched his arm. "Want a raincheck?"

"No." He caught hold of her hand, his fingers tightening until he was hurting her but she made no sound, made no attempt to pull away. "No. Sitting around and watching her rot. No!"

"We might be back before she goes."

Ignoring the walkers moving about them, Tibo lifted her hand to his face, held it against him a moment, kissed the palm and let it fall. "I'd like to be there when she goes, but I won't mind a lot if it doesn't work out."

"What about telling her why?"

Tibo started walking again. "No. Can't trust her now. She got it in her head you're bad for me. She'd blow the whole to Cidder if she could arrange to keep me loose and she's getting soft enough to believe his promises. Sorry, Skeen."

"You didn't know. Besides, according to the Buzzard it's clear to Riddler's Pit by now that Skeen's prowling after Rostico Burn and Rallen."

He reached round her waist, pulled her close. "Ah, the drawbacks of fame."

"You ought to know, you pirate, seeing what happened when Tibo's Streak ran out."

Both laughing, they pulled apart and moved to the slideway in the center of the Way, riding it from the Suburbs to the Bubble where Angy Darling ran her multiverse.

SCENE: *garden room on the ABODE OF WHISPERS.*
         Hopeless lies on her back on pseudo-moss beside
         a narrow stream.
         Dwarf trees, piles of artfully weathered stone, a
         stepping stone path that wound between patches
         of lawn, bamboo, ornamental shrubs, flower beds.
         Overhead, a patch of daylight glow crawling across
         the ceiling like a miniature sun.
         The Ship has three sections. Garden Room for
         living and sleeping; Cargo Bay, which is about
         twice the size of this garden room; Bridge, which
         shifts about, tiny bubble inside this large bubble.
         Except in emergencies, the Abode flies herself.
         Skeen sits beside Hopeless.
         Timka cat-weasel is prowling restlessly under the
         trees, the subtle shifting of her coloration making
         her difficult to see. She fits with the half-wild
         look of this garden tucked into the belly of a
         starship.

Skeen rubbed at her knee. "It'd be handy if the Eye would tell us where Rallen lies."

Hopeless stretched and yawned, scratched at her stomach. "Eye tells what Eye wants." She smiled vaguely in Skeen's direction, went back to watching Timka prowl. "Give her to us," she said.

"Ask her. She's no slave of mine. She'll do what she pleases."

Ti-cat came gliding into the small glade, crossed to Hopeless. She made a sound like a cross between a purr and a hiss, set a foot just above Hopeless' navel, extruded her claws enough to prick, then went stalking away, tail switching in whip snaps back and forth.

Skeen chuckled. "You've just been turned down."

"Hylattis! she understood me." Hopeless sat up, wrapped her arms about her legs. "I keep forgetting she's more than beast."

"The body might change, the mind doesn't." Skeen looked after Ti-cat, frowned. "I'm not sure that's right; degree of intelligence doesn't change, but I think the nature of the beast influences her outlook. Hmm."

"Where is your other strange one?"

"Petro?" In the workshop making more modifications on Picarefy. The two of them, you can't pry them apart." She sighed. "I'm divorced, Hopeless, that's what it is."

"To be saving a species." Hopeless sighed with pleasure. "If we manage this, Skeen, if we really can do it, maybe I'll think about another name." She looked ecstatic and just for an instant madder than the Virgin. The look faded, she couldn't sustain the effort. "You're going to pull Rostico Burn out of Pillory."

"Looks like I have to." Skeen sighed. "Otherwise I could hunt the Veil for a century and come up empty."

"Virgin has found a transport. Needs some fiddling, we'll take it round to Chanix and have Maskin run his tentacles over it; he works fast. Where should we meet?" She thought a moment. "And when?"

"Rallen's somewhere in the Cluster, not much question of that, and there's Abel Cidder to think about. Picarefy ran a plot for me when I managed to get her attention," Skeen chuckled, "and came up with three Pits that won't mean too big a swerve from the Pillory/Cluster line. Nymph's Navel, The Orphanage, Revelation. I know the Navel, I never got to Revelation and made The Orphanage just once. I've got no preference. Pick one."

Hopeless thought a moment. "No," she said, "no reason I can think of to choose one over the others. VIRGIN!"

A Disembodied Voice whispered beside them: "Revelation."

"Skeen?"

"Fine. Anything I should know about the place?"

"It's more a pimple than a Pit. Not much there. A small multiverse, some trading posts, a fuel dump. And the Hermit. Virgin and him have had some long loud arguments, you'd swear they're ready to chew each other into hamburger, but they enjoy it. Fun to watch."

Better you than me, Skeen thought. "How long will the fiddling take?"

"Maybe a month standard. What about you?"

"I can't see how I could do the dip under three months standard, travel times included."

"No chance you can ransom him and save this?"

"Tibo says not. Mamarana thinks we can, she's offered to put up part of the price. Trouble is, she's hostile to anything I do, better we let her go on thinking that's the way we're handling it."

A Disembodied Voice spoke beside Skeen's ear. "Good. Cidder is sniffing close to Mamarana's webs."

Skeen tried not to twitch. She'd been here enough to become accustomed to the oddities, but the Abode more often than not was too weird for her comfort.

"That's settled then. Three months after Picarefy unties here, we'll be in Revelation with the transport, waiting. We'll wait another two months before we give it up and go on to something else. Agreed?"

"Agreed. Um . . . watch out for Cidder."

"The Eye will take care of that." Hopeless laughed. It wasn't a happy sound. She stretched out again on the pseudo-moss and closed her eyes.

Having nothing more to say, Skeen got to her feet. "Ti-cat, let's go home."

"Well, Pic?"

"The Ykx were a sneaky lot, Skeen. If the Ralleners are like them, you better watch out. When Petro saw the schematics Hopeless brought over, she laughed. Said Kliu screens are so coarse she doesn't see how they keep anyone out. The Lander is finished except for the engines, they have to be reset, and Petro says she can use some extra hands. Which means you, Skeen, or Tibo. Timka won't do. Nor my remotes. Takes a feel we just haven't got."

"Can we get started while we're working on the engines? It's seventeen days to Pillory. Makes me nervous hanging around like this, Djabo's twitches, I hate, I loathe, I abominate deadlines."

"I'm fueled and reamed out, that's all right, but I made a package deal with Patipsa for supplies and half of it's still to come. Tipsy promised on his father's nose I'd have the rest by tomorrow." Picarefy's lights danced and there was laughter in her voice. "I said I'd turn Ti-cat loose on him if he let us down."

"Tomorrow," Skeen said. She ran her hands through her hair, fluffing it out from her head in spikes. "Tomorrow." She looked at her hands. "I think I'll take a bath."

PART II: THE RESCUE

PILLORY

The Pillory System controlled by the Kliu Berej, Pillory operated as a prison planet, the asteroid belt worked by Miners under contract to the Kliu.

gravity: 2.75 g standard
diameter: 17,384 km
three moons: (unnamed) 1,200 km, 1578 km, 939 km.

> hollowed out and converted into guardian fortresses, part of a net of spyeyes woven about the world.

Sun: a red giant alone in the Sword Rift
two other planets (unnamed) one inside, one outside the orbit of Pillory.

Asteroid Belt between Pillory and the outer planet, a heavily populated Belt, rich with heavy metals. Because the Kliu are uncomfortable in freefall or minimal gravity, they have contracted out the mining rights to the Belt and there's a lot of coming and going.

Kliu Berej: Lacertine centauroids; six short stubby legs supporting a broad, heavily muscled body; squat torso; short arms; wide eight-fingered hands, three of the fingers capable of opposing the others; boxy head, small eating mouth, much larger breathing and speaking mouth; huge ears, mostly rolled into minimal size, leaving only the ear hole open, when unfurled, they are mobile scanners each larger than the head and capable of hearing into the electronic spectrum; eye, round and tender as with most nocturnals and those who live with dim suns.

Prison planet: A large diamond-shaped island in the center of Pillory's major ocean with a wall across the waist. To the north is the recreation area where the Kliu on duty in the fortress moons go to recover from the stretches of low gravity. To the south of the wall is the administrative center.

Many small island chains as if some catastrophe had drowned whole continents leaving only the tips of the highest mountains above water. One major land mass like a misshapen dumbbell straddling the equator. Most mines and farms in the Northern section. Most of the prisoners are kept here, though a very special few are squirreled away on one of the islands.

The prisoners capable of working in the mines are sent there without regard to training or skills. Those of lesser strength work on the farms or in the smelters. The weakest work as clerks and cleaners and in other service jobs.

Bribery and other corruptions are close to non-existent; There is nothing a prisoner can offer any Kliu that would make it worth the danger of dismissal and being sent back to the overcrowded homeworld with its miserable underclasses or to the few colonies the Kliu Berej have managed to acquire where life tends to be short and harsh. In addition to the dangers in dealing with the prisoners, the Kliu regarded what they were doing as herding animals; one did not enter into negotiations with beasts unless one was a pervert of some kind.

Life for the prisoners was dull slogging work that wore the body out; even the strongest seldom lasted more than a dozen years in the mines; those who did lighter work had to cope with the gravity and lasted little longer.

While no prisoner had ever managed to get off-world without being ransomed, a slow trickle of men escaped from the mines and the farms into the wildlands where they managed to scrape a precarious existence ignored by the Kliu. They were a problem time resolved; there were no females of any species on Pillory; the Kliu refused to take them. The native beasts (no intelligent lifeforms there) were budders and splitters and completely asexual. The escapees went where they chose however they could, made some minor raids on Kliu installations and shipments, never sufficient nuisance to justify hunting them down.

Rostico Burn had been nearly two years on Pillory when Picarefy slid undetected into a quiet section of the Asteroid Belt.

Picarefy's lights seemed to blush as she showed off the warroom she and Lipitero had put together somehow in the intervals between other activities. "A surprise for your birthday," she told Skeen with patent insincerity, "nothing important." With a sigh in her voice, she added, "We haven't had time to finish incorporating some of Petro's innovations, so there are blind spots, but she's promised to work on that while we're splitting to Rallen." Her lights danced with pleasure, an exuberance that leaked out into the room and tickled Skeen into grinning. "I can see farther and faster than any ship living," she exulted, "I can wiggle through any screen I ever heard of and maybe some not invented yet. Petro has, listen to this, worked out a way to slice loose from set buoys if there aren't too many of them and . . ." dramatic pause . . . "even a way of maybe snapping back at a snagship." Remotes came rolling in with tea and sandwiches, laid out a light meal on the handsome conference table that took up part of the space in the smallish room. "Sit and let Petro tell you about it."

Being particularly fond of rare roast beef sandwiches, Lipitero piled them on her plate and spooned honey into her tea before she said anything. Tibo was amused by the situation, preferring to sit back and watch it unfold without getting involved. Timka too had nothing to say; the sleep teacher had inserted enough information into her head to give her some grasp of what was being offered, but none of it was felt-knowledge. Skeen was exasperated and amused, but far from detached; she had too much riding on the utility of Lipitero's offerings. After several minutes of silence filled with the soft sounds of eating and drinking, she said, "Well?"

Lipitero put down the remains of a sandwich, patted at her mouth with her napkin. "I'm not sure how much you know about the old Ykx?"

Skeen made an impatient gesture. "Assume I know anything you told Picarefy."

"I thought as much, but I wanted to be sure. Two things you should keep in mind. My ancestors turned elusiveness into a high art, and they lived in a region that had at least one minor war going at any given moment and sometimes several." She took a sip from her tea bowl. "There was always the chance one side or another was out tracing ships, and they weren't particular whose, and snatching them into realspace which was hard on the ships and crews and often deadly since the hooks were clumsy things and one time in three exploded the fish rather than reeling it in. They kept refining the snatchers, first one species then another, and the old Ykx fought to keep up with them. So. The Remmyo dug out and duplicated for me the flakes we had from the time before the Gate; that's his joychoice, he's a student of ancient things. On Mistommerk we didn't have much use for a lot of that technology." Again she stopped talking, sipped at the cooling tea. "No starships, for one thing. Lifefire's blessing on his playtime, otherwise no one would have remembered those cobwebby remnants and the information on them. Picarefy helping me, I've been reading them and transferring them into her files. So. We came across some of those old devices the then-Ykx used to defend against being snagged. Picarefy ran them against what data she had on this day snagships and out of this, that and the other, we think we've cobbled together something that just might work, it should induce waves of instability in the gravity sink which we hope would eventually blow the generator. Some hope. Better we don't have to test it."

"Amen to that." Skeen laughed and did a sitting bow, touched head and heart with the fingers of both hands. "And congratulations." She straightened. "If I put my mind to it, I could wish we'd done some more testing on the Lander. I never got near her top speed."

"You were the one in a hurry to get here."

"So I was."

"Skeen . . ." Timka was frowning at the world analog turning slowly in one of the screens. "That might be mostly water, still there's a lot of land to search. And a lot of prisoners to search through. I don't see how we're going to find one man. I came along this far figuring you knew what you were doing, you always have before, but if you don't mind, I'd feel easier if I wasn't jumping in the dark."

Skeen grimaced. "Sorry, Ti, I keep forgetting it's not just me and Tib doing this and other people can't read my mind like he does." She edged the floatchair closer to the table, leaned on her crossed arms. "This is how it goes. There's a hard way and an easy way; we'll try the easy first. Everyone who knew anything about Burn says he's a lot like me, in looks and in the way he acts. Buzzard was emphatic about it and he reads people better than most. Burn comes from the Cluster, I come from the Cluster, he acquired an Empire cruiser and escaped in that, I came out in a destroyer. Me, I never got snagged, but there were a couple times those early years when I missed it by the thickness of the sweat on my skin. He's thin but wiry and he's young; chances are better than good he was sent to the mines. Me, I wouldn't stay where the Kliu put me one minute longer than I had to, especially not in the mines. Mines or farms, he's gone. He'll be living somewhere in the wild making life hard for the Kliu when he gets a chance. We'll do a grid-scan of that north bulb . . ." she waved her hand at the screen, "see what's there, then I'll think where I'd go if I was him, go there and look."

"And if he's not there?"

"I exercise my talents on the Kliu files. Escapee or not, Kliu should know more or less where to find their prisoners. In case there's someone who wants to ransom one of them. There won't be all that much security in the headquarters building, who'd they need to keep out? But that Island's R and R for the guards so it's always thick with Kliu and there's not a lot of cover for nosy bipeds. And Burn could be dead already. I hear he has a flash temper. He might have goaded one of the Kliu into

stomping him. Or one of the fugitives—they won't be a
gentle lot, that bunch. If that's what happened, then
we're in for some more inspired guessing on my part,
backed up by whatever traces we can find as to where he
left the Veil. So. More questions? Right. Pic, clear the
table and spread the printouts, we'll be looking at ins and
outs, those are the critical times and I want to be sure
I'm not missing something that could come up behind me
and bite."

Lipitero and Tibo stayed with Picarefy. Tibo was annoyed, but there wasn't room for him and Timka both
and Ti's shape shifting was more valuable than his talents
here. Even on the way back it'd be useful; Burn was
another body to fit into a space that was cramped for
two. Ti could shift to her serpent form and tuck herself
into any available crannies. With so little space and nothing to do (the Lander flying herself) but sleep, eat and
excrete, it was a very long three days from the Belt to
Pillory.

When they reached the orbit of the outer moon, they
crept past so close to that moon Skeen felt her skin
crawl; she sat barely breathing, her thumb poised over
the abort sensor that would slew the Lander about and
send it into flight mode. In the screen before her she
watched the gun nodes, ports and zipships slide by, so
close and detailed it seemed she could reach out and
touch them. The near brush was deliberate; if Lipitero's
shield developed a leak, there was still time to back off
and get away.

The dark little moon went bumbling on; the silver
mayflies scattered about its surface caught the sun and
glittered, but they stayed put. The gun nodes stayed
shut. The shield was tight.

The Lander poked its nose into the atmosphere and
slowed yet more until it was creeping along like a fragment of cloud, reading air currents, sliding along them
with almost no disturbance, easing down and down toward
the dark side of the twilight line, gulping power like
a glutton. Skeen knew what to expect, she'd done some
testing on the way here, so she watched with knowing
gloom as the gauge line shortened.

They moved into the grid search, sucking up data through the array of sensors across the belly of the Lander until night over the continent ended. The little ship landed with the dawn, set Petro's spiders to weaving camouflage over her and sighed with pleasure as she took off the shield. There was more than a touch of Picarefy in her voice as she told Skeen and Timka, "Take a walk or something and let me sort out what I got; you make me nervous fidgeting in here."

They were down in the crater of a dormant volcano, tucked up close to some squat trees covered with a fine red dust. Red dirt spread around them, dropping in a gentle slope to a turgid smelly lake in the center of the crater. Several stands of reeds taller than the trees grew out of the water, a cross between tule and bamboo with short stubby leaves like knife blades, tough enough to stab with. Each reed was subtly different from its neighbors in color and configuration, a red like dried blood, a green so dark it was almost black, fire orange, a deep sapphire blue, shades and blends of all those colors, mottlings and stripes, a few with feathery sprays of seedpods bursting from their tops. The largest of them were bigger round than Skeen's arm. She worked on a blue reed with her knife for some minutes and barely scratched the surface. Panting with the effort she struggled back up the slope. "Virgin and Hopeless would adore those things," she said, pausing between words to catch her breath. She eased herself carefully onto a knotty root. "If they want them, they can come get them." She tried laughing, started coughing as the dust caught her in the throat. She spat, started, her heart thudding painfully as a hand-sized creature covered with stiff fur striped red, brown and gray, exploded from the dirt by her feet and went skittering away on a dozen short stubby legs. Timka-cat pounced on it, flipped it over, poked with long sharp claws at its plated underbelly, patted the frantically waving legs. Skeen rubbed her back against the rough bark, but nothing seemed to help the ache in her muscles.

When she stepped from the argrav environment contained within the Lander onto the surface of Pillory, the sudden increase in pull was a jolt to her system. She'd expected to breeze through acclimatization because she

was born on a moderately heavy world (1.3 g) and because she was fit, strong and had gone hard on weight
training while Picarefy was on the way here, but that one
step taught her the difference between 1.3 and 2.75.
Looking at the numbers, the difference didn't seem that
great, but the drag didn't quit; there was a constant
painful tiredness and even breathing was work.

Timka had less trouble. She looked frail and had been
reared on a light world, but she was Min with that
extraordinary Min body. All she did was shrink a little
until her muscles and the Min equivalent of bones were
denser, then moved about easily. Her cat-weasel form
was chunkier, squatter, more big cat than weasel and it
flowed across that powdery dirt as if she'd been reared
there the whole of her life.

They slept most of the seventeen hours of daylight. As
soon as the sun set, the Lander retracted the camouflage
and reset the shields. She rose cautiously, spiraled up to
search height and continued with the grid.

Five days later the Lander settled back beside the lake
and began chewing over and sorting out the data she'd
collected.

Skeen sighed and stepped from the cradle of the argrav
onto that clinging red dirt she remembered with distaste
from her first experience of it. The fist of gravity closed
more loosely on her this time.

Timka bounded past her and ran through a flock of
reddish leather-wings, scattering them like leaves on the
wind, kite-shaped fliers with thick hydrogen-filled veins
webbing the whole undersurface of their flat bodies. Head
canted, ears flicking as she listened to their scratchy
shrieks, Ti-cat sat on her haunches, her mouth open in a
hot red grin, her club tail sweeping back and forth,
stirring up a fine cloud of dust that settled swiftly back
only to puff up again with another sweep of that tail.
"Ti," Skeen yelled, "stop playing with those birds and
come help me set up the shelter." She rubbed at her
back, took hold of the pull strap on the dolly and started
for the small clearing in the trees Timka had nosed out
the last time they'd been here.

Timka shifted back to Pallah but kept a neat coat of

fur; there was a chill bite to the air in spite of the great red round of the huge sun just clearing the horizon. She capered over to Skeen, face stretched into a hieratic grin like some sylvan godling playing the mythic Fool; something about this world, maybe the heavier gravity, was intoxicating her. Singing cheerfully, if what she was doing could be called singing, bird warbles and animal calls and songs she'd picked up partying with Briony in Sundari Pit, she helped Skeen inflate the shelter, knock in stakes and chain it down. Beginning to grumble at the labor, casting eyes of desire at the shadows under the trees, swiveling her ears to catch the whispers, grunts, rustles that came out of them, she helped Skeen haul food and other supplies from the Lander to the shelter, setting her burdens down where there was open space not bothering to stow anything. When Skeen wanted her to help set up the guard ring with its shield dome plus generator, spyeyes, alarms and rotating cutter beams, she called a halt. She told Skeen, "I don't know anything about this stuff. Better I should do something I know, let me go on the prowl and see what's out there so we'll know better what to expect here and afterward."

Skeen watched her fidget, sighed. "All right. When you get back, stand off and yell so I know it's you and I can open a gate for you to come in. Um, be a little careful, Ti. Worlds like this can turn up nasty surprises."

Timka warbled a bit of wordless contempt for possible dangers, shifted back to the stocky cat and went bounding off.

Skeen sighed again and went to work setting up the guard ring. Ti was drunk with hubris and that could get her killed. She punched a spike into the hardpan and moved on. Wet kiss Bona Fortuna for me, old Djabo, and let the worst predators be nocturnal so Ti won't run into anything she can't handle. Tap in another spike and move on. She'd better sober up a little or she's going to be worth damn all in this business. Shit, I need her flying around scouting for me, that's the point of bringing her. Working quickly despite her growing fatigue, she finished setting the spikes and began slipping the caps on them, dogging them down with practiced ease, doing a swift check of power packs and circuits. When she was finished, she flipped on the system and moved around the ring, checking the web with a reader, making sure she'd left no holes and that every sector was functioning as it ought. Rubbing at the back of her neck, working her shoulders to ease the ache in the muscles, she moved to the shelter and looked around. The water comber next, so I can fill the tank. Then the miniskip. I should get that ready while it's still light, don't want to go fiddling around, dropping things in the dark. She stretched, yawned, groaned. Damn cat, Djabo bite her tail, she should be here helping me, not off playing somewhere. She grinned ruefully. And don't you wish you were out there with her. She started to turn off the web so she could get the water comber set up out by the lake but arrested the motion when one of the cutter heads swung around and a beam pulsed once, stabbing into the shadow under the trees. Wild shrieks, hasty rustles, then whatever it was went rapidly away. Skeen frowned. She shut off the general field but left several of the cutter heads on independent sweep, then she went to check with the Lander to see how the survey was getting on.

Crimson twilight. The sun a series of rubies laced between black peaks.

"Skeeennn." It was a whispered wail outside the perimeter.

"About time you got back." Skeen opened a gate between two spikes, pointed them out to the blackness under the trees. "Between here and here," she said. "Come straight to me."

It was the pale body of the Pallah that strolled into the ring. Timka looked exhausted and more than a little hung over. "Did you bring my clothes?"

"In the shelter. You hungry?"

Timka winced, shook her head.

"Bellyache?"

"I overdid the hunting. A lot." Timka rested a hand on her stomach; its shallow curve had acquired more definition and there was a drumtaut look to the skin that underlined what she'd said.

"Could be some of the life here is toxic. You want to watch what you eat."

"That's no problem. If something starts making me sick, I just shift and leave it behind."

"Min." Skeen started for the tent. "You're shivering. There's plenty of water, some of it hot, you can wash off that damn dust and get comfortable. Lander has finished sorting the survey and done the printouts. I've skimmed over them and I think I know where to look, I want to see what you think."

They sat cross-legged on the shelter floor leaning over a low extruded table examining a relief map of the northern continent.

"Mines are black," Skeen said, "farms, green. Administrative centers, flitter fields, that kind of thing, gray. What's interesting to us are these red blotches. Those are life-readings the Lander got not connected to any of these other centers."

There was a flurry of loud noises outside the shelter, the flare of cutter beams visible through the round windows of the shelter's largest living space. Timka shivered. "Aren't we being, well, rather noisy?"

"The satellites? Dormant volcano, that takes care of the heat. Heavy deposits of iron ore, that masks our metals, enough anyway for the crude sensors the Kliu have up there. Wouldn't make it with Petro's stuff, but we don't have to worry about that, she's on our side. The light show out there? Most of it's round the edges of the clearing where the canopy is thickest. Not a lot of light is going to leak out. Even if it does, we've still got our best defense, the Kliu mindset. Whatever they happen to see, they'll explain away because it's not possible to have intruders on the ground." Skeen frowned. "You didn't come across anything that big and mean?"

Timka shook her head. "Just small stuff like that skitter you roused this morning." More shrieks and flaring. "Are they going to keep that up all night?" She hugged her arms across her breasts. "What happens if some of those things whatever they are get through?"

"We run like hell for the Lander."

There were three clusters of life readings that might be escapee camps. The nearest was in what appeared to be a

cavern high up in the wall of a monstrous canyon which
lay at the boundary between mountains and plain about
fifty kilometers west of them. The river running along
the bottom of that chasm had its source in the lake they
were camped beside. The second cluster was in the same
mountain range but about five hundred kilometers farther north beside a long skinny lake. One of the mining
settlements was a short distance off, several small farms
with lush crops near harvest were laid out in a deep
valley a few kilometers beyond the mines. The third
cluster was far to the north out in the middle of the
Plain, no settlements or mines within many days' travel.

Skeen tapped the canyon. "Not this one. Look." She
fished among the fax sheets beside the map, pulled out a
halfsheet with what looked like several views of a stunted
root system. "The caves. No back door. None." She
looked up as another wave of whatever hit the defense
web. "Stupid gits, they should know by now they can't
get at us. Hmm. I suppose those things are why the fugitives wanted the safety they'd get in that rat trap. It gives
me itches to think of living in a hole like that with only
one way out." She moved her finger up the mountains,
touched the lake. "Let me come back to this one." She
rubbed her thumb over the Plains settlement. It was
much the largest of the three. "This is a possibility.
There are fots somewhere in this mess." She riffled through
the stack of papers but didn't pull any of them out.
"They show an organized settlement, sod houses, farms,
livestock penned in fields. Been there a long time. Probably have their pick out of the fugitives from the mines
and farms. From what I've heard of him, Rostico Burn
would be welcome. If he is there, it means he's given up.
That's why I say this is the second choice. Two years is
too short a time to lose hope and rage and settle down to
vegetate. Me, I'd be here." She tapped the lake camp.
"It's pretty well camouflaged by trees like the ones we're
under right now. It's close to a clutch of mines, offers
possibility for raids, close to farms to supplement what
they can scrounge out of the wilds. Might be the easiest
group for a newcomer to find; it'd also be the best
guarded and most dangerous. No vegetating there. What
do you think?"

"If it were me, I'd choose the Plains settlement. That's why I think you're right."

"Well, now that's settled, let's get something to eat. This is going to be a busy night. You hungry yet?"

Timka shook her head. "But I wouldn't mind a bowl or two of tea. And I wouldn't mind your telling me how we're going to get through that." Another wave of attackers had hit the shield web.

Skeen grimaced. "I was so busy being efficient and getting everything packed onto the miniskip . . ." She got up from the table, all angular, impatient moves, filled with nervous energy, crossed the to kitchen nook. "There's not one fuckin' weapon in this place, Ti, except this," she slapped the darter holstered on her hip, "and it's worth a load of spit against what's out there. This isn't my sort of thing, great hunter of the wilderness blowing beasts to shreds. If the fuckin' stupid gits would get the message and go away, let 'em live to arthritic old age, I don't care."

"So we sit in here until they decide they've had enough. You think they'll quit when the sun comes up?"

"Don't know and don't care." She shook some tea leaves into the strainer, tapped the water heater into high, then sent a stream of boiling water through the leaves into the pot. "I'm not going to wait them out, um, if you don't mind scrambling for the Lander." She punched up a meal for herself. "You sure you don't want something hot? Up to you." She shook the strainer, lifted it out. "Tea's ready, take it to the table, will you? I'll be over in a minute."

"You interest me strangely, Skeen my friend. Just what is it you want me to stick a claw in?" Timka came back for the bowls and the honey she liked in her tea (though Skeen made faces each time she spooned it in). "If you think I'm going to jump without knowing where my feet land, forget it."

Skeen pushed the fax sheets aside and set her tray down. Outside, the bests renewed their attack. When the light faded again, Skeen frowned, swung round to face the nearest window. "That one was, um, quieter, didn't it seem that way to you?"

"Not enough to mean much. Several of the hits have

been like that but they always come back heavier in the next or the one after. So. You've got a plan. What is it?"

"They aren't fliers; they're hitting the web from the ground, you can tell that by the way the cutters swing. The canopy is fairly thin over the middle of this clearing, you can take a look at it, see if you can fly through it, if you can't I'll have to think up something else. Once you're out, you get to the miniskip. You get the gas grenades out of the cargo-pod and fly them back here. I hate to waste them on those beasts but I'm getting nervous about this place, I think we should get out fast as we can. Not just this lake, away from Pillory altogether. Well?"

Timka gazed into the bowl cupped between her hands. "It might work. Yes. I'm willing to have a try." She gulped the rest of her tea, stood up. "Let's have a look at the leaves." Quick grin. "Or did you pack the torch too?"

"Now that's not logical, Timmy." Skeen laughed at the face Timka made and wondered, not for the first time, who'd first called her that and why she hated it so much. "With the kind of roots these trees have, I'd be falling on my face or otherwhere every second step without a torch. It's in the clip by the door. Come back and let me know what you think. I'm going to finish my meal in peace, you hear."

The air under the flickering forcedome stank of roasted meat and the deathvoiding of the beasts; the dead were dark piles their shapes still secret, lit by erratic bluewhite flickers from the web and the occasional stab of the cutter beams. Skeen stood close to the shelter, the control in one hand. She turned to Timka who was crouched in bird form close to the guard ring. "Ready?"

A rustle of feathers, a harsh squawk.

"I take it that means yes." She entered the command, activated it. The top vanished from the scrawled web of the dome. "Go."

The bird form rose from its squat, began running round the ring, long legs scissoring faster and faster until finally the choppy wings took hold and the bird labored up and up, it slid through the gap, went crashing through the thin layer of leaves and vanished beyond them, still working hard to overcome the pull of the dirt below.

Skeen sighed, strolled over to the ring and turned the torch on the body of a beast that lay apart from the rest though it was as dead as the rest of them. A disc-like body with a sharp hump in the middle, a head on a short thick neck, great round mouth filled with razor teeth, round staring eyes, black, beady, around the top of the head like a crown. Clusters of legs, longer than she expected, splayed out on both sides. "Ugly fuckers." She giggled. "No, I'm wrong, you do it on your own over here." She played the torch over the creature. "Just as well, I doubt even a mother could love something like that."

Timak dropped the pack of grenades, landed heavily a moment later. She shifted to Pallah and squatted, panting, while Skeen began working the straps loose.

Skeen glanced at her. "Any trouble?"

Timka swallowed, sucked in a long breath, exploded it out. "Nothing ah in the air. That stuff is heav vy."

"Put on some fur or get dressed. You won't have to fly again. I hope." Skeen squatted beside the pack and began snapping together the launcher. "Better stay biped. I've got nose plugs in here that will fit your Pallah form, but I'm not so sure about the cat." She dug in the bag, tossed a film-wrapped packet to Timka. "You can wait a while before putting them in, they're misery doubled." Holding onto the pack, she straightened until she was standing. "Got your breath back? The shelter's buckled down, the skitter discs can chew on it till next year and have their trouble for their pains. All we have to do is wait for them to come again."

"My clothes?"

"Round by the door with the rest of the gear."

"Another reason for me to stay Pallah, eh?"

"Why else."

"Your friendly neighborhood packhorse reporting for duty."

"Duty right now is get dressed and wait."

"Funny."

"What?"

"An hour ago we wanted them to go away. Now we dance in circles till they come back."

"Get dressed, Ti."

"Yeah, right, Sarge."

"What?"

"Briony taught me some things."

"Obviously. Can you chase pneumonia off by shifting?"

"What's that?"

"Never mind; get dressed and get back here."

They came out of the night and flung themselves at the force dome, snarling, warbling back-of-the-throat threats, screaming howling hissing as the cutter beams slashed through them without stopping them, dark garish pastiches of fur and shell and leathery skin, red, gray, vomit orange, green, purple-black, polyjointed forelimbs slamming into the field like clubs, scimitar claws trying to slash through the shimmer of pale light that was the only evidence of the impenetrable shell that kept them from the meats inside.

Skeen programmed loops into the dome, oval holes outlined in fuzzy buzzing blue, one over each of the spikes. Starting where the attack was the hardest and noisiest, she launched gas grenades through the loops, working methodically about the guard ring until she returned where she'd begun. The cutter beams sliced away at the gradually decreasing number of attackers, lighting up the pale blue, almost invisible puffs of gas spreading in a thick ring outside the dome, part of it seeping gradually away under the trees, part into the dome. The air that came through the nose plugs had the burnt smell that meant the gas inside was thick enough to put her out if she was careless. She slid the bagstrap over her shoulder, clicked three more grenades into the launcher and signaled Timka to follow her.

When she reached for the far side of the guard ring, she collapsed it and went trotting through, moving slowly enough so she wouldn't be tempted to open her mouth and gulp down the gas-laden air. She snapped her fingers impatiently. Timka grunted and switched on the torch.

Tense, alert, they moved under the trees toward the lakeshore. Timka swung the torch in wide sweeps across

the path ahead, but kept her exaggerated enhanced ears
tuned to the rear, listening for anything coming at them
from behind.

Multilimbs driving it in a hitchety swoop toward them,
the beast came silently out of the night, mouth open, two
forelimbs, twin claws like steel hooks reaching, ready to
swing faster than the eye could follow, coming at them
without snarl or threat, many feet setting down on the
uncertain footing, mold and knobby roots, surely and
without more than faint pats. Coming behind them, behind the sweeping fan of light, coming from the sleep and
slaughter around the shelter, faster, closer, reaching. . . .

Timka gasped, clamped her lips shut to keep out the
gas, snuffed up burnt air through the nose plugs, leaped
off the path into the trees, torch coming around, shining,
holding steady on the best despite the gyrations of her
arms and body.

Skeen swung at the gasp, launched the first of the
grenades into the gaping mouth of the beast, then put
another on the ground a step ahead of it, flung herself
around one of the trees and stood pressed against it,
watching the result of her shots.

The torch beam trembled a little but kept the beast
pinned.

The first grenade went off in its throat. It shuddered
and kept coming, head jerking about out of control,
body juice spraying from the holes in the neck. The
second grenade went off beneath it, drowning it in the
pale blue gas mist. It kept coming, breaking out of the
dissipating cloud.

Skeen waited, holding the launcher ready.

One meter, jerky pat-pat of the several feet, lurching
plunge that could have been comic if it wasn't so terrify-
ing. Two meters. Head jerking more and more wildly.
Legs starting to tangle, to lose sequencing. It tripped
itself and crashed to the ground, making more sound in
its fall than it had made in the whole of its run. Lay
scrabbling aimlessly at roots and mold, tearing up and
flinging away clumps of fungus and earth, small weeds,
bits of bark.

Timka kept the torch sweeping the backtrail, returning
to the beast, moving away, until Skeen snapped her

fingers and stepped onto the faint path once more, an
animal trail leading down to the drinking spot on the
lakeshore. They went on, moving at the same easy trot,
breathing through the noseplugs and fighting the need to
gasp in more air through the mouth.

The trees grew smaller and farther apart, then they
were on the stretch of red dust running in a gentle slope
to the water.

The camouflaged Lander was a dark mass a few meters
off, the low black miniskip lost in the shadow beside it.
Skeen stopped alongside it, tested the air. The burn
smell was almost indetectable. She grinned and shucked
out the plugs. "Gahh, I hate these things." She held
them in her fist, looked wistfully at the lake, slipped the
plugs into her belt pouch. "Ti?"

"I'm here." Timka moved up beside her. "The gear's
in the cargo pod. We going? It'll be raining soon." She'd
stripped off shirt and trousers and was wearing a dark
sleek coat of fur. Arms folded, shoulders rounded, she
was eyeing the skeletal miniskip with some distrust and
considerable disfavor. "Will that . . . that . . . thing fly
through the storm that's stirring up there?"

"We won't crash. Climb in. I want to reach the camp
area before sunup."

"Hmm. It's your funeral, I can fly out."

"Get in, grump, or you'll get your fur wet." Skeen
cracked open the pilot's pod, stretched out on her stomach and pulled the cover down. She fit the commandcap
onto her head, began a methodical check of the machine.
When she saw that the second pod was filled and sealed,
she tapped on the lift field and began a swift slanting dart
for the clouds.

After a cold, rough eight-hour ride twisting through
the mountain peaks, buffeted by powerful erratic winds,
battered into wild swoops by a monster thunderstorm,
Skeen eased the skeletal miniskip into a high dry cup just
over a ridge from the lake.

Timka uncurled cramped fingers and retracted her claws.
In a stiff silence she clicked open the pod cover whose
padding had proved so inadequate and got to her feet
groaning. When Skeen chuckled, Ti snarled then shook

herself through several transformations before retrieving the hybrid Pallah cat-weasel form she'd learned on that final rush to the Gate. She bounced on her foot pads, swung her arms and purred at the rush of energy that always accompanied the assumption of this form.

Skeen stopped laughing. Her own aches and bruises were going to stay with her. "Min," she muttered. Ignoring Timka's growing exuberance, she unstrapped the stunrifle, got the nightscope out of its case and snapped it in place. She shrugged her shoulders to make sure the pack and the groundsheet roll were sitting comfortably, then frowned up at the lowering sky. It wasn't raining here, now, but the storm was shifting north faster than she liked. It was very dark, a little over two hours till dawn. She fixed hooded stickums to her boots, straightened. "Ti?"

"Here."

"About two hours till dawn, that time enough?"

"It'll take a while to search the camp. Hadn't we better get started?"

"Be careful when you're down there."

"Take your own advice."

"Not much for me to be careful about. Just sit and watch the rain come down."

With Timka padding silent behind her, Skeen picked her way cautiously up the scree-littered slope, cursing under her breath as she started small rockslides every few steps; carefully as she tried to set her feet down she couldn't help sounding like a herd of tinks on a mating run, she could move like a ghost's dream through the most cluttered interiors in just about any city one could name and steal the sweat off a sleeper, but here. . . .

She reached the top and found a grassy hollow where she could look down the shallow escarpment at the lake while she lay concealed behind a dead bush with brown dead leaves clinging to branches crooked and knotty as arthritic fingers. She wrapped herself in the camouflaged groundsheet; it was waterproofed, would keep the threatened rain off her and the rifle, cut the bite of the knife-edged wind that swept over the top of the ridge and blasted down the cliff face. When she was settled she twisted her head round so she could see Timka. "You can fly in this?" She had to shout to break through the howl of the wind.

"Don't worry about me. You just be ready to drop the rope when I whistle."

"Bona Fortuna give us you have something to whistle about."

"You said it." Timka moved closer to the edge, swaying as gusts of wind slammed into her; after a swifter shift than usual she was the broad-winged bird shape she'd found most efficient at coping with the gravity and the thick air.

Skeen adjusted the night goggles and watched her circle out over the water then slant toward the thick woolly treetops. Seemed like every day now Timka grew more restless, more reckless; handling her was like juggling a bomb with the failsafe missing and the timer running. Skeen watched the Ti-bird slip like smoke into the treetops. The two of them bumped against each other more and more whenever they were together, whether it was on Picarefy or at a Pit Stop. Or here. It was becoming obvious they weren't going to settle into a team no matter how much they liked and respected each other and how effectively they worked together. Skeen smiled when she remembered the slippery submissive Min woman way back there on Mistommerk. Set that Timka next to the one fishing in the leaves down there and you'd hardly think they were the same species. Scratching at her nose she scanned the silent canopy then the lake some dozen meters below her. A large cold raindrop spashed on her cheekbone, rolled past her mouth, another landed in her hair. She sighed, pulled the groundsheet over her head and settled to what she expected to be a long wait. Patience, Skeen. It's a job, like all the other jobs, you know how to be patient when you're working. Don't think about what happens when this is over, you don't know what's going to happen. One step at a time and keep your mind on the step, or you'll fall on your face, old girl. The raindrops were falling more heavily. The dead bush in front of her was rustling with a curious almost-music, a complex of sounds that was like the world singing to her, scratches, long creaks, the rhythmic plop plop of the rain. She was warm, dry, comfortable, the soreness from the bumpy ride was easing out of her, the greatest danger she faced was falling asleep; how many times had she waited like this, casing a building, scouting a ruin? Enough times she knew how to deal with distractions and the powerful urge to sleep washing over her. Live in the present moment. Watch. Wait. Be ready to deal with anything Timka scared up.

The camp was a group of mud-wattle huts built around tree trunks, their floors a meter and a half off the ground. Rain dripping in sharp brittle tip tap tunks about her, Ti-cat slid through the deep shadow under the huts, nervous because those high floors suggested strongly that predators like the skitterdiscs prowled here at night. She circled the outer rim of the camp, but found no sentries. That made her yet more nervous. There should have been sentries. Either she was missing them in the noise of the rain and wind, or the fugitives who lived here depended on local predators for their security. Lifefire, I've haven't time to waste on this. She ghosted to the nearest hut, lengthened her neck and nosed aside the leather curtain blocking the small doorway. Two sleepers inside. She readjusted her vision, moved her head carefully so she could see the faces. No Rostico Burn here. She brought her neck back to normal, slid to the next hut, repeated the process. One by one she searched the huts, her stomach in knots, her ears flared to catch the slightest sound, hoping the watchbeasts had gone off to sleep since dawn was galloping closer, not really believing that. Hut after hut. Her neck muscles ached, the colloid was thudding in the veins in her temples, she felt like throwing up. Time passed. She squeezed down on frustration and impatience, continued with her careful controlled exploration. Long neck, nose about inside the hut, short neck, move on, slow slow, never relaxing, methodical, taking each hut as it came, working in ragged spiral deeper and deeper into the camp, cold uncomfortable, wet and angry.

She moved round a patch of berry brambles and stopped.

A rough cage made of lake reeds bound together with

thin tough cords about three meters across and two meters high. Someone inside stretched out on the mud, sluggish streams of mud or blood moving across pale skin.

She edged closer. Her foot touched cold metal sunk out of sight in earth the consistency of thick soup. A chain snaked past her, one end locked around the nearest tree, the other end about the captive's waist. A man, naked, prone, either asleep or unconscious. From the look of his back, he'd been severely beaten and raped before he was thrown in the cage. Her muzzle wrinkled into an unhappy snarl. I don't like this; Mala Fortuna, as Skeen would say. His head was turned away from the chain tree; she padded around the cage, dropped on her stomach in the mud and lengthened her neck again.

He twitched and shivered, groaned as her head moved toward him. What she could see of his face was contused and distorted, but enough like the fots she'd examined to leave little question about who he was. Rostico Burn, Mala Mala Mala Fortuna yes. And he was very like Skeen, more than she'd expected now that she saw him in the flesh. She retracted her head, shook herself into shape for running

A powerful kick in the side sent her tumbling over and over to crash into the chain tree. Dazed, she scrambled to get away, managed to throw herself around the tree in time to avoid a second blow though the skitterdisc's foreclaws scraped a deep furrow into her flank before the tree intervened. The thing was fighting as silently as the other had, the one that followed them from the shelter; praying that it would maintain that silence, Timka clawed up the tree until she pulled herself onto a broad limb springing horizontally from the trunk; the tree shivered and swayed as the skitterdisc slammed into it, the limb groaned under her weight threatening to drop her under the claws of the silent furious beast below her.

Flustered and panting, Timka clung a moment to the brittle bark, struggling to concentrate. She huddled next to the trunk, got herself propped as steadily as she could and finally managed the shift to her birdform. The shaking got more frantic. The skitterdisc whined, the sound rising and falling, growing louder and louder. Timka shuddered, her feathers rasping against the bark. She forced her mind away from her doubts and fears, began climbing higher in the tree using talons and beak to pull herself up. Nearly drowning as leaves emptied rain on her, fighting to hold on in spite of the soaking and the sway which got wider and more violent, she wrenched herself upward until she reached a level where there was a fragment of open sky. She launched herself into the rain, sank heavily until her wings bit into the air and powered her up again.

Unwilling to fight the windshears along the face of the low scarp, Timka flew the extra distance around the end of the lake where the slope and windspeed both were gentler, circled round behind the ridge and finally dropped beside Skeen, cawing a warning before she settled. She shifted to Pallah, shivered and grew herself a thick coat of fur. Though the rain had slackened a little, it cut deeper, combed into long stinging lines by the icy wind.

Skeen twisted round, pulling the ground sheet tight about her face, blinking away the rain that hit the side of her head and dripped into her eyes. "Well?"

"Found him," Timka said. "There's a problem. He's inside a cage and chained to a tree. And he's been pounded into chopped meat, he's not going to be walking out of there. Another problem. The men there don't bother with sentries, they sleep in huts they've built in the trees and let a herd of skitterdiscs handle their security. One of them nearly got me, came down on me before I knew it was there. Between the wind, the rain and the mud, I wouldn't have noticed a stampede of draft horses."

"Shit."

"True. You'll have to help me carry him. Will that thing keep the skitters off?" She leaned over and tapped the barrel of the stun rifle.

"I think so. Let's hope I don't have to use it. Noisy. If you and that skitter haven't already waked the camp, this will do it."

"Maybe we should wait till tomorrow night."

Skeen moved restlessly, the ground sheet rustling as it shifted about her body. "We probably should. No." She turned her hand over, looked at the ringchron. "We've still got an hour of real dark and there's more rain blowing up, I want to go now." She frowned. "You're sure it's him?"

"He's enough like you he could be your brother." Timka grinned at her. "A MUCH younger brother."

"Snip. You're going to have to swim me across that lake." She got to her feet, shook out the groundsheet and rolled it into a small neat bundle, then she took the rope and the piton that had shared the sheet's shelter with her, exploded the piton into the stone and dropped the rope over the rim. "Come on. The sooner we get started. . . ."

Timka flowed out of the shadow under the trees, shifted to the Pallah-cat hybrid. "As far as I can tell no one woke or noticed the noise the skitter and I made. There's a herd of the beasts poking in the mud around something that smells like a garbage dump, but none prowling in the rest of the camp, the one who chased me must've given up and gone back to his kin. Mud's getting deeper by the minute. If Burn doesn't wake up soon, he's going to drown in it." She dragged her arm across her flat muzzle, squeezing some water out of the short plushy fur on it, water immediately replaced by the hard rain now falling about them.

Skeen kicked at something obscured by the mud. "I cut two of the reeds in case we need a stretcher to carry the man."

Timka clicked her tongue against her teeth. "To get him across the lake, maybe. Better I carry him and leave you loose to guard us."

"If you can manage the weight . . ."

An exasperated snort. "Better than you, Nemin."

Skeen knelt beside the cage, cursing under her breath as the light blade labored to cut through the tough reeds. Built the fuckin' cage around the man and didn't include a door, stupid gits. Timka prowled about, nervously alert, watching for early risers and wandering skitterdiscs, feeling the miniscule changes that announced the arrival of dawn. Rain dropped around her, the drops splatting like bullets into the mud; the wind was turning erratic, the steady pressure changing to powerful gusts that swung unpredictably from side to side.

Setting the lengths of reed beside the stun rifle that she'd left leaning against the cage, Skeen crawled through the opening. The captive was blowing bubbles in the mud; as Timka said, a bit more and he'd drown in it. The light blade cut through the soft iron of the chain far faster than it had the reeds. She put her hand on the man's shoulder, cursed again. Hot. She lifted his head, slapped him lightly. He grunted incoherently, moved his arms, his hands in feeble aimless gropings, subsided into passivity. "Djabo," she muttered. She touched the butt of the darter, shook her head. "Better not." She got him belly down over her shoulder and began crawling through the opening.

Timka was waiting there. She knelt and took the body as Skeen slid it off. A hand on his wrists to hold him in place, she shrugged his body about until she was satisfied with her balance, then rose carefully to her feet. "Far as I can tell nothing's moving," she told Skeen.

"We better be." Rifle ready, Skeen went trotting off, heading for the lake.

They reached the lake in a gust of wind and rain; the sun was up and the darkness was diluted to a mottled gray; the water was gray, the jewel colored reeds were dark grays and light, the water was a choppy hard gray, small wrinkled chop that struggled with wind and gravity; the rain was gray, hard hammering drops that catapulted from the clouds with force enough to bruise Timka through her fur. Rostico Burn's body shielded her from some of it; for one fleeting moment she wondered what the beating was going to do to his already battered flesh, but the smell of blood, feces and mud that clung to him was powerful enough in spite of the rain to wipe away whatever charity she had for him; what she wanted most of all was to get him off her so she could shift and leave the stench behind.

She slid him off onto the hard dirt of the lakeshore, sighed with relief as she straightened.

Skeen knelt beside him, touched his face, tucked fingers under his chin to check his pulse. "Tough kid. Got fever but going strong." She scowled at the icy gray water. "Though what swimming the lake's going to do to him, I don't know. Or me. Djabo, that stuff is cold."

Timka glanced at the gray anonymity of the trees a few meters off, then at clouds that looked close enough to touch. "Not much choice," she said. "The sooner we get him to the miniskip the sooner you can do some temporary repairs on him." She waded into the water, shifted to her dolphin form and waited, jolted about on the rough surface, for Skeen to pull Rostico Burn into the water so she could take them across the lake.

Cross the lake. Skeen half-drowned and chilled to the point she is close to losing control of her fingers, her legs. Rostico Burn's pulse turning thready and uncertain, his body shuddering with waves of chill. Skeen swarms up the knotted rope, tosses the ground sheet down to Timka. Timka wraps it around Burn, ties the end of the rope about him, then scrambles up the rope to join Skeen and help her haul the man up the face of the scarp. Load Burn on Timka's back (still wrapped in the ground sheet which gives Timka a lot of trouble since it makes him slippery and less flexible), run recklessly downslope without caring what noise they make or what predators they stir up. Shoot him full of antibiotics, turn on a small heat radiator, fold him up in the cargo-pod, slam it shut over him and take off, vanishing into the clouds to begin the dangerous flight back, tossed about by the powerful but erratic winds, dipping into swift dangerous slides, only Skeen's quick reflexes and the longago craftsmen who built the miniskip for her keeping them off the rocks, eight hours of storm and slide, roller coaster ride, gravity exaggerating every drop and drift. Eight hours, eyes burning, head aching, body almost forgotten so intense her concentration on the sensor readings. Tempting to put down for a while, a rest, she can't maintain her alertness that long, so long since she's slept and the sleep so disturbed, yet if she stops to rest, Rostico Burn will surely die, he needs food and relief from the pull of the gravity, he needs his wounds cleaned out and bandaged, he needs plasma and more than the rough guess and go for it medicine she'd pumped into him so he wouldn't die on them right there. Eight hours, she felt her age as she hadn't felt it in years, so weary, so sore, so feeble, feeble as Mamarana, are the ananile shots being eroded? should she get them redone? they were supposed to last another ten years, all this effort, this drag of a planet, were those nullifying the shots? Don't get off on that, Skeen, don't let your mind wander. Pull up and away from the cliff that almost sucks them in, almost feel the surface of the miniskip scraping on the granite. Keep your mind on what you're doing, Skeen, you can worry about this nonsense later. If it is nonsense. Eight hours, interminable hours, then, finally, the crater and the round lake below them. Glide down beside the mound that was the Lander and hope, pray, will the camouflage to be sufficient, hope, pray that the Kliu have not located them and aren't waiting there, spider for the draggle flies they were.

They landed at the lake in a gray afternoon hush, high clouds, no rain, and the wind had dropped to a whisper.

Rostico Burn was babbling with delirium, fighting feebly against the constriction of the ground sheet and the four intrusive impertinent hands that struggled to pry him out of the cargo-pod. He shrieked and drooled and clawed at them with fever-driven strength, but they finally peeled him out and got him on Timka's back. With Skeen trotting beside her, the stun rifle ready, Timka hauled him to the shelter.

The tall spikes of the guard ring were kicked over, more than half of them with the caps knocked off and carried away, the hard packed earth was clawed into tatters, but the shelter stood where they'd left it, somewhat frayed and dusty but intact. The small clearing was empty. Skeen unsealed the entrance, Timka dumped her burden on the floor of the common room and shifted to Pallah to rid herself of the man's stink. Burn gabbled and clawed at the floor, managed to get onto hands and knees and started crawling toward the entrance. "Idiot," Timka said, "doesn't he realize he's been rescued?" Face twisted with distaste, she put her foot on his flank and pushed him over.

"Obviously not." Skeen was bending over the sensor

board, waking up the facilities of the shelter. "We're
going to need plenty of hot water and the medkit." She
sneezed. "Djabo's drippy nose, not just for him." She
shivered. "A bit more and I'm coming down with pneumonia. Ti, you think you could set up the water comber?
We all need baths. Here." She gave the small combox to
Timka. "You mind? Go talk to the Lander, she'll get
things ready for you, tell you what to do if you run into
trouble. I want to get some hot soup ready. And there's
enough water for me to clean the boy up some so your
tender nostrils won't be offended." She gave Timka a
weary smile to take the sting out of her words.

"Lifefire, yes." Timka closed her fingers about the
combox, concentrated and grew a covering of short thick
fur. "I'll bring the medkit." A last glance at the feebly
scrabbling form, then she left.

Skeen touched the back of her hand to her own forehead, grimaced as she felt the warmth there, acknowledged the boiled onion feel to her eyes and the prickle at
the back of her nose. No help for it, she was in for a bout
of coughing and sneezing and general misery. Ananile
shots to retard aging, regrowing limbs and organs, med-
dling with genes, but still no cure for the common cold.
She yawned, stretched, slouched across the room to the
kitchen nook, sidestepping as Burn reached for her ankles. She dialed hot broth and a tubful of water. Sipping
at the broth she ambled back to Burn, wrinkled her nose
at the stench rising from him. The bruises were coming
up nicely, plum purple with tinges of red and ocher. The
rain had washed some of the mud and blood away but
streaks and stains of both wound about his body in a lazy
calligraphy of violence. He was quieter now, weaker. She
emptied the mug of broth, wiped her mouth and knelt
beside him; setting the mug on the floor, she twisted her
fingers in black hair that felt distractingly like her own
when it was long unwashed and turned his head so she
could see his face.

She stopped breathing, closed her eyes but couldn't
erase the image. This was her uncle as she remembered
him, maybe a little younger, a little leaner. Opening her
fingers, she let his head thud down, she couldn't bear to
touch him a moment longer. They kept telling me he

looked like me, I couldn't see it, not in the fots. Ay, Djabo Djabo, Mala Fortuna, I can't. . . . She swallowed, her throat pricking with the developing cold, her eyes prickling with tears she refused to shed. He muttered, his hand came round and slapped down on her knee. She struck it away and started to get to her feet, changed her mind and settled back. Shivering convulsively, she forced herself to look at him. Slack mouth moving, half open eyes glistening wetly, swollen nose. Tongue clamped between her teeth, she lifted his head again and examined his face more carefully. He wasn't as much like her uncle as she thought, not really. Not when she took his features apart. Her stomach stopped knotting and she could breathe again instead of gasping. She set his head down, more gently this time, got to her feet. Poor young Rostico Burn, kicked about and left to welter in his gore. Time and more than time to clean him up a bit. She took him by the wrists and dragged him into the bathroom. By the time Timka got back with the medkit, she had him cleaned up and stretched out on a pair of towels. He was unconscious, breathing hoarsely, his pulse thready and uncertain.

Timka passed her the black box and stood behind her, staring down at Burn. "Now that you've got him washed up, he looks worse."

"Hmm. I've about used all the water in the reservoir."

"If that's a hint . . ."

Skeen moved her shoulders impatiently, opening the kit.

Timka scratched at her thigh. "Lander says the sky has been buzzing since morning, but there's no sign she's been noticed. Those were supposed to be fugitives, weren't they? It looks to me like they are in oddly close touch with the Kliu if that's so."

"Mmm." Skeen was working down the man's back, spraying every cut, scrape and bruise with a whitish mist from a small squat can. She paused a moment to rub the back of her hand across her nose, waited out a sneeze, then she was at work again on the lacerated flesh. She heard Timka go on talking then her voice fading; when she finished with Burn's backside, she rolled him over and straightened up and sat on her heels, shutting her burning eyes, letting herself feel the aches and rheums

that filled her body. After a moment she looked around,
but Timka was gone. She shrugged and went back to
work tending the boy's hurts. Not really a boy, she
thought, he'd reject the term with vociferous disgust, but
he couldn't be more than a third of her age. And I'm
feeling every year, this fuckin' cold, this Djabo-cursed
world that never lets up. I swear, once I get off here, I
swear by my soul or what's left of it, I'll never set foot on
a heavy world, it's g or less for me, for sure. She set the
kitprobe to dealing with the pneumonia flooding his lungs
and the rest of the ailments inflicting his inside and went
to check the water supply. Timka had managed, with or
without the Lander's help. The reservoir was filling quickly.
She drained off a tubful into the heating chamber and
started the pulser.

With the prospect of a hot bath sparking a new surge
of energy, she finished bandaging the boy, muscled him
into one of the bunks and set the heaters going. The
kitprobe was buzzing softly, steadily, not throwing one of
its hiccupping fits; that meant most of the infection and
the illness was cleaned out of his system and what he
needed now was what he'd get, uninterrupted sleep. Something she wouldn't mind for herself after the bath. For
sure, after the bath. She didn't want to leave before
dark, not after what Timka said about the sky sweep.
Even with Lipitero's shields there was always the possibility one of those flying eyes would pop up close enough
to get a good look at them; the Lander wasn't invisible,
far from it. She went back into the bathroom, stripping
as she walked, smiling with pleasure as the heat from the
radiators and the steam rising from the tub began to
work on her stuffed head and sore body.

Timka lounged in a pneumatic chair, stun rifle across
her knees; she was back in Pallah form, wearing tunic
and trousers, small slim feet buckled into heavy sandals.
She scratched idly at her wrist and watched Rostico Burn
snore. He was lying on the floor, a pair of blankets under
him, another drawn over him; the grayness was gone
from his face; apart from the snorting snores, his breathing was slow and steady. The bruises on his face and
arms were developing lurid colors, but the worst of the

swelling was gone after six hours of deep healing sleep and the efforts of Skeen's medkit.

Skeen came yawning in, mug in one hand, the other rubbing at her nose; her hair stood in soft crumpled peaks about her thin face, her eyes were shiny with the cold that was fruiting in her, her eyelids heavy, the tip of her nose red. She stood a moment looking down at him, sniffed and rubbed her nose again. "You talk to the Lander recently?"

"A few minutes ago. The sky has been clear since sundown except for some activity north of here close to the horizon."

Skeen emptied the mug, wiped her mouth with the back of her hand. "I don't know, Ti, every time I think about it I change my mind. What do you think? Question him here before he's had a chance to get his defenses working, or get him back to Picarefy where we'll have time and room and, well, be a lot less likely to kill him getting the data out." She looked at the mug and at the man, sighed and sank to the floor, all elbows and knees until she was settled beside the large black medkit. "He looks too much like someone I . . . I loathe, Ti, I don't trust myself on this. What do you think?"

Timka produced claws and clicked them on the stun rifle's latticework stock. "What I think is we should get out of here. I know, I know. Listen, from what Mamarana said, more than one has tried to get Rallen's location out of him and it hasn't worked all that well. Give him time to get organized and I wouldn't play Picarefy down, but I doubt if she's mean enough, you see what I mean." She turned a hand over and contemplated her claws. "Two things. One, he's never going to get off Pillory without you, make him buy his way off. Two, there's a reason for the shape he's in and why he was in that cage. Maybe the reason comes in two words. Abel Cidder. Uh-huh. Not so big a coincidence, don't you think? Given the interest he has in you with lagniappe like Rallen thrown in to sweeten the bait? Ah! Three things, this being the third: turn him over to me if nothing else works. Remember, I've got the Min mindreach, I'm fairly sure he's too weak to keep me away from whatever I want to know."

"Even with a mindlock?"

"I don't know mindlocks, but mindlocks don't know Min."

"True." Skeen ran her hand through her hair, towsling it yet more. "We'll need him awake. Um, Ti?"

"What?"

"Move back a bit more, will you? Watch him. Buzzard says he's like me, I wouldn't be too friendly right now." She tucked the holster flap behind the darter's butt, pushed into a squat, balancing on her toes as she reached for the medkit. She ran the dioscog along his body, sucking her teeth as the readings showed how fast he was recovering from the battering he'd received. "Ah, to be young again," she murmured. Across the room, her chair blocking the entrance, Timka snorted. Skeen looked round. "No comments from the audience, please." She dug into the kit, found the shotgun, slipped a stimtab in the magazine and shot him in the arm. She unfolded swiftly, kicked the medkit away and stepped back to wait for him to wake.

He stirred, his hands groped, felt the blanket over him, plucked at it, went still as he opened his eyes a crack. For an instant he looked startled, then his face went blank. He pushed stiffly up until he was sitting cross-legged with the blanket pulled about him. He licked his lips, opened his mouth, shut it, swallowed. "Hello," he managed, given Skeen a quick rueful look as his voice cracked in the middle of the word.

Skeen nodded. "Who are you?"

He glanced past her at Timka. Ti lifted the rifle, gave him a grim smile. He produced a grin of his own, as broad and charming as he could make it given a cut lip and assorted facial contusions. "Say who you want, cousin," he told Skeen, "and I'm him."

"Cousin?" A caustic disbelief in the word, Skeen looked him over. "Kind, maybe, but not kin."

"Ah, you crush me, you do." He shook his head with exaggerated melancholy. "But it's not polite to be pushy, so I'll drop that matter. What does Skeen the Marvelous want with me?"

"More know me than I know. Who are you?"

His battered face closed up for a moment then smoothed

out then reclaimed the grin. "Why not. Rostico Burn's the name I run under."

"Good. Talking kin, you want to give me line and sept? Not necessary, I'm just curious."

"Sure. Consider it a freebee. Rassta Abti soha Fahan, motherline Gyare-Ayf, fatherline Harac Farn, major sept Bryssal on Tor-Farran. We were a colony branch, you're Torska, I'm Lingaban."

"Hah!" Skeen sucked air between her teeth, glanced at Timka. "Would you believe it, Ti? He really is a cousin." She scowled at Burn. "I hope you don't consider that a recommendation, most Brissali I ever knew were about as loving as a set of gritchers. You look like an uncle of mine. . . ." Her mouth twisted, she made an angular gesture, annoyed with herself because she couldn't keep from picking at that ancient sore. "I've got a deal for you."

"I'm listening."

"You brought a shipload of artifacts to the Buzzard once. You called it Rallen work. Do you remember Rallen?"

"Why am I not surprised? I remember Rallen."

"You'll notice where we are."

"From the feel of it, on Pillory. Which is very interesting since according to a lot of people, that's impossible. Unless Cidder finally caught you and this is his price for letting you offworld."

"Hmm. I hadn't thought of that. Why were you in that cage?"

He hesitated, looked around at the shelter, frowned past Skeen at Timka.

Timka played her claw tips along the rifle. "Talking about Cidder . . ." she murmured.

For an instant an angry frightened ferret looked through his eyes, then the charming grin was back. "Were we?"

"My patience is limited, Burn." Skeen paced about, careful not to get between the boy and Timka. "The cage."

His grin got a little strained. "They didn't tell me much," he said slowly, "but Shyem the Rat showed up day before yesterday. Cidder's name came up in the, ahhh, party they played on me, what I heard, he and the

Kliu were tight, he gets me or the orodokk would be
erased down to the dirt."

Skeen slapped at her side, swore under her breath.
"He's here, then. That . . . that . . . he's out there sniffing after me." She straightened, angry, impatient. "This
is the deal. We'll get you off Pillory and out to a Pit, you
give us Rallen." Three quick nervous strides and she was
taking the rifle from Timka. "Try holding out, and Ti
here will suck it out of you. Give him some samples, Ti."

Timka stood; she stripped off her clothing and shifted
from Pallah to cat to rockleaper to owl and back to
Pallah. She got dressed again, crossed to stand in front of
him, a sweet mocking smile lifting her lips. "That," she
said softly, "is to show you I'm a lot odder than I look
and I've got talents you've no defenses against."

Skeen handed her the rifle and moved away. "Make up
your mind fast, Burn, the sky's full of lice and I want out
of here before they swarm me." She sneezed, wiped her
eyes. "Fuck. Skeen's word on it, you'll get off Pillory if
I do. And I will."

In spite of the sleep he'd had and the cleansing of his
system by the probe and medication, his energy levels
were at low ebb; though he fought to keep face and body
noncommittal, his desperation showed through the frayed
cloth of his control. "The Veil," he said, speaking slowly
with visible reluctance.

"Where?"

"Close to the Bell Rift."

One hand jigging impatiently against her thigh, Skeen
looked at him with exasperation. "I'm not about to pull
this out of you word by word," she said. "Get on with
it."

"You know what they call the Rope, it's off the shoulder end, a slit in the gases like a short length of rope
fraying off into the Veil. Rallen is in that slit moving
toward the Fray, going to slide into it fairly soon as those
things go. Their sun, they call it Nepoyol, is a singleton
solitary and a young star and with the Veil as close
around them as it is, you can't even get a hint of other
stars." He stopped talking and fixed his eyes on Skeen,
waiting to see what she was going to do. She'd given her

word, but he wouldn't fully trust that until he was off Pillory and free in some Pit or other.

Skeen turned to Timka. "What do you think?"

"Feels like he's telling the truth." Timka lifted the stun rifle, crossed her legs, settled it back on her thigh. "I'd have to get closer to deep read him."

"That's good enough for now." She ran her eyes over Burn, her mouth twitching into a half smile. "We didn't think to bring clothes for you."

He relaxed, though this too he tried to hide from them. "I can make do with a blanket and some pins," he said gravely, his eyes laughing at her. He jumped up, holding the blanket about him, looked down at himself. "My robe's a little long." He kicked at the folds. "It needs some redesigning."

She tossed him her bootknife. "You hungry?"

"I could eat this blanket."

"Kaff or tea and what else? The autochef waits."

"Ahhhh, oh, Marvelous Skeen, oh, queen of legends and slipp'riest slider in all known space, if you only knew how I've dreamed of ham and fried eggs and whole grain toast and thick sweet kaff that's half cream and thin thin slices of rangeo fruit. And if you'd come up with some safety pins, I'm ready to appreciate a fine home-cooked meal."

"There's a repair kit in the bedroom, part of the services. Home cooked I don't know about, but we'll do our best. The autochef will, I mean. If I tried to cook, well, forget it."

"Most unfeminine of you, cousin. I'm sure our kin would be terribly disapproving." He laughed and ambled out through the arch that led into the first of the small bedrooms.

Timka looked after him. "He's going to try something; what about the hatch in there?"

"He's not stupid, Ti." Skeen smiled at the doorway, feeling a surge of affection for her mischievous cousin; she wasn't going to trust him a hair beyond what she had to, but it was unexpectedly pleasant to find a member of her family who was worth more than the spit it'd take to drown him; she found herself liking the boy in spite of his face, the face of the uncle who had abused her from

the day she came to live with him and her aunt, who'd
made her life a misery till she killed him. Who still gave
her bad dreams when she was feeling low. Fleetingly she
wondered if there were more of her cousins about like
Ross, would it be worth the danger to look them up? She
tucked the thought away and turned to the autochef,
looking through its repertoire to see how closely she
could approximate Burn's menu.

"It's impossible." Rostico Burn followed Skeen out of
the shelter, shivering as the chill night air coiled round
his naked torso. The blanket had been reduced to a
knee-length kilt. Much of his earlier wariness was wiped
away and he looked younger than his double dozen plus
years. Part of that, Timka thought as she followed them
out, is euphoria about getting out of here, something I
certainly agree with; the rest has to be Skeen, she's
acting like she's found a long-lost son. I wonder how
Tibo's going to take this. "Nobody can get through Kliu
security, Skeen," Burn went on, waving a hand at the
sky meagerly visible through the leaves. "I don't know
how many have tried it, I've talked to some of them.
How . . ."

"A very good question." A rich mellifluous voice came
from the deep shadows under the trees. With the voice
came powerful light beams, pinning the three of them.
"Be still. I prefer not to damage any of you." A small
figure less than a meter high stepped into the fringe of
the lighted area. "Well, Skeen, we finally meet after
missing each other so often."

"Hunh. Better for me if we missed this one." Skeen
took a step toward him, ignoring a snapped command
behind the lights to stay where she was. Cidder held up a
hand and the protest subsided. She set her hands on her
hips, one close to the darter. "What now?"

"A talk, I think. That question your young friend was
about to ask."

Timka stared past Skeen, eyes wide, finding it hard to
believe what she saw. The Abel Cidder she'd heard so
much about was a tiny man, a doll of a man, but not the
sort that invited cuddling, a hard rubber man wide as he
was tall. Thick white wavy hair, broad beaky nose, wide,

thick-lipped shapely mouth, high cheekbones, large lobeless ears. Dark brown eyes, thick straight brows. Large hands, a sculptor would like them, veins and muscles sharply defined. Flexible bass voice smooth as chocolate cream, a wonderful voice so rich the ears were sated by it very quickly. From what she'd picked up about him from Briony and others, interested because of Skeen's reaction to his name, he was heavyworld born and bred, a deadly fighter, impossible quick, deceptively strong. Formidable as his physical equipment was (absurd to think of that doll as formidable, not absurd at all when she looked twice), his mind was far more dangerous; he had a capacity for assimilation of data and an ability to flip through combinations of unrelated snippets of fact that made him almost as eerie as Virgin with her disembodied companions, coming out of nowhere to take his quarry like a frog flicking his tongue to catch a fly. Bona Fortuna had cuddled round Skeen up to now; more than once he'd missed her by the breadth of a hair due to that luck and to her highly developed capacity for wriggling out of tight spots. A dozen times in the past dozen years, they'd come close to colliding but until now they'd never met. Until now he'd never had to stand with a crick in his neck looking up at her. In spite of his confidence in his own worth, in spite of his superiority to almost every being he'd met, he never got over having to look up into the faces of fools; he didn't mind them laughing at him, this evidence of their stupidity merely fueled his contempt for them, it was that eternal backbend in his neck that got to him and turned him mean. Watching him, Timka saw that meanness grow as he gazed up and up at the tall lean woman standing before him.

Rostico Burn had the good sense to keep his mouth shut and do his best to play shadow to Skeen; his eyes darted about looking for a crack he could dive through. The situation was hopeless right then, but he was ready to jump the moment he saw a chance, relaxed but alert, covering his intent with a layer of gloom.

Abel Cidder whistled, three-note birdsong. His forces came silently from under the trees, three Kliu and five bountymen (trust him to be sure his safemen outnumbered the local help), the torches that pinned Skeen, Burn and

Timka in the hands of the bountymen. At a gesture from one of them Timka rested the stun rifle against a tree and stepped back. Another gesture and Skeen began working with the buckles on the belt that carried her darter. Hardly breathing, the Kliu and the bountymen focused on her, watching her as if she were a live bomb about to explode. Cidder leaned toward her, tongue moving along his lips, his eyes glistening, an avidity in his face Timka found revolting; disarming Skeen, she thought, was getting him as excited as a bunch of feelthy pictures (the Poet's words, remembered from some long ago feast when he had to do the pretty for country kin, the Poet's disgust remembered and present in her now). She drifted to the edge of the light zone without drawing attention from Skeen and her slow scornful semi-strip, teetered on the verge of diving into the dark, but changed her mind when one of the torches flicked her way. She concentrated on standing very still and looking helpless. Fervently she willed the bountymen and the Kliu to overlook her, to forget about her, to cease noticing her.

Something happened inside her.

She felt gray, translucent. As if the torchlight speared through her without touching her.

Startled, she felt at herself, began to lose the sense she was a shadow among shadows. The torch flicked toward her again, away again.

Abruptly enlightened, once again she willed them not to notice her, making herself inconspicuous in a way she hadn't thought about before but had discovered in this moment of need as she'd discovered the hybrid Pallah cat-weasel at another such moment. It came so easily she was astonished. A gesture made by accident, then recognized.

Skeen lowered herself to the ground, began pulling off her boots. She set them beside her, tipped them over with a swing of her arm. "Satisfied?" Without waiting for an answer she got to her feet. "Or do you expect me to strip?"

The ghost of a shadow, Timka faded unnoticed into the darkness under the trees. As quietly as she could, she stripped off her clothing, tucked the bundle into a crotch partway up a tree, then shifted to cat-weasel and settled herself to wait until she was sure no one had noticed her desertion.

A skitterdisc shrieked a short distance off. Cidder looked away from Skeen. "What's that?"

One of the Kliu drew near, muttered something Timka couldn't hear. Skeen laughed. "They like this clearing and they don't like us. Nearly tore the place down last night. I expect we're cluttering up their dance ground and this is their week to party."

Muscles knotted beside Cidder's mouth, but he showed no other sign the disdain in Skeen's voice found any target in him. Ignoring her words he left two of the Kliu on guard by the lakepath and herded his prisoners inside. To Timka's relief he didn't notice one of them had decamped; she pressed her muzzle against her paws to push back the whining cat laughter, but as the shelter's entrance irised shut she stopped being amused and began wondering what her coup had gained her. It's like that time in the caves with Angelsin, she thought startled, happening all over again.

She began prowling warily toward the path, intending to get the stun rifle back into her hands. Before she could do anything useful she had to be better armed.

The Kliu left outside were jittery and unhappy, twitching with every sound, backing nervously together whenever a skitterdisc shrieked. Timka was nervous herself; the screams were getting closer, putting a time limit to her efforts; she had to get the rifle and break the others loose before that herd arrived. Her muzzle wrinkled into a silent snarl, her long ivory whiskers twitched and jerked. The Kliu were clinging stupidly to the path and the tree where she'd set the rifle. Boneheads, you should be out in the clear so you'd have time to blow the beasts apart, go on, get! Naturally they didn't listen to her and continued to cling to the illusory shelter of the trees. She crouched belly to the ground fuming with frustration.

Skitterdiscs screamed, the sound crackling about under the clouds, call and response. Close enough to make the hair stand up along Ti-cat's spine.

The Kliu expelled gases through their eating mouths, bubbling farts of fear, gabbled at each other through their breathing mouths and rocked deeper into the shadow

under the trees, looking for a place where they could
huddle together and feel a bit safer. Timka watched them
fidget off, willed them away away away, her mouth
stretched in a fierce cat grin as they disappeared into the
darkness. She crawled closer to the tree, moving slowly
and as silently as she could manage across the knife
edged grasses that grew in stiff clumps between the trees.
You made your fatal mistake, Abel Cidder, you left
these housepets out here instead of one of yours; you
were too afraid of Skeen escaping you again, yes, that's
it; she's managed it so often. She shifted her right arm
into a tentacle like one of Henry O's and sent it gliding
round the tree. She lifted the rifle, easy, easy, brought it
back around. Slow and quiet, she told herself, slow and
careful, don't you make a mistake, you can't afford it if
you want to get off this miserable world. If you want to
get home again. Sometime.

She crept awkwardly across the crumpled grass, knowing she left traces a blind man could follow, not worrying
much about it, those Kliu were worse than blinded, they
were blinkered, their attention resolutely elsewhere. When
she felt safe enough, she set the rifle down and shifted to
the Pallah cat-weasel so she'd have hands (and speech if
she needed it).

One of the windows in the first of the small bedrooms
was an escape hatch; it could be opened from the inside
with no trouble and from outside with a bit of fiddling.
While skitterdisc cries ululated more frequently around
the clearing, call and response orchestrated into a cre-
scendo of warning coming closer and closer, Timka chewed
on her lip and struggled to find the latches that would let
her into the shelter. She could hear a faint burring sound
through the wall, rising falling intonations, pauses, thank
the Lifefire, Cidder was still talking. She ripped the
latches loose, clenching her teeth at the unavoidable
squeals and scrapes; she peered in, the room was empty,
she rolled through the opening, landed on her feet and
stood poised, the stun rifle ready, listening.

Cidder was talking, that rich creamy voice rolling on
and on, ordering Skeen and Rostico Burn pinioned, de-
scribing the facilities for extracting information at the
Kliu headquarters.

Timak ghosted toward the open archway, staying close to the wall where she couldn't be seen. She waited until she heard feet scraping on the floor, the sounds converging. They were on their way out. She stepped into the arch and turned the rifle on them, the whiny twang filling the room and bouncing back at her, the stun field sweeping from side to side, mowing them down, taking Skeen and Rostico Burn with them. She jumped the fallen, raced to the exit. The sound of the rifle brought the outside Kliu running; she sprang through the door, got them before they could react, though that was closer than she liked, behind her the shelter began leaking air where a wavery beam from the hand weapon pierced the skin when the left side Kliu got off a pulse as he fell.

A skitterdisc screamed, so close it might have been beside her. She started, the hot-wired nerves of this form driving her into wild bounds as she swung round, hunting for the beast that made the cry, but the clearing about the shelter was still empty. She fought for calm, loped under the trees and reclaimed her clothing, reclaimed also the Pallah form. She could think better as a Pallah and she was going to have to do some quick hard thinking.

Weary and frightened she returned to the slowly collapsing dome, dragged Skeen and Rostico Burn out. She touched Skeen's face, pushed her head about, clicking her tongue as she felt the flaccidity of the muscles. She didn't know how long the effect would last. She looked at the bodies, she looked at the wrinkled folding dome. A large cold drop hit her in the middle of her head, another hit her shoulder. The wind was beginning to rise and the night was noisy with shrieks and creaks. She looked around, shook her head. "Stupid." She dragged Skeen and Rostico Burn back into the shelter, came loping out a big cat, the combox in her mouth, and raced off into the darkness.

She dropped the dolly's strap, swung up the rifle as two skitterdiscs came rushing at her, dropped them as she had their cousins, grabbed the strap again and raced for the Lander. She'd knotted some of the Kliu harnesses together and tied them down, but Skeen and Rostico Burn flopped about on the bed of the dolly. The rough

ride down the track had loosened some of the knots. She
worried about losing them when she could spare a moment to think of it which wasn't often.

The herd's forescouts had come tottering into the clearing as she was leaving it, they'd sounded their whining
shrieks and set at her, a lurching clumsy flinging of their
limbs that looked impossibly awkward but carried them
forward with a speed and impetus that made them formidable fighters. Timka shot the leaders then plunged on
along the lake path, the dolly jolting behind her, slowing
her with its drag and the need its mass placed on her to
shorten and thicken her legs yet more. Skitterdisc scouts
came at her, popping out of the darkness, out of the busy
small noises of the night, silent until they were on her,
shrieking, drooling, all teeth, claws and ugliness.

By the time she reached the shore she was bleeding on
arms, shoulders and thighs and her head was throbbing
from the twang of the stun rifle, the howls of the
skitterdiscs; Skeen and Rostico Burn were nibbled at,
Burn more because he had more bare flesh available to
their claws.

The Lander had stripped off the camouflage webs, her
lock was open and the lift ready to drop. Timka dug into
Skeen's belt (she was relieved to find it still wrapped
about one of the straps; Skeen would skin her if she left
the darter behind, or her tools), used the cutter to slice
through the straps that held the two bodies onto the
dolly. A blue-white light blade slashed past her shoulder
and she heard the scratch thump of more skitterdiscs as
they ran for shelter. "Thanks," she called. "Drop the
lift. We need to get out of here."

As soon as the lock was closed, while the Lander was
humming busily about her, Timka strapped Skeen and
Rostico Burn into the chairs and got her own cushions
ready. She thought a moment, then found some spare
wire and wound it about Burn's wrists and ankles. She
found the pulse in his wrist, sighed with relief as it beat
strongly under her fingers. She circled round, checked
Skeen, stood beside her facing the lights dancing across
the panels (she was still uneasy talking to a no-face like
this, uncertain about its limitations; Skeen called the

Lander *her*, but Timka couldn't think of that complex of
wire and metal and crystal as anything but an *it*.) "How
soon can we get out of here? Do you have to wait till
Skeen can pilot you? We'll have half the Kliu on Pillory
sitting on our necks if that's so. Unless you can tell me a
way to wake her faster."

"It would be better not to interfere with the recovery."
The Lander's voice was a pleasant countertenor, suggesting either male or female, whichever the listener chose to
hear. "There are flakes from the coming in, route and
instructions from Skeen; it is possible to retreat along
that line as far as the outermost orbit of the guardmoons,
but beyond that there is uncertainty. What degree of
stun? Maximum? Skeen will most likely be recovered by
then or soon after. Do you wish to start now?"

"Yes, yes. You can do the shields? This time the Kliu
know we're here."

"It is noted; the shields are integrated into the drive
unless Skeen orders otherwise. It would be prudent for
you to take your place, Timka; if you must speak, you
have the combox; it will be heard no matter what else is
happening."

Timka nodded, hesitated, then decided the Lander had
sensors enough and intelligence enough to interpret the
movement of her head. She curled up in her cushions.
"Go."

They burbled up off the surface, spiraling slowly out of
the atmosphere, skimmed past a moonfort and came to
rest an AU farther out.

Skeen blinked slowly, smiled with satisfaction as she
looked round and saw Rostico Burn coming awake in the
other chair. "Ti?"

"Yup." Timka rose from her cushions and moved round
to lean a hip against a bit of unimportant instrumentation.

"Cidder?"

"No doubt he's waking up about now unless the
skitterdiscs ate him, and I doubt they did, he looked like
too tough a mouthful."

Skeen unsnapped the straps, touched a control and sat
up with the chair. "When I saw it was just the two of us
in there, I thought you'd come up with something or

other Cidder was going regret." She examined the schematic in the viewscreen, stopped talking while she entered instructions, then she settled back and examined
Timka. "You don't look different. What did you do this
time? Melt?"

"One thing about traveling with you, Skeen, a person
keeps learning new things if a person doesn't want to get
stomped. I can now shift to a ghost's shadow. Something
no one feels like looking at or thinking about."

"Well, aren't you clever."

Timka grinned at her. "Aren't I just."

"If Cidder is awake now, he's going to be sure he's
cursed." Rostico Burn had contrived to free himself from
the straps and bring the chair upright. "I don't understand any of it, but I prefer my situation to his, poor old
Hound. Ahhh, I hesitate to bring my little difficulties
into this discussion, but this wire is damn tight and I'm
dryer than a hot day on Rabesk."

THREE DAYS TO KILL GETTING BACK TO THE
BELT, ANOTHER HALF DAY PROWLING
THROUGH THE ROCKS TO THE PLACE WHERE
PICAREFY WAITED. I COULD DO THE MAGIC
QUICK CUT AND IGNORE THOSE DAYS, ONE
OF THE BENEFITS OF TELLING A STORY RATHER
THAN LIVING IT. HMM, I THINK INSTEAD I'LL
USE THIS INTERVAL TO FLESH OUT ROSTICO
BURN'S PAST. PICTURE THE INTERIOR AS
SOMETHING LIKE THE INTERIOR OF YOUR
BASIC TV; PICTURE YOURSELF AS ONE OF
THOSE ENTERPRISING COCKROACHES THAT USE
A TV AS THEIR EQUIVALENT OF A
CONDOMINIUM AND YOU'LL HAVE SOME IDEA
OF LIFE IN THAT LANDER. A LITTLE STORY
TELLING CAN LIGHTEN A LOT OF TEDIUM
AND TAKE SOME OF THE CURSE OFF ENFORCED
PROXIMITY. BETTER TO TALK THAN TO GET
ON EACH OTHER'S NERVES TO THE POINT
WHERE DISMEMBERMENT LOOKS LIKE A
BARELY ADEQUATE RESPONSE TO INSULT.

Tors (Skeen's homeworld) and Lingaba where Rostico
Burn was born and raised were companion worlds captured by a multiple star (six elements in all) in a nearly
catastrophic passage not too long after life had begun to
develop on Tors; when the system settled down there
were still some stubborn lichens and small mobiles clinging to the churned-up surface of Tors and sufficient spores
had been leached over to Lingaba to kick that world out
of its pristine sterility. When the system was discovered
in the early days of the Empire, Tors was a lush green

world, a little too hot, but filled with fiercely competing
life-forms of which the most intelligent was a cat-like
predator with remarkably dexterous forepaws. Given a
few more millennia these beasts might have made the
leap to sapience, but they had the misfortune to be in
direct competition with a far more ruthless and efficient
predator. By the time the new Torskan population (fugitives from worlds the first Emperor was bludgeoning into
submission and fitting into his Empire machine) had multiplied sufficiently to control the temperate portions of
the landspace, there were no more caterills, only speci-
men skeletons in museums and rumors that a last pair
haunted the hills of the far north. Finally Tors was redis-
covered and absorbed into the Empire. The Consolida-
tion Wars had destroyed a lot of databanks and more
than one scout report had been lost; it took a while to
chase down those lost worlds and rather longer to convince them they'd fare a lot better under the aegis of the
Undying. The Torskans who held the threads of power in
what had become a stratified feudal society were reluctant to let go, then not so reluctant when the Imperials
showed no sign of pulling the rug from under them as
long as they paid their taxes and kept the plebs in order.
The rebellious were ruthlessly weeded from the population, exiled to Lingaba and left to make whatever they
could out of that austere and unwelcoming world. By
accident of topography and the nature of the settlers,
Lingaba had a considerably looser social organization
and a far less radically skewed distribution of wealth. It
also had a force of Imperial troops garrisoned there and
an Imperial governor with veto power over anything he
didn't like, but for the past two hundred years all or
almost all thought of rebellion had been thoroughly
squashed out of the one-time rebels. Since Lingaba was
rich in minerals scarce on Tors there was considerable
trade between the two worlds and some contact between
branches of the various septs though Torska generally
considered Lingaban crude, crass and untrustworthy while
Lingaban saw Torska as a treacherous snobbish bigot
strangling in the knots of his history.
     Ross was born into a desperately respectable middle-
class family living in the suburbs of a mid-sized city not

too far from the planetary capital. He was clever and showed it before he was old enough to know better. The weight of family expectations landed on him hard. He was surrounded by the clan, uncles, aunts, cousins, connections of the remotest kind, and worst of all, his younger brothers and sisters, his parents. Wherever he went, whatever he did, family eyes were on him, judging him, jealous of him, but depending on him, urging him on, whatever he wanted the family sacrificed to get him and never let him forget that sacrifice. Rebellion churned in him but he didn't know what to do with it. He did well in school because he liked the power knowledge gave him over adults he secretly despised, a secret continually on the verge of exploding out of him; he managed to keep his feelings hidden because they still had the power to punish him in ways he knew he could not endure. Collectively they were far stronger than he was, stronger in their terrible ignorance and even more terrible obedience to gods and rules that kept them from turning their anger on the invisible men and institutions that pushed them back into the mud whenever grinding endless work pulled them a little way out of it. By the time he won the Imperial scholarship to the sector techschool, he'd seen the feet kicked from under uncles, cousins, kin to all degrees. It hadn't happened to his father yet, but he knew that was only because his father had no ambition for himself and was content to stay a repairman on the jitt lines, putting in long hours for barely enough to pay his bills, feed and clothe his family.

When he won the scholarship, he was twelve. They told him (father, mother, all the clan from the fuddled ancients to the urchins running the streets) what a wonderful chance it was. They looked wistfully at him. You'll get out of here, they said. You'll get away. You're smart, you'll be important some day, really really important. They implied (though they didn't say it), then you can help us get out, you owe it to us, it's because of us you've got the chance.

He didn't believe it.

He'd already seen too much to believe that dream. He'd seen a great-uncle who had long ago gone up the ladder to success, the ladder they kept pushing Ross up,

had seen Momak co-opted by the kickers, whole-hearted
in his ruthless tromping on the heads of his kin. He was a
disappointment to the clan because he'd turned his back
on them, but he was also a matter of pride and hope.
Look, mothers told their sons, Momak got out, you can
too, never mind he's a rat who eats his own, you're
better than him, you won't be like that. Look at Momak.
He did it. Work hard and you can too. Ross had seen
Momak kicked back in the muck when his dancing feet
lost their skill on the ladder, when he was burnt out,
used up, when he was flung on the garbage heap where
he'd helped fling so many more, given a barely adequate
income and fancy titles that meant nothing. And when
their sons pointed to that, the mothers shook their heads.
You just be smarter, that's all. You can do it.

It seemed to Ross he had two ways he could go. He
could stay a kickee or join the kickers. The longer he
thought about it, the more clearly he saw that Lingabans
all came to the same end, whatever route they took
getting there. Down in the mud with Imperial heels on
their necks. Momak hung around him, offering him snippets of wisdom from his own experience of the world
beyond Lingaba, looking to ride his shoulders up out of
the garbage pile he'd been thrown into. He couldn't
avoid the man but Momak made the inside of his bones
itch; he loathed him. The thought of ending up like him
made Ross want to lie down in front of a jitt and let it
run over him. On the other hand there was nothing on
Lingaba for him but the whips of disappointment and
scorn in the eyes of his clan and a dull deadly slogging
life like his father's. He turned and twisted, seeking
desperately for some third choice, something that would
give him a chance at self-respect and surcease from
boredom.

A month before he was due to leave for the school that
third way appeared; he didn't recognize it at first, it
seemed only the cousin/uncle no one talked about except
in whispers. Kleys soheyl Fahan was much worse than a
black sheep, call him a black goat; he was a con man, a
thief, a smuggler, a pirate and whatever else he had to do
to scratch a living and keep out of Imperial hands. He'd
been scratching for somewhere around fifty years and

had managed to keep loose, but now and then when things got tight, he slipped back home to let the Cluster cool off. Though they deplored him publicly, the Fahan clan secretly delighted in exaggerated stories about Old Sneak and the coups he pulled off. Imperials came sniffing around Hadda Adda a time or two, but no Fahan ever betrayed him; whatever else he was, he was family and this branch of the Fahan line Bryssal sept had been surviving on Lingaba under Imperial rule of varying degrees of severity for more than thirty generations. Much scarifying and debilitating experience had taught them the value of presenting a bland unbroken face to authority. Uncle Kleys never messed on homeground and the clan never messed with him; he'd spend a month or two telling stories the children weren't supposed to hear (but always did) then he'd slip away from Lingaba and go back to nipping at Imperial ankles.

Uncle Kleys sneaked into Hadda Adda and moved in with one of his nieces, a broad-minded and marginally respectable female who earned a living of sorts from cooking and cleaning, supplementing her official earnings with presents from assorted lovers who appeared and disappeared in her life. She had a house full of children, hers and strays she took in, all of them under ten; she kept them fed and washed and more or less clothed, laughed with them, played games with them, organized them into squads that cleaned house, worked in the garden, took care of the littlest ones, scowered the streets for reusable scrap and brought in vast volumes of reusable gossip. Want to know anything about anybody? Ask Veesey. Uncle Kleys settled into that household with scarcely a ripple to indicate his presence. He played with the children, dug in the garden, made love to Veesey, spent whole nights talking and drinking with kin who dropped in to say hello and hear the new stories about the world *out-there*. Everything seemed to be going along as it always did.

But Momak was back in Hadda Adda. Not back enough, not really part of the clan again, still wanting, still hoping to climb back among the kickers, refusing to admit he was discarded. Hoping. Brooding. And then he saw Kleys in Veesey's back yard, mending her iron, a repaired com

unit by the box he was sitting on, broken appliances
ringed round his feet, his hands working delicately while
he joked and laughed with three of the older boys spad-
ing the garden. He saw Kleys and thought he saw a way
to buy himself back into influence.

Ross was slouching along these back streets heading
circuitously for Veesey's, taking a last sniff at places he
hoped and feared he'd never see again, looking as inconspicuous as he could because his father would skin him if
he knew his son was on his way to talk with that seducer
of pure youth, old Uncle Kleys, and he would know
sooner or later, there was bound to be some snitch about
who'd see him and draw instantaneous and regrettably
accurate conclusions about what he was doing in that
part of town. He saw Momak skulk from the gate in
Veesey's back fence and scoot furtively away; curious,
the boy followed the man.

Momak worked his way to the local platform and got
on a jitt going to Degali, the administrative center. Ross
slipped on after him, sliding in the back door and slump-
ing into a seat by the fender. Momak's bobbing gray
head turned constantly, his mean little squinted eyes
turned here, turned there though never back all the way
where Ross was sitting. For a while Ross kept his head
down, then he realized however much Momak peered
about, he was seeing nothing but his greedy hopes and
the fear that someone would snatch his chance from him.
Ross told himself he couldn't be sure what was happening, but that was just words; if one of his teachers set this
up as a moral problem, that kind of quibbling would be
expected in the discussion that followed, but this was
real. Ross knew by the sick knots in his stomach what
Momak had seen in the yard and what he was intending
to do about it. Otherwise, why would he be on this jitt?
But Ross' guess was not proof and he knew he had to see
for sure what Momak was up to if he wanted adults to
believe him.

The journey took an hour, the jitt clattering and swaying
along the rails, stopping, starting, folk getting on, getting
off, Ross in his seat at the back of the car watching
Momak, Momak sitting up behind the pilot column growing more eager and nervous as the kilometers clicked off

under the jitt's little wheels. At Degali Center Terminal, Momak stumbled off, almost falling in his eagerness. Shaken by the jolt, he ran his hands over his hair, straightened his clothing, arranged his face, then walked on, looking coolly contemptuous of the world around him. Ross followed. Momak strolled to Government Square, looked casually about, then started up the steps of a tall golden building, heading for the great black glass doors set into the austere facade; there wasn't a window visible anywhere in that glittering metal, vertical folds were the only breaks in the mirror surface. Air rushed down in a continuous gale that hammered the boy breathless. He lingered, making faces at himself in the golden mirror surface, drifting gradually closer until he could hear Momak arguing with the guard who stood before the doors and barred his way, a stun rifle held horizontal between them. Momak was shivering with rage and frustration, but keeping his voice down except for a few squeaky shouts. He made no impression on the guard for all his blustering until he flung a word at him: KLEYS.

Ross sidled away, driven by an urgency he could hardly control. Over his shoulder he saw the doors opening, the dark mouth swallowing Momak, but he didn't run until he was round a corner and away from Government Square.

Back at the terminal he hopped into a jitt heading toward Hadda Adda and sat with his hands fisted on his thighs, his mouth dry, a sick fear churning in his middle. Again and again as the jitt shuddered and jerked along, he wondered if he should have called com and passed word what was happening, but no one used the com for anything private. Everyone knew computers listened for key words and voice tones and scanmen took random samples from all com calls. He couldn't take the chance; even if he tried to give warning without appearing to do so, the Imperials would have a record of the call and the mere fact it was made would tangle all of his kin in the mess. He jiggled on his seat, willing the jitt to go faster. If Momak got through to someone important, THEY wouldn't have to use a jitt to get to Hadda Adda. There was just a sliver of hope. Momak was what he was; it would take time for him to convince the Imperials he really had something they could use. Gas collected inside

Ross's gut, he had to break wind, but, oh, God, he couldn't, that'd get him too much attention, might get him kicked off the jitt, the car was crowded, this was a halfday holiday, lots of men going home from work in the city. He wriggled uncomfortably, got a glare from the man sitting next to him, forced himself still. The very worst part of the trip was when he could finally see the warehouses and tenements this side of Hadda Adda. Where Veesey lived was all the way across the city; the jitt stopped and rattled on, stopped and went, emptying as it moved; the car seemed to vibrate in place, getting nowhere, ever and ever nowhere, but that wasn't really true, it was only his impatience exaggerating things. It finally reached his homestop. He swung off, forced himself to stroll (just a boy heading home on a warm summer day after enjoying the delights of the big city) until the platform was out of sight around several corners, then he plunged into the maze of alleys that led to Veesey's place, speeding to a skipping trot as if he ran solely for the pleasure of running, waving careless greetings to people he knew, whistling a snatch of song now and then, keeping a grin pasted on his face when he wasn't whistling.

He reached Veesey's backyard and slowed to an amble, stepped over Patcha and Chelly playing in the dust, waved to Erb and went into the kitchen where Veesey was chopping vegetables for the monster stews she made to feed her brood. There was a new tadling walking round and round the long narrow room holding onto cabinet doorpulls, either a visitor or another orphan Veesey had acquired. Two babies slept in a box on one end of the table where Veesey was working.

Ross fidgeted a moment, looked around; he didn't want to say anything in front of children old enough to understand. When the little boy reached the far end of the room, Ross sidled closer to Veesey, whispered, "Where's Uncle Kleys?"

"Now Rosta, you know better."

"Of course I do." He was indignant for a flash, then licked his lips. "It's important, cousin. Momak's in Degali selling him to the Imperials. He's got to get away."

Veesey set the knife down and frowned at him. "You wouldn't joke about this. Tell me."

Ross jigged from foot to foot. "Veeseee," he wailed, "there's no time." Pinned by her skeptical patient gaze, he cleared his throat, said rapidly, "I saw Momak outside the fence here acting sly, I followed him, he took the jitt to Degali, I followed him, he went to the Admin Building, the guard wouldn't let him in, he argued with the guard, I wasn't close enough to hear much, but I did hear him say Kleys, so I came back, I didn't call com, you know why, I was careful, Veesey, I played like I wasn't hurrying, Veesey, they could come any minute."

Veesey pulled her apron off. "Ross, scoot out of here, get over to Cesto's, tell him what you saw, then you get home, make like you know shit-all about what's happening." She was shooing him out as she spoke. "Don't bother your pa, he's better off doing his job, but tell your mum to get the Larday club over here. Tell her I said it's important, but don't you say why. I'll do the saying. Scoot."

When the Imperials arrived, they upended Hadda Adda, but found nothing, just a few unlicensed jars of homebrew. Never was there such an innocent, placid, law-abiding set of folk. The Guard tore Veesey's house into splinters and dug a five-meter hole in her yard, but there was not a smell of Uncle Kleys. They put Veesey and her brood under question and got sex, squalor and brute stupidity and were satisfied with that because it fit their prejudices so well. They used their probes on houses, huts, businesses and found nothing. Ross' father was deeply indignant and waved the Imperial scholarship seals in the face of the squadleader when the Imperials came to search his house.

The Guards left after three days, dumping Momak back on Hadda Adda though he begged them to take him away. He didn't survive the night. Official records said accident; he fell into a pool in the city park and drowned before anyone found him.

Kleys came to Ross a little later and they spent the night talking.

"Two years," Kleys said. "You can afford the time, Rosta. What'll you be then, fourteen? See how you like it. Just don't let them put the warp on your head, don't believe the line they shovel out. You owe it to your family to give it a try. Maybe serving the Imperials will suit you. Me, I don't think so, you're no Momak. Learn everything you can stuff into your head. Not just the technical side, get history and art and economics and martial arts, anything you're interested in and be interested as wide as you can. Shove it in your head, kid. They'll send you home for a visit every couple years, unless they've changed things since I went that route, I'll drop by and we'll talk again. I'm getting old, starting to move slow and think three times where I did once before. Time I had a younger head helping me think. If you want to scramble with me, I'll teach you the steps. And no, you can't come now, you're too damn ignorant."

At the end of two years Ross was torn. He hated life at school, but he liked what he was learning. He went home for his breakvisit, talked with Kleys, had a miserable time with his family because he'd lost the art of fitting in, lost the threads of daily life that once had woven so thick and warm about him. It took him most of his vacation to learn how to play the clan game again, pretending what he couldn't feel, but when he left he was comfortable with his kin and rather smug at how easy it was to fool them.

The smugness was quickly stripped away when he got back to school. He was starting to stand out from the crowd. The breadth of his studies (far beyond the usual specialization) began to pay off in ways that were not obvious, not startling breakthroughs into new insights, mainly an ease in understanding concepts and a capacity for thinking beyond his current knowledge. All the separate disciplines began locking together in ways he found little short of magical. His teachers talked about him, put pressure on him, showed increasing interest in him. His few friends melted away, most of the students turned hostile. The thing that brought envy, anger and contempt together like a boil was the clearly evident fact that he didn't care about all this preference; the good opinion others coveted came to him and he wasn't interested. He was regularly attacked by one group or another during the first year of this two-year session; one of those beatings nearly killed him. Nothing was done about it; he didn't expect anything would be. Instead, he nosed out a handfight instructor who was willing to work with an enthusiastic and talented student; he was naturally coordinated, came from a 1.2 g world, had unusually quick reaction times and applied the energy and concentration he used with his studies to learning everything the instructor could teach him. He was attacked once during his fourth year. He didn't quite kill them, but broke several important bones and tore loose a number of ligaments. No body shots, no ruptured testicles or spleens, nothing lethal; instead, a broken collarbone, a shattered elbow, a cracked jaw, broken toes and fingers, all quickly repairable and all painful enough to discourage any further attempts to harass him.

At the end of the fourth year he was recommended for advanced political training and offered eventual work in the Heart of the Empire. He accepted with suitable humility and went home for his scheduled breakvisit.

He told his mother about the offers. He was sixteen now and somehow grown much closer to her after the long absence, just as he'd grown impossibly far from his father. They couldn't even talk to each other any more. his father talked and Ross listened and inside he said no no no.

Two weeks before he was due to leave for school he took a jitt to the coast, rented a day sailer and didn't come back. Four days later the boat drifted onshore, belly up. They didn't bother looking for the body. The Imperials didn't try because of the heptopods infesting that part of the ocean, huge, carnivorous, faster than most jetboats. The Fahan didn't try because most of them knew quite well (though it was never spoken of) that Rosta had gone off with Uncle Kleys.

For the next three years Kleys and Ross did this and that (giving the Imperials a bad case of heartburn), visited Hadda Adda when they wanted a taste of home, generated a whole new set of fabulous stories for the clan to whisper when they were elsewhere. Ross was well on his way to joining the list of disreputable heroes the Fahan threw up every generation or so.

But Kleys for sure was getting old; he made a mistake.

Ross pulled him out with luck, energy and quick thinking, but the Imperials got close and stayed there; flutter
how they would, Ross and Kleys couldn't break loose;
then the Imperials started driving them toward what had
to be a trap. In his struggle to shake them, Ross too
made a mistake and Kleys got spattered across a cloud of
comets along with half the force herding them; in the
confusion that followed, Ross managed to take over a
cruiser which had some minor damage that knocked out
most of the crew; with the help of ship remotes he
dumped the crew into lifeboats, shot them out and took
off. On the way out of the Cluster he was chased into the
Veil and went to ground on a world called Rallen where
he traded Imperial hardware for help altering his ship
and acquired by stealth and accident his first Rooner's
load of artifacts.

INTERVAL OVER. PICTURE THE LANDER NUZZLING UP TO PICAREFY, BEING SUCKED INTO THE LANDER LOCK. ROSTICO BURN LEG-IRONED TO A SMALL REMOTE THAT ANNOUNCED HIS PRESENCE TO THE SHIP'S BRAIN. TIMKA WANDERING OFF TO SOAK A WHILE IN A HOT BATH WHILE SHE THINKS OVER EVENTS ON PILLORY AND WHAT THEY MEAN TO HER AND ABOUT HER. SKEEN THINKING ABOUT THE AUTODOC AND HER BRUISES, HEADING FOR THE BRIDGE TO GET PICAREFY STARTED FOR RESURRECTION.

Skeen strolled onto Picarefy's bridge. "Where's Tibo?"

"Sleeping. Want me to wake him?" Like the Lander, Picarefy's voice was androgynous, deep, musical, in the chasm between tenor and alto. A remarkably flexible voice, filled with nuance, with character. She tended to be acerbic, independent and ofttimes irritating; she was as close to being an independent entity as any ship in existence and Skeen cultivated that, no matter how annoying it was to have to talk Picarefy into doing things instead of just pushing a button and seeing it done. But Skeen didn't need slaves and the benefits of Picarefy's independence were enormous. She could bounce plans off Picarefy's brain and get ruthlessly honest evaluations, then sometimes reluctant, sometimes exuberantly enthusiastic cooperation. Skeen added to Picarefy's capacity every time she had extra credit and by this time Picarefy had grown like a fungus into every crack and cranny of the ship. Skeen bought her books and tapes and thousands of the smallest, most efficient spy eyes available so she could watch life even if she couldn't get out and experience it; she even established a line of credit for

Picarefy on every Pit Stop she patronized so Picarefy could order whatever she thought she needed (within the limits of fiscal prudence which anyway Picarefy was far better at keeping track of than Skeen). If she went overboard now and then on something esoteric and enormously expensive, well, Skeen always paid off. A lot of dealers had become familiar with Picarefy's taste and saved things for her, sending out news of finds through the low ways, the unofficial but efficient grapevine that connected the Pits.

Skeen lifted her shoulders, strained a little, groaned. "Let me have a bath first, I'm not fit company for a mudhog. You'd better get started. We ran into Cidder down there, take it sneaky, you know the scam. If Tib doesn't rouse when he feels us moving, stir him up and send him to the shower-room. Where's Petro?"

"Workshop," Picarefy said absently, busy with the complex problems of creeping out of the Belt. "Ah! This rock clutter makes me nervous. You're back faster than anyone expected."

"It didn't seem that fast. Tell her we're back. If she wants to talk to Ross, keep an eye on them but let her see him. Um, he might decide to be tricky; discourage him if you notice anything like that. And let me know about it."

"You'd better do something about that Cidder; how'd he miss you this time? Never mind. You should eat, Skeen. I'll fix something for you and Tibo." Sniffing sound, one of Picarefy's minor jokes. "After you take that bath for sure, otherwise I'll have to scrub the air with number two steel wool if anyone's going to feel like eating."

Timka looked up as Rostico Burn came in, the remote drifting along behind him. She smiled to herself as he strolled over to her and dropped on an electric blue hassock; he was being relaxed and unimpressed by it all. She could remember her own first reaction to Picarefy; Cream's *Slider* hadn't at all prepared her. "Picarefy's been working on the lounge again," she said. "It wasn't like this when we left to pick you up." There was a lot of glass and pewter work with accents of brilliant blues and greens. A cool room, the sort of elegance that makes you tuck your elbows in and hold your knees close together. Timka had shucked her shabby clothes and was wearing a sleek coat of silver-gray fur. She was curled up on a long low divan upholstered in a pale blue panne velvet.

Ross brushed at his trousers. "I've heard a lot about Picarefy."

Timka sat up, rubbed bare feet into the shaggy gray carpet. "Wait till you learn to know her."

Skeen came in, looked around, snorted and dropped on the divan beside Timka. "Pic, what the hell?"

"I thought I'd try house beautiful for a while." There was laughter in the voice that came, it seemed, from the air in the center of the room. "Don't worry, Skeen, I won't expect you to conform."

"Conform?" Tibo strolled in, glanced at Ross, settled on the rug by Skeen's feet; he smiled up at her, dropped his hand on her booted instep.

Chuckle from Picarefy. "Wear beautiful robes, burnish her body, maybe even comb her hair."

Snort of indignation from Skeen, soft laughter from Tibo. His hand moved up her leg to her knee. "Pic, oh, Pic, don't waste your imagination on her, play with me instead."

Ross kept his mouth shut during that exchange, but his yellow eyes (so like Skeen's) flicked from face to face: detached mysterious Timka, annoyed and amused Skeen, relaxed enigmatic Tibo. He lingered on Tibo, curious about the man he'd heard so much about, wondering how these two strong personalities managed to exist in any kind of harmony, wondering too how he could insinuate himself into the project they were working now; he needed more than freedom, he needed funding.

He was sitting with his shoulder to the door so he didn't see Lipitero until she was well into the room. He stiffened, fear rapidly replaced by wariness. Though he maintained an outward calm, he changed his position so he was ready to fight or run, whichever seemed indicated.

Lipitero moved past him and settled into a deep soft chair, its pale green velvet waking an answering green light in her crystal eyes. She smoothed her flightskins and smiled at him. "Relax, Rostico Burn, I'm not Rallen."

She turned to Skeen. "The way he's acting suggests we'd better not take him with us." Sliding her hands along the chairarms, she considered Ross. "Annoy them that much, did you? I wonder how. We'll have to talk. I need to know every nuance of your relationship with them."

The stiffness smoothed out of him. He gave her a broad grin. There was a tinge of artificiality to him, but a naive artificiality that offended no one, that invited others to share the game with him; he seemed to be saying, you know it's a game and I know it's a game, have fun with it. "What do I get for scraping my brain for you?"

Skeen sniffed. "I could always dump you into a lifeshell and let you find your own way to a Pit."

"I thought I already paid my passage."

"The price has just gone up."

"Not fair. Not kind."

"Isn't, is it."

"Hmm. Illusions die one by one." He smiled with practiced charm, rubbed his thumb against his first two fingers. "Duty is fine, but enthusiasm is gold and glory."

Timka stirred, raised herself on her elbow, examined the two faces, so alike and so unlike. Skeen was looking vague, sleepy. Timka waited to see how she'd jump; Ross' position was a lot shakier than he knew. Skeen was generous and unconcerned about power plays—as long as you didn't push her. Now that they knew where to find Rallen (and didn't really need his help talking with the Rallen Ykx), Skeen could easily dump him at the nearest freeport and let him make his way how he could. As the silence stretched on, she watched him become aware of this. Here in Picarefy, Skeen's will was law and there was no appeal. His eyes slid from Tibo who was studying the far wall, to Petro who wasn't interested, to Timka who gave him a feral grin like the cat she sometimes was.

Abruptly, Skeen grinned at him. "Rev up your enthusiasm," she said, "with thoughts of banking my goodwill." The smile vanished. "Or the opposite." She didn't wait for an answer, but got briskly to her feet. "Pic, how we doing?"

"Coming up on Teegah's limit. No pursuit." A pause.

"There's some fuss back around Pillory, no shape to it, no sense of direction."

"Good. I think we thank you for that, Petro. Um, don't take chances, Pic. What do you think about going a couple AU farther before we hit the insplit?"

"Hard on fuel." A pause. "We'd have the comet cloud to mask us. I think it's worth the cost."

"Do it." Skeen ran a hand through her hair, began pacing about the room, stepping over Lipitero's feet, circling her chair, touching the icicle moire on the walls, kicking at the gray shag of the rug, wandering about looking at the appointments of the room. "This place is dead, Pic, are you going to get in some plants or something?"

"I'll think about it," Picarefy murmured, "you might be right."

"You better believe it." Skeen continued to wander a while longer, poking into things, clicking her tongue against her teeth, whistling at times, lovely liquid trills. The others watched her without saying anything to her or to each other. Finally she ambled back, flung herself down beside Tibo, her shoulders braced by the divan's side, her head pushing against the seat padding, one leg drawn up, the other a black line scrawled across the rug. "So. Ross. Tell us about Rallen."

PART III: THE WORLD

Rallen Tuzeykken. Rallen Firesky.
Sun: Nepoyol
Planets:

1. NAMELESS. a blob of molten rock smaller than a mid-size moon, close enough to Nepoyol to spend most of the time brushing his corona.

2. NARAZAT. the dark sister, twin to Rallen, though much hotter, marginally habitable, some life, mostly fungal and bacterial, heavy clouds, infested with microscopic plant and animal forms which turn the clouds almost black.

3. RALLEN. 0.9 g
diameter - 12,783 km.

continents:

i. IZAKALA ZIGA - eastern hemisphere, mostly north of the equator.
ii. TALAHU ZIGARU - eastern hemisphere, south of the equator, subcontinent size, but too large to be classified as an island.
iii. TANUKA ZIGA - western hemisphere, long irregular land mass straddling the equator.

islands:

i. GALASSIT KISKUR - major island chain, four great islands, half a dozen large, several midsize and a

scatter of small islands. Sit-
uated close to Talahu Zigaru.

ii. a scatter of smaller islands, sown semé through
the various oceans, most though not all uninhab-
ited, a few developed as vacation resorts, those
close enough to the continents to make soaring to
them possible and reasonably safe.

4. ASTEROID BELT. as far from Rallen as Rallen is from the sun,
most of the asteroids are stone, but there
are several rich iron sources, also some lodes
of light metals. If the development problems
could be overcome and a means of getting
offworld could be constructed or acquired,
a number of Rallen's resource problems would
be removed or lessened.

5. EGGEN. gas giant, very close to star size, impressive ring
system.

A HISTORY OF THE YKX OF RALLEN FIRESKY.

The Kinravaly speaks:
This we know. There was a homeworld called Ysterai. There
were three colonies planted from Ysterai. Keelava, Tozeed,
Tovazh. Tovazh was a world in the middle of emptiness, a way
station more than a colony, a place for studies the Elder Kinra
considered too dangerous for Ysterai. A fourth colony was planned
for a world we named Rallen, not this world. We named this
world Rallen because we wished a reminder of what we had lost.
We skipped first to Keelava, refueled there and went on. During
that second skiptime the trouble happened. The three transports were com-linked while in skip space so they wouldn't
emerge in the wrong place. To save on cost there was only one
full computer; it was placed in the hen ship, the chicks were
little more than vast sleep-pods. It was the Hen that controlled
entry to and exit from skip space, though each of the Chicks had
a much less complex brain used mainly to regulate life support
and pass along data to the Hen. It is not clear what happened.
What survivors pieced together afterward was this: something
like an infection started in one of the Chick brains and leaped
from there into the Hen. It happened so swiftly that two-thirds

of the Hen's brain was wiped clean before anyone knew what
was happening. The links were broken then, the Hen isolated.
The wake crews labored with little rest, struggling to limit, then
control, then reverse the damage. The infecting pod was discovered, the sleepers and their support were transferred to another
pod brought dangerously close. That was a heroic time, you
must believe, we've got many songs celebrating the wake crew
and what they did. When the transfer was at last complete, the
pod was taken into normspace and sent off into a sun. Gradually
the links were re-established between the Hen and the remain-
ing Chick. Then the crew tried to recover the route to the
original Rallen. Unfortunately, during the Wild Time, the Hen
went into a blind panic flight. There was neither data nor
sufficient working computer capacity to trace what happened in
that Wild Time. The Hen's captain and the Kinra of the colonists consulted and had to acknowledge they were thoroughly
lost. They decided to break out into normspace and take a look
around to see if they could identify anything. They came out
into a strange sky. The computer proved incapable of star matching, but the ship's sensors did locate a nearby star that had
planets. It was Nepoyol and one of the planets proved suitable
for sustaining Ykx life. Again the Captain and the Kinra consulted. Having little real choice, they opted to land the pods on
the habitable world and wake the colonists who then could
consider what they should do. In the end, they brought the Hen
down also because they needed the computer and the memory
capacity. So much had been destroyed that almost no technical
information remained, little history, literature, music, little of
the culture with which they meant to make life warm and easy.
While crew and colonists did all the things necessary to sustain
life, they poured Ykx memories into the blank, frantic to gain a
more permanent record of what was left, what existed only in
the fragile organic brains of the living Ykx. Even the most
technical elements were more an incantation of the possible
than a vigorous development of argument. Ykx working at the
boundaries of any of the disciplines do not volunteer for colonial
expeditions where their special interests are useless and their
apparatus not available.

There was a primitive race on Rallen Firesky; they were at the
transitional stage between sedentary agriculture and hunter/
gatherer; they had several semi-domesticated beasts that provided food and fiber. They were six-limbed creatures, egg layers.
The females were larger than the males. Generally six females

were hatched for each male, each female produced no more than six eggs during her entire fertile life, two eggs at a time. The males tended to appear as one of the middle pair of eggs. It was not an easy relationship that developed between Ykx and six-legs. There were elements among the colonists who used genetic knowledge and manipulatory skills to enslave and breed the natives like beasts, doing some genetic tinkering to produce subsets of the basic form, lowering intelligence and inducing a docility that tended to result in a reduced lifespan for the six-legs so treated.

The chaos of the landing smoothed away. The world worked its slow changes on the Ykx. WATCHERS died, no more were born so Rallen Ykx lost that skill. Fate played a joke on us, giving us a world we could live on with comfort and even delight, but it was also a world greatly deficient in heavy metals. The elements beyond iron were rare to nonexistent and even iron was not abundant. The technology of Ysterai, even what was left of it, could not be sustained. It was a long slow struggle finding substitutes, most of them organic. We couldn't build lift belts, but we could develop the Wings using a helium-producing bacteria that was self-regulating and kept pressure at the desired level as long as it was exposed to the proper amount of light. By providing or removing the light with a simple on-off process we have since produced flight aids of considerable sensitivity and subtlety. More and more we turned from metals to organics as the millennia passed, using the metals at last primarily for sculpture and other decorative arts. The one thing we could not do was get offworld. By the time we had reordered our lives, by the time we were capable of fighting around the limitation of this world and ready to attempt solving the difficult problems of building a ship of organics, the double motion of the gas cloud and Nepoyol our sun plunged us into the Veils of Fire.

That was a difficult time. Weakened by our genetic tampering, the native six-legs died out except for a few of the hardier wildings. Many Ykx died also. Industry and commerce were shattered by the sudden extinction of many varieties of bacteria and fungi. But we survived this as we had survived earlier disasters. Out of shame at what we'd done to the native species, we did our best to help the remnants of the six-legs survive also, but all our efforts failed and it was a blot on our common conscience. Something we did not speak about or think about, something that came out in nightmares and severe depression.

An Ykx would leave his Gather, go out and poke among the ruins in the native preserves, then he would sit facing the west, he would neither eat nor drink nor sleep, just sit until he left his bones with the shells of the six-legs. Periodically one of the Kinra would propose we destroy the relics and put the event completely behind us since there was nothing we could do about it, but that seemed to many of us the final insult to the six-legs, that they be forgotten, so the preserves were left to melt slowly into the soil from which the six-leg structures had risen.

Rallen slid finally into clearer space and we began to regain stability, replacing what had been lost, honors going to those who could discover a new means for doing what had already been done. Redundancy became a never-ending search. But escape from Rallen was lost. The energies that once went into that project were needed elsewhere. The sky was fire curtains pulled across the stars, a symbol our poets have long noted and used. There was no moon to serve as a stepping stone, no nearby stars visible to call out to us, come see, you Ykx, come see what once you had. This was a disturbing thing. There is in us a profound need to soar. It did something to our souls to see a lid on aspiration, to feel our world as a cage we couldn't escape from. We can also see the time coming when we plunge back into the Fire. When that youth who called himself Rostico Burn burst through the Veil and landed here, he found a yeasty chaos that whirled around him, tempted him; he traded and stole, promised nothing, yet promised far too much by his presence and the possibilities he suggested. By the time he left, he had begun, I think, to understand and be afraid of what he had helped to create.

YEAR ONE AFTER THE COMING OF ROSTICO BURN.

Veratisca climbed the tower, carefully testing each rung. The Utaro Har Gather was long abandoned. Too close to the shame fields. You could look out over the patch of waste ground where no one plowed and planted, where here and there pale bones or the decaying remnant of a wall shone through the green and gray of the vegetation. She reached the crenelated platform, settled herself atop one of the uprights. Out near the horizon on her right side, a dustcloud rose where forty-four hitches of grubbers were plowing their horny snouts along, breaking up the earth so the seeders they pulled could drop their load into the furrows. She kept her back to the Wasteland, she hadn't come here to contemplate species shame but to find if there was any peace left inside her. There were times since the alien Rostico Burn left when she looked up at the filmy streaks of pale fire and felt them burn her face, times when she felt like going into the waste and sitting and stopping. Yet there was something jagged and intractable inside her that would not let her do that. In the end she still might and she knew it. She wanted so much, so many things she couldn't name; at times she felt as if she would explode from the pressure of that wanting. One day she might sit on the far side of this tower and stare into the Waste, into the Shame Death and she would cast herself from the tower, soar in a slow spiral downward and pull in her flightskins and give way to the despair that clawed at her.

It was a hardwind day. The wind blew into her face sharp and cold, teased at her flightskins though she kept these tucked tight about her. It brought her the damp dark smell of the turned earth, the leafy slickness of the grubbers. She heard the encourage-whistles from the handlers and the dull clack of the seeders as they bumped over the rough soil.

She scratched uncertainly with a stylus at the pad she'd
brought with her:

Dark, damp, secret, the soil—
Extruded womb—the seed implant—
Fervid ferment, and
Forms damp and dark
   and secret
What coils within the seed—
Waiting—

With a tongue-clicking curse at the impossibility, she
thrust the stylus through the loop and returned the pad
to her belt pouch. She began and began and began. And
finished nothing. Nothing eased the anguish, the wanting
that churned in her, nothing exhausted her, not the long
walk, not the perilous climb up the rotting ladder into
the tower. The Veils very faintly visible at dawn and
dusk and throughout the night, brighter then, streaks of
fire, they were cords wound round and round her head
and sometimes they tightened, until she almost couldn't
bear it. She got to her feet with awkward grace, stood
balanced a moment on the upright, then snapped open
her flightskins and fell off the tower into the wind.

Bohalendas put the welder down, passed his hand across
his eyes. He leaned back in the chair, eyes closed, dorsal
muscles twitching and sore. The power just wouldn't
cross the gap, he couldn't marry the cells. He lay like
that a few minutes, weariness pinning him down as effectively as brads nailing him to the chair.
He heard a bustling behind him but couldn't rouse
himself.
"Tata." A small hand touched his arm.
Making an effort, closing his hands about the padded
curve of the rests, he pulled himself up.
Lih stood beside him, patting his arm and Lah stood
half a step back, holding a tray with determined steadi-
ness. He dredged up a smile.
Lih pulled up a stool and Lah put the tray down so
carefully nothing jarred. Bohalendas smelled the hot spicy
bite of the iska and swung the chair around, ignoring its

creak though as usual Lih clapped her hands over her flower-petal ears, but grinned as she did it and whistled a much pleasanter version of the grinding rise and fall of the sound. Beautifully true. She showed strong signs that her joychoice would be music and her dutychoice would be something to do with animals. She had no interest or aptitude for submicroscopic herding and plants were things to eat.

Lah poured the iska into the thickglass drinking bowl, watched jealously by his sister. He was one year older and tended to take advantage of his seniority whenever he could. Unlike Lih, he'd manifested no strong interest for joy or duty and that worried Bohalendas. The time was rapidly approaching when the choice must be made. Lah couldn't earn his full name or move in adult circles if he refused either choice, nor could he stay among the children. Not for the first time Bohalendas felt a flare of anger at the fate that took Zuistro from him and made her Kinravaly, separating her from her family as irrevocably as death would have done. He thought about calling her, but it was very difficult and what could she know? She'd been gone for years. He didn't know what to do about his son, a grave quiet boy who made no trouble, but lived behind a mask where Bohalendas could not reach him.

As Bohalendas sipped at the iska and felt the lethargy that had taken so strong a hold begin to melt at the edges, Lah circled round him to stand at the work bench looking down at the failed transformer. Bohalendas watched Lah poke at the small handcom. "I haven't found a way to graft the two technologies," he said. "The power cells that were in it have enormous capacity compared to the ones we use. Yet it doesn't take more than a whisper of that power to operate that com, at least over short distances." He nodded at the com's twin propped in a chair across the room. "I have to understand how the parts work together," he said, "before I can think about producing equivalences." He grunted as Lih, feeling neglected, climbed onto his leg and lay stretched out against his side like she used to do when she was still nursing from the bloodnipples he'd resorbed into his body now that she was weaned. Her soft warmth woke pleasant memories that flushed away some of his weariness and despondency. "Having abundance where we have scarcity or lack," he said, "they Beyond the Veil made leaps where we still creep; I . . ." He stopped talking as he saw Lah reach out and touch the eviscerated instrument, finger tracing a printed circuit with an intentness and accuracy that made Bohalendas' heart ache as he understood what his son's joychoice would be. It was one he'd have little chance of fulfilling on Rallen. For a moment he was not a Seeker, but a father, cursing the fate that sent the alien Rostico Burn to this Gather, this Gurn. Absently stroking his daughter's baby down, he began pondering what he could do to find Lah a place where he could earn his welcome while he tinkered with the hard, stern and nearly useless field of heavy metal electronics.

Ykx like a flight of birds flew over the waste, circling and circling about one of them, trying to touch him. He was singing, spiraling up and up, soaring carelessly, losing the thermal lift and tumbling till his flightskins caught and steadied him. He sang a wild wordless chant at sky and sand and in the last of his erratic tumbles, he broke from his companions. He soared out and away. Abruptly, he burst into flame, wrapped his skins soft about him and plummeted, a burning shred of Veil torn from the sky. As he hit the sand and continued to burn, his companions soared in circles, mourning.

YEAR FOUR AFTER THE COMING OF ROSTICO BURN.

Zelzony walked restlessly about the long room, going over her report in her mind, glancing repeatedly at the rekkagourd looped to her wrist by an intricately braided cord.

The Kinra came in, all six of them, their official harnesses managing to glitter in spite of soft, indirect lighting. They settled into the wide, winged chairs, three on each side of the center chair which was a handspan higher and more elaborately carved. When they were all seated, the silence grew thicker. Zelzony felt unable to keep pacing. The Kinra of Rallen were oppressively solemn when all met together like this, carrying on their shoulders the responsibility for the well-being of all Rallykx and everything else on Rallen.

Zelzony knew them all very well, it was part of her job, knew their weaknesses and obsessions. She gave them separately the attention she felt they deserved (in two cases, almost none) but met together like this, their flaws vanished, as if they contained within themselves the soul of Rallen. For anyone who came here once or twice in a lifetime, this view of the Kinra meeting was awesome and inspiring; for Zelzony who knew too much about the machinations and maneuverings that won each of those seats, the sight of them all sitting there still woke a response to the meaning of their offices if not to the Kinra themselves.

The Kinravaly Rallen was chosen by elaborate lot when the former holder of the post died. It was a lifetime appointment and refusal was not allowed. It was ceremonial, but in the proper circumstances could be immensely powerful. Kinravaly Zuistro was still fairly new in her post, only there a handful of years. A middle-aged poet who'd borne her three children already and was not at all

maternal. She'd lost one child, stillborn, the last. Perhaps
that had something to do with her detachment. She had
almost bled to death with her stillborn daughter, a gush
of blood as if everything inside her had given way to
follow the ejected infant. Perhaps it had. Sometimes
Zelzony saw her as a shade walking in the shape of a
rather beautiful Ykx (she'd retained her beauty even
after her close brush with death). For a shade, she'd
done rather well, she'd made several near miraculous
pronouncements and had single-handedly settled a trade
war to the satisfaction of all sides, something Zelzony
would have sworn was impossible. Unfortunately, the
trouble Zelzony was bringing to the attention of the
Kinra and the Kinravaly was much worse than that conflict (though the trade war had threatened to split Rallen
into three factions that would neither speak to nor deal
with any of the others). The data Zelzony had gathered
suggested that species death was possible rather than
unthinkable. Perhaps even imminent.

Kinravaly Zuistro came quietly in and slid into the
center chair. Unlike the Kinra, her harness was old and
plain, and she looked a little frowsy as if she'd come
from digging in her garden without bothering to shake
off the debris clinging to her fur. She glanced around,
frowned briefly at Zelzony. "Sit," she said, her voice
husky as if she'd strained it to the edge of mutiny, but
that huskiness was curiously effective, made every word
she spoke slip under the listener's skin. Zelzony responded
to it always, whatever the circumstances, though she
tried to arm herself against it in public places. In spite of
her control, she shivered with pleasure when Zuistro
leaned forward, fixed quiet ocean-deep eyes on her and
said, "What have you found for me, my Zem-trallen?"

Zelzony lowered herself onto the cool black leather
cushions of the witness chair; she slipped the rekka off
her wrist and sat with it cupped in her hands, the glass
inset turned so she could read it when she looked down.
"Two years ago," she said, her voice quiet and controlled, "you called me to your garden and told me you
were uneasy about the health of Rallen. You asked me
to travel about, collect impressions, assimilate such sta-

tistics as I thought apposite, looking for patterns so you could determine if your uneasiness was justified or not."

She gazed down at the rekka without really seeing it, shook herself and lifted her head. "A report of my findings has been sent to each of the Kinra. Since it is thick as my fist, I'll sketch in brief what is there in exhaustive detail." She drew in a long breath, let it trickle out; what she had to say was painful to her and would be more so to the Kinra. "You will remember what happened after the six-legs perished, that an epidemic of suicides swept through the Ykx. For several years it was an open question whether we could stop the hemorrhage before we beld to death. It is possible another such wave of suicides is beginning to rise." Ignoring the exclamations, questions, indignant rejections, she gazed at the wood mosaic floor, rubbed her thumb slowly back and forth along the smooth bumpy surface of the gourd, waiting until the Kinravaly saw fit to silence the Kinra and let her go on.

When there was quiet again, she lifted her head, looked past them at the polished wood of the wall and returned to her quiet reporting. "Some background first. Around four years ago an alien male came through the Veils of Fire and found us. He was something of a mountebank, certainly a thief and smuggler, though he claimed to be a free-trader. You will understand that what I tell you of this Rostico Burn is largely conjecture. It was difficult to persuade those who had closest contact with him to answer my questions in any detail; there is also the problem of language." She cleared her throat. "The first Ykx he came across was Fafeyzar of Masliga Gather, a grubber handler on a tekla farm, doing some preplanting plowing. It took me some time and considerable persuasion to find young Fafey and then get him to talk; though we are a social, law-abiding people and pride ourselves on the easy friendly interaction between the classes, it would be foolish to deny there are frictions, especially between workers and managers. Rostico Burn, our enterprising alien, appeared to expect this. Considering his success in evading notice, I'd say he'd more than a little experience in exploiting such conditions. You may or may not know he was able to visit fifteen Gathers in six Gurns before we who have the responsibility for governing Rallen learned of him." She made an impatient gesture, the impatience directed at herself. "I wander from my course; I meant to speak about what Fafey told me. When Rostico Burn landed, he spoke no Rallyx, of course, nor any language analogous to it, but he was adept at communicating without words. With signs and gestures, he persuaded young Fafey to trust him and take a curious crown upon his head, then he played a silent symphony on an object about the size and shape of an unabridged dictionary which appeared to be a control of sorts, perhaps a compact computer. As Fafey tells it, he felt nothing and nothing seemed to be happening for a longish time. Then he felt a tickling inside his head. That was all. After that, the alien took the crown away, fitted it into slots in the top of the box and reworked the controls. When he was finished, that box spoke to Fafey in the Rallyx a baby might use. The longer he and the box conversed, the more adept the box became. On the third day, Rostico Burn put the box away and after that spoke with Fafey himself. It seems to have been some sort of universal translator, an interesting example of the technology beyond the Veil of Fire. Well. Fafey kept quiet about the alien, hid him in a shed outside Delsay Gather, something Burn and he agreed on, Burn not wanting to attract attention until he felt knowledgeable enough to talk himself out of trouble. This was obviously a tactic he was accustomed to using, which should tell you some more about him. As I said before, he visited fifteen Gathers and six Gurns before his presence became known to anyone in authority." She turned her head slowly, gazing at each of the Kinra in turn.

"I have mentioned in the report the names of a number of Gather officials who were especially negligent in their duties, creating severe frictions within the Gather which made it prohibitively difficult for rumors of the alien to reach their ears. It seems they were undisturbed too long in their office, developing bad habits those in authority over them ignored as long as no overt trouble erupted within the Gathers. In some cases these Remmyos acquired their positions by inheriting them from one parent or another, something we would do well to discourage because it leads to the overlooking of unbelievable incompetence. I have noted the Gathers where this practice is prevalent and have suggested that the Kinravaly allow a reasonable amount of time for the condition to be corrected, then go to all Gurns with her seccateurs and cut away the dead wood."

There were no vocal protests this time, only a variety of expressions and in two cases a lack of expression that was as revealing. *Sulleggen* and *Uratesto* from Tanaku Ziga on the far side of the world. Against her now and always. The slackest and most corrupt, their Gurn-sets (Marrallat and Urolol) were in an increasingly desperate ferment which they kept from surfacing by means that made Zelzony sick and angry, counting on their distance from the Reserve to keep all this from the Kinravaly, making sure no reports of disturbances got beyond their borders. For the Kinravaly's eyes alone Zelzony had taken time to make as thorough a report as she could on their activities and methods along with as true a picture of feeling inside Marrallat and Urolol as she could gather with meager resources and the limited time she was permitted to visit there. *Talahusso.* He liked comfort, but he'd jump if the Kinravaly said hop. There was considerable laxness and corruption in Oldieppe, but on the whole the Ykx there were content with his management; his Gurns were mostly coastal. The interior of Talahu Zigaru was a forbidding desert; it was rich in minerals (there was even an iron mine) but a punishment to live in; trying to tighten up that bunch of hardy individualists might cause more harm than good. *Hatenzo.* An enigma operating out of some inner harmony whose rules baffled Zelzony. His was the richest collection of Gurns and the closest to the Kinravaly's Reserve. He kept to himself, was seldom seen by any of the Ykx in his care. They were a little afraid of him, but that might be a good thing. The Itekkillykx were a fractious litigious bunch, but the Gurns were the best managed of any on Rallen, high standards of courtesy and competence demanded of all, from the most minor clerks to the High Justicer herself. Itekkill Gurns were heavily populated, with a large number of merchant families. These handled most of the commerce on Rallen. Itekkilli ships and wings went everywhere. The rekkagourd she held was grown and finished there; little food was produced in Itekkill, much of the land was given to the production of the organics that underlay the technology of Rallen. Hatenzo was the only Kinra to meet and speak with Rostico Burn; that he made no attempt to hold the alien or report on the conversation to the Kinravaly was disturbing, but not unexpected. When Zelzony discovered the meeting, she'd questioned Hatenzo about Burn and made little sense of his answers. Perhaps the Kinravaly could if she chose to call him in. *Selyays.* She was looking interested. She ran Yasyony University in the Galassit Kiskur with some of the most creative gentechs. The Kinravaly's once-husband Bohalendas lived there, a man capable of astonishing flights of intuition; Bohalendas also met with Rostico Burn and obtained some alien devices from him. When Zelzony spoke to him, he was charmingly rueful about his failure to report the presence of the alien immediately, confessing that his zeal had got the better of his good sense and duty to his Gurn; he waited until Burn was gone to report his presence to Selyays. *Tyomfin.* Eggetakk along the western rim of Izakala Ziga, mountainous, fertile with a large variety of ecologic niches. Gathers here were small and insular, producing some of the finest artists and artisans on Rallen. He was visibly worried and had reason to be; Eggetakk extended far to the north and in the icelands he was losing more Eggetakkykx than he was comfortable thinking about. He was a gentle intelligent Ykx, inclined to well-reasoned causes and the promoting of dreams; whatever the Kinravaly decided, he'd throw his energy and abilities into the project. Zelzony swept her eyes across them a last time and went on with her report.

"To get Fafey to speak at all, I had to give him Kinravaly's Hand, which I had leave to do if I thought it necessary." She spoke gravely, her gaze firm on Uratesto who sat with his teeth clamped on his lower lip, his barely suppressed fury turning his eyes bloodshot. "Who touches him now faces Kinravaly's Ire. Fafey took the alien to the next Gurn and turned him over to another worker he wouldn't name. I didn't press him on that. It happened over and over; he was passed from hand to hand about the world, paying for this help with stories of

Beyond the Veil and bits of silver and gold." She smiled slightly, amused. "No one told him how rare such metals are on Rallen. Other than that, from the tales I heard, he collected more than he gave and when Selyays heard of him and tried to pick him up, he got away from her ortzin like a greased mo worm and vanished. After considerable effort I managed to trace him to Tiksa Spat where he'd had a score of Ykx helping him modify his ship. He was gone several months before I found his traces, Fafey thought off-world and back through the Veil of Fire, which was why he was finally willing to talk to me." The Kinra stirred as she stopped speaking.

Selyays leaned forward eagerly, tapped the arm of her chair with her polished ivorine claws. "There's a list of the Gathers and Gurns the alien visited? You give us some idea of the items he traded?"

Zelzony glanced at the rekka. "The places, yes. The Beyond the Veil artifacts, for the most part, no. They've dropped so far out of sight they won't see daylight for a century." She waited for more questions but Hatenzo was looking dreamily at the wall behind her, Tyomfin and Talahusso were whispering together, Sulleggen and Uratesto were glaring into their laps, mouths clamped into thin lines. They'd go over their copies of the report line by line, probably even glyph by glyph, before they ventured any sort of comment.

She sighed. "The alien appears to have been a catalyst, touching off radical increases in certain behaviors." She dropped her eyes to the rekka readout, though she didn't really need help remembering the numbers. "Medicals have reported a 239 percent increase in claustrophobic seizures. Nearly half of these seizures result eventually in death, usually from depression-enhanced illnesses. In your reports you'll find Gurn and Gather breakdowns on specific types of seizure and death along with a distribution chart. I have not included the deaths from suicide but put those in a separate listing." She cleared her throat, called up a new set of numbers, then brushed a hand across her eyes, a futile attempt to brush away the memory that haunted her nights . . . a visit to her home Gather in Eggetakk on one of her many world circles during this investigation . . . agitation, wailing, curses piled onto her because her kin could not bear the blame they felt . . . her brother, her youngest dearest brother she'd cuddled, raised, loved fiercely, defended from everyone, her youngest brother had fled the Gather an hour before she got there, riding a stolen wing into the wildlands, cousins racing after him to stop him, her brother, her dearest brother a fireball spiraling down to crash onto the stone before she could reach him . . . why? That was the worst of it. No one could tell her why, nothing she learned about his last months could tell her why, the only answers she got came in the numbers she was about to recite.

"There has been a 973 percent increase in suicides," she said, her voice hoarse in spite of her attempt at coolness. "I include a frequency chart of the methods used. The most prevalent is the fade, where the individual stops eating, drinking, sleeping and simply dies in spite of all attempts to break through to him. More troubling," she swallowed, then drove herself on, "is a swiftly spreading fad, I don't know if that's the right word, but I'll leave it for the moment, a spectacular way of dying." She closed her hands tight about the gourd, fixed her eyes on the wall, willing herself to keep her anguish from showing, her words coming slow and flat when she spoke. "The individual often accompanied by friend witnesses who try to talk him out of it, this means of death seems to be confined to males, wings to the nearest wasteland, jettisons the wing, soars as high as he can, douses himself with the most inflammable liquid he can get his hands on, then lights up and plunges burning back to earth. The first of these fireballs occurred on the first Sorrow Day after Rostico Burn left the world. It was a minor poet with little recognition who was also a failed teacher working as a grubber's groom at Yahloc Farm. The death song he left behind suggested he was reacting to the closing of the Veils about Rallen and the name of the alien. Rostico Burn. It seems the second part of that name means wounding by fire. There were two such deaths that same year, one on the Day of Landing, one on the winter solstice. This year there have been so far forty-nine such deaths, though there are two or three that I'm not sure are real suicides; they could be disguised killings." Again there were protests, the loudest and most emphatic coming from Sulleggen; Uratesto clamped his mouth shut, contented himself with glaring at her. She ignored the noise and plunged on, speaking in a monotone that rode over their passions with the inevitability of a glacier. "I am sure I needn't remind you Sorrow Day arrives in three months. Can any of you prevent the rain of Burndeaths I foresee if this trend continues?" She didn't wait for an answer, but continued talking over their interjections. "Less serious, but still troubling is the drop in the productivity of workers. Absenteeism, apathy, drugs. Before this we've had some trouble with youngsters, the tweeners not yet adult, who have been creating their own bemusements. They always seem to know what drugs are available, how to grow and process them, what enticing new twists have been added by some crazy youth tinkering with them and with himself. Information of that sort seems to flow on the wind from tweener to tweener.

During the past two years the situation has changed. Someone has taken over manufacture and sale of the most popular items. Lom, gett, zars, gloy, keck, shey. Usage of these is up dramatically, the problem is widespread among younger workers who seem even more hopeless and alienated than their parents. Alienated. That's a pun of sorts, I suppose. And the dealers are beginning to get hold of our children; the infection started among the worker children, but it has been spreading to the pre-fertile adults in the professional and managerial classes. That is not generally known because in those classes, especially the managerial, the act of drugtaking is considered shameful as well as stupid; the parents are struggling to cope with their children and their respectability at the same time and finding it increasingly difficult. Which is another reason productivity is off in these areas. Your ortzin, Kinra, are also beginning to be affected, not so much by the drugs as by bribery and other such activities of the dealers. In most cases the rot hasn't spread far; if you act decisively and swiftly, you can cut it out. Where possible, I have listed names and the proof needed to sustain the accusation; however, I do not pretend to a thorough assessment of the orzala forces.

The Kinravaly Rallen will speak to you later, one by one, and has told me she will add her resources to yours if her help is requested." Zelzony straightened her back. "I have spent the past ten days in retreat, contemplating what is written in the full report. Obviously there are many causes of the malaise that has attacked our folk, each case is subtly different from every other. However there seem to be two factors that have hastened a development that otherwise might have taken decades rather than years to reach this state. The first is this: Each year the Veils of Fire are visibly closer to us, a potent reminder of what happened the last time we plunged into them. And by some unfortunate anomaly the section of the Veils closest to us is particularly thick and bright. Some nights even I feel uncomfortable outside looking up at them. The second factor is the arrival and even more, the departure of Rostico Burn. His arrival reminded us that there is a very large universe beyond the Veils, his departure reminded us that we are eternally cut off from it. These things combine to reinforce a loss of hope."

She sighed, slid her fingers over and over the smooth bumpy surface of the gourd. "When hope is gone, life's meaning goes; with meaning gone, the will to live and strive is gone. We need the hope of soaring, Kinra, Kinravaly Rallen. Before we entered the Veils the first time, we were beginning to work on a starship, gathering ourselves for the generations of hard sacrifice and harder work it would take to reach first for the asteroids and the metal there, then to relearn the old lessons and blend them with the new. Even now Bohalendas is working on ways to bridge the gap between our organics and the metal-based technologies of the items Burn left behind. If we can turn hopelessness into a vigorous new dream, and harness Ykx energies to that dream, then much of the malaise will vanish. It will be expensive in resources and personnel, but it can be extended over a very long period if our folk can see a steady succession of small successes and know in their bones that their grandchildren will see what they will not." Zelzony thought of saying more, but did not. Either they accepted the data in the report, or they rejected it, and they'd do that more on who and what they were, than on anything she could say or write. None is so blind as he who will not see. Sulleggen? Uratesto? If they acknowledged and acted on the information in the report, how long would they stay in power? Hard to say, but a little hope could be deadly in the soup they were cooking in their Gurns. I've been riding along too easy, sitting on the surface of things, she thought bitterly, I've played love with Zuistro and my others and forgot about my own. Eggetakk was a good place once, I suppose it still is, but Marrallat? Kinravaly and Zem-trallen should have done something about Marrallat and Urolol decades ago. When did it start? When did we lose control of the far side of the world? Not with Zuistro and me, no, long before us. But that doesn't excuse us. It should not have taken the chance coming of an outsider to alert us to the sickness on Tanuka Ziga. Whatever happens now, we've got to start cleaning that stable. Generations of grubber dung, layer on layer, it'll take more generations to muck it out. With the Sul clan and the Uras fighting us for every layer. That's another reason to get this starship project working, once the excitement starts seeping into those Gurns. . . . She sighed. Talahusso? He could go either way, hmm, if he has a hand in awarding contracts. . . . Hatenzo? Can't do without him. Can't read him either. Itekkillykx will get a lot of work out of this, but they'll be the ones called on to sacrifice most, can't help that. If he stays neutral, I'll probably lose Itekkill. Selyays? She's sold already, bless her. Can't do without the thinkers at University. Tyomfin? He's for it, thank the All-Wise. That's it, then. Two against, no matter if the sky is falling. One engima. One who could be bought, and fairly cheaply at that, inclined to be for something that will increase the importance of Oldieppe. Two for, no matter what. She gazed expectantly at the Kinravaly, waiting for her decision. Zuistro knew about Zelnozy's plan, but she hadn't commented beyond giving her permission to have the plan presented to the Kinra.

The Kinravaly stood. "That is sufficient for the moment, I think. You, our Kinra, will read and consider the report. Talk it over among yourselves if you wish, prepare arguments in support and against the conclusions drawn and the plan outlined on the final pages. Prepare challenges of any data you think distorted or out of context. Meet here seven days hence and present your arguments, your challenges. I will hear you and at the end of that session, however long it takes, I will give you my thoughts on the matter." A moment's pause. Her eyes moved over the faces of the Kinra. "During that time none of you will speak to the Zem-trallen and she will not speak with you. If you have questions, keep them until the Kinra meets."

Zelzony stood, watched the Kinravaly walk around her chair and out the small door with the lack of ceremony that characterized all of her public appearances. As soon as the door clicked shut, she turned and went out, friendly eyes, hostile eyes, noncommittal eyes following her; none of the Kinra tried to stop or question her and she felt a surge of gratitude to the Kinravaly for arranging that. Seven days of peace. Trouble was, that meant seven days of waiting and wondering.

Two days later Zelzony walked in the garden with Zuistro.

"I can give you twenty researchers and perhaps five agents. No doubt you're right and that precious pair know most of your people by now. Don't rush things, Zeli; you do, you know."

"Give me Borrentye with them, Zo; let me set him to work on the problem of clan Sul and clan Ura, that sort of manipulation is not my strength, you know that. Impatience, yes and the wrong twist of mind. I don't hesitate to admit it. Besides, there's a possibility I HAVE to look into."

Zuistro sighed. "The suicides that might not be."

"It's not something I can trust out of my hands, the evidence I have is too fragile; I shouldn't have mentioned my suspicions in that report, that was stupid. I am careless, Zo. And lazy with it. But this worries me more than the other thing. If Ykx have begun to kill Ykx for the pleasure of it . . . I don't know what to think." Zuistro murmured comforting sounds; Zelzony turned her head and kissed the hand that curved about her shoulder. "Are you going to let me have my ship?"

"How can I not, oh, wisest of my counselors? You argue the need so very exhaustively and I do not use that world lightly. Lightly," Zuistro repeated with a soft gurgle of amusement, "that's not an apt word either for that tome you had me reading the past two days." Another chuckle. "Your ship and as many rumors as my mouth can spread. Stay with me tonight?"

"That bitch Sulleggen is bound to have her lice following me, even if she doesn't dare meddle with you. I want . . . I want very much to stay, but I won't let her have anything she can use against you."

"My lice are smarter than hers, they've herded hers away from us, trust Borrentye for that." Zuistro sighed again. "I'll miss him, but he says his apprentice is coming along very well indeed. Yes, I meant to lend him to you all the time. Come. I'm hungry enough to eat a grubber without washing it."

In the year that followed the convocation of the Kinra, Rallen began to hum with rumor, a mosquito whine at first, hardly noticeable above the daily noises, but it grew rapidly in intensity and volume. We had ships once, we can have them again, the hum said. Where one has come, there one can go. We can soar again, WE CAN SOAR.

YEAR FIVE AFTER THE COMING OF ROSTICO BURN.

Veratisca spiraled down onto the ruined tower top. The night sky burned overhead; the Veils were brighter than last year, yet they seemed somehow frailer. Not bands that bound her head. She stretched her arms high as if she were reaching for the streaks of fire to shred them into ash and gone.

Excitement fountained in her. Her mind knew there'd been no real change but her body was rejoicing in a freedom that was as yet only a seed of possibility, a seed still unplanted. She took pad and stylus and wrote:

Barren soil
Too much bearing
    ere this
Yet
Might-be is planted
Will-be germinates
        Yes

In a scoop-walled ravine, hidden from the night sky by a great outslant of stone, three forms crouched about a fire drinking hot iska out of thick-walled mugs, talking in the comfortably weary tones of beings who have completed a hard but satisfactory day's work. In the dark behind them a thing moaned, but its sounds were faint and drained even of pain and after a short while ceased altogether.

Rallen crept closer to the Veils and completed a second turn about its sun Nepoyol. In the seventh year since Rostico Burn's precipitate departure, another alien stepped onto the soil of Rallen.

PART IV: THE CAMPAIGN

BACK TO OUR SEARCHERS.
SKEEN INTENDED TO DUMP ROSTICO BURN AT
REVELATION PIT, BUT HE APPEALED TO FAMILY
FEELING, PULLED EVERY STRING HE COULD
GET HOLD OF TO PERSUADE HER TO TAKE HIM
WITH HER. AS A CYNICAL RASCAL WITH AN
EYE OUT FOR PROFIT, HE TOLD HIMSELF IT
WOULD BE A SIN AND A SHAME TO LET
HIMSELF BE SCRAPED OFF LIKE MUD FROM A
BOOT. BEING IN REALITY A THOROUGH-
GOING ROMANTIC, HE COULDN'T BEAR THE
THOUGHT OF BEING LEFT OUT OF THIS
ADVENTURE. THE FOLK OF HADDA ADDA
WOULD WHISPER ABOUT IT FOR GENERATIONS
AFTER HE WAS DEAD, THE STORY OF HIS
RESCUE OFF PILLORY, HIS RETURN TO THE
CLUSTER WITH THE LEGENDARY SKEEN, TIBO
THE LUCKY THIEF, LIPITERO THE MYSTERIOUS,
AND TIMKA THE IMPOSSIBLE. IN SPITE OF HIS
VENEER OF SOPHISTICATION, IN SPITE OF
HIS MAULING BY LIFE AND THE DEPRESSING
EVIDENCE HE HAD FORCED ON HIM OF THE
INIQUITIES OF HIS FELLOW BEINGS, HE WAS
PLEASED WITH HIMSELF, EXUBERANT IN HIS
ENJOYMENT OF LIFE AND YOUNG ENOUGH
TO THINK IN GRAND ABSTRACTIONS LIKE
GLORY. SKEEN WAS IN THIS SEARCH TO PAY
OFF A DEBT, TIBO BECAUSE HE WENT WHERE
SKEEN WENT, SHARED HER DEBTS AS SHE

**SHARED HIS; LIPITERO WAS HERE TO SAVE HER
ADOPTED GATHER AND HER OWN SOUL;
TIMKA WENT ALONG BECAUSE SHE HAD
NOWHERE ELSE TO BE AND MIGHT AS WELL
AMUSE HERSELF. ROSTICO BURN WENT TO
WRITE A NEW STANZA FOR THE SONG OF
HIS LIFE.**

Picarefy danced a deceitful jig through, around, up and
over the patrolling ships of the Ancient Evil, the Undying Emperor of the Cluster, and at last nosed into the
Veil where Ross had burst from it seven years before.
Sensors screaming, speed reduced to a crawl, she dipped
in and out of an insplit curdled by the overflow from the
tangle of forces in normspace; backtracking Ross' route
out, dug from his memory (he'd destroyed the trip flakes,
he told them, the Buzzard's advice after he refused to
sell them to him, and got himself the best block he could
buy. I could work my way back if I had to and I wasn't
about to let some bastard steal my life); with some trepi-
dation he disengaged the block, let Picarefy put him
under and pry those memories from his mind.

While Skeen and Tibo combined with Picarefy to out-
wit the traps of Cidder's kind, perhaps Cidder himself
(though that was less likely since they got away a bit too
easily to have that Hound sniffing after them), while
Lipitero brooded alone, too fratchetty to endure company, while Timka prowled about in cat-shape or slept
away her boredom, Rostico Burn nosed about the ship.
Picarefy told Skeen about his prying during one of the
short intervals of straight-flight and they had a quiet
laugh together. Picarefy was far too complex and too
illogically arranged for the cleverest mind to understand
her even in her parts; Skeen had long ago given up trying
to comprehend what was happening as Picarefy built
herself bigger, only warning her that if anything went
wrong there was no one anywhere who'd have a hope of
fixing her, so she'd better build in one helluva lot of

redundancy. Take the organic brain as model, Skeen said, then giggled at the loud brrruppp that was Picarefy's answer to her suggestion. But Picarefy had taken her advice, providing abundant redundancy and repair mice that scurried endlessly about the sprawl of the brain, repairing any small breaks, replacing parts and acting as guard dogs against interference from the outside. (A short time before the ill-fated trip to Kildun Aalda, when Skeen was arguing about the need for some expensive new components the cost of which would seriously cut into her playtime and send her on the hop after more Roons, she was moved to shout: Who owns who here. You've got the papers on me, Picarefy said, but I prefer to think of us as partners. Neither of us can live without the other. Mmf, Skeen groused half-seriously, let me know when I'm redundant so I can make other plans.)

"No moon?"

"Not even a collection of dust."

"How's their astronomy?"

"Look, I wasn't doing a survey, I was skipping ahead of the local law and trying to make a sliver of profit. Not much of it, the little I saw. What have they got to look at? Can't see any stars but their own. They keep track of the streaks of the Veil and how fast they're heading through the rift, hobbyists watch comets and use hand-ground lenses to plot the orbits of the largest asteroids in the Belt. I didn't see any dishes; either I missed them or they haven't developed radio astronomy, they're poor in the heavier metals, maybe that's why. No long-range weapons, they've never had a war on Rallen, I know, it's hard to believe, but the Rallykx are like that."

"So. If I go into high orbit, it's likely they'll see me, but they can't reach me."

"Unless they've changed a lot in the past seven years."

"Would they? Your impressions, that's all."

"No. Wrong mindset. You'll be safe enough."

"Skeen?"

"Geosynchronous, eh, Pic? I'll feel better with you in sight, so to speak. Basepoint, hmmm, that lake in the Kinravaly Reserve, that's what they call it, isn't it, Ross? Where their high Poobah lives?"

"Gotcha. Consider it done."

Tibo grimaced at Skeen. "Old broom, take it out when you need it, shove it in a closet when you don't."

Skeen ran her hands through her hair, turning it into wild spikes. "Who else can I leave?" Ti-cat lay curled up under a large bright-leafed plant dripping down one corner of the lounge, watching the two of them, Tibo on the divan, propped up on spare cushions, his legs crossed at the ankles, Skeen prowling restlessly about. She looked defensive, Timka thought, and her usually slow, melodious voice was shrill. "Ross? Be real."

"Pic can handle herself, she doesn't need a nurse." He looked amused, but there was an interesting edge to the words. Timka lay very still, willing herself inconspicuous again. She had a suspicion that the prickly unease between these two was there because of the intruders into what had been a private space. Two acute, obstreperous individuals, both quick to resent any attempt to dominate them, they'd worked out a comfortable give and take that balanced the needs of both. A balance we disrupted, Timka thought. No room even for three, and now there's five of us. Not counting Picarefy. Should I count Picarefy?

Sound of clearing throat, sound of clapping hands. Picarefy asserting herself. "Listen to the man, Skeen."

"Butt out, Pic. Tib, I don't want to turn Ross loose down there."

"Don't be silly, Skeen. Keep him in the shadows until you can smooth the Rallykx down if they need it, then let him do his thing. He's got contacts you'll never reach, he's a clever kid and he's got a heavy thing for you, he's hot to show you what he can do."

Skeen made an impatient sound, close to a derisive hoot. "He's a con artist, Tib."

"So? What's wrong with that?"

"Aaaah! You are the most . . . most . . ."

"Handsome? No? Intelligent? Dashing?" He grinned at her.

"Pigheaded is more like it."

The argument went on, intensifying to the point of violence where Skeen and Tibo were circling about each other like angry cats, carefully not touching. Timka watched the man, more interested in him for the moment. He'd been polite but cool to her from the beginning; she meant nothing to him and he was more than content to keep it like that. In a number of ways, he was very like Skeen; he shared Skeen's attitudes toward money and pleasure, shared her aversion to exercising control over others (an aversion almost as powerful as his distaste for letting anyone control him). Much more than Skeen he was a watcher on the sidelines, getting a vast amusement out of the idiocies and idiosyncrasies of so-called sentients. Not a particularly endearing trait, but he was polite enough to turn his all-too-knowing gaze off you if he saw you growing uncomfortable under it. Unless you threatened Skeen. He was astonishingly protective of that tough resourceful woman, understanding her with an empathy that was the one thing he took pains to conceal from her, reading her moods and responding or not according to some interior set of rules Timka couldn't fashion.

So suddenly Timka found herself blinking, they reached agreement. Tibo and Ross would stay in Picarefy for three days, then, unless something unexpected happened, they'd join the groundside party, leaving Picarefy to amuse herself spreading her flying eyes about, keeping watch over Skeen and sucking in as much data as she could.

They gathered about the screen on the bridge, looking at the lake beneath them, the rolling scrubland around it with its patches of forest, the complex of buildings that seemed more like calligraphy than architecture. At a word from Skeen, the viewpoint darted down until they could see Ykx walking and soaring about the buildings (one structure was halfway around the lake from the others and far quieter. An Ykx was pottering about in a large half-wild garden, another was stretched out on a lounge chair watching the first).

"That the place?" A touch of Skeen's finger and a black arrowhead pointed toward the lone building.

Ross scratched at his nose. "I heard a lot of talk about the Kinravaly's Garden; I suppose that's it."

Skeen moved the point of the arrow to an open grassy space beside the garden's outer wall. "Pic, program that into Workhorse, that's where I want to put down." She laced her fingers behind her head, stretched, got to her feet. "We'll make a loop round the world, buzz 'em low and noisy so they know we're here." She grinned. "Stomp around and stir up the natives."

After they buzzed the first Gurn they had to go more carefully; Rallykx of all ages spiraled up to soar about them, riding wings or wind according to air quality and their own abilities. Skeen was flying the Roon harvester she called Workhorse, a powerful shuttle-tug nearly ten times the size of the Lander tucked into its belly.

Skeen raised her brows. "Yes, they've noticed us."

Lipitero was breathless, unable to speak, the hair on her arms and along her spine erecting with the force of her emotion. Ykx everywhere, a world full of Ykx.

Timka yawned, beginning to be bored by this meandering trip. Skeen had planned a route that took them looping over all the major land masses, a long, tedious, essentially uneventful journey without a hint of comfort, hot, noisy, rough. The tug was built for strength, speed and maneuverability, not for an easy ride.

When they came back to the lake, Skeen put the tug into a tight hover-circle some hundred meters above the spot she'd chosen as a landing site, handed the Hailer's pickup to Lipitero. "Speak your piece, Petro. Here's hoping they listen; I don't want to squash anyone when we land."

Lipitero had worked out her speech with care, using the limited vocabulary she'd lifted from Ross, augmenting it with words from the Old Ykx she'd learned from the flakes the Remmyo had given her. Universal literacy, a longish lifespan, slow breeding and the conservative nature of the Ykx meant that language change occurred with the deliberation of glacial drift, but centuries do add up to real time if you have enough of them and Rallen was colonized a long long LONG time ago.

"Ykx of Rallen," she said, "hear me. We will not harm you. We will not let you harm us." She swallowed, closed her eyes. She'd meant to pause here, giving them time to react to the first words. She had to pause, want to or not, because her throat had closed on her. A cough muffled behind a hand, a few experimental workings of her mouth. She continued, "This ship (heavier than air flier) will (immediate future, less than an hour forward from the present moment) land in the open space (grass grown and uncultivated) on the out side of the garden wall. It is our hope (fervent wish accompanied by firm will) that we harm nothing other than the grass when we come down (controlled descent involving deceleration). We ask (favor of importance, a good conferred on speaker and listener) that all who hear me will keep clear of the ship by at least two of its diameters since there are powerful forces working around us that would endanger (throw about, break limbs, kill) any Ykx approaching too close to us. There will come a moment when we are committed to the landing and cannot abort. We must land, whatever (being, beast, artifact inclusive) is beneath us. I (female, beyond breeding years) will (immediate future, less than an hour forward from the present moment) come forth (leave this shell and become vulnerable). It is necessary (great urgency, a matter of supreme importance to the speaker) that I speak with the Kinravaly Rallen. I will come with bare hands, claws retracted, I will wait the pleasure of the Kinravaly Rallen."

Lipitero walked into the thin cold sunshine, Ti-cat limber and lethal beside her. Behind her the brutal black form of the tug squatted like a spider, its hoists were legs drawn tight to its mass. Ykx soared above her and the Garden, a swarm of wasps smoked from their nest, but they kept their distance, wary of her, frightened by the promise of power in that monstrous beast of a flier. She wore a harness she'd designed for this moment, plain, with no weapons, only spyeyes, so Skeen could see and hear what she saw and heard.

There was a gate in the wall about a score of meters from the landing site. When Lipitero reached it, she hesitated, wondering whether it would be locked against her. She hoped not, she'd rather start this talk on a friendly basis. If Skeen had to burn the gate open for her, well she didn't want to think about that. The gate was simple, planks of a velvety tight-grained wood polished by weather to a soft smoky gray. She flattened her

palm on the wood, gave a short sharp push. The gate
swung smoothly open, the hinges were oiled and silent.
She stepped inside.

Two Ykx waited alone beside an immense tree that
spread great russet limbs across a moss garden and a
small noisy stream that came round heavy beams of
roughcut unpainted wood which formed part of a structure that was mostly hidden behind clumps of bamboo,
flowering bushes, trees and climbing vines, a stream that
continued across the glade to pass under the wall a short
distance beyond the gate. A quiet, peaceful place, filled
with the music of the water, scattered trills of birdsong
and the soft buzzing of hidden insects. With Ti-cat following half a meter behind her and slightly to one side,
Lipitero crunched along a gravel path to a wooden foot-
bridge. She stopped on the bridge and examined the two
strange Ykx.

A stocky golden Ykx, no longer young but so astound-
ingly beautiful the breath caught in Lipitero's throat when
she looked at her. Her harness was ancient leather, worn
and comfortable, patched in several places with leather
thongs, probably by her own impatient hands. The lacing
was hastily done, with no attempt at disguising the utilitarian purpose of the work. Her fur had been brushed
sometime in the recent past but not since she'd done
some pruning, if the bits of leaf and bark dusted along
her forearms meant anything. She was smiling a little,
deep glowing eyes watching Lipitero and Ti-cat with gentle amusement and considerable curiosity. Beyond all
doubt, the Kinravaly Rallen.

At her side, a tall Ykx, female in her prime, couldn't
be much past her bearing years. A silver-gray like Lipitero.
Stern handsome face. Sleek, rangy, strong. She stood at
the Kinravaly's shoulder, looking like she wanted to be a
step ahead, her body interposed between the Kinravaly
and Lipitero. Seething with a suppressed anger that found
expression in the unnatural rigidity of her body, she fixed
her amber-crystal eyes on Lipitero as if she dared the
stranger to make a hostile move. Obviously she didn't
want Lipitero anywhere around the Kinravaly, strange
scarred Ykx whose motives were suspect, who could
threaten the woman she protected so earnestly.

Lipitero waited.

The gold Ykx smiled. "I am Kinravaly Rallen. You asked to speak with me."

Lipitero spread her arms, letting her flightskins fall free, showed her hands, empty, claws retracted. "I am Lipitero the Bereft who come to speak for the last Gather on Mistommerk."

"Bereft?" The Kinravaly took a step forward, ignoring the wordless protest of the silver-gray. Her ocean-deep eyes swept over the scars that marred Lipitero's face and torso. "You've been hurt."

"My children are dead, my kin are gone, my Gather lies empty and broken." Lipitero felt uneasy with the contrast between the formality of her speech and the quick fluid response of the Kinravaly (words and body language both), but the Kinravaly's accent and some of the words she used demanded hard listening and puzzling out at times; speech would grow easier as she grew accustomed to the accent, but at the moment she felt safest keeping to the most formal of exchanges.

"That's a terrible thing. Do you come from Ysterai? No, of course, I mix myself up, you said Mistommerk. Is that a colony settled after Rallen? Do you have trouble there?"

After sorting out the questions and puzzling out what the Kinravaly actually said, Lipitero dug for words. "Colony, yes. Settled not from Ysterai but from Tovazh. I am come a beggar from Sydo Gather to say this: The Gathers of Mistommerk are empty and Sydo is alone. We cannot exist alone. I am come to plead for colonists to fill the empty Gathers."

"I see. We must talk about this more." The Kinravaly turned to the silver-gray Ykx who was grinding her teeth with frustration. She looked up into the rigid face and smiled. "Zem-trallen, go reassure the Kinra, will you? Be sensible, my friend. Our visitor wants help, why should she harm me, what good would that do her? Go, before I have Sulleggen storming in here foaming at the mouth and demanding answers to questions I haven't even thought of yet."

The Zem-trallen clamped her lips together, threw a searing glare at Lipitero, swung round and stalked off.

The Kinravaly beckoned to Lipitero. "Come round to the patio, we can sit and chat there, be more comfortable. I've ordered some iska and cakes. Do you know iska? No? It's a sweetish herbal decoction drunk hot or iced, very refreshing. We've been a long time apart, but I don't think it would be dangerous to you. I've heard that the young alien who visited us a few years back ate and drank with Ykx and had no trouble from it. Hmm, was it him who guided you here?" She laughed suddenly, a warm accepting sound. "You probably don't understand half of what I'm babbling."

"That is true, Kinravaly." Lipitero spoke slowly, carefully. "But I am growing accustomed to hearing you and understanding becomes easier. Please continue, but be patient with my thick head."

The Kinravaly laughed again and continued a steady flow of conversation as she led Lipitero and Ti-cat to a covered patio looking down a long slope of grass and flowers. Carved wooden screens were placed about to block the wind and several braziers provided enough heat to keep them comfortable in spite of the chilly air. When Lipitero was seated, her feet on a low hassock, Ti-cat stretched out beside her, the Kinravaly pulled a bell cord, then settled herself in a worn old chair, her feet propped on a three-legged stool.

Anki came in with a heavily loaded tray. The Kinravaly took a cup of iska and sipped at it as the young Ykx brought a cup and a selection of wafers to Lipitero and set these things on a small table at Petro's elbow, then glided out. The Kinravaly set her cup down, laced her fingers over her stomach fur. "Tell me why you are here. More detail now. Take your time, I will listen as long as you need."

"It requires preamble," Lipitero said. The iska warmed and relaxed her. I should take some plants back with me, if I can talk Skeen into carrying them. She closed her eyes a moment. The words were starting to come easier, but this chase between two similar languages was hard on her head, long habit came constantly out of the shadows to trip her up. "I do not know how much the Rallykx remember of the seedtime, the time when the colony transports were sent out?"

"There was an accident to the memory of our main computer, what we know of that time comes from the colonists who recorded what they remembered. The knowledge we retrieved that way, even the technical data, is more incantation than information. So. Assume we know a little of our history but that knowledge is spotty. Be sure that if you mention something unclear, I will stop you and ask for explanation.

"I hear," Lipitero said. "You know nothing of what happened after you left Ysterai?"

"There was no way to learn anything."

"I see. There are hard things for you to hear. To get the hardest over with, Ysterai is ash. A lifeless cinder. Victim of a three-way war between Pallah, Nagamar and Funor. This happened less than a century after the Rallen transports vanished. I know little of Keelava and Tozeed. Skeen tells me she hadn't heard of our species prior to her Leap through the Stranger's Gate. Yes, yes. I'll explain in a little, let me finish this first. As far as anyone knows, the only Ykx alive exist here on Rallen and in the Sydo Gather on Mistommerk. I told you before that Mistommerk was colonized from Tovazh which now has the name Kildun Aalda. There are no Ykx on Kildun Aalda." She drank the last of her iska, sat silent as the Kinravaly brought the pot to her and filled her cup again.

"My folk came from those planted on Tovazh. I don't know how much you know about that colony, it was a place where some very radical and esoteric experimentation was happening. Remember these things. A gathering of the finest and no doubt wildest minds among the Ykx. Trouble between the Balayar and the Chalarosh. Tovazh's star a flare star, something not generally known because of the length of its cycle, something discovered serendipitously in connection with other research by a group of Ykx Seekers. The time of the flares approaching rapidly. Soil cores indicating the burning off of all life above ground during previous flares. The Tovazhi Kinra begin planning for the evacuation of the population before the flares make living there impossible. Before the evacuation can get under way, the Balayar and the Chalarosh move from irritation with each other to open

warfare, and both refuse to recognize the neutrality of
the Ykx. Ships of both species swarm about Tovazh,
coveting that planet for its strategic location halfway
between their home worlds. They establish a blockade
about Tovazh. Neither Balayar nor Chalarosh listen to
Ykx warnings about the flares and they will not permit
the Ykx to desert that world unless the Ykx cede owner-
ship of it to one or the other. But Chalarosh will not
permit the Ykx to give the world to the Balayar. Balayar
will not permit the Chalarosh to take it. A few Ykx
chosen by lot get offworld when the Balayar and the
Chalarosh are busy sniping at each other, but not one
tenth of the population manages to leave.

"The perturbations grow more intense. The weather
turns unpredictable. Food begins to run out, impossible
to grow sufficient in the few hydroponic gardens. It looks
like a race between starvation and cremation."

Lipitero paused, sipped more iska. "You see the bind
they were in. They did find a way out of it, I'm here as
evidence of that. This is how they did it.

"Among the wildest and most brilliant of the Seekers
on Tovazh was an Ykx called Mierzel ap Xon; like the
Tovazhi Sun, he was hot and bright but unstable. He
required adulation like some require drugs and gathered
about him a small band of sycophants who worshiped
him as a genius, almost a god, and got him funding for
his experiments. The greater part of those on Tovazh,
though, ignored him and his work. More orthodox Seekers thought he was either crazy or a charlatan or both,
and had good reason for thinking so from what I've read
off flakes made around that time. Inclined to acerbic and
megalomaniac pronouncements about things entirely outside his field of competence, he was a bigot, a snob,
dishonest in small things and large, cruel, incapable of
sympathy or compassion, with a severely inflated estima-
tion of his own worth. Within the very narrow limits of
his specialty, despite his delusions, despite the general
inadequacy of his persona, despite the unsavory nature
of his acts and ideas, he really did have flashes of genius.
Withdrawing to the compound his acolytes had built for
him and furnished lavishly, scrambling desperately to
escape the death he refused to countenance for himself,

throwing together insights and data from his prodigally various researches, he drove a bridge across the insplit gap into another universe, collapsed that bridge into a Gate that he thought he alone could open. A way for him to leave Tovazh and take his faithful with him, along with as many pre-fertile females as they could gather up in the time left to them. The Gate opened on another world, you see, a habitable world. Mierzel's Luck, he wanted to call it, Mistommerk it was, named already by those with a better right. Being what he was, he proposed to take his chosen few and let the rest of the Ykx on Tovazh be what he called Purified by the Flare.

"Fortunately for my ancestors, that was too much for three of his acolytes. However fervently they adored him, however thoroughly they were cut off from their kin because of that adoration, they could not persuade themselves to run to safety and leave brothers, sisters, cousins, whatever, to burn. They duplicated Mierzel's records and took them to the Tovazhi Kinra. Dishonest in almost every phase of his life, the one thing Mierzel wouldn't fudge was his data. He kept meticulous records of every experiment and noted down every step of his thinking. The acolytes added their own testimony; they'd looked into that other world, they had taken samples of its air, its plant life, they had even trapped a small rodent and brought it through into the courtyard of the compound where the Gate was built.

"Mierzel ap Xon learned of the defection of the Three. Frightened, he gathered those present and fled through the Gate. He was never seen again. In opening the Gate he had drawn from someplace between this universe and that other one an amorphous Thing we later named the Ever-Hunger. Ever-Hunger ate him and his minions and the young females he took with him.

"Perhaps the forces unleashed by the opening of the Gate hastened the onset of the flares, perhaps the Seekers were wrong in their timing of the cycle, but there was just enough time to recreate the Key to the Gate and gather the folk. The Kinra collected all Ykx left on Tovazh; skim sleds were piled with food, tools, texts, instruments and the youngest children if their parents couldn't carry them. They stripped Tovazh of whatever

was valued and useful and brought it to Mierzel's
Compound.

"Tovazh's Star was pulsing, throbbing, so the flakes
tell it; the air burned mouth and lungs, the earth groaned
beneath their feet. Cubs wailed. Adults quarreled, fainted,
fought; some died. Seekers struggled with the Gate; there
was much the acolytes didn't know about its workings,
perhaps only Mierzel ap Xon ever really understood what
he created. At last they got the Gate open. An advance
party stepped through and discovered the Ever-Hunger;
two out of twenty got back to describe what had happened. The Kinra and the Seekers struggled to deal with
that, but time was running out; finally they had no choice,
they began sending Ykx through with instructions to flee
from the Gate as swiftly as possible.

"There was another danger waiting for the folk widecast
through that Gate. Mistommerk was already inhabited
by native sentients who called themselves the Min. They
were not happy about this influx of intruders and they
were frightened by our gear. They attacked. Much not
lost to the Ever-Hunger succumbed to the depredations
of the Min."

The lounging cat-weasel shifted, put a paw on Lipitero's
foot, claws out enough to prick her.

Lipitero looked down, chuckled. "I get the points,
Ti." She cleared her throat, gulped down a few mouth-
fuls of the lukewarm iska; she was more tired by this
talking than she'd been any time during the long trek
across Mistommerk, her head ached and her throat felt
raw. *A little more, I'm halfway through. Back to work,
old woman.* "Depredations isn't exactly the right word;
the Min were defending themselves against invaders. After the initial hostilities, Ykx and Min established a fingertip, tooth-end peace that very slowly developed into a
limited trade between the two species. We . . . yes, I will
say we, since I am born of them and what they did . . .
we established five filled Gathers scattered about Mistommerk and a sixth Work Gather close to the Gate. We
had inflicted the Ever-Hunger on the Min of Mistommerk,
we owed it to them and to ourselves to remove the
scourge.

"After Mierzel loosed the Hunger, it raged the hills

about the Gate destroying all animal life, including the Min living there. Though it was tied to the Gate, it grew and grew, reached ever farther to feed on the life around it. It was amorphous, invisible and as far as we could determine, it was unkillable. We tried to drive it back through the Gate, but could not. We tried to destroy the Gate, thinking that might cause the Hunger to wither and die, but we could not. In the end we managed to confine the Hunger into a space a kilometer square behind a white wall that generated a most peculiar field which the Ever-Hunger couldn't pass. For decades after that Ykx came to Gate Gather to study the Hunger, but as the years passed interest in the beast diminished. We were too busy recreating the life we'd enjoyed on Tovazh to bother with it.

"Decades turned to centuries. And the time came when we learned how badly we'd botched our work on the Gate. Tovazh's sun flared again and the Gate opened. Not only did it open, but it summoned to it the Chalarosh living on Tovazh. They'd won control of the world a few decades earlier. Chala aren't noted for their interest in abstract science; they stole their technology, then bought experts to keep it running. They forgot about the last flares or maybe they thought that was a one-time thing, so when the cycle came around again, it caught them unprepared. Except for the Gate, they would have fried, those Chalarosh holding Tovazh. Instead, they came pouring through the Gate, falling into the throat of the Ever-Hunger. The Wall frustrated the Hunger a bit, but it dined well that year, feeding on the weakest and most suggestible of the refugees. That was the second Wave of invaders to hit Mistommerk. Again and again, right on schedule, the Tovazhi Sun flared, Wave after Wave of refugees tumbled through. Balayar. Funor Ashon. Nagamar. Aggitj. Skirrik. Pallah. Lot of trouble, lot of turmoil. We avoided most of it, we Ykx; our Gathers were away from the trade routes and migration lines. More centuries slid past. We diminished. For the longest time we didn't realize what was happening. Then one Gather was empty. Another withered. The other Waves were sometimes hostile, hunting us, that is how my children died. It is not an easy place, a safe place, our Mistommerk.

There is another thing you should know. Something on Mistommerk depresses fertility. Our Seekers have tried to isolate it and failed. Skirrik have been working on it with their cleverest growmasters; they've learned enough to suspect a synergism of some kind, unfortunately a different one with each species. Ahh! Are the words the same? I'm getting tangled. Do you understand what I'm saying?"

"I believe I've got the heart of it. You're being very candid."

"I have to be. I need volunteers who know what to expect; otherwise, they'll die."

"Tell me why I should allow my Rallykx to listen to you."

Lipitero smiled wearily. "I could play tricks, but I won't. I can offer you copies of our records from the ancient times, including starship/insplit technology, the history and literature of Ysterai, there are some gaps but not huge ones, all of Mierzel's studies and experiments with the Gate between universes, a selection of the history and literature of the Ykx on Mistommerk."

The Kinravaly chuckled. "Do you know, I think I'd kill for a moiety of that."

"Have you anything more you would like to ask me?"

The Kinravaly rubbed her palm back and forth along the arm of her chair. "It's hard to know where to start. The Min, I think. We encountered natives here and they found the experience unfortunate; they died of it."

Lipitero laughed. "The Min? They're alive, healthy, some friendly, some hostile. There's not a chance we could wipe them out if we wanted to and we don't."

"So you say. Another universe. Another species. What are they like?"

"You wouldn't believe me if I told you."

"Playing games?"

"Just a bit. You see my bodyguard?"

"A beautiful beast. Well-trained."

"Hardly a beast." She nudged the cat-weasel with her toe. "Wake up, Ti-cat. Show the Kinravaly what a Min is."

Ti-cat yawned, got to her feet, stretched, then walked lazily to the center of the patio. She showed her teeth again, flexed her muscles, flicked ears and tail, purring all the time. Then she shifted.

A large owl stood blinking huge golden eyes at the Kinravaly. Ti-owl spread her wings, hooted, powered into the air. She made a single circuit over the garden, landed beside a couch that had a bright throw tossed on it.

A slender pale-skinned Pallah woman with long curly black hair stood beside the couch. She pulled the throw off it, wrapped it quickly and neatly around her, took a dagger pin from Lipitero and stabbed it through the cloth. "Min," she said. "A short sample." She pushed Lipitero's feet off the hassock and sat there. "It's a complicated world."

The Kinravaly closed her mouth, then closed her eyes for a moment. She lay back in her chair, body rippling with short spasms of laughter. "Min," she said and opened her eyes. "What is your name, shape-changer?"

"Timka."

"Timka, if you pull that trick a few times more and tell my Ykx that thousands like you live on Mistommerk, you'll have to beat them off with clubs. There ARE thousands like you?"

"Several million."

"Ah. I wish . . . no. Do you think some of your folk could come to us?"

"I don't know. Some might like to . . . Petro?"

"Not soon. Aalda's sun is due to flare before the year is out. Tovazh's sun. It will be some years after that before anyone can put down on that world. If you could get another Gate open to Mistommerk . . ."

"Yes. I see. Tell me, how did you Tovazhykx ever deal with . . . with shape-shifters who could look like your long lost cousin if they chose?"

"They're not so flexible as all that. Not many of them can match Timka shift for shift. When we came through, the Min were herders and farmers. Those bodies, you know. No incentive to industrialize. Wrong mindset. They've changed since then, of course. Rubbing up against all the Waves. New plants, new beasts, new languages, new ways of thinking, new shapes for their bodies. Interesting world."

"Very." The Kinravaly brooded a moment, looked up. "Rostico Burn?"

"Yes. Skeen found him and he brought us here." Lipitero traced figure eights in the soft wood of her chair's arm. "What sort of welcome would he get if he showed his face down here?"

"You mean would we tie him to a pole and set fire to his feet?"

"Something like that."

"My influence is perhaps more limited than you think."

"I *am* Ykx."

"Our branches have diverged for a very long time."

"Perhaps I delude myself."

"And I." The Kinravaly frowned thoughtfully. "My responsibilities always seem to outrace my reach. About Burn. He'll be safe in the Reserve, otherwise, you had better talk to the Kinra. I won't give him my Hand, if that's what you're asking. A suggestion. He should stay on this side of the world if he decides to put his toe to ground. Sulleggen or Uratesto will fry his gizzard for him if they get hold of him. Hmm. If I send you out with my guards, I'm setting my seal on you; if I let you go about as you please, the All-Wise alone knows what disasters you'll tumble into. And I'd still be putting my seal on you, because I haven't stopped you or sent you away." She dropped her head back and stared up at the carved wooden squares that ceiled the patio. "And either way, I feel like I'd be selling Ykx. I want what you offer. I want it badly, Speaker. I just don't see how I can justify letting you loose to talk Rallykx into following you."

Lipitero sheathed her claws and stroked her fingerpads over the scars on her chest. Timka re-crossed her ankles, wiggled her toes; she slid the dagger pin out of her wrap, retucked it and stabbed the pin back. She was restless, nervous. Distracted for a moment by Timka's fidgeting, Lipitero found herself wondering what the Min thought about this business; if I succeed, there'll be more Ykx on Mistommerk, more invaders. She brushed the thought away, no time for it now. "Volunteers, Kinravaly Rallen. I can't deal with conscripts."

"And I can't throw Ykx into the void without some check on them. Even if they are volunteers."

"Ah. Yah. That's a problem. I told you. There's one working Gate. One. It's on a world that's due to cook for a few years so no one can get in or out of it. Not till the surface cools enough for a ship to land."

Timka looked up from the cloth she was pleating over her thighs. "Send someone you trust with us. He or she can see a bit of Mistommerk, see that Petro is telling the truth about the Gate. You don't need more than that, do you? Your agent can come back with Skeen and report what happened."

The Kinravaly's lips twitched into a tight smile. She shook her head. "If you are slavers or something equally dangerous, that's giving you one more victim, not a guarantee of good faith."

"I know that." Timka shrugged. "Wasn't meant to be; 'twas a suggestion for shortening your worry time. It'd make this a bit less like jumping into a bottomless pit. What it comes to, you trust Petro and the rest of us, or you don't."

"Hmm. I'd feel more comfortable about this if someone in your party was committed to something more than this one visit to Rallen. This Skeen. He? She?"

"She," Timka said; she straightened her back and looked interested.

"Would she be willing to discuss trade agreements with the Kinra?"

Timka chuckled. "Willing isn't quite the proper word, eh, Petro?"

Lipitero felt her mouth trying to stretch into a broad beaming grin; before she could speak, she had to damp down the joy starting to bubble in her blood. It was going to happen, it was, it really was. The Kinravaly was biting on the bait. When she had her voice under control, she said, "Yes. For a lot of reasons Skeen would be delighted. Um. Don't let that fool you though, she's a wily bargainer."

"I see. You have told me how the Tovazhykx got to Mistommerk. I'd like to know how you yourself got back through the Gate and where this Skeen fits in."

"Ahh." Lipitero emptied her cup for the third time; the iska was cold now but drinkable and it soothed her throat. "It's a long story. And complicated."

"More iska?"

"If you don't mind."

The Kinravaly pulled the cord. "Anki will bring another pot. Do you want to wait?"

"Timka knows the first part better than I. Ti?"

"Why not." The little Min smoothed her hands along her thighs, looked thoughtfully down the grassy slope toward the dark hump of Workhorse showing above the walls. "This is what Skeen told me. . . ."

"That's what they said." The Kinravaly walked to the front edge of the patio and stood looking at the weave of the Firestreaks drawn across the night sky. "That improbable creature and Lipitero the Bereft. What a story. Do *you* believe any of it?"

Zelzony clicked her tongue against her teeth. "Do you?"

Zuistro wandered back, stretched out in her chair, laced her fingers over her stomach fur. "Oh, yes. Lipitero is *so* transparent and *so* determined to be honest, poor thing. Her Remmyo's clever to send her; she'll be very effective in the Gurns if the Kinra allow her to speak. You know which will and which won't. They're fools, aren't they, that happy pair. Zeli, make sure the folk in Marrallat and Urolol know about our visitors."

Zelzony looked down at her, began laughing. "Ayy, Zo. Ayy, Zo." She sobered. "I suppose I shouldn't laugh, it won't be very funny what's going to happen there."

"I know. Borrentye's apprentice Singlow is working on ways of easing the pain. Zeli . . ."

"You want me to go with them."

"Do you mind?"

"What good would it do having me there? They'd scrag me with the rest and sell us all. If that's their plan. One middle-aged Min ignorant about everything past the Veils, I'd be worth a handful of spit against their weapons and their guile."

"At least I'd know. If they sell you, being you, if you're alive, I count on you getting back here. With a starship, too. Then we'd figure how to deal with them and get our folk back."

"Saa, Zo, you don't expect much."

"Saa, Zeli, I know you."

"Am I flattered? No. Only a fool. I'll go."

"They know a lot we don't, our aliens, but they don't know organics like we do. You'll go equipped with our best, Zeli, and you'll bring back a lot more than reassurance for an aging lover. I'm convinced of this, my Zeli, what Lipitero told me is no sly trick, but the truth. That doesn't mean we have to be quite that candid, yes?" She reached up her hand, smiled with pleasure as Zelzony took it and held it tight for a moment. "You're to be careful, my Zeli, you're to come back quickly. These are yeasty years ahead of us, my love, I need a shoulder to hold me steady." She freed her hand. "Pour yourself some wine and bring me a glass. What have you found out about the newest deaths?"

Zelzony took the stopper from the decanter; her hand shook a little and the glass stopper rang musically against the neck of the container. "Two of the missing have been found. A ravine in the Leposare Reserve." She concentrated on filling the glasses, set the decanter down with slow care; it nearly slipped from her fingers, she had to snatch at it, then bend to retrieve the stopper she'd knocked onto a floor cushion. "I shan't want to eat for a week. The second was just a cub, Zo, her flightskins soft with new down. Violated." She stammered over the word, got hold of herself and carried Zuistro's glass to her, went back and gulped down too big a mouthful of the wine, nearly choked on it. When she could speak again, she wiped her spattered fur, said, "Her heart was cut out. Part of her brain was gone. The other damage . . . if you need to see it, I have a record in the imager. Signs of a fire by the body. Which suggests some sort of ritual eating of the dead."

"A ravine?"

"Yes. Not far from the Tekala River, no water in it now, snowmelt in the spring. There's a high stone overhang so a fire wouldn't be seen from above. They're cautious, those horrors." She shivered with rage, her eyes misting over so she couldn't see, could just stand trembling and blind until the spasm passed. "Dry season," she said finally. "Not a time many folk visit the Leposare. No one about to see them though they seem to have camped there several days. And no one to hear them. It must have got noisy at times." She looked at the glass in her hand, set it on the table and walked to the edge of the patio. After a moment she folded her arms over her ribs, pulling her flightskins tight against her body.

Zuistro grimaced, finished the wine. "How many have you found now that they haven't bothered disguising as suicide? Yes. Nine. All of them pre-adult. How many killers this time?"

"Three, might possibly be four."

"Anything at all to identify them?"

"Scrapes on rock from boots or sandals, a few flakes of leather off a harness, no bigger than a shred of meat someone might get stuck between his teeth. Common grubber hide, nothing idiosyncratic about it. No way to connect it to anyone specific." She gazed up at the blazing sky. "The Veils are brighter than usual."

"Are they?"

"I've failed, you see. I'm floundering. I don't know where to go from here. I've tried every way I can think of to penetrate this darkness. My people have pried like corpseworms into the lives of the victims. We've run those lives through the computers a hundred times. There are dozens of correlations, but nothing that means anything. They were all young and except for this last cub who wasn't long off weaning, they were all well-grown, pre-adult, on the verge of committing themselves fulltime to their dutychoice. There could be sane reasons for choosing victims that age, no one would miss them for a month or more, tweeners are expected to flit about like that, their last freedom flights. Going off who knows where. No way to link them with anyone. Scattering like leaves before the wind. I think it must be chance. Those horrors come across a wingrider alone. Doesn't have to be anyone special. Can be either male or female. Class doesn't matter, though worker tweeners aren't likely to have wings. The victims we've found have all belonged to the managerial or professional classes. These creatures must go hunting whenever the urge is on them; no lack of sport year-round, not for them, they just change their killing field." She snapped her arm out, reaching toward nothing, her fingers starred. Her flightskins swayed, caught the light from the oil lamps, burnished silver shimmering over the surface of the down. The gesture meant nothing, it was only that she had to move, to dissipate some of the tension coiling in her. "Chance. The throw of the dice. How can I fight that, Zo? We've investigated friends, relatives, acquaintances, any connection we can think of, however remote. Sometimes there will be links between two or three, nothing nothing never anything linking all nine. We tried making patterns of killing sites, of dates, of Gurns and Gathers the victims started from. Nothing, Zo. Do you know how many killings we've had since we landed on Rallen? Not connected to the six-legs I mean. Fifty-seven. In almost as many millennia. Do you know how we caught the Killers? All but three turned themselves in, nearly paralyzed by their horror at what they'd done. Two were caught at their second attempt to kill, one was never caught, but stopped killing for some reason; no one then or since has ventured a guess as to why. I can't think about this any more, Zo. I try, but my mind slips off somehow onto something else. It's not real for me. I can't believe it. I've seen the bodies, I know what's been done to these children, but I can't make it mean anything, Zo, I can't visualize the Ykx who is capable of such things. When I try to concentrate, to force myself into thinking carefully, logically, into applying reason to this thing, I cannot do it. I have to come at it sideways now, but even that doesn't work. After three years of struggle, I am no closer to finding those monsters that I was when I stood there in the Common Hall and blathered on about the malaise in the soul of Rallen. Give this to someone else, please. I have failed and I will continue to fail."

"Who, Zeli, who among your people would do better?"

Zelzony jerked her arms in another impatient gesture, the silver sheen racing like spilled mercury across her fur. Zuistro couldn't see her face because she kept her back turned, but she didn't need to see it to know the pain of that failure. Her Zem-trallen crossed her arms, the skins pulled tight against her once again. "No one," she said, "They are capable workers, all of them, good thorough investigators. Borrentye is a marvel at what he does; he

squeezed time out from his other concerns to try his hand
at the puzzle, but he gave it up some months ago. He
said there was no point in him wasting his time any
longer. Besides things were getting a bit difficult in
Marrallat, some of his agents were disappearing and he
didn't like the rumors he was hearing about what happened to them. And no, he didn't think that had anything to do with this other thing. Just ordinary political
disappearances, Sulleggen dropping her adversaries down
a hole somewhere; he doesn't think they are dead, no,
just suppressed until Sulleggen can think of some way to
cancel out what they learned." She started prowling about
the patio, picking up worry stones, running her thumbs
over them, setting them down again, touching the decanter but leaving the stopper in place, picking up glasses,
running her fingers down the stems, setting them down
with exaggerated care. She stopped by Zuistro's feet,
stood gazing down at the Kinravaly. "Odd. People know
what's happening. We haven't tried keeping the deaths
a secret. Or suppressing how they died. They know, but
no one talks about it. Worker, artisan, manager, trader,
justicer, professional, they all refuse to think about this
thing. The tweeners flutter about as freely as always on
wing and skins as if nothing has happened. As if we all,
and I'm in it too, my love, as much as any, as if we all
can't absorb what's happening."

"Rallykx, ah, the Rallykx," the Kinravaly said. "They
can whip up some twisty tricks. Hmm. When the copper
vanished from the Narassen Gather's storehouse, what
did you do to find out how the thief did the impossible?"
She smiled affectionately at Zelzony. "Thinking sideways, my love. You went through orzala records and
found yourself that thoroughly reprehensible old thief
Tokalle who had fallen victim to the age of his body, not
his mind and you saw he got two years taken off his
reparations when he told you how he thought the thief
had done it and once you knew how, you knew who.
And Narassen got its copper back."

Zelzony threw herself into a chair, sat with legs splayed
out before her, hands clutching at the arms. "Thieving,
yes. But Zo, we've got no expert practitioners at murder
for me to consult."

"Perhaps we have."

"What?"

"Everything Rostico Burn said about Beyond the Veil tells us it's a violent place. Lipitero confirms that. No, I don't suggest that you ask her for help. She might live in the midst of violence, but Mistommerk Ykx are still Ykx. Think about Skeen. Grave robber. Smuggler. Thief. Remember what Lipitero told us about her and the way she lives. It's likely she knows quite a bit about killers and how they're hunted, though she's not a killer herself. Lipitero likes her, there's no misreading her feeling for the alien. She approves of her, she told me the woman is tough, perhaps and a bit crazy, but you can trust her if she gives her word. I will be talking with her tomorrow morning, I could make helping you a part of our bargaining."

Zelzony twisted around to frown at Zuistro. "She's the kind I'd be chasing if she were Ykx. Isn't this getting ourselves too deeply involved with her? Besides, how much can she know about lawful hunting?"

"How much did Tokalle know about thief-catching?"

With a flurry of elbows and knees, Zelzony jumped to her feet and trotted to the edge of the patio. For several minutes she stood there staring into the darkness. Then she shivered, the light dancing seductively along her lean body, over the graceful fall and fold of her flightskins. She turned her head, looking over her shoulder at the Kinravaly. "I was hoping . . ."

"That I would take this burden from you?"

"Yes. Yes. Yes."

"Ask Bohalendas how kind a Kinravaly can be. Ask Lah and Lih."

Zelzony dropped beside the chair and began smoothing her fingers along the solid muscle in the Kinravaly's leg. Down along the dark golden fur, the paler gold shimmering with buttery lights, up to the knee, down again to the long toes. "Kindness. If fate is kind, the monsters will take fright and volunteer to be colonists."

Zuistro was silent for some minutes, her breath roughening as she responded to Zelzony's touch. Finally, she said, "No, my dearest, I think they'd be the last to leave. I think they are terrified that they've lost themselves and

everything important. I think they need control, order. I
think they loathe change, they want everything eternally
the same so they won't feel inadequate or afraid. When
they do these things that sicken you, and me, however
calmly I talk about this, Zeli, I feel like screaming and
cursing, but neither helps much, does it? No, not even to
ease my horror . . . where was I, yes, when they catch a
flier in their nets, they have power in their hands, power
over life and death, pain and not-pain. I can hear them
laughing when they force their victims to do this and that
like training a grubber to plow. The laughter of complicity, of total control, master and mastered. These days,
my love, you can see change happening. Yeasty times.
I've said that a lot, that doesn't make it less true. A time
when workers are filled with the hope of escaping their
drudgery, a time when managers find their positions and
honors precarious. Especially the honors. You and I, my
Zem-trallen, have never cared much for the formalities
of our offices, but if we wanted, we could put on such
parades of pomp the dead would stare. I am locked into
this role by far more than the pleasures of power, but
you, my love, you could walk away from your office
tomorrow and all you'd miss would be the work. Do you
think Sulleggen could stop being Kinra the same way?
Do you think she doesn't know that if you stripped away
her honors you'd leave her a naked worm? And she at
least has some talents to cushion her fall. What about
Uratesto? He's a figurehead for the Consortium that
really runs Urolol. What would he be without his official
harness? Too much change will kill them, Zeli, that's
why they are fighting you and Borrentye with every wind
they can raise. They'll not allow Lipitero in their Gurns
and they won't let their folk out to hear her. And they
are right, my love. She is the match that will set off the
explosion they've contrived to create under them. Though
maybe I'm wrong about Sulleggen, maybe she will see
this as a chance to drain off the most dangerous of her
malcontents. Where was I, yes, I don't say your monsters
are Sulleggen or Uratesto, I think that's unlikely, but I'd
say look for similar types among the less successful of our
managers." She sighed with pleasure as Zelzony continued stroking her fur. "I will arrange a meeting between

you and Skeen tomorrow afternoon, ahhh, do you know how marvelous that feels, mmmm? A minute and I'll return the favor; if the woman agrees to help you, see if you can get her to give us star charts from Beyond the Veil. Ahhh. . . ."

"How many?"

"Nine in the past two years."

Skeen was startled into laughter then had to apologize. "Etjillos on Tor where I grew up, well, nine dead in a night would be a night unusually calm. My uncle's house was a few streets over from the Menagerie, um, that was where the dross of Etjillos was dumped, I would see the dead vans clanking past after the meatmen collected the corpses off the streets. They used to bet on how many they'd find, the meatmen I mean, no one who knew the place would put his money on nine. More often it was twenty or thirty; one night they pulled out seventy-three."

Zelzony shook herself, tried to comprehend what seemed to her an impossible anarchy. "Dead left in the streets? Their families . . ."

Skeen shrugged. "What families? Besides, if you stuck your head up to claim a body with half a hundred stabs in it, you'd probably be hauled in by the traiches and thumped until you confessed killing him. The local archon generally paid the meatmen a copper or two per corpse, ground these up and sold the result to the local farmers to use as fertilizer or kebir food. If someone important, especially a Citizen, went slumming and got himself offed, the Imperials came stomping in, rounded up whoever they could get their hands on, turned their brains to mush with hard probes; since they didn't bother asking the right questions, they almost never learned anything important; after that, they lined the leavings against a handy wall, shot them and fed them into the fertilizer mills. They never bothered hunting down whoever really did the job, the object of the exercise was to convince the locals they shouldn't lay a finger on a slummer no matter what he did to them."

Zelzony stared at her, shivered. "I can't see how you could live like that."

"Nice to have a choice."

"Forgive me, fer Skeen, consider it ignorance speaking. Then you don't have any suggestions for me beyond what I've already done."

"I wouldn't say that. I'm no good. But it's not me you should be talking to, it's Picarefy. Come out to Workhorse with me. Uh, the ship."

"Picarefy?" She followed Skeen across the grass. "Another member of your crew?"

"No. The ship. Not this one. The starship up there." She waved a long arm at a sky thick with dark clouds threatening rain.

"What?"

"Oh, you have a treat ahead of you, my friend. My Picarefy is something else, though don't tell her I said so. She's already too conceited."

The lift carried them smoothly to the airlock. Zelzony followed the tall, thin alien inside. Even the round surfaces in this thing seemed harsher, more rigid than the plastics, plants and cultures she was accustomed to considering technology. There was an odd cool smell around her that wasn't unpleasant, just unfamiliar. It seemed to Zelzony to hold some essence of the alien and her way of life.

Zelzony settled in the padded chair that was almost as comfortable for her as it was for the alien; she watched with a twinge of envy and desire as Skeen's long, rather bony fingers moved with swift assurance over the console.

A face bloomed in the oversize screen.

"Eh, Tibo," Skeen said, then said more in a rapid patter of words that Zelzony couldn't follow. She was startled by how frustrated this made her feel; she wasn't accustomed to dealing with strange tongues, even the few dialects that had developed in the more widely separated Gurns were quickly comprehensible to one who took a moment's thought and listened carefully. Ykx were conservative by nature, literate, and no group had ever been totally cut off from another so any changes in the language made their way swiftly around Rallen. She had a sudden vision of herself lost in a sea of meaningless sounds and it frightened her more than anything, even these murderous cretins she was trying to locate and the fear that they were a portent of Rallen's future. In a moment of panic she wanted to run from the place and tell the Kinravaly she hadn't the courage to leave Rallen and plunge into that kind of uncertainty.

The alien in the screen grinned suddenly and stopped talking. Another voice came through the speakers, using Rallyx smoothly with a subtle blend of accents. "How goes the bargaining, oh, Partner and Friend? Please may I send you these ants in my belly? Tibo and Rostico Burn aren't meant to be soulmates."

"You've been taking language lessons," Skeen said, laughter in her voice.

"Self-defense, I swear it."

"Live with them till tomorrow like we planned. Pic, I've got a sweet little problem for you to play around your circuits. That's Rallen's head cop you see there." She chuckled. "Quite a change from the usual scenario, isn't it." More soberly, she went on, "Help her all you can, Pic, it's a mean one. She'll give you the layout. Um, she's called Zelzony." Skeen swung round to face Zelzony. "Just talk, the sensors will catch your voice and send it up. Her name is Picarefy, please use it when you speak to her."

Feeling odd talking to a mechanical thing (though it helped that the other alien, Tibo, continued to watch from the screen, giving her the comforting illusion she was talking to him), Zelzony repeated once more the list of deaths and what she'd done to discover the authors of them. It was not easy, baring Rallen's troubles like this to strangers who had no stake in them, but she was at the end of her resources and she kept seeing the mutilated cub. She finished, swallowed a sigh, waited for some response.

"I am going to ask questions which you might find irrelevant and even embarrassing," Picarefy said. Her voice was a lovely thing, warm and friendly, a blend of alto and tenor Zelzony found soothing to ears and spirit. It struck her as odd, another odd thing to add to the many she was accumulating as she associated with these people, that this voice moved her almost as much as Zuistro's did, yet it came from a machine. The voice made it easy to forget she was talking to a machine. She accepted that gratefully and relaxed yet more. "Some questions you will think unnecessary because I must already have the answers from Lipitero and the flakes she has allowed me to read. Please answer them nonetheless. Rallykx are omnivorous?"

Zelzony opened her eyes wide, then smiled and settled herself for a long chat. "Yes."

"What about the Old Ykx?"

"As far as we know, yes."

"On Ysterai were there predators large enough to threaten an adult?"

"That's a bit hard to answer. Have you been told about the accident that brought us here?"

"Yes."

"Ahh, yes. Piktar packs. There's a lot about them in children's cautionary tales. *The Piktars will get you if you don't watch out. So don't you go out alone, you fidgety cub.* A Piktar was small enough to hold in one hand." Zelzony held out a cupped hand, cupped the other over it. "Like that. But they ran in packs of fifty or more. Sometimes several hundred, if the food supply permitted it. Adults could outrun them or soar away from them, especially the latter, since Piktars never gave up on a meat trail. They generally went after children, especially cubs before they could soar, got round them and overran them. Some of the best stories are about summercubs who vanished down the gullets of the swarm."

"How did you get the meat you ate?"

"Nets. Soar over a herd, pick your beast, preferably one on the outside, spook the rest into running off, cut the throat, bleed the beast, butcher it on the spot and distribute the sections to the hunting party. The most dangerous part of the hunt was getting the meat back to the Gather. Cutting the carcass up reduced the weight enough so the band could fly it back. If possible they hunted around escarpments or gullha trees so they would have a height to launch themselves from."

"Before you had nets?"

"I really don't see the point, never mind, it's all speculation anyway. Story goes this way. One day a swarm of Piktars stampeded a herd over a cliff and a wandering band of Ykx got there first. The Ykx had a wily old female for their point. She decided she liked fresh meat better than carrion and put her mind to getting it."

"Ah. Male, female, how were the roles distributed?"

"Who knows. Listen, I'll tell you what happens now. A female Ykx bears alive. During the later part of her pregnancy, she is too heavy to soar, so I suppose back then that meant she couldn't hunt during those months. Once the child is born, the male feeds it from blood nipples he develops when he lets the cub lick and suck at him. You see what that means. Males and females trade responsibilities; in early times they probably took turns doing the hunting. A female Ykx tends to be larger than a male, she needs the mass to provide for the fetus; what happens is females tend to do the heavy work, ah, and I suppose most of those old hunting bands had female points, while males did more of the fine work; from the old tales, they did the courting, preened like bright birds and fought a lot, being, as a whole, more aggressive than females. Now, the fertile period in females is short, just six years, and the maximum number of children she can produce is three. Male fertility lasts longer. Do you want to know about copulation? It starts a few years before either sex is fully fertile and continues a long time beyond the child-getting and bearing years. A bonding mechanism, our students of custom tell us in their dry, cold way. You talk of sex roles, do you understand how fuzzy the edges are for us? We Ykx spend the greater part of our lives as not-parents. So gestation and suckling mean rather less to us than to other species. You see me? I used up my patience raising my youngest brother, my mother died when he was born. My own children, well, I had my three as soon as I could and left them with their father to raise; to speak honestly, they bored and irritated me; not him, he liked holding and tending them. Sometimes it happens that way, sometimes the mother takes over after weaning, sometimes the parents share the raising. It depends on temperament not custom."

"I see. The roles are diffuse, but family bonding is strong; I understand that your Gathers are actually clan holdings, one large extended family."

"It's rather more complicated than that. Still, I suppose all of the Ykx in a Gather are connected one way or another to a smallish family grouping among the original settlers."

"Lifespan?"

"A healthy female Ykx can expect to see her Four-hundred. Male lifespan is somewhat shorter. They have more complicated metabolisms, burn up faster."

"Local years?"

"I don't . . ." She stopped, blinked. "I never thought that years would have different lengths. It depends on how far you are from the sun, doesn't it. How strange. If someone says I'll see you two years from now, how do you know when to meet? I suppose you have some sort of standard time length you refer to. Never mind explaining now, we can talk about that later. Local years, yes." She looked doubtful. "Do you need some sort of measuring guide to tell how long that is? Our years are a fraction over three hundred ninety-eight days."

"Thank you. From what I have seen of Rallen, your ties to Gather and Gurn are very strong, much stronger than other species I have observed. Yes. Your technology forces you to be less flexible than you were in earlier times, you have less freedom to express your idiosyncrasies. Your classes are shut within boundaries without the elasticity they once had, too many possibilities are foreclosed. No, Zelzony, don't protest. I'm not saying you've a society that grinds its people into faceless clones. You don't. I know a number of people who'd say you've done very well indeed for yourselves. I am saying that there is less looseness in the mix. With some notable exceptions, you Rallykx can't shake time loose from the demands of work and Gather to fool around with unstructured nonsense. You've codified dutychoice and joychoice and work hard at both and in a sense you've squeezed the juice out of your lives. I know, yes, I know that's overstating the case, you have your poets and singers, your thinkers and your seekers, those folk who ignore the pressures I'm talking about because they've got something that they are so passionate about nothing else has much reality for them. What percentage of the population are they? Listen, this is what I'm telling you. You Rallyx have developed your technology and the work structures created by it to the point where they are beginning to overload your

institutions and suck the life out of your traditions. Add
to this the oppressive effect of the Firestreaks coming
visibly closer year on year with no way to escape them.
Add again the deeply driven need of your species to
soar, actually and figuratively. Add the impact of Rostico
Burn's arrival, the reminder of the vast spaces beyond
the Fire, spaces forever locked away from them, as far as
they know. You tell me that suicides have increased
ninehundredfold since Burn's appearance; tell me this,
isn't suicide violence against the self? Your murderers
have turned outward when others have gone in. Well,
none of this is particularly helpful for finding them. Yes.
Before the arrival of Rostico Burn, were there any suspicious deaths?"

"No."

"You say that with certainty."

"Too much certainty?" Zelzony shook her head. "I
could be wrong, but I don't think so." Se picked at the
chair arm with the tips of her claws, frowned unseeing at
the screen. "Each suicide had a history of depression and
growing disturbance. There were witnesses registered to
swear to the circumstances of each death. The first mutilated bodies were found some considerable time after
Burn's departure. Rather ineptly camouflaged as Burn-
deaths."

A long silence. Then Picarefy said quietly, "Do you
have a list of witnesses at that first Burndeath and the
genuine suicides of all types after that?"

"I could get some part of the names; you should understand, circumstances make it difficult to get data out
of Marrallat and Urolol. Why do you want those names?"

"In the long ago on Ysterai a hunter acquired a taste
for fresh meat and arranged to get more of it. Some of
your Rallykx have acquired a taste for death. In the
beginning it's likely they sought out suicides to indulge
this craving. Because they didn't know what they were
going to be doing, they wouldn't bother hiding their
presence, why should they; in appearance, they were
there like all the others to urge the suicide to change his
mind. Who could read their hearts and know they were
really there to feast on death? So they wouldn't hide
their traces like they did later. Look for witnesses that

show up on several lists. Look for names that don't fit, strangers from other Gurns. All you really need is one name, the end of a thread you can pull to unravel the camouflage over them all."

"I am a fool! Why didn't I see that? Something so obvious, so simple?"

"Not so simple as all that. You were concentrating on the victims."

"Yes. And there was nothing to point to the killers. They were chosen by chance, no more."

"Um, I doubt if it was wholly chance; I think you'll find that your hunters observed their prey for some time before they snagged it. The lack of clues is a clue in itself. You told me not one of the dead was reported missing less than fifteen days after his or her disappearance. Everyone of these youngsters was expected to be gone for a fortn't or longer. Even that last cub, she was traveling with an older cousin to visit her father's kin on one of the resort islands, travel time a minimum of ten days. They weren't listed as missing until they were five days late. From what you say, no one has reported strangers asking questions about any of the victims. How do the killers know which travelers are going where and how long they will be gone? Are there expeditions of a solitary nature that require licensing or offices where the victims would report the intended absence from their home Gathers? Who would have licit or illicit access to such reports? The descriptions you have given me of the condition of the bodies indicates a certain delicacy of touch, as it were, suggesting a being adult enough to savor his or her pleasures, postponing ultimate gratification as long as possible. In eight of the nine cases, the victims were raped with traces of semen present, though, unfortunately, too much time had elapsed for typing, so at least one of the killers is a sexually active male. And finally, what individuals of working age could disappear for five to seven days without causing comment? Answer these questions and compare them with the lists of witnesses, then you might have an individual or two you can concentrate on."

Cursing softly at the incompatibility of the two systems of recording, Zelzony worked frantically at the rekkagourd,

entering notes in her personal shorthand. She looked up
after a moment, saw Skeen watching her with a sympa-
thetic smile. Her face crumpled, the hard elegant lines
shattered by anger, frustration, selfblame. "I knew all
this, why why why didn't I see it? The Kinravaly said it,
why didn't I hear what she was saying? If you know how,
you know who, she said. If you know how. . . ."

"You were looking so hard in one direction you lost
your peripheral vision. That's a benefit of living Beyond
the Veil, you learn to watch back and sides as well as
what's in front of you. Thanks, Pic."

"My pleasure." A silence that was hesitation rather
than a finish. Skeen leaned forward, waiting; Zelzony
stopped her work with the rekka, wondering what was
coming next. The voice that came from the speakers was
wistful, a sigh implicit in the slow words. "Skeen, I . . . I
have enjoyed this consultation. Watching is good enough,
but do you think someone else down there would like to
talk to me?"

Skeen turned to Zelzony. "If the Kinravaly lets us out
to talk to your folk, we'll be using skips, um, two-seat
fliers. Takes less energy and easier to handle, put down,
less likely to damage anything or anyone. Workhorse will
be staying here as a base of sorts. I could seal off anything I don't want touched and make sure a visitor can't
harm herself, himself or the tug." Laughter in her voice,
she said, "You can send your cleverest spies, my friend,
Pic's a lot more discreet than I am."

Zelzony produced a smile. "Let's talk a bit. Favor for
favor. The Kinravaly would like starcharts and a reasonably detailed sketch of the political situation outside the
Veils."

"Set starcharts aside for the moment. Talk for talk.
Send your, um, Seekers to chat with Picarefy and while
they're chatting, she'll answer what questions she thinks
she can or should. That acceptable to you?"

"Hmm." Zelzony rearranged her flightskins, pulling
them over her knees. How much can we trust these
people, how do we know this . . . this machine would
give us anything like the truth? We've got no way to
check on it. All-Wise give me patience. This wasn't her
metier, she felt incompetent and found the feeling dis-

turbing; Zuistro should have Hatenzo doing this. She squashed down a sudden surge of anger at the Kinravaly. Zuistro was asking too much; it wasn't fair. She had other lovers, other Ykx she trusted, Zelzony knew that with a coldness that rapidly washed away the remnants of anger and left her with a sick uncertainty that was exacerbated by the need to conceal it from these aliens. She made a sharp, slicing gesture, get this over now, she thought. "For the moment. You can talk to the Kinravaly about more time later."

"Good enough, eh, Pic?" Skeen was stretched out in her chair, relaxed and smiling a little; she looked lazy and hardly interested in this give and take, but Zelzony didn't believe it, not a drawled syllable or a smiling eye.

"Good enough." The ship's voice was almost purring.

Skeen yawned and stretched. "I'm a sucker for Pic's interests. Those organics of yours, you might be able to trade some basic texts for the starcharts you want. I hear you Rallykx are working on ways to interface the two sorts of technology. No one better than Pic at that sort of thing, chances are she could give your Seekers some useful tips." The voice was slow and lazy, the offer slipping out with such a lack of emphasis Zelzony almost missed it as she worked over the rekka trying to get down a detailed account of the conversation before it leaked out of her head.

She realized suddenly what she'd heard, jerked her head up. "I don't know," she said, more sharply than she intended. She caught herself, closed her eyes a minute, went on with more calm, outwardly at least. "You'll have to talk to the Kinravaly about that."

Skeen smiled, waved a languid hand and turned to the screen. While Zelzony finished her notes, the alien spoke at some length with the man and the ship. Leaving the screen on, she led Zelzony outside again.

They stood a moment beside the massive ship. Skeen ran her hand along the cool slick flanks of the beast. "You might mention that Workhorse here could be put out for rent if you come up with a good offer. With her in your hands and a little training, you could get out to your asteroid belt. There's considerably more heavy metal out there than you have on this world." She patted the nearest landing leg. "It would have to be a very good offer, the old girl is a powerful beast with good cargo capacity."

Zelzony tightened her mouth into a thin line, hating the casual arrogance of that offer; the alien knew what a temptation that ship was to everyone on Rallen, only the All-Wise knew what she'd manage to squeeze out of them for the use of that worn-out piece of junk. No, it wasn't that bad, it was a good machine, but old, the alien probably wanted to replace it anyway and now she could twist its value out of us while she kept hold of it. And I've got to go with them if they persuade our Ykx to follow them. They will, I know it. They will and I don't know how I can stand it. Unable to respond without shouting her rage, she waited in silence, saw the alien shrug and turn away. Still silent, she followed her back into the Kinravaly's Garden.

FOR REASONS OF HER OWN THE KINRAVALY
AGREES TO SPONSOR LIPITERO AND SEND
HER TO ALL GURNS AND GATHERS WILLING
TO HAVE HER SPEAK.
LIPITERO AND TIMKA START OFF ON THE TALK
SHOW CIRCUIT, TAKING WITH THEM A HERALD
FROM THE KINRAVALY'S STABLE, FLIPPING
FROM GATHER TO GATHER IN A CROWDED
BUT FAST LITTLE SKIP (EVERYONE WHO SEES
IT COVETS WITH A PASSION TOO POWERFUL
TO BE CONCEALED; PETRO GETS ENOUGH
OFFERS FOR IT TO LEAVE HER RICH FOR LIFE
IF THE SKIP HAPPENED TO BE HERS). NEWS
OF HER IS CARRIED AHEAD OF HER BY
WINGRIDERS COMMANDEERED BY THE
HERALD.
SKEEN AND TIBO GO TRAVELING ON THEIR
OWN (THEY ALSO HAVE A THIRD IN THEIR
SKIP, A COURIER FROM THE KINRAVALY'S
SERVICE WHO SITS IN ON ALL TALKS, TAKING
COPIOUS NOTES OF THE DEALS ARRANGED;
SKEEN IS IRRITATED BY THE NECESSITY, BUT
TIBO KEEPS HER TEMPER REASONABLY LEVEL
AND, WITH HER, CROSS TEAMS THE RALLYKX
WHO ARE NOT SO BAD THEMSELVES AT
WORKING UP A DEAL). SKEEN AND TIBO BUY
ON THE SPOT A CERTAIN PERCENTAGE OF THE
ARTIFACTS THEY ARE OFFERED, PAYING FOR
THEM WITH GOLD AND SILVER BITS FERRIED
DOWN FROM PICAREFY, ALSO THEY SET UP
FUTURE EXCHANGES CONTINGENT ON THEIR

RETURN. RALLYKX TECHNOLOGY HAS SEVERAL
CONSPICUOUS BLANKS. NO LONG-DISTANCE
COMMUNICATIONS. COURIERS RIDING THE
MOST EFFICIENT OF WINGS, HAND CARRY
LETTERS AND REKKAGOURDS. THE RALLYKX
HAVE NO CAPACITY FOR REPRODUCING
SPEECH, INSTEAD THEY HAVE DEVELOPED AN
EFFICIENT SHORTHAND AND WRITERS SO
SKILLED IN USING IT, THEY COME CLOSE TO
BEING FLAKE-MACHINES. THEY HAVE
SUPERLATIVE IMAGERS AND
PHOTODUPLICATORS OF REMARKABLY SUBTLETY
AND FIDELITY (SO MUCH SO, THAT THERE IS
AN ARTFORM ON RALLEN PREDICATED ON
THESE DEVICES). THEY ALSO HAD
INTERESTING COMPUTERS WHOSE CAPACITY
RATHER ASTONISHED SKEEN WHEN SHE SAW
HOW LITTLE POWER WAS INVOLVED IN
THEIR OPERATION AND WHAT THE RALLYKX
COULD DO WITH THEM.

PICAREFY IS REVELING IN MARATHON
CONVERSATIONS THAT HAVEN'T STOPPED FROM
THE MOMENT THE KINRAVALY VOICED HER
APPROVAL. WHEN ONE SET OF SEEKERS
WEARS OUT OR HAS ALL THE DATA IT CAN
ABSORB FOR THE MOMENT, ANOTHER SET
REPLACES IT.

HAVING BEEN STERNLY WARNED TO BEHAVE
HIMSELF, SKEEN SAYING I DON'T WANT TO
SEE YOU KILLED BUT IF YOU MESS UP OUR
WELCOME HERE, I'LL LEAVE YOU TO FACE
WHATEVER THE RALLYKX SEE FIT TO DO TO
YOU, ROSTICO BURN TAKES A SKIP AND

**GOES SLIPPING IN TO VISIT FRIENDS HE'D
MADE ON HIS LAST VISIT.
ZELZONY AND HER FORCES ARE BUSY HUNTING
DOWN THE RITUAL KILLERS AND WORKING
ON THE MESS IN UROLOL AND MARRALLAT,
BUT NOT TOO BUSY TO SAMPLE REPORTS ON
THE ALIENS AND THEIR PROGRESS ABOUT
THE WORLD.**

or

**STIR UP THE NATIVES AND WATCH THEM
EXPLODE.**

Marrallat. Government Reserve. Office of outGurn activities,
records department.

Present: Data Retriever, Kinravaly Reserve. Name: Haraka Purpose
        of the DR's visit: the annual collection of statistics
        from all Government Reserves on Rallen.
        Clerks assigned to assist the DR (2 young males, minor
        functionaries with no influence or seniority but a rea-
        sonable competence at their work) Names: Dugohuzh
                                                Alleyeth
        Liaison from Kinra Sulleggen's Office (intermittently
        present, there to make certain Haraka didn't go prying
        into things that were none of his business, the clerks
        also being warned to report any activity they find un-
        usual) Name: Sullaplon

Scene: Haraka running through records the clerks bring him.
        He is a russet Ykx with gray spreading through the
        red-brown fur on his head and shoulders, less conspic-
        uous but present in the warm cream of the fur on his
        inner arms and stomach. A mild harmless little Ykx on
        the edge of being old. Calm blinking eyes with a tinge
        of green in the crystal. A comfortable smiling wrinkled
        face, everybody's favorite uncle. Soft unassertive voice.
        Formidably competent at his work, his shorthand al-
        most sleight-of-hand. Given to a mild chatty flow of
        stories as he worked, adept at drawing similar stories
        out of his co-workers even if they began the collabora-

tion sullen, suspicious and silent. Which they did, a
state that lasted less than a single workday, its
vanishment coinciding remarkably with the departure
of Sullaplon.

"Hmm, yes. Interesting. The number of exit visas has
halved itself, and most of those are wanderflights; you
Marallese are turning into homebodies, getting wisdom
as it were. Hy yai, if I had my druthers, I'd have my feet
up on a hassock reading Veratisca's latest poems." Haraka
lifted his head and stopped the dance of his claws for a
moment as he watched the short square figure of the
Liaison swagger out, then he went back to entering the
figures from the screen in front of him and to the gentle
flow of chat that didn't require any response, quoting
snatches of poetry he'd read recently, murmuring comments about a drama he'd watched in another Gurn,
praising the felicities of the land about the Reserve which
he'd observed as he winged in, blessing the pleasant
spring weather outside, an unobtrusive, soothing sound
that insensibly smoothed away the jags his presence had
torn in the quiet lives of the two clerks, jags exacerbated
by the intrusion of Sullaplon who had stumped about the
computer rooms asking stupid questions and using his
scowl and his connections to intimidate the Ykx working
there.

By the third day Sullaplon no longer bothered showing
his face and the three workers had settled into comfortable habits; Dugohuzh and Alleyeth took Haraka around
to inexpensive eating holes, to a drama put on by a
well-respected group of amateur players, and finally (after some anxious whispered consultation) to a vaguely
illicit poetry reading.

Haraka began edging the exchanges in the office toward
the topic of nepotism, relatives of justicers, high admin
officials, Remmyos, anyone with influence of whatever
kind, who went poking into recordrooms and messed up
the files so thoroughly that staffs had to work extra hours
to get things straight. He had several stories like that,
with names and dates, keeping things gently humorous,
showing a mild disgust at such stupidities. One story led
to another; Dugo and Aleth capped his stories and didn't

notice he was noting down the names and dates they provided, just reveled in the chance to vent their resentment without endangering their jobs. Haraka would leave the Reserve in another day or two and most likely wouldn't return; he certainly wouldn't do any talking to those authorities they were grousing about. The agents of the Kinravaly were tolerated here but not welcomed; Sulleggen resented furiously the need to let them in to gather the data that ancient tradition granted the Kinravaly Rallen; there was a fixed though unstated policy of ignoring the presence of these insects. If any ears were safe, his were.

Two days later he left Marrallat with three gourds of data and seven names of outsiders poking in the lists with no apparent reason behind their curiosity.

Around Rallen, in every Government Reserve, Kinravaly's agents (all carefully selected by the wily Borrentye for their artful natures) used their various skills and assorted personalities to tease out similar lists of prying outsiders.

Itekkill. Korika Gather. Ishtayll Arena. Early evening, rainy outside, chill wind blowing off the sea. Interior of the Arena brightly lit and warm, though rather drafty as great fans pushed air about to keep the hundreds of Ykx hunting seats around the stage reasonably comfortable.

Saffron and Mauvi elbowed through a noisy, pushing, excited throng and climbed to one of the darker corners of the Arena's second balcony; there were fewer Ykx up here, leaving them their own path of shadow and a privacy that Saffron immediately began to exploit once they were comfortable on their cushions. He leaned into Mauvi and began playing with the soft curling hair that covered the nape of her long neck.

Mauvi giggled, a faint breathy sound inaudible two steps away. She danced supple hands down his body and began tickling his knees.

The noise below them hushed suddenly. Mauvi sat up with a jerk, spilling Saffron off her. He bumped his head on the ledge of the row of seats behind him. "Ohf. Ay Mau, what . . ."

"Shush. I want to hear this."

Lipitero was sitting on a stool in the center of the stage, the light teasing glitters from her silver-gray fur and deepening the shadows in the terrible scars that marred her face and her torso. Stretched out on the polished planks of the stage floor near the stool, a sleek, dangerous beast twitched its long tail and yawned, its tearing teeth like curving yellow knives crisply clear against the dark red of its gullet. Mauvi sucked in a long breath, whispered to Saffron, "I wouldn't want to meet that in the dark."

More interested in her, here only because she'd talked him into coming and it was something to do that didn't cost the earth and was out of the rain, Saffron looked past her, muttered agreement and went back to playing with her shoulder fur.

Speaking with halting earnestness in a husky, emotion-filled voice, Lipitero recounted the history of the Stranger's Gate and the Gathers on Mistommerk. She finished with a listing of the flakes she had given into the hands of the Kinravaly, saying no matter what decision her audience made, she'd leave these (with a flake player, of course) so the Rallykx could regain parts of the history they'd lost coming here. She slipped off the stool to stand beside the beast, her arms held wide, her flight skins glistening. "Come with me." Her broken voice sang through the Arena, filling it with the intensity of her need. "Come fill the empty Gathers. Come with me or Ykx will fade from Mistommerk, my Gather will die as my children have died. Come with me, see the wonders of another world, face the dangers your ancient ones faced so bravely. Come with me. It won't be easy or comfortable or safe. Come with me."

As that last terrible cry swept the hollows of the hearspace, Lipitero shook out a rectangle of crimson yley cloth that had been folded and draped over a rung of the stool. The silky material caught the light and turned to liquid fire as she snapped it out of its folds and sent it sweeping through the air. She pulled it in and draped it over her arm. "Mistommerk," she sang, "Mistommerk, my kin. Behold a piece of Mistommerk, behold a woman of the world I call you to. Timka, a Min of Mistommerk."

The beast rose to its feet. It stretched and yawned,

leaped lightly to the stool's round seat, balanced there a moment, then was a great wild bird with hooked beak and vicious talons, with burning golden eyes, a white head and a brown-gold body. It stretched its wings wide, posed for them, a figure from myth and magic with the secret power of such things hanging like perfume about it, then it powered into the air and swooped back and forth across the cavernous bowl of the Arena, its harsh eerie cries tearing through the gasp and buzz of the audience. It swung back to the stage, landed beside Lipitero and was suddenly a graceful four-legged runner with lyre horns on a long thin head; it caracoled about the stage, the tak-tok of its hooves turning the hard wood into a tympanum, beating out a kind of song as it kicked and leaped and danced back to the stool. In the awed hush (the Ykx had got beyond comment, almost beyond surprise) it changed a last time into a bipedal form, roughly like an Ykx without flightskins or fur. Small stature, mammary glands rather like the keeskey had, though rounder with small pink nipples, skin the color of skim milk, naked except for an exuberant growth of curly blue-black hair on the head and a much smaller, coarser patch of black at the juncture of the legs. It took the yley rectangle from Lipitero, wound the cloth about it so it covered its body from armpit to ankles, stabbed a dagger pin into the cloth over one of the mammaries to hold the improvised robe in place, then it turned to the goggling Ykx and said, "I am Timka, I am Min, I am of the blood and bone of Mistommerk, of the people who dwelt there before the Gate was opened. I am one of the dangers you'll face there, if you come."

Kinravaly's Herald came onto the stage and tweener ushers flooded into the audience holding lightrods. The Herald cried: "Who among you have questions, come to the rods."

"Question to Timka the Min." A strong voice from the floor near the stage, a familiar voice to Mauvi, the justicer who owned a third share of the stable where she worked. "You say you are one of the dangers that colonists would face. Explain that please. Why are you here if you are a danger to us?"

Timka smoothed a slim hand over her hair. "I spoke as

a symbol of what the colonists would face. I in myself am
no threat; I have learned to live in peace and even liking
with Nemin like you."

"Are you in any way captive or slave of those you
travel with? If you wished to stay among us, could you
do that?"

Timka threw back her head and laughed, a full-throated
joyous sound that filled the Arena. "No. Who could
keep me if I wished to go? Skeen is my friend and
companion, I travel with her to see the wonders of another universe than mine, I travel with Petro here because I like her and want to help her. One day I might
return to Mistommerk, or I might not. As I choose, so it
will be."

Mauvi pushed Saffron's hand away. "Oh, quit it, Saff,
I'm not in the mood. This is important. Let me listen."

Mauvi was Worker class. She was good enough with
beasts to have a job she liked as a groom in a stable of
racing yauts, but she wanted a thousand things she'd
never have. Most of all she wanted a chance to use her
greatest gift. She played the habold, one of the smaller
ones with only fifty strings, and knew she could be more
than good given a chance and the proper teaching; she
wanted to create music as well as play it, but there were
no scholarships for such as she, her kind weren't supposed to have sufficient sensitivity to merit development
of their rudimentary skills. It wasn't very likely that this
new world would have the resources to train her the way
she wanted, but there was a chance just a ghost of a
chance . . .

"Yes," Lipitero said, answering a question put in another voice Mauvi thought she recognized though she
couldn't be sure. "We welcome anyone who is willing to
come, whatever his skills, whatever class he belongs to
here, but there's something I must make all of you understand. Mistommerk is dangerous, you must not forget
that; you can't bring antagonisms and resentments with
you, you'll die if you can't work together. You must be
able to leave old ideas of class and capacity here on
Rallen and learn to know the person behind the labels. If
you can't do that, don't come. Please don't come."

*   *   *

. . . a chance. an opening to possibility. Maybe there
would be no teachers, no music, but there had to be
something more than here. Failure, disappointment, she'd
faced them often enough and lived through them and
could do it again as long as there was hope. Hope and
the possibility of change. She knew with a deadly certainty what her life on Rallen was going to be unless she
took it in her hands and changed it. One day like the
next repeated over and over and over. She hadn't told
anyone yet, but throughout the long days and longer
nights she was thinking about suicide. As the Veils closed
on Rallen and the iron bands of her life tightened about
her, hope was draining out of her, leaving her dry and
limp and so weary there was no bearing it. She loved the
boy beside her, but that was not enough to light the
darkness within her and about her. That Ykx down there
on that stage, Lipitero bereft and scarred and afraid, that
Ykx had cracked the darkness wide and the light was
blinding.

"Trade," Lipitero said, "yes, there's a great deal of
trade on Mistommerk; let the buyer beware is the core
philosophy of a large part of that trade. There is also
considerable piracy at sea and more than a few outlaw
raids on land caravans. The Balayar are sharp traders but
generally honest. They have their hands firmly on just
about all major water transport. They build the best
ships and are certainly among the finest sailors and navi-
gators on Mistommerk. Though I must add, one of the
most respected of the sea captains is the Aggitj woman
who carried my friends and me halfway round the world.
Very competent she was at sailing and at chaffering. Yes,
sailing. Wind power. Ninety percent of the folk on
Mistommerk are in a pre-industrial stage of development; the desperate flight through the Gate before Kildun
Aalda's sun flared and ashed them, meant that many of
the refugees came through with little more than they
could carry on their backs; then they had to fight the Min
and the earlier Waves for a place of their own. A lot was
lost in the process. If any of you are med-techs or medics
or Seekers doing medical research, you will find an al-

most untouched market if you can develop and deliver species specific antibiotics for Balayar, Nagamar, Chalarosh, Aggitj and Pallah, perhaps even the Min. Surgery and anesthetics, vaccines, there's almost nothing available except among the Skirrik who will deal only with their own needs and perhaps among the Funor Ashon who keep themselves very much apart from anyone non-Funor. And there's whatever it is that depresses fertility among the Nemin, that's everyone not Min, another reason for embracing anyone who can bring medical knowledge with him or her."

In the beginning, even during Lipitero's impassioned plea for colonists, Saffron was more interested in cuddling with Mauvi than in what was happening on the stage. Timka's startling metamorphoses chased away his indifference; he leaned against the balcony's railing and began listening to the questions and answers, though he was still not as involved as Mauvi until Lipitero began talking about med-techs. He was in training as a med-tech. He wanted desperately to be more than that, but like Mauvi he was Worker class. If he'd proved unusually brilliant in his schooldays, the admin might have made a rare exception and educated him further. He wasn't anything like a genius, merely a bright intelligent tweener with a slightly better than usual facility for making things and nowhere to go with that intelligence and dexterity. He'd survive, of course; he was already a bottom-level med-tech and that was better than most of his kin had managed, a bit of luck for him. But he wanted so much more. As passionately as Mauvi, he wanted more than Rallen could give him.

Urolol. Masliga Gather. Rainy twilight. A grubber stable outside the Gather, with a leanto where a handler slept when one of the grubbers was sick or about to lay a clutch and the handler had to be there to see she didn't eat them. Yellow lantern light leaking out of the cracks in the wall of the leanto. Two figures inside, sitting at a shaky table (one leg replaced with a thin barrel that once held salt fish), a stone bottle between them and heavy mugs partly filled with a murky liquid before each of them. Rostico Burn and Fafeyzar, his first contact on Rallen.

*   *   *

Fafeyzar was deep into his fertile stage, but he hadn't changed much from the stocky young Ykx whose stolid sedate exterior gave no hint of the rage that smoldered deep within or the capacity for organization and manipulation that lay behind those dull brownish eyes, more like muddy water than crystal. His fur was a smoky gray fading to silver along the inside of his arms and legs and across his belly. His hands were broad and blunt, heavily callused with several of the claws broken near the tip; they were painful when he retracted them but he gave no sign he felt anything. He wore a harness of grubber hide, old and stained, without even a touch of ornament. For a moment, when he grinned at Rostico Burn and his face lit with delight and welcome, he was almost handsome; the charm he ordinarily kept hidden but could use like a weapon flowed out from him and surrounded Ross with warmth. He reached out, touched the tip of a forefinger claw to Ross' palm. "I hoped you would come."

Ross produced a tight smile more like a grimace. "I didn't know if you'd be here. I've been hearing things. Like it's really gone rotten over here, folk disappearing, slave camps behind shocker fences. You're a slippery son, Faz, but well, you know, it happens to the best of us, falling off the highwire."

Fafeyzar widened his eyes. "Not you, Rosta?"

"Even I. Bona Fortuna be blessed, though, I've got a cousin who can get in anywhere. She pulled me out. Skeen, yes, one of them that's going round now doing deals."

"They promise a lot more than they show."

"Oh, they can produce, if the price is right. Believe me, Faz, Skeen's a wonder when she puts her mind to something. The stories I've heard about her, hah! And I saw her work, she pulled me out of a place no one has ever escaped from."

"Why?"

Ross gulped down a mouthful of tuvviz, coughed, cleared his throat. "Blood calling to blood, maybe. You b'lieve that? No. You right. She needed me to find Rallen. She owed Lipitero, you hear that story? Hey, it's a hummer, ask me later, I'll give you the gist. She owed Petro a debt

and she always pays her debts. No, no, that IS true, Faz.
Everyone knows it. Do her good, she pays you back;
mess with her, you get paid too, but you won't like it."

"She's set her hooks deep in you."

Ross shifted uncomfortably. " 'S not like that, Faz, it's
just I heard stories 'bout her since b'fore I c'd walk.
What'd you do 'f Elezar the Wise came in now and sat
down and poured herself some of that tuvviz and started
talking to you?"

"Elezar is a child's story, no more substance than the
smoke from that oil." Fafeyzar waggled a thumb at the
lantern. "If she walked in now, I'd look up the nearest
headmed because I'd be seeing things that aren't there."

The warmth of the tuvviz rising in him, Ross laughed
until Fafeyzar had to quiet him. He looked at the tuvviz
left in the mug and pushed it away. "This stuff gets you,
don't it. Whew, that makes the world go round. What
you need, Faz? I'm down to my skin right now, but I can
maybe talk some gadgets out of Picarefy, she likes me a
little; I think it's b'cause I look like Skeen. My cousin."

"And which of them is Picarefy?"

Ross tried another grin; Fafeyzar was going soft around
the edges and the walls of the hut were tilting ominously.
"The starship," he said, taking care to shape the sounds
carefully, because his esses were starting to slur on him.
"She's sa wonder too, she is."

Fafeyzar examined him closely, got to his feet and
moved to a shadowy set of shelves. He rummaged in a
coarse-weave sack, came back to the table with a handful
of hard biscuits. He fetched a jug of water and a cloudy
glass, set these beside Ross. "Eat something, Rosta; if
you want to get serious, I want you sober."

Fafeyzar was deeply involved with an illicit association
that spread like a fungus across Urolol and Marrallat
with threads into Itekkill and Oldieppe, an informal coming together of workers and others to provide an outlet
for furies and frustrations that seethed among those without any hope of changing the conditions locking them
into roles that cramped the spirit and twisted lives into
ugly shapes. Being Ykx, there was no blood in this, but
Fafeyzar and a few others were adept at devising strate-
gies to disconcert and embarrass targets in authority,

especially those belonging to the Consortium in Urolol and Sulleggen's pets in Marrallat; in effect he ran a consulting service for rebels. Or had been running it. The situation in Urolol was deteriorating so fast he was being sucked into a full-blown conspiracy to overthrow the Consortium. When Rostico Burn knocked on his door, he was sitting, staring at the jug and trying to adjust himself to the hurry hurry pressing in on him. He was not accustomed to feeling the earth turn liquid under his feet; always before this he'd been one step ahead of everyone else, his feet firmly planted for the next. Now his deftest scheming served to keep him afloat but no more than that and he was contemplating the necessity to change his outlook and his goals, to completely revamp the way he worked.

He watched Rostico Burn breaking up biscuits and soaking the shards in the water so he'd have a hope of chewing them into something he could swallow. The young alien was caught in the tuvviz melt, having reached the stage where he had to concentrate mightily on whatever he was trying to do; he was frowning at his hands, moving a finger at a time as if he didn't trust them to act in unison. *Hit him hard, I shouldn't have given him that brew when I didn't know how it was going to take him. Saa, saa, I hope it doesn't kill him, I need him if I can get a grip on him.* A little over three years ago he'd used Rostico Burn as his ante in a dangerous game with the Zem-trallen where he'd exposed more than he was comfortable remembering. It was worth the danger because he won what he'd been fishing for, the Hand of the Kinravaly Rallen held over him, protecting him from the malice of Uratesto and the Consortium. It was still protecting him, but the shelter was beginning to fray and if he wasn't careful he'd be up to his neck in wet shit. The Zem-trallen was no fool, the reason she didn't flay him and hang his skin to dry had to be what she thought of the mess she found here in Urolol; what she'd said about him to the Kinra made him look harmless, what she might think of him was something else. *If the Kinravaly ever got around to cleaning up over here, we'd better have a hole to dive into,* Zelzony wanted the world to stay the way it was, just prettied up a bit. She was an ally now, come the day she'd be his most dangerous enemy.

Time passed slowly, Fafeyzar's impatience slowing its passage yet farther, but the melt faded eventually and Ross was back in cinc with the world. He glared at the jug, massaged his temples. "Mala Fortuna, Faz, I've got one humongous headache. Hmm. Seems to me I was asking you what you need that I might could get."

"I've been thinking. Two, three things come to mind. How do I get folk out of the slave camps? How do I get an ear into the high councils so I know before they do it what they're going to do? How do I get news from my . . . mmm . . . call them yautboys out there without having to go meet them or having to wait for messages to come to me? Going or waiting, both are dangerous, to me and to them. Any ideas?"

Ross set his elbows on the table, dropped his head into his hands and sat that way, rubbing long thumbs back and forth across his temples. After a silence, he muttered, "Some." More silence. He cleared his throat, winced, sighed. "Don't know about the camps." Another sigh. "Ears, yah. I can get you bugs that'll pick up a hair falling and pass it three kilometers, and maybe more here where there's no interference, to a receiver with a recorder." He lifted his head, blinked bloodshot eyes at Fafeyzar. "How much of what I just said do you get?"

"Not much."

"I'll have to show you, I suppose." Ross straightened his shoulders, winced again as his head jogged with the movement. "It's getting late. I'd better slip away before someone spots me. Look, I'll bring you some samples, show you what they do, then we can get to figuring out how to pay for them. Maybe goods like I took before, hmm? I have to chat Picarefy into agreeing to make the bugs and receivers, maybe some radios. That'll take a while, hunh, getting through to her is going to be a pain, She's in this marathon talking jag with clots of Seekers. No big deal getting in here, Ura's lice haven't a chance of spotting me. The most dangerous part of it was getting from the skip to here. And back, I suppose. Look, give me three, four days to set this up, after that, what's the best time for you?"

Fafeyzar extruded his claws, inspected the fleck of blood on one of the broken ones. "Four days on, same hour. I can't guarantee I'll be here, by the All-Wise, I'll do my best." He pushed back the short bench he was sitting on, got to his feet. "I'll see you on your way."

Ross nodded. "I set the skip down on the far side of the grove. Ah. I didn't tell you about Lipitero and her proposition." He fidgeted from foot to foot as Fafeyzar turned a bucket over the lantern, plunging the hut into darkness.

A hand on Ross' back to guide him, Fafeyzar opened the door and followed the young alien out. Rain was dropping in a steady drizzle, dripping from every over-hang, not likely there'd be watchers around now, but there was no point taking chances. And he wanted to see the thing Rosta called a skip. He pulled the door shut, tapped Ross' arm to start him going and walked at his side, listening as he sketched Lipitero's history and the plea she was making for colonists.

"You might think about jumping the Gate, Faz. If things get too tight here."

Fafeyzar stumped along, hands cupped together, left thumb sliding back and forth over the right, listening to the viscid suck of the mud under Ross' feet, letting the sound guide him. It was tempting. In a way. He got tired of scheming, be a rest to lay it down. He shook his head, a denial meant only for himself since Ross had no way of seeing the movement. His place was here, now, doing what he'd always done. Ah! but the folk in the slave camps, now they were something else. All-Wise give me a way to get them out of there and to wherever the colonists are assembling. He peered through the dripping darkness at Rostico Burn, shook his head again. No, Faz, Rosta's friendly but he won't stick his neck out for you; you'll buy whatever help he gives you, nothing comes free from these folk. Four days. I'll think of something. Must get word of this to Gondol. The Consortium will be twisting the net tighter. We have to have those longcoms, can't let Rosta see how much I want them or he'll have my blood for them. Cursed merchants, doesn't matter what the shape or species, they're all alike. We'll have to steal the things Rosta wants, tchah! he'll want blood and bones. The sooner it's done, the safer it'll be; with that offworld Ykx stirring everyone up, the Consortium will be having fits, shit scared out of those gutless wonders. Rosta's taking a big chance, coming here where they could get their hands on him. Hmm. He has to want this junk a lot. So. We've got a wedge, no, fer Rosta, you won't bleed us without a fight.

A touch on his arm. He stopped, wiped the muck from his eyes. The skip was a dark blotch ahead of him, rather like a tureen with a soupbowl reversed near one end. Ross brought his mouth close to Fafeyzar's ear. "Better not come any closer, the lift field could suck you up, wouldn't hurt you, but you'd be damn uncomfortable." He squeezed Fafeyzar's shoulder. "Four days. Take care, Faz."

"And you, Rosta, no fool's dance; leaving aside your bugs I wouldn't want you stomped."

Itekkil. Skeen. Tibo. The Courier Zagaro. In the skip, taking the Corridor between Stonaril and Penso Gathers, Ports on the east coast.

Skeen was stretched out, sitting on spine and neck in the offside seat, half-asleep and suffering from a growing boredom. This hopping about sweet-talking skeptical Ykx (actually sitting back being charming while Tibo did the talking, he was far better at it than she'd ever be) into trading their treasures for lumps of gold, silver, platinum, even hanks of copper wire, it wasn't how she chose to spend her life, it was dull, dull, d u l l, dull. Not like digging into ancient records on University and Heavenlyhome, hunting possible Roon sites through tons of garbage, wearing carefully crafted personas because neither of those worlds would let her near their readouts if they knew who she was; not like sliding past hungry Hounds to slip down on a target world, never sure there was anything there worth her trouble, taking time to flake everything she could find out about the Roon sites, and finally, oh, ultimate gratification, going like a sievebill through the Roon sucking up everything that might bring a price. Now *that* was interesting. It got tedious sometimes during the aftermath, what she had to go through to sell the things, working her hard-gained experience and her contacts to secure for herself something like the real value of the objects. If it got too boring, though, she could dump what was left with brokers like the Buzzard and get on with her playtime. She'd made expenses already, there was no real need to keep up this hop hop about Rallen, but Tibo enjoyed the game with its snip-snap and I'm the One, so she kept on trekking; besides, she owed him the stash he spent trying to get her off Kildun Aalda.

The skip was warm and filled with light, humming with drowsy peaceful sounds. Tibo was doing the piloting with a fragment of his attention, watching the coast flow past and chatting with the Courier. Skeen cracked her eyes, listened a moment. Talking about the dance troupe they'd seen yesterday. She stopped listening and dropped deeper into sleep.

"Skeen." Someone shaking her.

Head clotted with sleep, body expressing itself in cricks and assorted small nigging aches, Skeen wriggled up. "What?"

"It's Pic. She wants to talk to you."

"What the . . . that fuckin' kid?"

"Don't know, why don't you ask."

"Toss me the headset." She caught the helmet, settled it on her head, pulled down the shield. Courier Zagaro wouldn't know synspeech, but she didn't believe in taking chances. "What is it, Pic?"

"Two things have come up. That Zelzony, the cop, you know, she's got a list of names and she wants to talk to you about them."

"What's your reading on this?"

"Tibo can handle the dealing."

"Ehhh, Pic, you know me, don't you."

"I should. I'll drone a skip over to you tomorrow morning. Second thing. Rostico Burn."

"Shit. What's he done?"

"It's what he wants to do. Far as I can tell, he's clean with the Rallykx admins, but that won't last if they catch him passing out bugs and comlinks. He's murky about who's getting them, but I haven't much doubt it's some group our cop and her friends would like to stomp out. If one of those gets caught with our equipment on him, this world could turn unfriendly fast. He wants me to make them on spec for him; he's going to pay me materials and labor when he sells his take."

Skeen chuckled. "He keeps trying, doesn't he. Ahhh, Pic, how many days left here?"

"Twenty-five, thirty, around there, it's hard to say with any certainty. After Petro finishes the circuit, we've got to set up an embarcation area, you might talk with Zelzony about that when you see her. From what I've seen, Petro will make her cargo and then some. You want me to send a message rat to Virgin and Hopeless?"

"Might as well, it'll take them a while to get here. Burn. Stall him some, tell him you'll need a week to manufacture the bugs and comlinks. He'll be wanting samples, take some out of stock for him, but tell him you want them back; he can show them so he can make his sales, but he can't let them out of his hands. Tell him why, though he'd figure that out soon enough. We can't mess up Petro's chances. Right?"

"I hear you." A bubbling chuckle, almost a giggle. "Knee-jerk subversive."

"I resent that, Pic. I won't jerk a knee for jerks. I pick my causes, I do."

"Like a dog picks fleas."

"Little tin fascist. I'm glad you called, Pic, I was starting to petrify. My grin first."

THERE IT IS—A SAMPLER OF KEY EVENTS.
THE INTELLIGENT READER IS REQUESTED TO
ADD INCIDENTS OF HIS/HER OWN DEVISING,
TO EXPLORE AND EXPAND THE POSSIBILITIES
PLANTED IN THE SAMPLES.

INTERMISSION

NOTES
DAYDREAMS
ASSORTED IMAGININGS

INTERMISSION continued
more notes
more dreams
more imaginings

END OF INTERMISSION

SO WHAT'S HAPPENING.
A LIMIT OF ONE THOUSAND COLONISTS
ANNOUNCED.
AN ASSEMBLY POINT ANNOUNCED: THE
GRASSLANDS NEAR THE LAKE IN THE
KINRAVALY RESERVE.
ZELZONY HAS NARROWED HER SUSPECTS TO
SIX.
WITH SKEEN'S HELP AND PICAREFY'S
COOPERATION, BURR SPIES ARE INTRODUCED
ONTO THE HARNESSES OF ZELZONY'S
SUSPECTS, THEREAFTER THEY ARE TRACKED
WHEREVER THEY GO, THEIR ACTIVITIES AND
WORDS RECORDED AND ANALYZED.
LIPITERO HAS VISITED ALL THE GURNS IN THE
EASTERN HEMISPHERE AND IS IN MARRALLAT,
BEGINNING HER ROUND OF THE GATHERS
THERE. UROLOL STILL REFUSES TO ADMIT HER.
ROSTICO BURN HAD FINALIZED HIS DEAL WITH
FAFEYZAR AND IS ON THE POINT OF
DELIVERING THE PROMISED EQUIPMENT.
FAFEYZAR IS SCRAMBLING HARD TO GET HIS
PEOPLE OUT OF THE SLAVE CAMPS AND PASS
THEM UP TO MARRALLAT WHERE THEY MIGHT
BE ABLE TO JOIN THE RUSH OF THE COLONISTS
TO THE KINRAVALY RESERVE.

THE SUSPECTS:

Eshkel, Jufagga Gather, Itckkill. Second son of the Damm of Esh, head of one of the wealthiest merchant clans on the East Coast. Works at a sinecure, a position created for him by his Clan Justicer mother, few friends, joychoice the breeding and training of yauts, no success at it, lost interest in his runners during the past year.

Yumotz, Hivato Gather, Oldieppe. Ascribed to Clan Yu, parentage uncertain, has been groom, handler, breeder of grubbers and caravan-type gekkols, fired from all subordinate positions, failed as breeder, drafted as miner for the interior, managed to slip away (which shows some ability as most don't succeed at this), current means of support unknown, suspected smuggler, could be involved in transfer of large shipments of keck and gloy out of Oldieppe into Itekkill, Eggetakk and Yasyony.

Laroul, Elleyes Gather, Yasyony. Youngest child (only male) of a mid-level manager, clan Lar, father (clan Lar also) dead of a stroke shortly after weaning him. Lecturer in basics of gene manipulation at an unimportant branch of the University. His only visible ability seems to be his capacity for making a dull subject duller. Unpopular with students and colleagues. Recorded a joychoice at the proper time—bird watching—but one can suspect he did so primarily to comply with tradition since he did nothing with this purported avocation for a number of years, to be precise, nothing until a little over two years ago, when he began showing a strong interest in tracking avian migrations and applied for leave to follow the greater blueback on its biennial flights.

Aneskat, Hordoz Gather, Yasyony. Second of three sons born to the poet Antereylla who has been called one of the greatest singers of the age. Father unknown. Antereylla has had many lovers and has always declined to name the fathers of her sons, which has made life rather difficult for them since she despised barriers of all kinds and took her lovers as she pleased from all classes; there are rumors that Aneskat's father was a netman on a fishing lugger; children can be cruel, that was shouted at him more than once during his school years. A withdrawn child, an unsatisfactory adult; Antereylla used her influence to get him a sinecure, but will not see him otherwise; he drifts about from group to group,

generally on the fringes of whatever he works up a tepid
interest in.

Vettok, Vesset Gather, Yasyony. Youngest child (only male) of
the Historian Estrinevok and the Seeker Trontalevok; neither parent much interested in their children; Trontalevok
refused to suckle any of them, gave them out to nurse (all
the nurses were indigent young males, dependent on scholarships and the stipend they were paid to grow blood nipples; this service gained them the patronage of both scholars
so there was no lack of applicants for the position). The two
elder daughters proved gifted beyond the ordinary, one has
become a noted dancer, the other is gaining a reputation as
an innovative technician, already has five patents bringing
in enough royalties to keep her for life if she chose to retire.
Vettok has shown flashes of brilliance in several fields but
grows bored too rapidly to bring to fruition any of his
schemes. Occasionaly hallucinates. This may be due to
drugging, his parents have wrung him out more than once.
For the past two years he has been drifting, not doing much
of anything, calling on his parents when he runs out of
credit.

Jatsik, Sully Gather, Eggettak. Parents wealthy farmers, vine-
yards, winery, tannery producing top class leathers,
highfarms with large herds of prime juhlammas, the annual
clipping brings in a healthy count of bales of the finest
fleece. Father is Hemm of Jassery, you have to be top level
management to afford the product of his looms in your living
areas. Jatsik is the oldest child, there is another son and a
daughter. He was groomed from cubhood to take over for
one of his parents, according to his talents and interests,
but something went wrong when he was a tweener. The
circumstances are not clear. Eggettakkers are a closemouthed
bunch even among their own. Outsiders haven't a prayer.
Whatever it was, Jatsik left the mountains and has been a
rootless wanderer since, picking up a living however he
can. Has been in minor trouble a number of times, usually
excessive roughness in his sexual habits, sometimes verg-
ing on violence; however, he has never come close to
damaging his occasional partners. It seems he's unusually
strong and has a hasty temper. Evidence taken indicates
the females involved have no fear of him, they just think he
should have some manners pounded into them.

The oversize viewscreen on Workhorse's bridge was divided into six hexagonal cells, each cell a bright image showing what one of the suspects was doing at that moment. Zelzony scowled at them. "None of them doing a thing they haven't done a thousand times before. You'd think with all this brouhaha going on it'd be an ideal time for whoever it is to pick another victim."

"Depends on how addicted they are to their feasts of pain." Picarefy's voice was a bit thinner than usual, she was being extended near her limits, working with Zelzony, keeping an eye on Tibo, recording his deals, checking on Rostico Burn, keeping miniature bombers armed with nonlethal darts flying around over him so she could pull him out of anything he stepped in, labeling her conversations with the Seekers and routing these to dumps so she could sort through them later, keeping an ear out for signals from Virgin and Hopeless. "And there's a measurable chance," she said, "that the six we're watching have got nothing to do with the killing. Calm, calm, Zem-trallen. I don't think that's likely."

"All-Wise, I hope not." The words exploded out of Zelzony, their force a result of her own secret doubts. She flipped a hand at the divided screen. "A more worthless lot . . ."

"What did you expect? Contented successful Ykx with well-integrated personalities?"

Zelzony slapped at the back of the chair she was standing beside. "Hai! Nothing. Nothing. I expect nothing."

"That's what you have so far."

Zelzony's head jerked up and back, she clamped her lips hard over the words that rode her tongue. The voice was casual, no touches of sarcasm or mockery, but the words flicked her where her soul was raw. She looked toward the doorway, would have sold that battered soul to be out of here. She glanced at the screen, blinked and forgot her anger. "Two of them, who are they? They're meeting."

"Hmmm." Picarefy scanned her inputs, dropped four of the cells and magnified the two concerned; each had two Ykx and the same background though seen from slightly different angles. "You have there one Eshkel and one Laroul, mmm, together outside Laby Youl Gather. Let's have a listen."

Zelzony started, steadied herself. Moving with stiff care, she circled round the chair and lowered herself into it.

There was a faint hissing sound, then the distant crashing of the ocean and a whine of a sharp wind, the squawks of unseen seabirds, the crunch of sandals over small pebbles. Eshkel and Laroul walked on parallel tracks a double arm's length apart, not looking at each other nor talking together. After a moment Picarefy collapsed one of the cells and let the other fill the screen.

The two Ykx kept walking until they reached the lip of a rutted cliff that dropped steeply to a thick crescent of sand and rumpled blue water streaked with a webbing of foam. Still ignoring each other, they spread small rugs over a pair of boulders and sat looking out over the water. Laroul cleared his throat. "I've got three good ones. One of them is nursing a girl cub, a cousin, for his uncle who is on loan to the Kinravaly, has been since before the cub was born, he's a mathematician. The boy is taking the cub to see her father day after tomorrow, going to wingride. The plan he filed has him crossing the Channel to the north coast of Oldieppe, hop from Gather to Gather on no set .schedule, cross the Narrows to the Tail of Itekkill and work his way up to the Kinravaly Reserve."

"All that way alone with a cub?"

"The child's mother is unwell, nothing serious but she's going to be in the care center for a fortn't or two. With the number of wingriders going north to volunteer or witness the embarkation of the colonists, she thought it would be a good chance for the father to see his cub."

"A cub. I like it."

"Have you heard from Peeper yet?"

"Just a note. Said he'd be down soon as he could slip away. Sulleggen has been a real bitch. Kinravaly keeps her stirred up till she bites whoever says word one to her. That old sow who's trolling for colonists has been touring Marrallat; Sully hates that too, but she figures she's going to get rid of the creeps making trouble for her so she goes with the flow. Got her private lice imaging the crowds so she knows who's where. When the sow leaves, Sully's bound to make a lot of folk unhappy.

"Want to hear about the other two?"

"Why not. Have to tell you, you'll go some to top the combo of the kid and the cub, but you're the host this time."

"Turn it down, I can't hear more of this." Zelzony rocked back and forth, moaning, her eyes squeezed shut.

Picarefy continued to record, but shut off the sound and faded the image to black and white ghosts shifting and gesticulating in silence. She waited until Zelzony had calmed enough to speak, then she said, "What do you want to do?"

Zelzony forced herself to lie back in the chair, she uncramped her fingers and flattened trembling hands on the chair arms. "The worst thing, the most nauseating thing is . . . is the way they were talking, so . . . so . . . so . . ."

"Banal?"

"That and juvenile, it's as if they stopped developing when they were early tweeners. Eshkel is coming up on firsthundred, he left his fertile time years ago. Laroul is about half his age, but long past his tweens. *Listen* to them. Think about what they're saying. I can't . . . I don't . . . I . . . I . . ." Her hands fluttered in short angular movements, her shoulders hunched up as her body tried to say what she'd couldn't find words for.

"They don't fit, do they, the bodies you've had to look at and that pair of zeros. You expected the evil to match its manifestations."

"I suppose I did." Zelzony laced her fingers and rested her hands on her stomach. "They make those deaths seem so futile. The final insult to the dead."

"I'm recording image and sound. Can you use that to convict them?"

Zelzony closed her eyes. "No. I've only seen what you chose to show me. No no, I do believe it, but it could be argued you're faking the whole. Especially the part about Peeper. Do you know who that is?"

"I assume someone close to Sulleggen."

"Her youngest son. We have to see him in the act of

torture, that's the only way we can do anything about him."

"Ah. You've got an ethical problem here."

"Oh, yes, I do know that. A cub, a nursling cub." Not that boy, not that cub, especially not that cub. I'm not going to talk about that. "If it was just the tweener boy, it would be bad enough. I can't let that go on, I have to stop them. But if I intrude myself, this triad backs off and we lose them. They won't stop, they'll just be more careful with their leavings. We have got to let them take their victim and start working on him or her; we have got to have eyewitnesses and imager prints to back them. Not the cub, though. Not that baby."

"Hmm. Selyays. How far can you trust her?"

"Far enough."

"Talk to her. Skeen can fly you down in a skip, get you to Government Reserve in three hours if she hurries."

Zelzony hugged her arms across her broad flat chest, fur standing up along her spine; she knew she was going to accept yet more help from these aliens, but she needed a moment to gather the will to say so. She sighed and with the sigh, relaxed. "What time is it?"

"Five of your hours to sundown this meridian, let me see, seven hours till sundown in Government Reserve, Yasyony."

Zelzony pulled herself out of the chair, glanced at the ghosts walking across the screen. "Keep following them. If Peeper shows his face, make sure you get him, voice and image. Can you make a copy of the record, one I can take with me and show Selyays?"

"Certainly. Won't take more than a breath to do, so you can call for it when you're ready to leave."

"Thank you." The words came out thickly, with a reluctance she couldn't suppress. She nodded and went stalking out.

Selyays was a smoky blue, with a blue tint to the crystal of her eyes. She was in her thirdhundred but looked less than half her days; tall, lanky, never pretty even when she was a child, a moment after meeting her everyone forgot what she looked like in the warmth of her smile, the intelligence and humor in those brilliant eyes, the extraordinary voice that made the harshest of words like organ music. Even as Kinra, she spent part of every day with gifted children, coaching them in singing. Her lifemate was a mathematician and a near hermit, speaking to perhaps a dozen Ykx a year beyond his immediate family. He was her second such, link-riting with her a number of years after her first mate was caught in a freak storm and dashed to earth by a windshear.

The page led Zelzony into a light airy room where mirrors danced lumen lines into sculptures that changed position as the angle of the sun changed and gradually acquired a flush as it sank toward the horizon. One of Selyays' proteges came in with a pot of iska and some wafers; she smiled shyly at Zelzony, put her burdens down on a long low table between two curved couches. "The Kinra will be here soon, she is finishing a conference with a group of Remmyos, it was planned some weeks ago, she hopes you won't be offended by the wait." The words poured out in a rush, her voice sounded richer, more mature than her appearance suggested. Even shaking with nervousness, it was a lovely voice.

With a pass of her hand, Zelzony brushed away any idea of irritation. "Of course not, young friend. Selyays had no warning I was coming and my visit is not so urgent I expect her to drop everything to meet me."

The tweener ducked her head in a sketch of a bow, then hurried out, moving with an awkward grace that made Zelzony smile. She crossed to the couch that faced the entrance arches, put her impedimenta on the table and poured herself a cup of iska, noting absently that her hands were shaking now there was no one to see it. She took the folder filled with prints and began leafing through them, it was like tonguing a sore tooth, she couldn't stay away from these horrors, sick as they made her.

"Zem-trallen."

Zelzony got to her feet. "Kinra."

"You didn't bring the alien?"

Zelzony bowed. "As you see." She was amused at this oblique way of informing her the Kinra was aware of how she'd got to Yasyony. "Perhaps we might be alone?"

A small gesture indicating the pages and others hovering by the arches leading into the room.

Selyays widened her eyes, but didn't comment on the request. With a gesture of her own, she dismissed her attendants, then settled herself on the couch across the table from Zelzony. "You don't ordinarily make mysteries, Zem-trallen."

"I don't ordinarily have occasion. Kinra, will you please examine these prints, read the accompanying notes and the summary of conclusions."

Selyays took the folder and opened it. When she saw the first image her face went still with shock. Her head snapped up, she stared a long minute at Zelzony, then she lowered her eyes to the folder and began reading. The prints rustled as she turned them, examining each with blank-faced care, reading the notes clipped to them. When she came to the last, the image of the mutilated cub, her face didn't change but the folder shook. She set it on the table and took up the summary. Zelzony had sketched in the steps she'd taken, including a list of witnesses to suicides, the names the Data Retrievers had teased out of record clerks, the movements, the match-ups, the results of investigations as to where the Ykx culled from the two lists had been during the days just before the victims were reported missing, the list of those cleared for one death or another, the final six who remained. She put the summary on top of the folder and sat for several minutes gazing at the list of six and the notes beside the names. Finally she sighed and looked up. "Is this all?"

"No." Zelzony picked up the leather case before her, began undoing the buckles. She coughed, cleared her throat. "I was fighting shadows, Kinra. For two years. Then the aliens came. The Kinravaly· suggested I ask them for . . . for help since they came from a more violent society." She swallowed and went on, speaking quickly, flatly, all emotion excised from the words. "They suggested . . ." she wasn't about to tell Selyays about talking to a machine, a thing, "gathering the names of Ykx who kept turning up as witness verifiers of suicides and comparing these with the names of Ykx who had improper access to records of young folk seeking permits

to travel." She drew the player from the case, pulled
the earphones from their slot, set them on the table,
unwrapped a tiny brownish seed. "Look at this. Gently."

Selyays took the seed, rubbed her finger over it. "Ah.
It bites." There was a drop of blood on her fingertip.
"Burr. So?"

"Keep it a moment. Let me see if I can work this."
She fiddled with the machine, pushing buttons with awkward care. "There. Look at the screen."

A small image, clearer than any mirror. The room,
everything in front of Selyays' hand, a full half circle, was
there in the screen, the other couch, Zelzony, the light
sculptures now flushing blood red as the sun set, everything was there. Selyays eased the seed off her hand and
put it on the table. "A transmitter," she said softly.
"Bohalendas spoke of this, he had some . . . ah . . . com
sets he called them, but they were much larger." She
looked from the tiny seed to the player. "The purpose of
this show?"

"The aliens gave us a number of those seeds. As you
saw, they have sharp hooks. They were placed on the
harnesses of the six and everything these Ykx have done
since has been recorded and reviewed."

"Ah! Zem-trallen, I don't know about this. . . ."

"The Kinravaly was informed and she gave her approval, with the proviso that every record not directly
concerned with the deaths be destroyed once we have the
killers."

"Yes, I see. I also see that the Kinra and Kinravaly are
going to have to draft laws controlling such spying, if
contact is maintained with the Beyond-the-Veil. However, that's for later, isn't it. What have you got to
show me?"

With the same tooth-clenched care, Zelzony changed
the setting on the player and showed Selyays how to
put on the earphones. Then she sat back and waited while
the player went through the meeting of Eshkel and Laroul,
then the additional bit, the meeting of Peeper with them
and their gloating over the images of the victims.

Selyays slipped off the earphones and set them on the
table; she straightened and shuddered, eyes closed, teeth
clamped on her lower lip until blood came. The shudder-

ing eased, she exploded out a breath, sucked in another, opened her eyes. "Fiuli and Tissa. MY Fiuli and Tissa."

Zelzony nodded. "I saw that."

"Did you tell Kilenc?"

"No. I came to you first. There is a knotty ethical problem here."

"Yes. I see." Selyays nodded at the player. "You can't use that to prove anything."

"Right. We have to see them doing these things, we have to have image prints to back up the witnesses, so we have to let them take a victim and hurt that person. And Tissa is your grandson's daughter and Fiuli is your grand-daughter's oldest son. If you save them, you are condemning another Ykx's child to torment. I'll tell you this, Selyays, if it were just the boy, I would not be here. But a nursling, no. We'll go in as fast as we can, once we have the evidence. I think we can get to them before they do serious damage, but I can't be certain of that. So many things could happen. No one can prevent the working of chance."

Selyays rubbed her hands together and stared at the objects on the table without really seeing them. "They have to be stopped," she said finally.

"Yes."

"Why are you here? Tell me why you're here."

"Because I don't know enough about Laby Youl to protect Fiuli and Tissa without warning the killers."

"Ah!" Selyays pressed the heels of her hands against her eyes. "How long do I have to think about this?"

"Fiuli is starting off three days from now."

"Saa saa, ah! You don't give me long."

"That meeting took place today, a few hours ago. I'm here now because I asked the alien to bring me."

"Which one is it?"

"The tall female. The one called Skeen."

"Where is she?"

"In the skip, the flier, keeping out of sight."

"They are generous, those aliens."

"They want to keep us sweet until they have the colonists for their Ykx." She shrugged. "That's what I think. I don't know."

"You don't trust them?"

"I don't know them, I don't know the world they come out of. I do what I have to."

"I want to talk to her."

Zelzony frowned. "That *I'm* here is bad enough."

"I can hold house, Zem-trallen." There was an edge to the rich voice, annoyance in the thin face. "Bring her."

"I hear, Kinra." Zelzony got stiffly to her feet, stalked out without another word.

"Kinra."

"You are called Skeen."

"You have it."

"Why are you doing this?"

"What's my price, you mean?"

"That is part of what I'm asking."

"Right. One, it costs me nothing much and I was bored with dealing. Two, Picarefy enjoys using her talents. Picarefy, that's my ship, but don't think of her as a machine, she's as much a person as any of us. Three, it earns us good will. Four, I'm not a robot, I saw those pictures and I don't care species or shape, whoever did that should be stopped. That's about it."

"Good enough. Will you and your Picarefy be in the hunt when the Zem-trallen goes after the killers?"

"Depends on what you mean. I understand well enough that too much alien will taint your evidence." She flipped a hand at the player still lying on the table. "We can provide communications and transportation, if you want. Courtesy to our hosts, that should provide sufficient justification. Once the Zem-trallen has those crazies, we can transport them to the Kinravaly Reserve, that will avoid certain difficulties the Zem-trallen might face, considering who one of the killers is. Also we can transport the victim quickly to the nearest Care Center so he or she can be tended, mind and body."

"Yes." Selyays pulled her hand across her mouth. "Thank you. I . . . ah . . . appreciate your clarity of vision." She got to her feet. "I have to think. Zem-trallen, fer Skeen, Posi will show you to a room where you can be comfortable. If you need or want anything, ask her to bring it."

A quiet back court in the rambling complex belonging to the Sel clan in Laby Youl Gather, a port Gather, the one closest to the digressive impressive essentially lunatic aggregation of structures that constituted Yasyony University and to the Government Reserve. Reserve workers at all levels live in Laby Youl as do many of the students at the University, though there are living quarters available on the University grounds. An outside room, one in a cluster of such rooms forming part of the south wall of the court. Inside this, a young male Ykx in his late tweens packing for his wingride, a nursling cub crawling about on the floor dragging with her a much chewed rubbery grubber doll.

Fiuli clicked his teeth and emptied the wingsac on the bed for the fifth time. There was no way he was going to get everything in. If he was packing for himself, it'd be easy, but he had to include Tissa's things especially a fur cloak that developed a bulk so intransigent he'd given up trying to deal with it and intended to tie it to the baby web Tissa was going to ride in. He rubbed his hands together slowly as he eyed the three chaotic piles on the bed, then began sorting through them again.

"Fiu Fiu Fiu," a high warbling voice, alone at first then joined by a chorus of others, punctuated by laughter. He went to the door and looked out.

Dropping out of the sky like a flurry of falling leaves, what seemed a swarm of tweener Ykx touched down on the courtyard paving flags and came rushing toward him, separating into seven laughing friends. The foremost was one of the rare pale golds; she ran to him, her flightskins shimmering, a triumphant grin splitting her elfin face. "Fiu, guess what, guess, guess, you'll never guess." She flung herself at him, hugged him exuberantly, danced back. The others gathered behind her, matched grins straining their faces.

Fiuli leaned against the door jamb and took his time examining them. "So," he said, "Tink. What's this noise?"

She laughed. "You! We're going with you. All of us. On that scuzza great fly. The Mas and Pas they finally turned loose. History happening, hooo hah, never mind, that's just parents going on like they do, who cares, we can go, we got credit, we got wings, we got passes. What you think of that?"

He straightened slowly, stretched out his arms slow slow slow and beat his hands together over his head, whooped wildly, capered about, caught hold of Tink and danced her around, passed her on to Bar, grabbed Lolloy, whirled round with him, passed him on, danced around Tissa who heard the noise and came crawling out to laugh and sing her incomprehensible cooing songs, and finally collapsed with his friends in a laughing breathless pile.

The overgrown neglected garden of an ancient tower, once a watchhouse for a group of amateur astronomers, now co-opted into the University as part of its farmlands. A half-hour's easy soar from Laby Youl. Late afternoon, sky reddening with sunset. Three Ykx present: Laroul, Eshkel, Peeper.

"I wanted that cub." The strident whine blasted out of the speakers. On the screen a heavy brown was stumping about, throwing a royal snit.

Laroul winced back from him, huddling on a bench that was being overgrown by an ancient vaddlin bush. The three plotters were in a weedy glade whose gonewild lawn was riddled with kunik holes, whose dusty paths had lost all their gravel. "You had the best of the last one," he muttered.

"What? What did you say?"

"Nothing, Peep." Laroul smoothed out his face. "Look, could I help it if those smik-eating stoup-nosed krats decide their kids should be there at that doodin historic smik?" His voice rasped with vitriol. He wasn't really afraid of Peeper, but a life-long habit of withdrawal had more influence on his actions than his malice did.

Eshkel scratched at a callosity on his palm; he was twitching nervously as he squatted on a clump of grass. He whined a protest at the noise Peeper was making, but the other two ignored him.

Peeper continued for several minutes to rave and claw at anything soft enough to shred satisfactorily. Then he came back to Laroul and hunkered down by the bench. "What can't be helped," he said. "Schemer, you start figuring how you can get us some cubs. Sweet young flesh for us, ahhhh, that was soo gooood, I have to have more. Meanwhile, let's look at your alternates."

A round room at the top of the Kinra's Residence, the walls pierced by tall oval windows less than an armlength apart; darkness outside, thicker than usual, there was heavy cloudcover and every few moments a flurry of rain drops spattered against the thick glass; darkness inside, except for the soft cool glows about glass globes filled with ecologically stable collections of luminescent fungi and bacteria. A ring of padded backless chairs gathered about a table covered by electronic gear. Kinra Selyays, her head ortzin Elexin (a smoke gray Ykx male with a lined clever face), Zelzony and Skeen are sitting where they can see a meter square screen propped up toward one end of the table.

Selyays lifted a hand. "Turn it down, I don't want to hear more of that . . . that evil!" She spent the next few moments breathing hard and getting herself in order, then she said, "We can't use that record in their trial, but I think it might be useful afterward. Will you give us a copy and a reader, fer Skeen?" When Skeen nodded, the Kinra managed a brief smile. She glanced at the images silently playing out the drama in the garden. "Will you listen for me, friend from Beyond-the-Veil, and tell me who they chose? I am shamed by my weakness, but I cannot, can not look at them any longer. Saa saa, they have to be stopped. Going after cubs." She swallowed hard, forcing back the nausea that threatened to send her retching. "Zem-trallen, how . . . how far do you have to let them go?"

Zelzony plucked absently at the fabric covering her chair. "You know the answer to that, Kinra. They have to commit themselves to the point that there can be no possible denial of what is going on."

"Zem-trallen, hear me." Selyays enunciated each word with fine crystal care. "If there is the slightest chance of the tweener dying or sustaining serious, permanent injury, you will go in immediately and pull the child out, whatever you think about the evidence."

"I hear." Zelzony brooded at her hands, retracting

and extruding her claws, watching the small muscles work in her fingertips. "Do you think I'm a fool?"

"I think you have been working too hard at this for too long. I think your judgment might be unreliable."

"Then cut it off now."

"Saa, Zelzony, Zeli, all I want is for you to keep your balance." She swept her hand in a half circle as if to cancel her doubts. "Tell me what you want, Zem-trallen, tell me how I can help. Agents? Doctors? Name it and it's yours."

"Ah." Zelzony leaned forward, face turned to the head ortzin. "Yes. I want ortzin, Elexin fej, your best. I want them watching the tweener, keeping records of everything that happens, building the chain so we have witnesses from departure to capture. I want agents who won't be tripping over their own feet. That triad is nervous enough now at having to change targets, I don't want them spooked. If they drop this one, the next might be in Marrallat. You know what that means." She turned to Selyays. "Kinra, as soon as they take off, I want you to alert the University Care Center. Not one second before, rumors spread faster than the winds can blow them. I'm leaving you one of the hardest parts; you'll have to get the parents and close kin of the tweener and take them to the Center. Skeen was right, it'll be best to haul the triad straight to Kinravaly Reserve and put them in the holding center there." She straightened her spine, rubbed at the back of her neck. "After this is over there's a lot you can do. . . ." Frowning at one of the glow globes, she began talking slowly, thoughtfully.

The grasslands outside the wall of the Kinravaly's Garden. A crisp bright morning with a brisk wind whipping out of the north, turning lakewater into white-capped chop. Shadows long and intensely black. A skip darts out of the south, settles beside the lake. Skeen and Zelzony emerge, walk quickly over to join the Kinravaly who stands beside the wall, waiting for them. Already inside Workhorse, Tibo booms a greeting at them, then sets the tug to work. The huge folded legs begin to move about, changing conformation, unfolding into a crane that is half metal, half forcelines.

Tibo winched the Lander out of Workhorse's belly onto the drone dolly, while Skeen stood beside Zelzony and the Kinravaly watching the crane work. When the Lander was far enough from Workhorse so the two lift fields wouldn't interfere, he put the tug on seal and came out to join them. "Cargo's stowed," he told Skeen, using synspeech to keep their business private, this being the first time he'd seen her since she'd left to set up the spy link, except for brief conferences over the com, conferences conducted in Rallyx to avoid making their hosts nervous. "Got the last load in before sunup this morning, the hold's locked. We've covered expenses and more." He grinned. "Rallen ware won't be so pricey after this load. The pictures, hey; University will make us honorary scholars if that's what it takes to get them."

"They'll still bar us, Tib."

"So they will." He turned to Zuistro, switched languages. "The bridge is set up for you, Kinravaly Rallen. You and whoever you choose to join you will be seeing everything that happens. The instruments are deactivated, they're being controlled now from Picarefy. There'll be a slight lag, less than a minute, the time it takes for the signal to complete its travels, you'll be aware of it at first, but you'll soon get used to the wait. The pin spies don't have much range, but Picarefy has set small drone receivers along the route the boy has registered; she can move them quickly if she has to, say the triad traps the tweener and heads off with him in some unexpected direction. The drones can move much faster than the fastest of your wings. The Zem-trallen has arranged for Lipitero and Timka to be in one skip with two of her agents, the ones doing the imaging. Timka will shift to cat-weasel and take them as close to the triad's camp as she can without alerting our targets. She'll move closer herself, she's a ghost when she wants to be, but she won't do anything unless your people call her in, she's backup in case things fall apart. That can happen and does. Zem-trallen, your chief agent, what's her name, ah, Marrin, she knows Timka's signal? Right. I'll be flying the second skip and Ross will take the third. One of us with two more agents can follow the tweener as he leaves Laby Youl. You have good night glasses and night lenses for your imagers;

Ross or I, whichever, can stay far enough away so the boy won't be able to see the skip. If one of the triad is watching him, he won't see anything either. At a guess they won't follow him out, but wait somewhere along his line of flight. Once they've got him and they've made up their camp, the three of us can ferry the Zem-trallen's people and their wings to a staging area far enough from that camp so the triad won't hear the noises of the skips. Marrin will have a com set with a silence hood so she can talk without being overheard; she can be in touch with the Zem-trallen at all times. The Zem-trallen will be aboard Picarefy who has already moved her groundzero from here to Yasyony Government Reserve, she'll be able to see everything from Pic's bridge, keep touch with you in Workhorse and the agents in the field moment by moment. Questions?"

In the Lander, rising.

Zelzony watched the land fall away beneath her, held her breath as joy rushed through her; she was soaring as she'd never dreamed of soaring, even when she seized the idea of the starship and ran with it in the hope of healing her kind. The world dropped and seemed to shrink, details lost definition, colors changed and merged; at some point, between one blink and the next, it folded back on itself and was a cloud-streaked sphere hanging against fire-streaked darkness.

"Coming up on Pic."

Skeen's voice shattered Zelzony's pleasure in this flight, reminding her that it wasn't her flight, but this alien's, that she was riding along like a baby in a carryweb. She closed her hands about the chair's arms, her claws out, though she didn't know it, the struggle to subdue an explosive mixture of anger, fear and most of all desire was absorbing all her attention.

"That's her, that's my Picarefy."

Zelzony sighed and opened her eyes. She blinked. At first she thought the fishshape in the screen was small, not much larger than Workhorse down below, then she took a look at the firestreak behind the sleek black shape. It was one of the thicker streaks with a familiar braid of whorls and blotches, even from here familiar.

She took several minutes to realize just how much of that braid was occulted by the black fish, an epiphany further delayed by the intimacy of their conversations. Talking with the ship without seeing her, she'd somehow developed the image of a being her own size, perhaps even her own shape; consciously she knew that was absurd, nonetheless the image was there. The reality of the ship, her immensity, was a physical jolt.

A hole opened in the flank of the fish and they the minnow swam into it.

Surrounded by metal, drowned in metal, metal so thick it didn't respond when she touched a claw surreptitiously to it, hardly a sound, as if it swallowed sound. Swallowed hope too, because if it took metal like this to make a starship, it would never happen. Somehow she hadn't thought of that with the tug, the metal there was as thick, as present, but not so much of it, never so much. She followed Skeen from the lock into a tube. The alien looked over her shoulder. "This could be startling. Don't worry about it, go with the flow." A long unfurred hand, flat useless nails, reached out casually, brushing touched a part of the wall.

Gentle but utterly irresistible, something untouchable unseen closed about Zelzony and MOVED her. Like sliding on ice multiplied tenfold, she WENT. Between one breath and the next she was someplace else. And was angry again because she wasn't given time to be afraid and conquer the fear.

Another casual flick of Skeen's hand and the wall opened.

Zelzony followed her into a room that once again surprised her. She'd expected something vast and echoing, commensurate with the area of the hull, but the bridge was a homey size, her parlor down below was larger. There was one oversize thing, an immense screen that curved across the whole of the front wall which, since the room was wedge-shaped, was considerably broader than the back wall where the entrance was. Two complicated chairs rode on thick round pedestals in front of the screen, and there were several smaller simpler seats scattered about behind these. No instrumentation visible; if there was any, it was tucked away behind what looked like wood panels, the wood waxed and polished until it glowed with life. The floor was a dark brown wood with red and gold lights. There were several plants in pots, even a small tree. Skeen saw her astonishment, grinned at her. "Pic keeps reading ancient magazines and redecorating her inside. Whenever I leave her alone a few days, I come back and get lost."

She settled Zelzony in the left hand chair and took the other. "Let's have a look, Pic."

Zelzony bit back a startled exclamation as the chair shifted under her adapting to her form.

Skeen turned her head. "If you want something, Zemtrallen, just ask, Pic will provide."

Zelzony said nothing, she had a lot of sorting out to do before she felt able to speak. This last bit of unnecessary instruction was a match to kerosene and still she kept the flare inside. The alien hadn't the faintest notion how she was feeling, no doubt the woman didn't really care. Zelzony turned to stare at the other. Skeen was stretched out in her chair watching the screen come to life. So suddenly she didn't understand herself, Zelzony wondered what the alien really thought of Rallen—and, a question much more painful, of her. She writhed inside as she realized how much she craved approval from this dubious stranger. As if she needed the validation of an outsider to know her own value. She couldn't deal with this, not now. She didn't want to think about it, now or ever. She had to think about it. Later, when there wasn't so much pressure. Later later later. . . . She swallowed and lifted her eyes to the screen.

Like the smaller one in Workhorse, it was divided into a number of hexagonal cells, each one with its own image.

*The Kinravaly in Workhorse. Borrentye with her. Hatenzo? That was a surprise. Tyomfin.

*Tibo, looking rather demonic, his dark face lit from below by the faint reddish light coming from the skip's controls. Tavva and Uszer crowded in beside him. The image switched momentarily to show dark water rolling beneath them. They were out over the sea waiting for the boy to leave. Sunup was the departure time he'd regis-

tered, that would be about a half hour away now at the
Laby Youl Meridian. A daylight flight to South Island
and the wild yaut reserve; he was keeping a record of the
changes in a single family of those lanky six-legged predators whose domestic counterparts were bred and trained
for racing. They looked awkward, even comical but they
could cover ground with astonishing speed. And they
were extremely dangerous if the observer got careless; it
spoke a lot for the boy that he was being allowed to go
there on his own. Zelzony beat her hand twice on the
chair arm then forced herself to relax. He was going to
be hurt by another predator, but he wouldn't be killed,
he might even be proud of what he'd done to save other
lives. No matter what, he was going to know what he'd
bought with his injuries. She swore that to herself, swore
a loyalty to the boy over all other loyalties. It was the
only way she could live with what she was doing.

*Lipitero in her skip, her scars like ink spilled across
her face. Timka dimly visible curled in the other chair
looking as limber as her cat form. Kert and Fescan behind them, recognizable only because she knew who was
there. Again the flicker of another image, dark rugged
moutain peaks with conifers like mangy fur. The Yaut
Reserve.

*Rostico Burn in the third skip, alone, looking stern,
the All-Wise only knew what game he was playing. Flicker.
Image of an enclosed court, a soaring tower on his left, a
tower with lighted windows near the top. The Kinra
Residence, Yasyony.

*Kinra Selyas, Elexin at her side, in the Round Room
with the table of electronic gear and the circle of windows. Several of the windows are open and a strong
breeze catches crumpled papers about Elexin's feet and
sends them rustling across the room. At the moment he
is reading a note, a grave-faced young page at his elbow.
He scrawls an answer, tears it off a pad, gives it to the
page who darts across the room and flings herself out one
of the open windows.

*In the Round Room with the Kinra, but over to one
side, near the windows, Marrin ortza-fej, playing terg
with Ellum and Pekkal to pass the time until the call
comes that the boy is safely off from Laby Youl. Then

they will crowd into the skip with Burn and run for the staging area where Lipitero and her passengers are waiting, a high mountain meadow not far from the camp area where the boy plans to spend his double fortn't.

*Three wings with dark cloaked forms strapped to the carry bars, speeding across dark choppy water, runner lights muffled, the middle one badly, so a few streaks of white burn out of gaps in the black felt.

"Would you care for something to drink while we wait? You could try a wine I like at times like this, not much alcohol in it so you won't fuzz your brain, or I could have Pic brew up some iska for you. Petro likes the stuff so we've laid in a supply of it." Skeen chuckled. "Don't be so surprised. I'd get insulted at the look on your face if asking you wasn't Pic's idea, she scolds me all the time about neglecting my guests."

"Iska would be best, I think." Zelzony tried a smile and found it fairly easy to manage with most of her mind distracted by the screen and what was happening on it. "I don't believe this is the best time for experimenting."

"Could be you're right."

In the Round Room. "He's off. A half-hour late, but what boy ever got out of bed on time."

To Rostico Burn from Picarefy. "Get ready for your passengers, you're clear to go."

To the Kinravaly, Zelzony speaking, voice transmitted by Picarefy. "It begins. The boy has started. Elexin reports the triad left Laby Youl separately three hours ago. The seed spies show them still traveling across water. Lipitero and Timka have landed in the Reserve. They're waiting."

From Tibo, a report. "We're moving; some clouds about, enough to keep him from spotting us. We're some seven hundred meters above him and about as many northeast. Tavva has glasses on the boy, no trouble at all keeping him in view."

To Lipitero. "He's on his way. Anything happening around you?"

Lipitero to Picarefy. "Nothing. There wouldn't be, would there. It's a twelve-hour wingflight there to here. We wait."

Rostico Burn to Picarefy. "Passengers in, we'll have to come back for the wings and gasbombs and the rest of the junk. Probably need Lipitero if we're to do the hauling in one trip. Those wings are bulky and gassing them up doesn't work, we should have done a bit of experimenting before we tried hauling them."

Picarefy to Rostico Burn. "You didn't think of it either, chirk, so don't go holier than on me. I'll get the message to Petro."

To Lipitero. "Ross is on his way, be there in an hour. The equipment has turned out to be bulkier than expected, so be ready to help him ferry it. Should be ample time. Tibo can let us know when the boy is getting close. Swing wide on your rounds to the Residence and back, don't want the targets spotting you, you can afford an extra half hour's flying time."

Lipitero to Picarefy. "Just as well I've got something to do, sitting around here is making me crazy and I'm not the only one, Ti-cat is out and prowling."

Skeen to Lipitero. "When you see her, tell her if she's got ants, she should make wings and hunt round the boy's campsite. The triad won't play with him anywhere near that camp, but they might try ambushing him there. And tell her if she isn't back by the time the boy hits the coast, I personally will dump her on a waterworld where she'd have to spend the rest of her life as a fish."

Picarefy to Tibo. "Give a shout when the boy's about an hour from land. We've had to do some revamping of arrangements, equipment foul-up."

Tibo to Picarefy. "Hear you. Isn't there always. The boy's sailing along easy in clear skies, no sign of the triad. Me, I think twilight's when they'll do it. Catch him flying, probably half asleep."

Skeen to Tibo. "I say they'll wait till he's on the ground."

Tibo to Skeen. "Double or nothing, the take's the stake."

Skeen to Tibo. "Done."

Time passes. Lipitero, Ross and Timka have something to do to help it pass. They work hard, loading down the skips until they're dragging tail, then sweat them back to the staging area where Marrin and the other agents work off some of their nervous energy unloading their gear. In Picarefy, watching the screen cells has lost whatever charm it had originally. Skeen has vanished somewhere into Picarefy's entrails, Zelzony has settled to a painful brood over her explosive and ambivalent emotions, trying to wrestle them into a shape more pleasing to her and more conducive to maintaining her self-esteem.

Tibo to Picarefy. "Coastline of South Island ahead. Hour away as requested. From his level, the sun's almost gone. Tavva says after he hits the coast he's got another hour and a half before he reaches the camp. Where are the targets?"

Picarefy to Tibo. "Everything is set at the staging ground. The targets are in the air again, heading toward the boy. Estimated intersect, forty-five minutes. The sooner they do it, the better we'll all feel."

Tibo to Skeen. "My game."

Skeen to Tibo. "Looks like, but we'll wait till they take him just to be sure. Hmmm?"

Zelzony to the Kinravaly. "The boy has reached the coast. It's getting dark. The triad is in the air, moving toward him. Soon now."

Kinravaly to Zelzony. "Please ask ship Picarefy to let us witness the capture. We must see how it is done."

Picarefy to Zelzony. "With your permission, Zemtrallen, I'll comply with the request."

Zelzony to Picarefy. "Given. Thank you."

Picarefy to Skeen in shower-room. "Hey, get your butt up here, things are starting to happen. I'd rather you were here, Skeen, makes me feel more secure."

Skeen to Picarefy. "Crock of shit, that; I'll be there soon as I dry off."

Dark wings, dark cloaks wound about them, the triad drifted toward the boy, riding higher than him, silent shadows slipping closer and closer. When they were a short distance from him, they separated and came at him from three directions. One slipped into a long glide that would take him into the airspace in front of the boy. The

other two slanted more steeply, dropping until they were
beneath the wing and close behind their prey. He was
limp, half asleep, not bothering about what was going on
around him. The sharp crack as one of the riders behind
him snapped a net out of its folds and tossed an end to
the other rider broke through his weariness. He started
to look around, but it was too late. They swung the net
up, tangled him in it. The rider in front of him slipped in
until the noses of the two wings were rubbing against
each other, then he swung a yautwhip at the boy's head
and put him out with a neat precision that spoke of
considerable practice.

"Eshkel and his racing yauts," Zelzony muttered.
Skeen rubbed at her nose. "They've had a lot of practice at that maneuver. You've found nine bodies; I'd say
you better look for more."
"Saaaa smik!"

Picarefy to Lipitero. "Capture complete. They're on
the move, going somewhere. I'll advise when they settle."
Zelzony to Marrin. "Capture complete. Be ready to
move when they settle."
Zelzony to Kinravaly. "Capture complete. Now we
have to let them go to ground. Marrin and the crew are
in the air, waiting. Timka is after them already, bird
shape, she'll be on the scene before anyone else so she
can take care of the boy until we get there."
Kinravaly to Zelzony. "The All-Wise guard and guide."

The sandstone canyon was deep and rugged with a
shallow creek wandering along the bottom between thin
stands of shuddering longleaves. At several points wind
and water had washed deep recesses into the walls. The
triad flew the boy into one of these.
Ti-owl glided past, circled round, came back. Glad of
the darkness which turned her into a faint smudge against
the pale stone, she hung about trying to work out a way
of getting into the hollow without alerting the triad. One
Ykx left, Peeper, picking his way carefully over the scree
slanting from the recess to the bank of the creek. After
water, she supposed, and gave herself a metaphorical pat

on the back when she saw the dripping bucket the big brown was hauling up. She grinned, also an inward thing since owls aren't equipped for ironic grins (or any other kind), as she watched that murderous thug struggle back up to the recess, his toe claws gripping the scree, the leather bucket giving him enough trouble to start him cursing violently as he fought to keep the water from spilling.

As he disappeared into the shadow, sour-faced Laroul came out, carrying a hatchet. Ti-owl clicked her beak. None of them trust the others enough to leave alone with the boy, has to be two in there so they can watch each other. Ah, shit, as Skeen would say. For a short while longer, she watched Laroul hacking at downwood, then she spiraled up out of the canyon and started back toward the staging area.

Ti-cat ghosted between the trees. Kert and Fescan drifted after her, almost as quiet despite difficult conditions; along with the soft flowing flightskins that threatened to catch on every stub, they had imagers with long lenses (night adapted) strapped to their harnesses, instruments both heavy and awkward. She led them into a thicket of small trees growing palely in the shade of a giant conifer that had extracted sufficient nourishment from the thin coarse soil in the bottom of the canyon to grow to twice the height of the longleaves; at that point it began dying from the top down, going bald in its old age. Using hand and toe claws they climbed past the fringe of needles and onto the doubled trunk, each finding a crotch to sit in so they could turn their imagers on the recess and start recording what was happening in there.

Timka went back to guide another cluster of agents in, these with night glasses. They were to be witnesses and arresting agents when the time came to stop the torment of the boy.

Zelzony clutched the arms of her chair, watching the central cell which had been expanded a dozen times larger than the others.

*   *   *

The triad carried the boy into the great hollow, a space large enough to swallow a sailing freighter. They put him down. Laroul began cutting the net off him. Eshkel checked his pulse, then settled back to watch Laroul work, his eyes flickering over the boy, his tongue pulsing in and out between his lips, a fine film of sweat gathering on the bunched glands in his forehead and cheeks. Peeper stood with feet apart, his hands clasped behind him though that must have squeezed his flightskins into tight uncomfortable folds. His eyes, like Eshkel's, were fixed on the boy, but his face was an unreadable mask. As Laroul finished removing the net, Peeper said, "I'll fetch water, one of you better be ready to get in a load of wood when I come back. Toss for it if you can't decide who." He turned and left.

Laroul touched the swollen spot where the yautwhip had landed. "He's been out a long time. If you've spoiled him, Eshko, Peep and I will make a meal out of you."

Eshkel's hand jerked. He glowered at Laroul. "He'll be coming round soon enough."

"So you say."

"Yes. So I say."

"You're a lazy duggen, Eshko. Peep and I have done most of the work; make yourself useful, go fetch the wood."

"Saa saa, you'd like that wouldn't you, leaving you alone with the boy. We draw lots for who gets him first. You heard Peep, we draw lots for who gets the wood too, and that 'un don't leave until Peep gets back." He pulled a handful of terg counters from the pouch on his belt, held them in his fist. "Put out your hand."

Laroul hesitated, then thrust out his long lean hand. The claws were partway out, a half-threat which Eshkel ignored. He shook the counters in his fist then let one fall. Laroul examined it. "Tree."

Eshkel shook his fist again, let a counter fall on the stone floor, left it there. Laroul picked it up, turned it over, swore. "Fire," he said. "Fire takes tree."

Eshkel shrugged, reclaimed the two counters and returned all of them to his pouch. He got to his feet, found a blanket roll and dragged it into a position where he could see the boy and look out into the canyon whenever he wished. He dropped onto the blanket, shivered a little. "It's supposed to be spring down here. I thought it'd be warm."

"Early spring, you're up high, it's a clear night so the heat radiates away fast. I wouldn't be surprised to see frost on the ground come the morning. We'll need more wood than I can bring in one load." Laroul sniffed. "Want to or not, you'll have to do some work or freeze. You try dugg'ning out on us, Eshko, Peep and I will pop those lots to see who gets your blankets."

Eshkel glared hate at Laroul but the Yasyonykx ignored him.

Peeper came stomping in with the bucket, set it in its frame. "Who gets the hatchet?"

"Me for the first round." Laroul got to his feet. "Who's doing the supper?"

Peeper snorted. "Neither of you. I want to be able to eat it."

A moan from the boy. The triad stiffened and turned as one. Their captive moaned again, stirred feebly, tried to move his arms. His wrists and hands were bound, he tugged at the bonds before he was fully awake, whimpered when he couldn't dislodge the thongs. He lifted his head, gazed with bewilderment at the blotches of thicker darkness a short distance from him. "Who are you? Where am I? What happened?"

Rasping breath. One of the shadows swayed off from the others, bent to take something from the stone, the boy couldn't see what it was but there was so much menace in the silence and that hoarse breathing that he went rigid with fear.

One of the shadows moved toward him. Teeth clamped on his lip to hold back the fear whimpers, the boy tried to wriggle away. Large gentle hand took hold of him, lifted his head and shoulders, held a cup to his lips. "It's only water, Giulin. Drink. You must be thirsty."

The cup was cold and wet as it pressed against Giulin's mouth. His throat was dry and painful, his lips cracking; confused and still afraid, he managed a few swallows, then turned his head away. The strange Ykx lowered him back to the stone, moved off a few steps. Giulin lay silent a moment, then, trying to speak with easy unconcern, no fear, only an understandable curiosity, he said, "Why am I tied like this?"

"So you won't run away, my dear."

The voice came from the other shadow, husky tones, a quaver in them like that in the voices of the very old, though Giulin didn't feel that the speaker was old, not in that way. There was something else in the voice, something he didn't understand, something that made him shiver from a cold not caused by the chill from the stone that was striking up into his bones. "Why would I want to run away? Where am I?"

"Yaut Reserve, of course. Wasn't that where you were going?"

"Are you poachers?"

"Poachers, you hear that, Peep? He thinks we're here to net us some yauts for the running game."

"Clever boy." The second voice was amused, almost playful. This was the one that had given him the water.

Giulin's fear increased; a little more and his sphincters would let go. He felt a searing shame at betraying himself that way and struggled to control the fear, but though they'd done nothing to him so far, nothing but tie his wrists and ankles, though they hadn't threatened him or hurt him, something was going to happen, something terrible. Don't be stupid, he told himself, keep cool and you'll get out of this. All right, so they aren't poachers, that doesn't mean they haven't got reasons for being here. You just ran into those reasons without meaning to. All they're going to do is keep you tied up here, out of their way, until they're finished with their business. Though he didn't quite believe any of that, he calmed down enough to realize that part of his despair came from the cold that was sending spasms of shivering along his body. He steadied his jaw, cleared his throat. "I'm freezing. Would you bring me my blankets please?"

"Of course, how thoughtless of me." It was the big one being genial. "We don't want you catching pneumonia, now do we. Eshko, get the young man's blankets. I'll lift him so you can spread them under him."

"Y y you c c could just un untie m me."

"Nooo. I don't think so."

The big one, the one called Peep, lifted him. His fur

was thick and rough and smelled smoky-acrid, his chest was hard and hot. As he stood holding Giulin, his fingers moved a little, small caresses that nearly shattered the boy's control. He began thinking about rumors he'd heard, tweeners who'd gone off and hadn't come back. He didn't know anyone who'd disappeared like that, but there were stories . . . about . . . about bodies turning up, bodies savaged by beasts. Or something. I have got to get away, I have got to get out of here. Docile. Yes. Let them think I've given up. Peep laid him on the blankets, moved his big hands over the boy, fondled his penis sheath briefly, then straightened and moved off.

Giulin tested the thongs binding his wrists and came close to tears. Whichever of them had tied the knots knew what he was doing. He turned on his side and began exploring the stone beyond his blankets, hoping to find a fragment of stone or a bit of bone or shell. What he found was dust. He shivered, recovered, brought his wrists to his mouth and began chewing at the tough leather.

The third Ykx returned to the hollow carrying a load of firewood. He dumped it a few paces away from Giulin, came over to look down at the boy, the scrape of his footsteps barely enough warning so Giulin could stop gnawing and turn on his back. This one was skinny, what the boy could see of him looked dry and dessicated. He grunted and went over to the wood pile. "Eshko, your turn on the wood line."

The quaverer protested, citing his age, his arthritic hands, his bad back. The thin sour one waited him out, handed him the hatchet. "As much again as this," he pointed at the wood he'd brought, "or you go back out, you hear?"

"Peep?"

"Hurry back, old friend, or we'll start without you."

"You wouldn't, you can't, you . . . ."

The big one just laughed. Eshko snatched the ax and hurried out.

Giulin went back to gnawing at the thongs, grinding as hard as he could at leather that seemed more like plaited steel. Firelight. They'd see him, stop him. All-Wise give them good appetites, let them concentrate on the supper they were talking about. The thongs were weakening, he could feel the give.

Peep was whistling as he shaved long curls from a bit of dry wood, the skinny one worked at building a small compact pile of lengths of wood more or less the same size. Stopping a second to catch his breath, Giulin looked over his shoulder at them, fought down the panic that threatened to engulf him. They've done this before. Lots of times. They know exactly what to do, they don't even have to think about it. His breathing broke on a sob, then he went back to worrying at the thongs that bound his wrists.

Zelzony leaned forward tensely, eyes moving over the cells.

*Marrin was wedged in a crotch of a quivering longleaf, glasses fixed on the hollow, agents like dark fruit in trees around her, like her, watching. Her body was stiff with insult, the hands clamped around the night glasses had the claws out. Beyond her, deep inside the hollow, dark figures moved back and forth between the fire and a recumbent figure.

*Tibo, Lipitero, Rostico Burn in their separate skips waited up above, settled on the stony barren earth a short way back from the rim of the canyon. If the triad flew up there, they would see the skips, but there seemed little chance of that.

*Peeper, Laroul and Eshkil were finishing a meal of bread, cheese, meat and roasted tubers, taking turns poking food into Giulin. The boy accepted their tending and its attendant caresses without resistance, his passivity disappointing and angering Eshkel. Peeper wasn't fooled, he grinned at the boy, his attitude one of amused complicity. Laroul was stiff and impersonal, even when he rubbed his hand over one or more of Giulin's erogenous zones, as if he were pushing buttons to test out the responses of some machine.

A remote came in with a table, a pot of iska and some sandwiches, arranged these beside Zelzony.

"Zem-trallen." When there was no response, Picarefy spoke again, louder. "ZEM-TRALLEN."

Zelzony started. "What?"

"They're taking their time, it might be hours yet before you can move. Eat something. Hunger plays games with your head."

Zelzony pulled her hand down her face, left it pressed over her mouth. Two rasping breaths, then she took it away. "Yes. I suppose." Her eyes drifted back to the screen. "Why don't they do something I can pin them with," she muttered. "So I can stop this hideous . . ."

"Eat, Zem-trallen. There's nothing you can do. The boy will survive it. Remember what the dead tweeners looked like, remember the cub, remember the work you've done so there won't be more dead. Your agents are there, they'll move in the minute you give the word. You'll know when you have what you need to put those sorry sick monsters where they won't hurt more children. You know you can't act before then. So?"

With a broken-in-half gesture that was meant to signify both her reluctant agreement and how much she loathed having to agree, Zelzony filled a mug with iska, chose a sandwich and after a brief surprise at how hungry she was, began eating.

TIME OUT FOR ARTISTIC AND ETHICAL CONSIDERATIONS. IN THE INTERESTS OF VERISIMILITUDE, I COULD DO ACTION AND COLOR ON THE TORMENTING OF GIULIN, CONDUCT YOU INSIDE HIS MIND AND SHOW HIS STRUGGLES TO COMPREHEND AND DEAL WITH THE GRUESOME THINGS HAPPENING TO HIM (A CHILD RAISED IN A WARM, LOVING, WHOLLY NONVIOLENT ENVIRONMENT), SHOW A CONSIDERABLE INTELLECT BLOTTED OUT BY THE GRADUAL ESCALATION OF PAIN AND TERROR UNTIL ONLY AN ANIMAL WAS LEFT, WHIMPERING AND FUTILE. ON THE OTHER HAND, HOW MUCH WOULD THIS INVOLVE WRITER AND READER IN A KIND OF COMPLICITY WITH THE TORTURERS? ME, I THINK I'LL LAND ON THE SIDE OF THE LESS AND TRUST YOUR IMAGINATIONS TO SUPPLY WHATEVER DETAILS YOU NEED TO MAKE THAT SCENE REAL FOR YOU.

Marrin to Zelzony (though the clear baffle drawn down over her face prevents sound from escaping, she whispers). "Zem-trallen, let us stop this. I don't know how much longer the ortzin will hold."

Zelzony to Marrin (pressing her hand across her mouth, frowning at the screen. Without taking her eyes off the scene in the hollow, she pulls her hand away, slaps at the chair arm). "I know! I . . . ssss haaah . . . we have to be sure there's no question what's happening. It won't be long before they start cutting . . . ahh . . . give the order to go in when you see blood on the boy. When YOU see it. Don't wait for me and don't let the agents push you."

Marrin to Zelzony. "I hear. Thank you."

Eshkel brought a handful of counters out of the pouch.
He rattled them in his fist, held out his hand. "Peep?"

Peeper inspected the counter Eshkel dropped onto his
palm, grunted. "Yaut."

"Lar."

Laroul accepted his counter, examined it without change
of expression. "Wing."

"And me." Eshkel rattled the counters again, dropped
one into his other hand. "Annnd . . . behold, Sun. Sun
takes Wing, Wing takes Yaut. Saa sa." He knelt beside
the shuddering boy, passed his hand over the blue-gray
skin of Giulin's chest, smiling as he felt the jerk of the
chest muscles. "Saaa yes, the sweet sweet pain." He
groped through the shadows on the floor, found what he
wanted, a sheathed scapel and a small vial, an artist's
brush for painting fine lines held against it by several
twists of a rubber band. "We're going to feel things
we've never experienced before, we're going to be alive,
little love, alive. . . ." He slipped the sheath off, danced
the knife over Giulin's chest, cutting shallow hashmarks
from his shoulderblades to the fine curls at the edge of
his belly fur. At the first touch of the knife, the boy
gasped and writhed, tried to pull away, but Peeper at his
feet and Laroul at his head held him still. When his body
absorbed the lack of real pain, he relaxed a little, still
frightened, but puzzled as well. With an absurdly prim
neatness, Eshkel wiped the blood off the scalpel using a
soft white cloth, then fitted the sheath over the blade and
set the scalpel back on the floor. He shook the vial,
thumb over the cork, forefinger under the rounded bottom, then pulled the brush from under the band. "Sweet,
sweet . . ." he murmured. He pulled the cork out, held it
between the last two fingers of the hand with the vial,
dipped the brush into the orange red liquid. "Nowww. . . ."

When she heard the hoarse terrible scream, Marrin
blew the two-note signal to take them. More screams
whipped at her as she dropped down the tree and ran full
out toward the hollow, crashings around her and ahead
of her from her agents, all of them driving themselves to

their limits so they could get into that hollow and stop the sounds coming from it.

By the time she got there, younger fleeter Ykx had the three pinned and were in the process of pinioning them. Kert was sobbing, but he had his imager going, getting pictures of everything that was happening around him. Fescan was kneeling beside Giulin, trying to cut the thongs off his bloody wrists and ankles, failing because the boy was still shrieking and writhing, in such terrible pain he was unaware that help had arrived, that the torment was finished. Marrin hurried to help. She held the boy down until Fescan managed to cut the thongs.

"MARRIN, MARRIN." Zelzony's voice broke through her concentration and the clamor in the cavern.

Marrin pressed a hand to her diaphragm, managed a croak, then, "What?"

Listen. Skeen says don't touch the cuts, flood them with water. What Eshkel was using, it has to be some kind of concentrated irritant. What? Not you, Marrin. Ah! Hatenzo has just this moment sent up a suggestion, sap of the eggetchuz weed. What? Yes. Yes. He says flooding is a good first step, then . . . you've got med kits with you, any puna salve? Bless the All-Wise. When you've dumped a bucket or two over the boy and can't see any slime left, spread that salve on so thick no air can reach the wound, then get the boy to a Care Center fast."

Picarefy to Tibo. "Can you take the skip to the canyon floor without crashing it?"

Tibo to Picarefy. "There's a gravel flat about five hundred meters east of the hollow. That's the only spot open enough."

Zelzony to Marrin. "As soon as you've got the boy quieted, send him south along the creek. About five hundred meters on there's a gravel flat. The alien Tibo will be waiting there with a skip; he'll fly Giulin to the University Care Center. Send Fescan and Uszer with them, tell them to keep talking to the boy, I don't care what they say, just make sure he hears friendly voices all the way."

Zelzony to Selyays. "Giulin will be on his way north in twenty minutes or less, he'll be at the Care Center before

the hour is out. Did you hear that about the eggetchuz?
Yes. About the Center . . ."

Selyays to Zelzony. "Medic First Okkaman has been
watching since the boy's capture. I thought seeing what
happened would give the medics at the Center a better
idea what to expect."

Zelzony to Selyays. "All honor to your foresight, Kinra."

Zelzony to Marrin. "The Center is prepared for Giulin.
I see the flooding and salve were a success."

Marrin to Zelzony. "He's stopped screaming, but he
still shudders when we touch him."

Zelzony to Marrin. "All the more important to get him
out of there. Do you have enough agents to handle
THEM?" (she spat out the word *them* as if she couldn't
bear to have it in her mouth).

Marrin to Zelzony. "We're going to basket them, given
the Kinravaly's permission; we don't want suicides or
escapes."

Zelzony to Kinravaly. "Kinravaly Rallen, Marrin re-
quests she be allowed to basket Peeper, Laroul, Eshkel
for the duration of the journey north to the Kinravaly
Reserve. Her reasons, to prevent suicide, injury to her
agents, any possibility of escape. The duration of the
basketing would be less than four hours, the journey
time from South Island to the Reserve."

Kinravaly to Zelzony. "Granted. The circumstances
are extreme and extreme measures may be taken."

Zelzony to Marrin. "Basket them, then get them north."

Zelzony fell back in the chair, limp and flat as a
discfish three days dead. "Haaaaah."

Soft laughter from Picarefy. Short silence. "Mind if I
ask a question?"

Zelzony signed, cracked an eye, dropped the lid again.
"Ask."

"Basketing. What's that?"

"Turning a person into a bundle with staves and rope.
Leaves the head free and nothing else."

"I see. Sounds uncomfortable."

"It is. More than uncomfortable. That's why ortzin
can't use it without permission from Kinra or Kinravaly."

"Hungry?"

Zelzony grimaced, yawned. "Tired. I might try some of that wine Skeen offered. By the way, where is she? I should be at the Reserve when Marrin arrives with the prisoners."

"I'll call her. Would you like to stretch out some more? I can change the configuration of the chair."

"No, don't do it or I'll never get myself back on my feet."

**HIATUS TO ALLOW FOR THE PAPERWORK AND
OBFUSCATION THAT APPEAR TO BE AN
INESCAPABLE PART OF ALL GOVERNMENTS
DEALING WITH GROUPS LARGER THAN TEN.
SPECIES AND DEGREE OF DEVELOPMENT
ARE UNIMPORTANT, ALL THAT IS REQUIRED IS
SOME FORM OF WRITTEN LANGUAGE.**

The Kinravaly's Garden. A warm golden autumn afternoon. Zuistro and Zelzony standing beside a small pond, throwing out bits of bread for some migrating waterfowl who'd stopped there for a moment's rest, scattering handfuls of seeds and melon bits for the land fliers.

"So it's over." Zuistro stood quietly a moment, her hand in one of the pockets of the many pocketed apron she was wearing. Her eyes narrowed to laughing slits, her head was back, turned slightly toward Zelzony.

"Over, hah! I've a year's worth of papers on my deak waiting to be read and signed."

"Saa saa, love, be glad you don't have to write them." Zuistro began breaking up a bun and tossing the bits onto the water. "Or have to face Sulleggen in a snit."

Zelzony crumpled her face into a grimace of distaste. "She's not in a believing mood?"

"Not half." Zuistro dropped onto a boulder roughly chiseled into a seat, dipped into another pocket and began scattering seed. "I had to call in Hatenzo and Tyomfin and just about tie her in the chair to make her watch the recordings of her son and his friends. Saa saa, that's not a scene I want to repeat. She foamed at the mouth and yelled fake at us." Zuistro sighed, stretched out her legs, wiggled her toes. "We showed her your reports and the imager prints of what they were doing to Giulin. More fakes. We showed her the confessions Eshkel and Laroul wrote. All lies. Peeper was a victim not the leader, Peeper was seduced by those two, he was innocent, he wasn't even there, it was all trickery. You and your ortzin were corrupt and probably did it yourselves and dragged Peeper in to blame it on. Well, I don't need to go on. She's going to fight us, Zeli. I was afraid of that. It's going to be messy."

"Mmf." Zelzony dropped to a squat beside Zuistro's knee. "What are the aliens doing? Nothing about them has seeped into my offices."

"Waiting. I heard from Lipitero yesterday. They've had a message from the other starship, it's in the Veil, on its way here. Supposed to arrive around ten days from now."

"All-Wise! Zo, let me off this. I've got tons of work, there's no way I can be ready to leave. Ten days, ay yah, there's no way."

"Borrentye can handle it, it's slogging flack work from now on. You know that as well as I."

"Sulleggen . . ."

"Is my problem. What is it really, Zeli?"

"I don't want to go."

"Why?"

"Aaaah, a thousand things, Zo. I don't . . . I . . . don't . . . LIKE . . . them, Zo. I don't trust them. They make me feel . . . I don't know . . . perhaps . . . like a stupid child. Like a speaker in the middle of signing deaf. Gestures. What do they mean? I keep thinking every twitch means something, I keep thinking . . . I keep thinking they're saying things about me knowing I won't catch it, they're planning things . . . and I'm dragged along like a baby in a carryweb . . . helpless . . . I loathe it, Zo. I'm angry all the time. Knots in my belly and acid in my mouth. Languages. Hundreds of them. Thousands of them. Me swimming in them understanding nothing, incapable of understanding. Like a yaut on a leash."

"Ah, Zeli, Zeli, give yourself time, give yourself credit, believe me, I understand. Oh, yes. I haven't worked with them as closely as you, my dear, but I've rubbed against that unthinking arrogance of theirs. I have sat and listened to Skeen explaining something, skipping ahead in such long leaps I'm left so far behind I can't even ask

SKEEN'S SEARCH   233

questions, and sitting some more while she does it over
again in careful babytalk. Trying to read her when I
haven't a smell of what kind of world bred her. The
others can be worse, harder to read, even Lipitero though
she's Ykx. Perhaps because she's Ykx, but different.
Expectation continually denied. I wonder and I worry
about the thousand we're sending with her. Zeli, do you
think it's easy for me, sending you out like this? There's
no one else who can do the job, my dear. No one. Will it
help if I send an aide with you?"

Zelzony pulled a handful of seed from the pouch she
carried, gazed at it a moment, let the seeds trickle through
her fingers, then brushed her hands together. Mouth
twisted in a wry grin, she looked up at Zuistro. "Two?"

Zuistro smiled affectionately down at her. "Why not.
Two it is. You want to choose them?"

"Yes."

"Very definite about it."

"Yes."

Zuistro got to her feet. "By the way . . ."

"What now?"

"Picarefy wants to talk to you. She's interested in the
judging of the triad." She untied the apron and took it
off, snapped it briskly several times to shake out the last
of the seeds. "What do you think of her?"

"I don't know. What can one think of a machine her
size?"

"Machine?"

"Yes. Ah, you're right, one doesn't see her as a machine. She reminds me a lot of Selyays. The same inquir-
ing nature." She fell silent, stayed silent thinking about
the question while Zuistro rolled the canvas apron into a
tight cylinder and tied the strings about it. "The same
sort of absentminded courtesy." Zelzony laughed uneasily. "It feels strange to be talking about a *thing* this way."
She got to her feet and stared past Zuistro, startled and
rather frightened by a sudden thought. "Zo . . ."

"What? You look like a chagga bit you in a tender
place."

"I just wondered, quite suddenly, what is a person?
What does it mean to have a soul? To be a thinking,
feeling, self-aware . . . you know, all the ways they . . .

oh, not that shapeless faceless they . . . let me say, all
the arguments someone like your brother the philoso-
pher marshals to explain how we're different from beasts.
Are we that different when we produce specimens like
Peeper?"

"Saa saa, you insult the innocent beasts. None I know
of would do that to another of his kind."

"No, love, don't. I haven't any humor in me right
now. Not about this. Listen. Is Picarefy a person, or
merely a clever counterfeit of a person? Our own computers can come close to approximating a playful creativ-
ity with the proper software, but it's not real, there's no
more self-awareness in them than there is in a dauber tist
making palaces of mud. It's all program. And look at
that zoo she brought with her. Skeen and Rostico Burn
at least match, but the others? And it's worse Beyond-
the-Veil; did Picarefy show you images of the kind of
things we'll have to be dealing with if we leave the Veil
somehow? I mean after this is over. Enough to put one
off one's food forever, some of them. I mean, what
makes a person? I . . ."

Zuistro laughed and patted Zelzony's arm. "Forget the
conundrums, Zeli, you're too old for this kind of silli-
ness, making mud pies to throw in your own face. Resign
yourself to it, love, you are going to go out there and, I
know you, Zeli Zeli, you're going to enjoy yourself enormously once you're there. Now, go talk to Picarefy and
let her take your mind off ineffable unanswerable nonsense."

WARNING: EXPOSITORY LUMP AHEAD.

"I loathe and detest unfinished stories, Zem-trallen. I have an itch in my flakes for months when I come across one. So tell me about what's ahead for those three."

Zelzony settled herself into the pilot's chair on Workhorse, noticeably not so comfortable as those on Picarefy's bridge. "Well, in a senn't they will have their judging. . . ."

"Judging?"

"Hmm." Zelzony scratched the tip of her nose with the tip of her right foreclaw. "If this were an ordinary case, say willful doing of damage to property or theft or even sale of drugs to tweeners, a local case, then the Zem-ortzal of the Gurn or, more likely, the ortzal-fej of the Gather would investigate the wrong with as much thoroughness as he or she was capable of. Let's say she, since I don't want to have to continually he or she this explanation. She'd get everything in writing, including whatever diagrams were necessary, the testimony of witnesses, if any, the valuation of goods involved, the past history of the accused. When she completed the report and caged the suspect, she would go to the Remmyo of the Gather or, if the offense was more than merely local, to the Zem-ortzal of the Gurn. In cases involving official corruption of whatever sort, she'd report to the Kinra of the Gurn-Set." Zelzony made an impatient movement of her hand. "Fah, I'm no good at this sort of thing; you sure you want me to go on? I could send you a book that explains all this much better."

"Please do, I'd appreciate the favor. Go on, you're giving me a sketch of the background so I can flesh out the story and bring it to an end. I want to hear it *now*, please."

"Oh, well. What happens next is three justicers are chosen to preside over the judging. One comes from the clan of the accused and serves to watch over her rights, make sure all mitigating circumstances are excavated and

presented. The local Remmyo names this one. The other
two, called neutrals, they're chosen by the Kinra or someone appointed by the Kinra to handle such things. That
last is more usual since most Kinras have a lot more to
worry about than naming justicers, um, this choice is
subject to review later and if improperly made might
invalidate the judgment. The justicers read the ortzal-
fej's report. This takes three to ten days, those things can
be heavy enough to give a grubber a hernia. They make
notes of anything not clear, any assumption they find
questionable, then they question the ortzal-fej. That can
be over fast, or the miserable woman might find herself
reduced to shreds after a week of picking and pounding.
If they find it necessary, they can re-interview witnesses
or anyone else the ortzal-fej talked to, though they usually don't bother. Then, finally, they interview the accused. When that's finished they work on their judgment.
Determination of guilt is usually quick, without much
argument. Conviction requires a unanimous verdict. Two
out of three can acquit. If two out of three are convinced
of guilt but the third will not acquiesce, an arbiter is
called in, usually the Kinra of the Gurn-Set, though if the
Kinra happens to belong to the clan of the accused, the
Kinravaly will be the arbiter. Once they have guilt settled, the justicers will search among the lists of Gurn and
Gather projects and assign the convicted a length and
type of reparation that seems to suit the crime she committed. Ah, yes, she will be supervised, we're not so
trusting as all that. She'll work on the project during the
day and at night will sleep in the local holding center.
That's how it's supposed to work," a shrug and a grimace, "depends on what Gurn-Set you're in how close
you get."

"What kind of reparations can those three do, what in
the wide universe can repair the harm they've done?"
The emotion in the ship's voice made Zelzony squirm in
her chair, waking again her ambivalence toward this amal-
gam of metal and personality.

She looked down at her hands, watched the shadows
on the skin alter as she moved her claws in and out. "It's
difficult. We don't know why they did what they did and
until we do know, all we can be sure of is that they won't

stop trying to do it again. We'll have to keep them caged one way or another. What the Kinravaly wants to do is have their flightskins cut away and their hamstrings severed, then give them to the University for study. Especially the geneticists. If the cause is something physical, we don't want it showing up again in our children. Did I say difficult? That is perhaps the biggest understatement any Ykx has made since we landed on Rallen. Sulleggen has already appointed herself as the homeclan justicer. Which means the Kinravaly will have to name the two neutrals. They'll be Tyomfin and Hatenzo, no question about that. She won't let Uratesto anywhere near the judging and Talahusso is too corrupt to trust. And she wants Selyays kept clear because of her connection with University."

"Neutral? I don't see . . ."

"Oh. No. They're called neutrals but there's no need for them to be neutral in fact. Or ignorant of events. Yes, they've seen your records, but those won't be mentioned by anyone, not even Sulleggen, and they won't be part of the official record of the judging. If we didn't have sufficient other evidence, we'd have to let the three of them go. Why do you think I've been working so hard on placing them close to the other killings, and providing image prints and eye witnesses to Giulin's torment?"

"So, they end their lives as lab animals."

"If things go the way the Kinravaly wants. Tell you the truth, I wouldn't be terribly surprised if Sulleggen snatches Peeper, takes him home to Marrallat and closes the borders against us. She's a fool if she does, the whole place would blow. There's no way she can keep word of what that monster has done away from the Marrallese."

"I see. The Kinravaly has said you're coming with us. Does this postpone embarkation until after the judging?"

Zelzony sighed, dealt firmly with the sick churning in her stomach. "No. I wasn't a direct witness, my part in this is sufficiently described in the reports. So, we leave when everything's ready; it's better that way. Having us gone will clear the Kinravaly's mind and let her concentrate on dealing with Sullegen and her miserable dropping."

"Sometimes it seems as if everything comes at one all at once."

"Sometimes."

My dearest friend:
  Will you accept Bohalendas either as one of your aides or as an addition to your party? He wants to observe the Gate in operation and take an infinitude of measurements he says he cannot possibly describe to anyone else.
  If you agree, dearest one, will you take very good care of him? It will need tact and ingenuity, he was ever a man bound to make his own way without help from those who love him. Take very good care of yourself. I cannot count the ways I need you with me.

                                                          Zo

Ykx began arriving at the lake, settling down in family groups on the rolling grasslands to the west of it. Every day more arrived, some as volunteers, some as witnesses to this historic event, an event both groups hoped would be only the first of many such departures.

Itekkillykx were everywhere, running cookshops, hawking souvenirs, selling matrices for the imagers almost everyone was carrying.

Poets declaimed, artists did portraits, soardancers played their graces in the air overhead.

Children swarmed over the grass, running about, soaring in short leaps, playing every game in the Rallykx repertoire. Their parents and other adults sat in groups, chatting comfortably, exchanging stories of their home Gurns and Gathers, glancing continually at the sky, using that as a kind of punctuation to the talk.

The crowd grew and grew, but maintained a vast good humor, Ykx packed against Ykx, accepting such crowding with an amiability that fascinated Zelzony. Day after day she stood for hours on the Kinravaly's flight tower watching the carnival on the grass, seeing in it contradictory things; on one side it was a folk-wide expression of her own aching need to soar beyond the visible limitation of the Veil, an affirmation of the validity of that need, on another it was a run from responsibilities at home, it was a rejection of traditions, it was a vastation of her ideal of civility which was woven about a proper appreciation of place, of the value of the class system with its beautiful

symmetry of interaction, class with class. She knew well
enough how far from that ideal civility most Ykx lived
out their lives, but she refused to allow that knowledge
to invalidate the dream. In that genial soup on the grass,
Ykx from all classes swirled together, from all Gurns, all
parts of the world. Every day Zelzony saw growing numbers of workers come struggling in, soaring dangerous
distances on their flightskins, living off the land like
swarms of locusts, here for a hope mostly unexpressed
even to themselves, a hope of breaking free of the limits
Rallen clamped about them, here to drop their names in
the great drum that would be churned and turned after
the starship arrived, when a thousand names would be
drawn from it, called out, a thousand Ykx summoned to
apotheosis. One thousand out of ten, twenty, the All-
Wise alone knew how many would be there by then,
watching, waiting, celebrating the occasion.

Zelzony watched and worried about what she and her
few ortzin would do when the ship was gone and thousands of stray Ykx remained, many of them tweeners.
The first senn't the crowd had been relatively clean of
druggers and drunks, but as day blended into day that
was changing, helped along by Itekkillykx peddling
hardbrews of every complexion and Oldieppykx dicker-
ing over cachets of every brainscrambler Rallen produced. She could not do much about these illegal
merchants without disrupting the good nature of the throng
down there, starting something she knew she couldn't
stop (though she could and did have her agents out
getting images of them at work to stow away for later
action). While that was frustrating, what worried her
more was her fear that what was happening below
portended drastic and troubling changes in the Rallen
she knew and loved. A yeasty time, as the Kinravaly
kept saying. Zelzony more and more thought she was
going to hate the bread leavened by this yeast. More
and more, she began to play with the thought of joining
the volunteers, of leaving Rallen so she could hold it
whole in her heart as it was when she was a child, leaving
so she wouldn't see what these changes made of it. Another part of her knew this was fantasy, that she'd be lost
and miserable among Ykx so eager to leave their Gath-

ers. Looking down at them from the top of that massive
tower, she tried to understand wanting to leave forever,
without a chance of coming home, never ever coming
home again. She could not. It was incomprehensible.
Hard enough to leap into nowhere with those aliens
when she had the promise of return, but cutting oneself
off completely? No and no and no. She looked down at
them, brown and gold and gray and brindle, all the same
despite the different colors, all Ykx. What would it be
like to live on a world where almost everyone else was a
different species? They were in for more shocks that they
knew, those poor idiots dreaming of a better life. She
shivered at the pictures her mind presented her and
repeated to herelf no and no and no.

Ykx continued to pour in; the grassy knolls were thick
with them and a new drum had to be provided to take
the names of the hopeful.

They watched the sky. All of them. Waiting.

The transport swam out of the Veil and whispered up
to Picarefy, dwarfing her as it floated next to her. Skeen
sipped at her tea and watched the immense teardrop
tremble daintily as it nudged into orbit a shiplength away.
A last flirt of its tail, then the screen in front of her
bloomed with the transport's bridge. Virgin and Hopeless looked out at her.

Hopeless' face split into an electric grin. "Ta, Skeen."

"Ta, Hopeless, Virgin. How's it going?"

"Sweatin'. This beast is a cow for handling and there's
a swarm of snaggers outside the Veil dipping their hooks
in the insplit."

Virgin was twitching and jitsy as an epileptic flea, her
eyes widened until the white showed round the tarry
black irids, tics did a dance in the muscles of her face,
her mouth writhed around a spate of silent words. She
never did well when separated too long from the Abode.
The Eye hung above her, invisible but almost palpable,
throbbing, twisting, expanding and closing in, mocking
the movements of her mouth. That powerful vortex of
nothingness made Skeen nervous. She did some twitching of her own as a Voice sounded behind her, deep and
sepulchral like a basso shouting down a tube. "Cidder is

out there waiting, crouching in the Essher Group like a spider, waiting."

Hopeless nodded. "He kept the Eye spinning, Cidder did. He's got Imperial harriers spread along the Veil's Edge. He's got thirteen sets of snagships and maulers parked. He's got a score of snaggers trolling. You can feel his fury, Skeen, it's like a cloud of poison gas, cold, brrrh."

Tibo came in, stood leaning on the back of Skeen's chair, smoothing a hand slowly along her shoulder and neck. "Got the snaggers mapped?"

Hopeless waggled a hand. "Ta, Tib. Ah yah, got it. Want us to shoot it over?"

He chuckled. "About six ways I could answer that, luv."

"Gotcha. Ready, Pic? Here it comes."

While Picarefy sorted out the data squirted over from the transport, Skeen sipped at her tea and listened to Hopeless and Tibo spar with careful amiability as they speculated about Cidder and what he meant to do once he discovered Skeen was out again. Hopeless insisted (and the Virgin's surrogate Voices irrascibly concurred) that Cidder hadn't got a smell of them when they slid in, that he was so focused on Skeen they could have gone in behind an array of trumpet ships blasting fanfares and he wouldn't have noticed them. Tibo countered that Cidder didn't care who went in, it was who came out he was going to go for. He was a patient man, and thorough. He wanted them all and was maneuvering to get them.

Tibo: The time he was after Harpo the U Know, he sat half a year on the back of Trouble's third moon with his pet snagger powered down and making like a rock. All on a guess and a wish it was, because even Harpo didn't know he was going after Trouble, that year anyway, but he blew his stash in a yatso game and needed something sure.

Hopeless: Harpo never lasted more than six months after a hit and he was an idiot. Yeah yeah, a lucky idiot except with any game you ever saw, but he pressed it, you know he did. Dipping twice into Trouble, tsing-bohhh, Tib, he was asking to get clipped. Nothing special in that.

Tibo: Ignorant, ignorant, you travel in circles too rari-
fied, Hop. Harpo had twenty digs he was storing up for
that kind of raid, a couple of them so overdue even the
sundoggies had forgot about them. What it was, he was
doing the infinite regression thing. He thinks that I think
that he thinks, you know, no one would go back so soon
to his last Roon, so he might as well go. Cidder untan-
gled all that and was waiting.

Hopeless: Hop? You're picking up bad habits from
Skeen. Hmm. I can think of a better one. Poutar Psoum.

Tibo: Who?: Sounds like a Roggaslang.

Hopeless: Right, that one was Roggaslangger. A
gahslang neut that lost its nid and turned feral. That one
didn't give shit about Roons, its thing was prowling treasuries; folk who knew swore that one melted into smoke
and oozed through walls, some of the things it did, ooz-
ing seemed the only way. It got above itself, though; it
went after old Ugly's summerhouse and got off with the
Undying's crystal harp which meant it had Cidder on its
tail. That one hooted when we warned it to watch where
it put its feet, you've heard gahslanggers hoot, doesn't
encourage empathy in the listener. It hit a couple more
treasuries, dropped into Marigold Pit for some playtime
in the Mimpi Hells. Thing you have to remember, Tib,
even when that one was Mimped to the gills, it never
talked about its jobs, yeah there was a leech or two who
Mimped with that one, trying to pry its mofo out of it but
no go. And it never repeated itself, it wasn't a chirkhead
like Harpo the U Know. And that one never went straight
anywhere, it zagged about and if it was kiting a tail, it
burned it off and if it couldn't burn it, it didn't do the
thing. Well, it oozed down on Thallex and into the vaults
of the High Church and there was Abel Cidder, waiting
for it. The way we worked it out, Cidder must have spent
a year studying everything he could dig up on Psoum,
then he spent some more time thinking about it, then he
went straight to the vault and collected his prize. He took
Psoum back to the Cluster and gave that one to the
Undying Emperor who made him, Cidder I mean,
Shadowknight of Charranor and deeded him half that
world to play with when he got tired of Hounding. You
and Psoum didn't overlap long, Tib, so I'm not surprised

you never heard of that one; hmm, it was a couple years after you showed up at Resurrection that Cidder gathered it in. Ever think of what he'll collect if he snags you, Skeen? If he can bring himself to hand you over. Hunh, maybe half the Cluster, say you keep twisting Old Ugly's nose the way you been doing. So, listen. He knows you better than you know yourself, starbait. The only reason you keep getting away from him is you've had the luck of Sweetbriar the Popole who broke the bank on Honeypot and got it offworld. And you keep coming up with the weirdest bunch of friends and partners who just happen to slide you out of the shitpool. And you're maybe just a little smart.

Skeen: Thanks a lot, Hop.

Hopeless: I'm no damn rabbit, Skeen.

Skeen: You and Timmy, sensitive.

Hopeless: You better believe it. I give myself this name and I don't want to be called out of it. (Another electric grin, but it didn't reach her eyes). Hear what I'm saying, or I pick up my counters and leave this game.

Skeen: Humblest of apologies, O paragon of exquisite sensibility, I abase myself before the delicacy of your soul. Shall I crawl on my belly and lick your feet? Hopeless. Hopeless. Hopeless. Hopeless.

Hopeless (her grin considerably more real): Gahh, nauseating idea. So. What do you think? How do we handle this?

Tibo: The Eye tell you what way he'll jump?

Voice (gloomy and disapproving, Virgin sitting very still, hands fisted, eyes closed): For us to say, not for you to ask.

Skeen: I'd say we go out separately like we came in. You'll be carrying the Ykx so you go quiet and pray the Eye can thread the needle for you. We go out noisy and pull most of what Cidder's got after us.

Tibo: Point isn't how but where.

Skeen: Virgin, any idea if the In-side of the Veil is infested like the Out?

Several Voices (Skeen can pick out three and maybe a fourth): Don't . . . don't go inside . . . no . . . spies . . . fear . . . inlaw and outlaw . . . paranoia . . . focused

toward outsiders . . . too long a flightline . . . traps out
. . . all probabilities negative . . . no . . .

Skeen (wrinkling her nose, drawing down her thick
brows): That's out, then. Hmm. You could drop straight
down. It'd be easier to spot you there, but you might be
able to get a lead on the snaggers and keep loose while
we make noise somewhere else. No, not down. Up. Up
feels wrong, don't you get an itch thinking about it?
Nobody seems to go up when they're wiggling off a
hook. So. Yes. Tib, it's more than likely Petro's shield is
still good unless we land right on top a snagger. We need
a distraction. You're the house magician, what do you
think?

Tibo: Harriers. What if we took out a few harriers?
Make Cidder notice we're around.

Picarefy: Eh, Tib, this is me, remember? I can outrun
'em, give me a decent start, but outgun a harrier? Forget
it.

Tibo: Listen. When I was young and generally ignorant, I shipped out with Humbolt on the Heller Madre.
One of his last prowls. He was in the middle of a delivery
to the Shingalaree rebels when Hound Zachs stumbled
over him. Zachs came cruising through the Swarm, looking over the scene, who knows why, with a harrier to
watch his tail, if he had a friend nobody knew it. His
snaggers were sitting back at his base over by Orion's
Knee because he was too cheap to spend the fuel when
he didn't think he'd need them. Humbolt did some fancy
flying, swung the sun, got behind the harrier and rammed
a missile up its butt. Almost got Zachs too, but he hit the
panic button and flamed out of there with the missile
chasing him all the way to Teegah's Limit. He split
intact, so Humbolt dropped his cargo fast and careless
and went to ground in the nearest Pit. Humbolt was the
only one I know of who ashed a harrier solo, but I
suspect there were others who discovered that weak arse,
because now harriers run in pairs or packs.

Picarefy: Pairs or packs. Tib, I still say what do you
think I am?

Tibo: You've got Petro's shield in place by now. No
harrier's going to detect it if the Kliu didn't, so we hunt
up a harrier pack with plenty of space between them and

the nearest snagships, get into them long enough to thread missiles through their jecters, all but one, we need one to squeal for help and fetch Cidder running, then we split fast as you can drive us, Pic, and we hunt up another pack and play with them a bit. Cidder should be hooked by then, so we get the hell out of that section of space.

Picarefy: With an armada after me.

Skeen: Eh, Pic, didn't you tell me you could outrun just about anything?

Picarefy: Given a good start.

Skeen: Well, we'll just have to arrange that. Then we have to lose them.

The Virgin was talking inaudibly with her disembodied companions, detached from the discussion, looking inward at something she approved of because she was smiling and nodding her head. Then she blinked, looked straight into the pickups, turning her smile on Skeen.

A Voice boomed behind Skeen: The Shoals.

Skeen: Virgin, what. . . ?

The Virgin had tuned out again and the Voices weren't talking.

Skeen: Djabo's horny toenails, Pic, what's The Shoals?

Picarefy: A collection of vortices, soft spots and other miseries that penetrate into the insplit. It pulses so you never know when you're going to find yourself in the middle of something that proceeds to eat you. Or pull you out like cold taffy. Or reduce you to subatomic powder. It's generally out by the Brown Betty stars, but sometimes it moves. I do NOT want to go there.

Skeen: Hopeless, was that the Eye talking? And does the Virgin mean we should go there or we will go there?

Hopeless: Eye says will. Doesn't say what happens when you get there.

Skeen: When WE get there?

Hopeless: Ah yah, nothing to do with Virgin and me.

Skeen: Lovely. You ready to go down?

Hopeless: When you give the word.

Skeen: I'd better let them know you're coming. Pic, is there anyone in Workhorse? Good. Tell him I want to talk with the Kinravaly.

*   *   *

"Zem-trallen."

Zelzony turned. Anki was standing in the arch where the stairs led onto the tower's roof, her body vibrating with excitement. "What is it?"

"Kinravaly asks that you join her in the tug."

"Ah! Thank you, Anki." Zelzony crossed to the ramp, stopped at the Lip and looked over her shoulder. "Join me?" Without waiting for the page's answer, she stepped to the edge of the Lip, spread her flightskins and dropped into the wind.

"The transport has arrived. We can land whenever you're ready for us."

The Kinravaly touched the end of a pointed tongue to the fold in her upper lip, frowned at the screen without really seeing it; she glanced at Zelzony but said nothing and Zelzony felt no urge to break the silence. "It is midmorning here," the Kinravaly said. "There are fare-wells that have to be made, blessings to be given. We have waited to draw the names of the volunteers until the transport arrived, that has to be prepared. You gave us a list of necessaries for each of the colonists. The packs are in storage here and have to be moved to the site. We have gathered a thousand wings, these too are in storage, plus seed packs, ova and surrogate wombs; don't worry, we have managed to stay under the weight limits, there is very little metal involved so weight for bulk is relatively small, but all that must be transported to the embarka-tion fields. Ah, give us two days, if you will. Day after tomorrow about this time. Does that suit?"

Skeen's eyes shifted a moment, her mouth moved but no sounds came through the speakers. She nodded, then looked back at them. "Yes, that's fine. Um, we'd like to put down in the lake. There'll be some flooding, but less damage to the land, also, it will be easier to control access and guard against harm to your people. The water will rise about fifty wings, Kinravaly Rallen; your garden could get damp in the lower reaches."

"It will dry again. You know your capacities better than we can, but what you say sounds reasonable. You have our leave to use the lake. Is there anything else we should do?"

"Nothing I can think of now. If something occurs, I'll let you know."

"All-Wise Bless, we wait your coming."

Zelzony lingered after the Kinravaly left. "Picarefy?"

"Zem-trallen?"

"The young one. Rostico Burn. He's still on Rallen?"

"Yes. Certainly. We informed you he wished to roam about a while more."

"Will you call him, please, and ask if he will transport me to Yasyony this afternoon?"

"One moment."

Zelzony sat stiffly erect, claw tips clicking a staccato rhythm on a metal plate set into the chair's arm. Time . . . time . . . Picarefy said something about the pressures of time . . . squeezing out the juices from Ykx lives. All-Wise Weeping, what must life be like when moving across half a world north to south takes hours not days. Or east to west, for that matter.

"Zem-trallen."

"I hear you."

"Ross says, be glad to. He can be there in somewhere around two hours. When would you want to leave?"

Zelzony tilted the rekkagourd hanging at her belt, read off the time, called up the time at Laby Youl. "Ah, yes. Two hours from now. That will be quite satisfactory. Thank you."

Giulin was in his studio (two small rooms in a free-standing structure that was mostly given over to work-rooms for the gardeners who tended the plants in the small and large greenspaces in the huge Giu clan compound at the south edge of Laby Youl). He was going through a batch of freshly sealed prints, sorting them into piles. More of his imager work was pinned in clusters on two walls, other prints were hanging from a line strung up by a densely screened window where air could move across them and help dry them.

When he saw who had come in, Giulin got hastily to his feet. "Zem-trallen." He looked apprehensive; shadows from the memories she evoked settled onto his face.

"Your parents have said I may speak with you." Zelzony

spoke slowly, his haunted mistrustful look dismayed her. With an abrupt movement of her hand toward the prints, she said, "I have an offer for you that concerns your skill with the imager."

Giulin glanced at the sheets he still held, set them on the table, looked around the small cramped room. "Maybe we better talk in the court, it's generally empty this time of day . . . ah, Zem-trallen."

"Yes. Of course." Zelzony followed the boy outside into the pleasant grassy garden enclosed within two wings of the compound and a six-sided outer wall. It was a crisp spring afternoon, the sunlight brilliant and not too hot, a breeze wandering through treetops and occasionally dipping to wind across the flowerbeds and curl about several small decorative fountains. Giulin led her to a bench beside a fountain constructed from water polished stones and pebbles, planted with small curly ferns. A pair of budding lacetrees spread a delicate tracery of shadow over the wooden slats of the bench and the pale gray gravel of the path. Giulin waited until Zelzony was seated at one end of the bench, then perched himself on the other end.

As uncomfortable as the boy, Zelzony dredged up a smile. "Kinra Selyays showed me your prize prints; she was pleased with your eye and your technical skills."

Giulin's nostrils flattened with embarrassment, he looked away, scowled at the water cascading over the stones. "Thank you," he said after a moment, gruff and abrupt. "What's the offer? . . . ah, Zem-trallen."

Zelzony drew her hand across her mouth, wiping away a smile the boy wouldn't appreciate. "The starship will be landing day after tomorrow, the colony transport. I assume you've heard of the Mistommerkykx Lipitero and her quest? Yes. Well. Kinravaly Rallen has won from the aliens the right to send observers. Bohalendas will be on board to take measurements for the society of Seekers. I am to be the Kinravaly's representative, there to make sure the aliens fulfill their contract with us, ortzin Marrinfej comes as my personal Aide. And there is one more place I can fill, that of Marrin's Aide. If you wish it, Giulin, that place is yours."

His hands closed into fists, opened, closed again; he swallowed several times, sat staring at the water, his shoulder turned to her, courtesy forgotten in the intensity of his reaction. He swung round, stared at her. "Why me?"

She frowned at him, then spread her hands. "To be honest, the offer's to help me sleep better."

"All that smik about my prints?"

"Not smik, Giulin, for me it's a pleasant extra, but you'll be doing the Kinravaly a service if you image the trip and the transfer through the Stranger's Gate for her. Perhaps some images of the Other Side."

"The family knows about this offer?"

"Yes. The decision is yours, your parents insisted on that."

"How long do I have to think about it?"

"Ah. It'll take a while to get the volunteers and their gear on board. Hmm. Take a senn't if you need it."

"Ah umm, how long will I be gone?"

"The aliens say a round trip will need a bit over half a year." Zelzony got to her feet. "I'll leave you to your thinking, Giulin. All-Wise Bless."

Giulin got to his feet, looking shaken and uncertain. "Wait. A moment, Zem-trallen. I want to talk to my parents. How long are you going to be in Laby Youl?"

"I have to return to Kinravaly Reserve tonight, but I can spare another hour here."

With a smile that came and went, excitement and uncertainty lighting his eyes, Giulin edged closer to her, touched her arm briefly, hesitantly. "I want to go. I think . . . I have to talk to my parents. Zem-trallen, you . . . I don't know . . . I can't . . ." A nervous giggle, a flare of his nostrils. "Thank you. In an hour. Please. I'll say for sure then. All-Wise Bless."

"Zem-trallen, yes yes yes. What do I do, what do I bring, when will I leave here, how, will you come fetch me, can the family go too, what . . ." Giulin shut his mouth and danced from foot to foot as Zelzony held up her hand.

"One at a time, tidal wave. Let me see if I can remember them. You don't have to do a lot, fill a pack with a few things you'd like to have with you, put something in it to amuse you, bookfiches, games, fancy work, whatever you can fit in; the aliens tell me that starflight is rather like spending a long time in a small room with nothing much to look at. Ahh, I'll send a skip for you about a week from now. Perhaps two skips if I can talk the aliens into it, so you can bring your family. If I can manage only one and they don't mind a cramped ride, you can bring your parents but not the rest. The trip from Laby Youl to the Kinravaly reserve lasts a little over three hours. Bring your imagers, but don't bother about matrices, the Kinravaly will provide them. When you get back we'll sit you down in the University labs and apply the whip until you make history prints for every Gurn-set." She smiled at the excited boy. "We're going to work the tail off you, Giulin."

"Ehh scuzza." Visibly containing an urge to whoop and run up the house tower to do a soardance through the clouds, Giulin contented himself with a grin that threatened to split his face in half.

"Anything else?"

"Ahhh, that Min woman, will she be around? I want images of her more than anything."

"The observers will be on the transport, not on Picarefy. Ah, that's the alien Skeen's starship. Picarefy tells me there's some danger Beyond-the-Veil and Skeen wants to keep the Rallykx clear. Once we land, you'll most likely get your images."

"Saa saa scuzzAH!"

"I hear you, Giulin. One week. All-Wise Bless."

The transport drifted downward, a long black teardrop; one moment it was no more than a dark speck passing through the thin high clouds, the next moment it was an immensity so awesome a sigh passed like the wind across the crowd. Down and down, settling feather light on the lake's surface, nudging the water aside with deceptive gentleness, down and down until it reached equilibrium floating a handspan off the bottom. The water welled up with much the same gentle inevitability, swallowing the lakeshore and the surrounding hillocks, moving out and out with an eerie almost-silence, but Zelzony and her ortzin had moved the watchers and waiters to higher ground and none of the Ykx got their feet wet.

Breath caught in their throats, eyes wide, Saffron and Mauvi watched a round section of the black skin blink away and light shine out of a sudden opening that seemed tiny, like a pin prick, until a dark figure stepped into it and stood looking out at them. In an odd jarring switch, at first the lanky hairless alien was a doll less than a hand high carved from the darkest brown bitternut wood, then, abruptly, she was taller than most Ykx, and the pinprick was a portal three wings high.

"Woo ow, Mau, do you believe that?"

"Have to, don't I." She shaded her eyes, then pointed. "Look, isn't that the Kinravaly?" A gold Ykx shimmering in the sunlight rode a gilded glittering wing soaring in high circles over the transport and the crowd.

"Must be."

The Kinravaly looked down over the vast throng, faces turned to her like flowers to the sun. Her throat closed up and for several minutes she couldn't speak. She swallowed and sighed, lifted the borrowed loud hailer. "Ykx of Rallen, the starship is here, the time has come to know the names of those who will leave us. The Talan fej Vosslar, servant of the All-Wise, will draw the cards, I Kinravaly Rallen will call the names, those called will come into the area set aside for them." She stopped talking a moment, feeling battered by shuddering waves of hope and yearning, fear and excitement coming at her from the crowd, it was like wingriding over the caldera of an active volcano. "Begin, Talan fej, begin."

Jatsik, Sully Gather, Eggettak.
   A massive brindle Ykx whooped and started pushing toward the roped off area.

. . .

Kulishka, Kevari and children, Lahusshin Gather, Oldieppe.
   Weeping, laughing, dragging friends and kin with them, a family of browns with a tiny gold daughter

started from near the back of the crowd, hands patting them as they passed other families.

. . .

Veratisca (poet), Laby Youl Gather, Yasyony.
Slender russet Ykx, laughing and crying at once, silence and a kind of mourning about her, sense of loss passing like a wind across the crowd when they heard her name.

. . .

Saffron and Mauvi (first pairing), Korika Gather, Itekkill.

. . .

Alazin, Elleret and children, Tikka Gather, Eggettak.

. . .

On and on the naming went; saturated by emotion, the crowd turned quiet and sad, kin hugged and nuzzled departing kin, friends touched and patted and hugged departing friends. Hour slid into hour, the Kinravaly sucked at a squeeze bottle of cold iska as her voice went hoarser than usual. The drums squealed and rustled as the Talan fej's acolytes turned their cranks. The volunteers in the roped off area sat or walked about, a few talked, broken bits of sentences, most were quiet, watching the Kinravaly, looking about with eyes like sponges, soaking in sights they knew they'd never see again. At the end of four hours, she called a halt for an hour's rest, retreated to the tower to eat a hasty meal, speak with Zelzony, Lipitero and Skeen who were on the towertop watching. When the hour was done, she winged to the waitingfield and went back to calling names.

Orica, Segetes and children, Filla Vam Gather, Urolol.

. . .

Esaros (soardancer), Masliga Gather, Urolol.

. . .

Yagara (sculptor), Trann Gather, Eggettak.

. . .

On and on, four hours, a break, four hours more; when the dark came down, beams of brilliant light sprayed from the transport, playing on the Kinravaly, lighting up the hillocks and the silent waiting Ykx.

On and on, throughout the night and most of the following day, until the last name was called, the last volunteer came through the ropes.

Shadows were long on the grass, then lost as the night came on; clouds thickened in the west and passed from vermilion to magenta to a vibrant midnight blue. The transport's lightbeams came on again, turned the Kinravaly into a shimmering wonder, bright against the black clouds overhead. "It is done," she cried, her voice breaking under the strain of calling out all those names and the swirl of contradictory emotions filling her. "It is time now to bless those leaving us and be blessed by them. They go into strangeness and danger, they go and will not ever return. Take my blessing and my sorrow, children of Rallen, my admiration and my admonition to remember those you leave behind."

I LOATHE PROTRACTED GOOD-BYES. YOU KNOW WHAT I'M TALKING ABOUT. YOUR WELL-MEANING FRIENDS AND RELATIVES COME TO THE THE AIRPORT WITH YOU AND STAY FOR TWO HOURS AND YOU FIND YOURSELF WITH A DECAYING GRIN PASTED ON YOUR FACE MAKING CONVERSATION OF SUBLIME BANALITY AND YOU FINISH WITH GOOD-BYE REPEATED UNTIL THOSE TWO SYLLABLES CEASE TO HAVE ANY MEANING WHATSOEVER AND BECOME A HABIT IN THE MOUTH THAT LEAVES A SOUR TASTE. SO, SUPPLY FOR YOURSELF THE RITES AND RITUALS OF OF YKX LEAVE-TAKING (IF YOU FEEL THE NEED). ME, I'M MOVING ALONG.

PART V: THE ESCAPE

Skeen watched the transport climb past her, slanting upward with massive buoyancy, intending to leave the Veils behind by leaving behind the galactic plane, moving up and over the area of dust and disturbance, then serpentining down again weaving a secret way through the traps and toils of Empire and Empire's agents. She smiled at Tibo, lifted her glass, then sipped at the seablue wine. "Well, Pic, time we were leaving too, the dust is thicker our way."

"Moving." Picarefy's voice was dull, almost a monotone.

"What's the matter?"

Silence.

"Sulking, Pic?"

"So I'm going to miss her. Petro."

"It happens to us all, Pic; friends move on. We miss

them a while, then there's someone else. Or things start popping around you and you haven't got time to think about sore spots, then when you get a free moment, the spots aren't as sore as they were."

"Thanks. That helps so much."

"Sarcasm doesn't become you, Pic."

"That's one woman's opinion. Tk."

"Where'd you acquire that?"

"Buzzard's party. Blue did it to irritate whoever he was arguing with. Tk."

The lounge had changed again, it was a rough approximation of a long oval, heavy dark wood paneling, dozens of alcoves in the walls, shelves in them, books and bibelots on the shelves, a window seat, a window at the back of each alcove with a moving holograph behind it, each vista brilliantly detailed, each vista from a different world. Scattered about the room, chairs and tables of tight-grained dark wood, heavy, carved in sinous curves. A working fireplace, paintings and tapestry, imager prints in ornate frames, a dark green carpet with black tracery through it, plants in bright ceramic pots, ceramic lamps with pseudo fires burning pseudo oil. Timka was stretched out on a long elegant daybed upholstered in dark gray galatee. She wore a short kimono of heavy silk printed with huge flower forms in shades of pink and coral on an ivory ground, wrapped loosely about her and tied with a wide silk sash. A slight smile on her face, she was watching Rostico Burn prowl restlessly about, pulling down books, fingering small objects that were mostly hold-outs from Skeen's Roon raids, things that pleased her so she kept them. What he wanted to do was beat it out of here and head for the bridge where he'd be in on what was happening, but he didn't quite dare. He was clever enough to see behind Skeen's casual manner and recognize how ruthlessly she'd handle any trespassing. When Ross' perambulation began to irritate her, Timka crossed her legs at the ankles, laced her hands behind her head and spoke in a lazy murmur, "Picarefy, is there a screen in this room? Be nice if we could see what's happening."

"Sorry, Ti. Didn't mean to let you slide like this.

Here." The huge dingy painting over the fireplace flicked
out of existence; inside the gilt frame was a view of the
Veils drifting around them and the increasingly distant
spark that was the transport. "Teegah's Limit coming up.
There won't be much to see after that." A fragment of a
laugh. "Though we will be sticking our nose into realspace
often enough, the insplit around here looks like lumpy
mush."

"Leave it on, Pic. Looking at the mush might just give
us the notion we know what's happening."

"Gotcha."

Timka watched Ross glance at the screen, then start
prowling again. With a snort of disgust, she sat up. "Get
off your feet for a while, Ross, you're making me jitsy as
the Virgin."

Quick brilliant smile thrown at her over his shoulder,
angled brow lifting, flattening, a bright-eyed fox pretending ease and doing it well, he said nothing, but kicked a
hassock over to one of the bulging overstuffed chairs,
flung himself into the chair and sat watching the screen,
feet up, ankles crossed, hands laced together over his flat
stomach.

Timka watched the Veil bands change and grow until a
soft chime announced the Drop. She closed her eyes.
When she was still new to this universe, she'd teased
Picarefy into leaving a screen open so she could see what
happened when they translated into the insplit where
they whipped along at speeds that were meaningless in
their immensity and absurd in the tiny numbers that
named them. One light. Two. Twenty. Fifty. Once was
enough. She tossed her lunch and what felt like every
lunch she'd eaten for the past month. Eyes closed, the
translation was quite endurable, a subtle alteration in the
subliminal hum that pervaded Picarefy's shipbody when
she was moving.

When Timka felt the change in the hum that meant the
translation was complete, she opened her eyes and lay
watching the mother-of-pearl irridescence of the insplit.
After she recovered from her nausea and nerved herself
to look at the screen, Picarefy told her that the subtle
shifts of color were full of information about conditions

outside, but she couldn't see it; apparently it took Picarefy's peculiar virtues to make sense of the flows. Moving, she thought, on our way to the Gate. A sudden flooding of homesickness squeezed her insides into knotty strings, surprising her with its intensity. She had enjoyed herself here, she had acquaintances she could make into friends with a little time and effort. She could be whatever she wanted here and the possibilities seemed endless. This convoluted odyssey Skeen had drawn her into had taught her comforting things about her capacity for transformation, not merely the old kind, the shifts she could put her body through, but a transformation of mind and spirit, a destruction of barriers she'd once seen as impenetrable. A frightening, beckoning, dangerous, exhilarating, fascinating universe. But when she thought of the Gate and the Mountains beyond, she ached with need to be back there, a need that didn't seem to diminish with time. Lifefire, what am I going to do? Hmm. I wonder if Telka went down the Ever-Hunger's gullet or wiggled away. She frowned at the rippling shimmer on the screen and knew, surprising herself again, that she wanted to find Telka alive and strong, that she needed to face her twin and finish one way or another the battle that had started the moment their mother cast off their buds, that she was bone-deep sure of the outcome.

A sudden change in the s o u n d. Her eyes flew to the screen, the flows were bunched into a knot of painful jags, the image rippled. A warning chime. Hastily Timka closed her eyes. Here we go again, she thought, remembering the in-and-out creep through the Veils when they were feeling their way toward Rallen. She sighed and got to her feet.

Ross looked round. "Going?"

"As you see." Timka shrugged. "We've done this before, I think I'll sleep through it this time."

"Good idea. Nothing will be happening for days yet."

Belly down, teeth bared, Picarefy crept from the Veils, stalking a pack of three harriers ambling along in the insplit, sweeping the Veils' Edge with such lackluster unconcern they couldn't be expecting anything to fall

into their nets. The nearest snagship was five lights off,
hugging the brown half of a yellow/brown dwarf double.

Ross and Timka were on the bridge, permitted there
after a stern warning that they should make themselves
invisible and inaudible. Timka curled in one of the smaller
chairs watching what she could see of Skeen and Tibo.
They were talking in single words and long silences,
grunts and gestures, something approaching a cued telep-
athy. It amused and amazed her that these two could
meld so closely they hardly needed to talk, yet Skeen,
away from Tibo, could suspect him of abandoning her
and stealing her ship. The two sides of the woman wouldn't
fit together, no matter how Timka shifted them about.
This fascinated her; anyway, speculating about Skeen
filled the emptiness of waiting time. She called up the
memories she'd acquired from Skeen when she attempted
to use the Min inreach on her, that long ago time (no, it
was less than—the realization was a jolt that knocked
Timka breathless for a moment—less than two years ago
though it seemed like another lifetime) when Skeen's
hand was rotting off her arm and doing a good job of
slowly killing her. The uncertainties hammered into Skeen's
soul during her rotten childhood had surfaced and wiped
away the certainties of her mind; her trust was betrayed
time after time by those who professed to care for her,
who should have cared, her perceptions were constantly
negated by such betrayal until she mistrusted her own
judgment almost as much as she mistrusted the surfaces
and professed intentions of those around her. There was
a sense of kinship in the way that Skeen had managed an
accommodation with herself; had devised a mode of living that seldom triggered her underlying paranoia, an
accommodation much like Timka's, survivors both of
them. Skeen was generous as long as she could set the
terms of that generosity. Like me. She had friends that
she would help without counting the cost as long as that
help didn't threaten her independence. Like me, the
now-me. She accepted with comity all beings who drifted
into her notice, but few got close to her. Tibo? Yes.
Watching that wordless coordination, Timka had to con-
cede an intimacy of mind between those two as complete

as any intimacy of the body. Even so, how much would Skeen grieve if Tibo left her? Hard to say. The one being, though, that she'd ever really mourn was Picarefy, who was child, sister, lover, friend, clone in a complex and peculiar mix. Fascinating.

Picarefy tasted the harrier's probes as they slid un-knowing over the Ykx shield and used these to visualize the harriers without having to send her own probes out and possibly trigger alarms aboard them. Skeen and Tibo watched the ghostly green lines drifting about in the center of the screen, the intensity of their concentration visible in shoulder and neck.

Tibo snorted. "Sloppy."

Skeen nodded, one short sharp jerk of her head. "Cidder'll have that chirk's hide."

The formation was looser than it should have been, with the high third several degrees out of position. Even Timka could see that none of the crews expected a ship to come out of the Veil and didn't really care whether it did or not.

Picarefy crept closer. Hours passed. Slow stretched out hours, not a sound on the bridge except the ragged breathing of the four and the subliminal hum from Picarefy, on and on, edging closer closer, interminable, drawn-out stalk, sometimes it seemed they were running and run-ning and getting nowhere as in a nightmare, tension climbing high and higher, dropsical distended instants bulking in Timka's stomach, hands wrapped tight about the chairarms, worry worry will the shield hold? It worked against the Kliu Berej, but about a tiny lander not a thing that massed like Picarefy. Would that make a dif-ference? No answer from Picarefy, none from Skeen or Tibo, no comment from Lipitero before she crossed to the transport. Closer. Closer. Until the screen could no longer hold the pack and divided into three cells. Until the jecter fronds of the harriers filled those cells.

"Missiles ready." Picarefy's voice broke the silence. Timka twitched. The pleasant countertenor sounded harsh; she could swear the ship loathed what she was doing though she was resigned to the necessity of doing it. "Two full, one ten-percent. Which one gets the tenner?"

Skeen flipped a hand at Tibo. Unlike Rostico Burn
(who was doing an internal wardance but had just sufficient tact to keep his whooping to himself), she wasn't
enjoying this stalk; dipping in and out of tight places,
relying on wiliness and skill was something she did with
pleasure and artistry, but here she didn't trust her in-
stincts and passed the decision to Tibo.

"High third," he said. "That's apt to be the leader;
he's the one you want able to squeal. It's likely his
message rat is pre-targeted to the snagship orbiting the
dwarf and that snagger will split over here in a blink or
less. Those devils are fast, Pic, and Cidder will have the
best of them on watch."

"Oh, is that so?"

A bark of laughter from Skeen. "I mentioned that
sarcasm, didn't I, Pic?"

"Could be. Could be I didn't happen to agree with the
context. Um. Click home your crashwebs. I'll shoot, roll
and drop, that's no problem, but shield, acceleration,
lifesupport will take all the oomph I can put out, little
niceties like g-normal will be on hold for the duration.
Yes, yes, I will remember that you're fragile creatures,
but I won't be worrying about your comfort, not right
then."

"Timka. Ross. You heard? Need help? No. Good. Pic,
goose 'em and let's get the hell out."

"I hear and obey."

Picarefy collapsed the Shield, spat the three missiles,
dropped into the insplit without waiting to see what
happened; she pulled the Ykx shield around her again
and built to her top speed as rapidly as she could without
breaching her sides and turning her passengers into goo.
If the crew in the crippled harrier was reasonably competent, they would take no-time to pinpoint the source of
those missiles and come after her claws out. There was
no way to be sure the weakened missile would do sufficient damage to prevent the harrier from following. For a
minute or so she couldn't be sure that she hit any of
them, she was suicidally close when she released the
missiles; there'd be maybe a breath between alarm and

explosion, but if Mala Fortuna was riding her back, that'd be time enough for an alert crewman to hit the panic button and lift his ship into realspace with half a chance of leaving the missile behind. Picarefy didn't expect such alertness and quick reflexes, but stranger things had happened and she didn't want to chance them happening to her.

One minute. Distortion in the flow, two knots. Dead ships.

Two minutes. Diminishing whine. A message rat on its way.

Three minutes. Weak probes ranging, spherical pattern, tips barely touching the surface of the shield. One harrier, crippled, going nowhere.

Five minutes. She eased off. Sparks of relief flooded her circuits as the strain passed out of her. She released the brake on the argrav, started the repair mice checking on her brain and body, started the medasource playing through Skeen's body (this was something she'd added without telling Skeen, the medasource instruments and program were costly, putting it mildly, and Skeen would have spent years arguing about the need for it when she already had the Autodoc, itchy because Picarefy would be intruding more deeply than ever into her life, she knew Skeen through and through, in a way she was Skeen, Skeen's thought patterns were incorporated in her own). She managed some sneaky repair, careful to do nothing Skeen would notice, then moved on to Tibo and Rostico Burn. By the time she was ready for Timka, the Min had clicked open the web, flipped through a pair of shifts and was pulling on her kimono.

Skeen unclipped the web and sat up. "Status, Pic?"

"Minor damage, a few unimportant breaks; the mice will have them sewn up in a minute or two. We'll be on target for the second hit coming up ninety minutes."

"The pack?"

"No pursuit, two flares on the field, whine of a rat, probes from the crip, less than halfpower. I'd say we got three hits and the news out as planned."

"Slickery Pic, hah!"

                    *   *   *

The threepack of harriers Tibo and Picarefy had elected
as her second target had been patrolling between two
micro clusters near several long thin pseudopods extend-
ing from the main body of the Veil; the nearest snagship
was over ten lights off, the pack was the last in the line of
harriers, it was roughly in the direction of The Shoals,
everything they were looking for. Unfortunately, by the
time Picarefy got close enough pick up their probes, the
ships had gone off patrol, had surfaced to realspace and
were drifting near a red giant, positioned just inside
Teegah's Limit, nose out. To get behind them she would
have to surface and swing round the sun, and after the
strike, she couldn't split without another long run. She
hadn't picked up a rat trace, but that was such a chancy
occurrence, she wasn't bothered by the lack. She knew
the pack had got a warning and was waiting for her. That
all the other packs would be waiting like these.

Skeen looked at the schematic and cursed. "Cidder!"
she snarled.

Tibo was gazing intently at the ships. "Mmm."

Picarefy threw an inset onto the screen, showing the
ships in relation to the star and the sphere of Teegah's
Limit. "Quick little viper," she said. "I'm picking up
feelers from three snagships, all of them moving from
their parking orbits, two coming toward us, one going
away. I assume they're closing in on the harrier packs."

Skeen ran her hand through her hair. "We wanted him
to notice us, I say we've done enough, let's get out
of . . ."

Picarefy jumped in before she finished. "No, that's
wrong. If we don't hit him again, he'll start seining the
place, but give him a line, he'll be on it, coming at us
with everything he's got, giving Virgin and Hopeless a
reasonably clear run. That's what you were setting up,
Skeen, you might as well follow through."

Reluctantly Skeen agreed; they had to twist Cidder's
tail again. "No tricks this time," she said. "Pic, those
missiles go with a full load."

"Oh, yes, no playing with that pack," Picarefy said,
fervor in her voice, "Bona Fortuna bless us."

Tibo passed a hand across his face, cleared his throat.

"The way the pack is positioned, you can see they are
waiting for you to come out of the starglare should you
be running this line. Cidder has to have some idea about
the Ykx Shield seeing what happened on Pillory, but he
hasn't had the time or data to bust it, so he's trying to
outfox it. Either him or the Lead in the boss harrier.
Lead knows he can't see you before you spit the missiles,
but I'd bet the family jewels he's got someone's thumb
on the panic button in each of those ships, with the
orders to squirt past the Limit and drop out the instant
anything at all appears on their screens. Him or Cidder,
one of them has guessed that you have to lift the Shield
before you can fire. Drop out, switch ends, surface again,
take out the missiles and pin you against the sun. With a
little luck the Lead can do all of that. Look at them, you
can almost smell the confidence. Hmm. Which brings up
another point. Pic, you think this is one of Cidder's
Fancies? You think he guessed Skeen would break out
this direction and put his prime pack here to catch her?"

"This threepack is light-years sharper than that other.
That's all I'd feel happy about saying."

"Hmm."

Skeen moved restlessly. "I'm not into suicide, Tib."

"There's a way to do it."

"So?"

"I just haven't seen it yet."

"Riiight. So how long do we hang in Limbow waiting
for inspiration to strike? There's two snagships heading
this way fast, like you said, Cidder requisitioned the best
of them."

"You want inspiration, hush and let me think."

Silence on the Bridge. Timka glanced at Rostico Burn,
but he showed no eureka signs; he was scowling at the
schematics and chewing his lip like a cub at a math test
he hadn't studied for. She agreed with Skeen. Suicide
didn't appeal to her. It seemed to her that all they
needed to do was stand off and fire a few missiles at the
ships; it didn't matter if they missed completely, Skeen
would have announced her presence and spat in Cidder's
face. Being on the easy side of Teegah's Limit, Picarefy
could drop out and split for The Shoals before those

harriers had a chance to get organized. She thought about saying this, but after a few minutes watching Tibo and Skeen she decided intrusion wouldn't be welcome.

Tibo rubbed his agile actor's hands along the chair arms, his amiably ugly face blank with the intensity of his concentration. "Ha!" He snapped thumb against finger. "Pic, how close can you get without triggering something?"

"Insplit or realspace?"

"Start with realspace."

"Visuals and ultramags, where *they* can make me, the Shield doesn't count. I can get lost for some distance in the starglare, but about half an AU from the pack most visual systems I know about can filter out that glare. Ultramags will kick in about then, reinforce the visuals. That's realspace. Insplit is trickier to judge, how far they could pick me up depends on several variables, reading capacity, interpretive skill, experience, and . . . I suppose you could call it intuition . . . the ability of the reader to make accurate calls on inadequate data. Given those, they could spot me several lights off. That's without the shield. With it? I don't really know. I don't know how it changes the flow. I'd like to do some testing . . ." a brief cascade of laughter, ". . . wrong time, you don't need to say it. There's some precedent that says the shield smooths out the knot my mass ties in the flow, so a visual read would miss me. I suspect that a truly talented reader would see something there. What he or she made of it would depend on other factors. That help any?"

"You could come up nose to nose with the boss harrier if you stayed in the insplit and under shield?"

"I wouldn't mind trying it."

"They're waiting for you to jump out of the starglare; if you don't, you'll have a few milliseconds before they can shift mind set. Here's what I suggest. Start above the plane, slide over to Teegah's Limit, going fast as you can without making waves in the flow, translate to realspace, coming down top speed, steep slant, one limb of a hyperbolic, hold the shield in place until you're on their tails, drop it, get the three missiles off, drag the shield on, hit the other limb, whip through the Limit and split. I think you can do it and get clear."

More silence on the bridge as Picarefy thought it over. Skeen had her chair almost flat; she was stretched out staring at the ceiling, her face unreadable. Rostico Burn was grinning, he had his hands wrapped around his chair arms holding himself down, his body shouting yes yes go for it. Timka wrinkled her nose at him, but he was too involved to take notice of her. She sighed, bored rather than frightened, convinced to her bones that those harriers, however expertly handled, were no match for Picarefy. She wriggled around until she was as comfortable as she could make herself, she was getting very tired of this chair, pulled the crashweb over her and locked it in place. There might be some more quibbling, but Tibo had set the game and Picarefy would play it out, so she might as well be ready for what was probably going to be a rough ride.

Picarefy laid on the acceleration, feeling the flow begin to pile against the Limit. She drove as close as she could, translated to realspace, spat like a melon seed from the insplit, body straining, her passengers pasted into their chairs (she spared a fraction of herself to tend the chairs and keep her internal symbiote Skeen reasonably intact). Her own brain and body a silent scream of effort, she whipped through the point arc of the hyperbola, nose toward the harriers' tails like a comet whipping around a sun. She snapped down the shield, released the missiles, covered herself, wrestled herself around and scooted for the Limit.

She hit the Limit a hair ahead of half a dozen harrier missiles, dropped out and accelerated again until she was slicing the flow at her personal best.

Limit plus 15 seconds. Diminishing whistle of a message rat.

Limit plus 20 seconds. Twitch in the fabric. Scratch one harrier.

Limit plus 21 seconds. Twitch in the fabric. Scratch second harrier.

Limit plus 22 seconds. Glitch. Scratch one wasted missile. Mala Fortuna rain shit on that harrier and cover him with sores.

Limit plus 30 seconds. Diminishing whine of a rat.

What the hell? who's that for? First was to the snagger, this has to be for Abel Cidder. Ouch.

Limit plus 39 seconds. Powerful probes ranging the flow. Djabo's lazy gonads, as Skeen would say.

Limit plus 45 seconds. Disturbance in the flow. Harrier coming after her. Mala Mala Mala Fortuna, looks like he's got a reader.

Limit plus 50 seconds. Probe ranging stops, ripple coming behind, tracking her wake.

Limit plus 55 seconds. Ripple dropping back, but hanging on.

Picarefy cut some of the powerdrain to the shield, brought up the argrav to .6 g, set the mice to working, activated the medasource, everything as before, gnashed her nonexistent teeth at the persistence of that ripple in the flow. When the medasource had dealt with the wrenches, bruises and small rips invading the organic fabric of her passengers and her symbiote, (Timka took care of her own body as before, shifting twice and returning to her Pallah shape with all damage repaired), she made a throat-clearing sound. "Skeen."

Skeen yawned, blinked at the screen, saw nothing there. "So?"

"We've got a tail."

"Didn't you say . . ."

"Mostly I said I suffered from congestive ignorance. It's a visual tag. I couldn't get far enough fast enough to break clear. They've got a flow reader, Skeen, and he or she or whatever is the best I've seen, almost as good as me. I've got legs on that harrier but not enough to lose him before we hit The Shoals. As for the rest, two dead harriers and one wandering missile, ours, way behind and washed out, missed the third harrier, our tag, Mala Fortuna gift him with boils. Um. Dead or gone, those harriers got off half a dozen missiles. Bona Fortuna's pretty thumbs, they missed me by a hair. Tib, you were right about them, that wasn't your ordinary pack, reactions that fast when I popped out at them from a place they didn't expect. Ah, well, a hair's as good as an AU, considering."

Tibo drew his hand along his jaw, scowling at the play

of irridescence on the screen; Picarefy hadn't bothered throwing up schematics of the pursuing harrier. "You can lose him in The Shoals?"

"That I'm sure of. The turbulence there will cancel out the blip we're making in the flow. What I'm not sure of is getting out of the Shoals intact. I . . . do . . . not . . . like . . . that . . . place. It's apt to open a mouth that wasn't there a minute before and bite large pieces out of me. How'd you like to be the garnish for one of those pieces?"

Skeen snorted. "You're getting giddy, Pic. I think that shield is making you drunk."

"So?"

"Hmm. Spare a cell or two to fix dinner for us? It's been a while since we ate, me at least, I'm hungry."

"I hear and obey, O mistress sublime."

Minutes creeping past, changing imperceptibly into hours. The harrier is left farther and farther behind until its knot slides off the screen and out of Picarefy's perceptions, but neither she nor Skeen have any hope that it has given up the chase. Turbulence growing ahead, the flow knotty and swinging in dizzying swirls, enough to give one vertigo watching it. Picarefy is tense, afraid of that morass waiting for them, she slows, begins to curve away from the densest of the twists, slows yet more, tiptoes along, sensors ranging as far as she can reach, ready to swerve at the first sign of threat.

On and on, hours hanging imperceptibly into a day, a night, ship time, lights bright, dimmed, bright again. Threading between scattered knots and whorls, Picarefy with her elbows tucked in, her eyes wide and straining, hoping she'd cast the tail, unsure, pushing a little farther to make herself more certain, a little farther, a little. . . .

She slammed into a wall. Addled for an instant, she shivered, sparks leaping wildly, bits of her twisted and jarred, more breaks, blankness. Garfish on a sharkhook, struggling. . . .

"Pic!" Skeen's voice in the blankness, shouting a string of syllables that cued the mice and remotes to furious activity. By the time the snagfield had stabilized her in realspace, pinning her there with its enormous pseudo mass, Picarefy was almost back to full capacity.

Tibo was on his feet, acrobat still, tough and nimble, flashing from the bridge. He came back a few breaths later with a remote hauling a large locked case, hand weapons for the boarding fight. Ross was gathering himself, his face registering a raging helplessness, hands fisting and opening, he'd been through this before that time the Herren snagged him, took his ship and dropped him into Pillory. Timka stripped off her kimono, shifted to her cat-weasel form, the boarders coming after them might discount a beast. She couldn't do anything about the snagger, but she was going to make the Imperials pay for every inch of ground gained.

Picarefy did some fishtailing and twitching to test the strength of the hold, but the Hook was set solid. She wasn't going anywhere. The snagger was an anchor, holding her until the much slower mauler arrived to peel them open, until the harrier who'd tracked them and pointed them out to the snagger came up to watch the peeling. Snagships were shells built around the Hook and immense drives, (the newest snags were pushing at the limits of speed, even in the peculiarities of the insplit), they had no armaments or defenses, they needed neither. This snagship couldn't get at Skeen and the rest, but with the gravity sink between it and Picarefy, she couldn't get at it. If Petro's Shear didn't work, Cidder had them all and there was nothing they could do about it. The old Ykx had worked out a theoretical method of inducing waves of instability in the field that produced the gravity sink; they built the device, tested it, found it gulped power and couldn't be used for more than a few seconds, but it blew Hook generators seven times out of ten. With the help of Picarefy and her remotes, Lipitero had built and installed this device; they did some minor tests on it, enough to make sure it did SOMETHING when a twitch of power was run through it, but there was no guarantee the thing would work against a real rather than theoretical Hook.

Skeen frowned at the screen. The snagship, the pseudo mass and the surround were drawn in pale green contour

lines about a green square that represented Picarefy.
"Status, Pic?"

"Repairs complete, fuel level down, close to half mark.
Not much margin, Skeen."

"Petro's Shear?"

"Intact, whether it'll work or not . . ."

Skeen glanced at Tibo, bit her lip. "Ti, Ross, web in, I
don't know what the fuck's going to happen. Ready,
Pic?"

"Ready."

"Go."

Picarefy shuddered and shook, the surges pulsing
through her blinded her, pulled silent screams of deep
hurt from her tortured mind/brain; she concentrated on
holding herself together as the torment went on and on.

Skeen clung grimly to consciousness, driven alternately
into the chair and the web (the shaking was so intense it
produced a play where there should have been none),
mouth bleeding where she bit through her lip, nose bleeding, sphincters giving way. SOUND battered her. WILD
COLORS crawled out of the screen and wheeled round
her.

Tibo and Ross writhed and groaned, bled and leaked
from all orifices.

Timka was thrown into compulsive and uncontrolled
shifting, losing all sense of herself as individual. Parts of
her broke away, shook out through the web and went
into independent shifts, like drops of water flung from a
weightless swimball, tiny reflections of the main mass.
Bit by bit she oozed through the web and went caroming
about the bridge, flung apart, crawling painfully together,
drawn by bodyNEED into reforming the whole.

Picarefy noted this as she noted the rest of the damage
within her, she suffered for them all, but she couldn't do
anything about what was happening. She struggled to
keep awareness flowing through her body, drawing in
what data she could, keeping it reasonably free of distortion. She held on until she felt the snag field throb . . .
throb . . . THROB, felt it swelling, attenuating. . . .

She cut the Shear, kicked in the sublight drive and

scooted away, the edges of the snagfield yielding with the reluctance of old gelatin. As soon as she was completely clear, she pulled the shield over her though she continued to draw in data, swerved round a sucking sump and began easing out of The Shoals.

The throbbing stretching field reached critical, hung for an instant that seemed to last an eternity, then BURST. The field collapsed so suddenly that space itself seemed to implode, creating an expanding suck in realspace and insplit that tugged at Picarefy. But she was far enough away for the Ykx shield to deflect the suck, she dropped out and split for elsewhere as fast as her depleted fuel store would let her.

Skeen recovered first. "Status, Pic?"

"I'm running low on parts, Skeen. This is the third time I've had to sew myself together since we left the Veil. Fuel near redline, not much leeway on where I get topped off. Ah, Timka is in trouble, you'd better see what you can do about her. I'll deal with Tibo and Ross."

"What the fuck. . . ." Skeen clicked off the web and tumbled from the chair. She ran to Timka who was a shuddering amorphous lump, all the scattered bits had been resorbed but the Min was in Chorinya, being wrenched through uncontrollable shifts. "Pic, get me Ti's bag, fast." She caught hold of Pallah hands before they could change again, held onto them when they went boneless and slippery. Her grasp seemed to help Timka regain some sense of herself, the shifting slowed and became less radical. When the remote reached her, Skeen freed one hand, dug through the bag till she found what looked like a tuning fork, the thing Timka had used to stop the Min Skirrik boy's Chorinya, banged it against the remote and held the base to the next head that appeared, took it away, watched until she saw Ti's Pallah face, then she set the humming fork against it and held it there. The shapeless body quivered into shape, and the Pallah Timka lay panting on the floor. She sighed and managed a weary smile.

Skeen sat on her heels, the fork on her thigh. "It needs a bit more work. The Shear, I mean."

Timka looked up at her. "You could say that," she whispered. She started to push herself up, collapsed. "I think I'll stay here a while."

Skeen nodded. "Let me see if your quarters are in shape, then I'll whistle up a remote who'll ride you there. Want something to eat?"

"Some tea would be nice. Hot and sweet. Mostly, I want to sleep for a year or two."

"Wouldn't mind that myself." Snort of laughter. "After a bath."

Ross standing beside him, Tibo was talking to Picarefy, assessing damage. He looked around as Skeen came toward him, wiping at her nose, rubbing the dried blood off her lip. "Shook all over, but still together. Like us all."

She nodded. "Pic, what about Ti's cabin, it in shape so she can sack out for a while?"

"I tucked the cabins up before this started. Yes, right, I've got it unbuttoned, she can go over whenever she's ready."

"Good. She needs a remote, she can't walk it yet. What about some tea?"

Ripple of laughter. "Can I bribe you all with tea? Hit the shower-room. Please."

"On my way. Coming, Tib?"

He slid from the chair, stretched, groaned. "Aaahhh, I feel like Cidder's tiny feet have tromped all over me and him wearing spike heels." He followed Skeen to the flow tube, put his hand on her back just above the swell of her buttocks. She leaned against him, sighed with pleasure at the warmth of his hand, reached behind him and brushed the sensor. They WENT to the shower-room, stepped inside.

Tibo wrapped his arms around her, pulled her tight against him. "A good day to have behind us." He chuckled. His breath was warm on her shoulder. "Cidder will be curling round the edges."

"Maybe he'll spontaneously combust."

"Fortuna would never be that Bona for us, luv. Mmf, you're my heart and all that, Skeen. . . ." He patted her buttock, moved away and began to strip.

*   *   *

"We're redlining it right now, Skeen. Twenty lights more and I'm running on empty."

"What's available around here?"

Starfield schematic, assorted symbols. Three green squares marking Pit Stops. A dozen yellow dots marking refueling stations dedicated to Company shiplines (they'd occasionally sell to transients if properly bribed). Nine red dots, scattered along the nearest edge of the Cluster, military depots.

"We'd better avoid the Pits," Tibo said. "And not just because we can't afford the fees. I wouldn't be surprised if Cidder was primed for sending a snatch team into a Pit after us if we went to ground in one. It'd make a lot of trouble for Cluster traders who use the Pits, but me, I think he's hot enough to chance it."

Skeen nodded. "Wish I didn't agree with you, but I do." She scowled at the yellow dots. "Fuckin' vultures."

Tibo leaned over the back of her chair, moved his fingertips in slow circles over her head, down her neck, along her shoulders and back. "Don't matter, luv," he said, "we won't be buying fuel or fiends. Pick a target and we'll jack him."

She sighed with pleasure as his hands continued to massage her. "You're relaxing me so much, I'm going to sleep. Mmmm. The nearest is that one at Potheree. We don't pass that way very often so we won't be laying mines for our own feet. What do you think, Pic?"

"It's small, lax and most of all close."

"Let's do it, then."

Hemallassar Harmon ran the fueling station at Potheree; that is to say, he was nominally in charge of its legitimate functions and personnel, answerable to the HomeOffice that owned the facility and the small airless world that housed it. Nominally in charge, because he paid almost no attention to those functions and personnel, spending most of his time on his hobbies and the collecting of credit sufficient to maintain them. He was a Gamesman whose dream was creating a living world in miniatures. He had genstructed miniature plants, piscians, crusta-

ceans, assorted mammals (vast herds of prey beasts, finger-
long tigers and other predators, bird species ranging from
songbirds the size of mosquitoes to vultures with the
wingspan as wide as his hand); after a century and a half
of labor and vast expenditure he had an ecologically
stable, self-reproducing world two kilometers wide under
a dome just over the horizon from the station. Until now
he'd played his games there with tiny androids, but these
were expensive, always breaking down at tense moments,
spoiling the scenario for Harmon, wrenching him out of
his dream. And they didn't bleed, die or feel real pain,
only simulated these. Most unsatisfying. He was attempt-
ing to genstruct miniatures of the various types of sentients he used in his Games. To pay for all this he'd set
up illegal fleshlabs on the far side of the world, where his
mechanics did surgery on those too notorious to venture
into the Tank Farms, created monsters to order for use
as bodyguards or victims, restructured contract workers
bound for worlds where their current shapes would make
them inefficient (their consent or lack thereof being ignored as beside the point), ran cloning services to cater
to the unhealthier appetites of assorted power brokers,
anyone who needed a certain amount of privacy about
his or her habits. As Picarefy ghosted up to the fueling
satellite, he was in his genlab, talking with the head
mechanic about the crew's progress toward his latest
goal.

"We're having real trouble with brain capacity. You
want a speech center, self-awareness, a degree of sen-
tience, and physical agility. That's a lot to ask from a
brain the size of a macadamia nut."

Harmon poked at a rubbery pink infant about the heft
of a mouse, a male whose type Ross would have recognized with a shudder, a miniature Herren lacking that
species' intimidating and antagonizing energy. It was le-
thargic, with no intelligence in the dull watery eyes. "I
see."

"The skull cavity is simply too small to allow for adequate complexity. To get around that, we're thinking of
providing a secondary brain, probably sited in the buttocks. The secondary would handle mobility and auto-

nomic functions, leaving the cranial brain for sensory input, thought and speech, so on. In those miniature bodies the distance between the two brains won't be a factor we have to consider. So what you'd have would be legions of fat-arsed soldiers with an additional vulnerability, at the moment we haven't got a practical way of protecting the buttocks brain. Even with the two brains, you shouldn't expect too much out of them. You might consider hive-minding them by socketing them into a computer. You could leave the leaders loose to provide a wisp or two of free will."

Harmon used his fingertip to push the baby about, then picked it up. "This is useless. Try the secondary brain, we'll see how that works." He carried the mute creature to another section of the lab, dropped it into a nid of landcrabs, stayed a moment to watch it being torn apart then went gloomily back to his games on his worldboard. His disappointment was such that he had to demolish three android towns and a small army before he settled to serious gaming.

"At the service hatch." Tibo's words came through the speakers on the bridge, a soft mutter from a throat pickup, transferred through the Lander to Picarefy, the Lander snugged behind a ridge rising beyond the armored dome which housed the crew and computers that controlled the fuel transfers from the feed Burr in synchronous orbit above the dome.

"Alarm bypassed."

Skeen sighed, still annoyed because Tibo had talked her into staying behind, letting him and Rostico Burn handle the crew. You're too well known, he said. What about you? she said. More men with their own ships, he said, not saying it's right, just that it's so. Bigger pool of possibilities. Nonsense, she said. You think you're going to fool Cidder about who took the fuel? You're getting back at me for making you sit and wait. Watch that paranoia, luv, he said. All right, all right, she said, go have your fun.

"Hatch open, going in."

                    *   *   *

Three men standing duty watch in the authorizing chamber. Two sitting at a table, playing a desultory game of grott. The third was on his side on a rutted couch, knees drawn up, face turned to the wall, his breathing slow and loud in a silence filled with small regular sounds from the computers and lifesupport.

The door slid open. The grott players looked up without much interest, expecting to see a familiar face.

"Keep it like it is." Tibo's voice was a husky growl, he spoke through a distorter in the mask that covered his head; owl-round holes filled with one-way glass concealed his eyes. He held a burner in his left hand, thumb on the sensor. Rostico Burn wore a similar mask; he stood a step behind Tibo, a burner in his right hand, a stunner in his left. He took a step aside so he could have clear lines on the three.

The man facing Tibo lay down his cards. He was a tall lean Shartzer, a stubble of whisker covering his face from eyes to chin. Red patches stained his dark skin, the end of his nose; he pressed his thin lips together and glared at Tibo. For a breath or two the situation balanced on a pin point, then the Shartzer drew a deep breath and the stiffness went out of his body.

Tibo waggled the burner at him. "Feel like dying for the Company?"

The Shartzer shrugged. "No."

Picarefy nosed up to one of the Burr's spines, positioned her flank to receive the umbilical, dropped the shield and sent a beep to Tibo.

"Start processing. There's a ship at the Burr, top her up."

"You're in shit to your neck, chirk. The Company will come after you, can't run from it, it'll get you."

Tibo answered with a jerk of his burner.

The Shartzer stood, strolled to the control board; he glanced at Tibo and Rostico Burn, shrugged and tapped in the release code.

The umbilical snaked out, socked home into Picarefy's fuel feed. The precarious uncertain shift began from the

Burr's massive bunkers—not quite a flow, not quite an instantaneous translation. Picarefy purred with satisfaction as her stomach filled and a new vigor coursed through her.

Beep in Tibo's ear. "Enough," he said. "Back off."

The Shartzer tapped in the close code. Another jerk of the burner. He returned to his seat. "What now?"

Rostico Burn turned the stunner on him, tapped his thumb on the triggersensor. Two more taps and the other men were laid out, the third without waking; whatever he was on, it had a powerful hold.

"Right," Tibo murmured into the throat pickup, "crew under. We're on our way back."

SOME STEPS BACK IN TIME AND SOME DEGREES DISTANT IN SPACE, WE LOOK IN ON THE COLONY TRANSPORT.

Giulin fidgeted. The Zem-trallen, Marrin fej and Lipitero were talking to the tall alien called Hopeless. He didn't have anything to say to them, nor they to him. Bohalendas was fiddling with his boxes, looking up now and then to gaze with fascination at the swirls of pallid color flowing across the screen. They were in a smallish room; the inner side was a flat square wall, the outer was a long angular curve, multiply faceted with the viewing screen like a window set in the center of the bulge. The room was bare, a few benches, some chairs bolted down, a rough drugget on the floor, foot trails worn in it, little attempt beyond a coat of paint to soften the sense of being locked inside an odd-shaped metal box. Voices acquired a metallic tinge and subtle, nearly imperceptible echoes. To hear what was being said, you had to be close to the speaker, otherwise the words would be so chopped up, so distorted, fall so dead on the ear, you couldn't understand a thing. Giulin fingered his imager. He'd already got enough images of this room and the people in it, he wanted to get out, go below and visit the colonists, see how they were getting on, get images of people beginning to adjust to this strangeness. He wanted to see how they were being treated, how much room they had and how their living spaces were arranged. He was in a four-sleeper cubicle with the Zem-trallen, Marrin and Bohalendas; it was barely big enough for them to turn round in. The bunks were hard and too narrow, furnished with pallets that grew harder every hour you slept on them, at least his did, and from the sounds in there during the shipnight—how odd to think of night as something arbitrarily determined by whoever ran the ship— the others weren't all that comfortable either.

The tiny alien, Virgin, came wandering in, talking and laughing with quavers in the air that swept along beside her. Giulin didn't quite know what to make of her. She might be crazy or this might be some weird alien behavior that was perfectly sensible when looked at from the viewpoint of her peers, certainly the tall one was unperturbed by it. He moved warily closer, lifted his imager, waiting for the pattern of line and expression that suited his eye, growing bolder when she didn't seem to see him even when he stood directly in front of her. He followed her about, entering images onto the matrix with a swift flurry of touches.

She smiled at him, held out her hand. He stumbled back several steps, startled. Her mouth moved but no sound came out; a moment later, slightly off sync, a Voice spoke behind him, "Bored, young artist?"

Giulin swallowed, frightened a little but also indignant at the condescension implicit in the words. "Oh, no," he said. "How could I be?"

Basso giggle, an absurdity sufficient to restore his equanimity, though he didn't quite know how to react to invisibilities speaking behind him while a visible enigma mouthed silently in front of him. Courtesy urged him to turn and face the speaker, but he knew in his bones there was no one there. Besides, wherever the Voice sounded, there was a real question about who or what was talking. "Come along," the Voice said, "they won't miss you. We'll show you the holds where the volunteers are stashed. You'll want images of them, won't you? Sure you will." Virgin reached up and put her hand on his arm, nodded gravely, then she turned and ambled out again.

Giulin glanced around, shrugged and followed her, a disconcerting mix of laughter and whispers trailing along behind him. He couldn't separate out all the voices though he thought he could recognize six different speakers which confused him even more since he'd in a way come to terms with the bass voice, accepting it as the expression of Virgin's thought. Six, though, even more, it was enough to addle any reasonable Ykx.

She led him to a dimly lit hole filled with noises that seemed to echo from eternity. He came from a cave-dwelling species, at least that was what he told himself, but that was then and then was millennia and millennia and millennia ago, and now was a bad-smelling hole filled with scratchy creaks and deep shuddering groans. Not enticing. She looked over her shoulder with that charming meaningless smile, beckoned to him. "Catch hold," the Voice said, "g-free slide, ride it down." She pushed off from the sill, drifting up until she could catch hold of a loop attached to a moving chain. Eyes wide, he stumbled after her, had to deal forcibly with a stomach in revolt as the weightlessness hit him, and only remembered to catch hold of a loop after one of them hit him in the head.

It wasn't at all like soaring, but after he got used to the noise and the odd sensations in his interior, he started to enjoy the ride. He gave a small tentative whoop and grinned as it echoed away down the tube and came back at him. There was more laughter around him and several of the voices wove their own whoops in and out of the echoes. He started whistling a jingle he learned when he was a cub and the voices joined him, improvising harmonies of their own.

He tumbled from the tube swaddled in laughter and snatches of song, Virgin dancing round him with a bright-eyed exuberance that convinced him (though he wasn't so much thinking as reacting) that if she was crazy, more people should be skewed that way.

The first hold was a vast cylinder divided into a maze of pipes and gratings with solid panels thrown in to provide sleeping cubicles where the travelers could get a measure of privacy. Already Ykx cubs were making themselves thoroughly at home, g-pull being half what they were used to, they were playing tag through the pipes, swinging from level to level, spreading their downy flight-skins and soaring for short hops, laughing, whistling, shouting, chanting count rhymes, playing with the echoes. Tweeners were scattered in small groups, some gathered around habold players, dancing and singing, others worked off their energy in races through the crooked lanes between the cubicles, some were pairing off, talking intensely in whispers. Adults were stretched out on tumppads, dozing, reading, thinking, or they sat in groups drinking iska, reminiscing or speculating about what was waiting for them, or they exercised in groups or alone, working off surplus energy. The lighting was clever, areas of creamy glow, other areas of shadow, light shifting with dark, slowly but continually (except in those few spots where a reader had flipped on an auxiliary light), the eye never tired because there were always new shapes, textures, intensities to look at, something to break up the stark stiff horizontals and verticals and mitigate the deadening effect of so much metal. Giulin turned to Virgin. "Did you plan this . . . ah this stage effect?"

She knew what he meant, nodded. The bass Voice chuckled behind him. "Amazing what one can do with such recalcitrant materials."

Giulin blinked. "Yes," he said, uncertain what attitude he should take. He sucked in a breath, got his imager ready, took a few panorama shots then plunged into the noisy busy hold to get closer more detailed images, forgetting everything else in his fascination with the task.

UNLIKE PICAREFY'S HECTIC JOURNEY (HECTIC IN
THE FIRST PART, THOUGH THE LATER LEGS
PROVED MORE SEDATE), THE TRANSPORT
TOOTLED PEACEFULLY ALONG. AT FIRST
ZELZONY HELD HERSELF APART FROM THE
COLONISTS, SPENDING HOURS WATCHING
THE CONVOLUTED FLOW OF FAINT COLOR
IN THE COMMONROOM SCREEN, TALKING
OCCASIONALLY WITH BOHALENDAS, THOUGH
HE SPENT MOST OF HIS TIME WANDERING
ABOUT THE BRIDGE AND THE ENGINE ROOMS,
USING LIPITERO TO QUESTION HOPELESS.
LATER, ZELZONY DESCENDED TO THE HOLD,
SEARCHING FOR SOME CLUE THAT WOULD
HELP HER UNDERSTAND HOW THESE
APPARENTLY SANE AND SENSIBLE FOLK COULD
DO SOMETHING SO EXTRAORDINARY AS LEAVE
BEHIND FOREVER EVERYTHING THEY KNEW
AND HELD DEAR. GIULIN SPENT THE FIRST PART
OF THE VOYAGE IN THE FIVE HOLDS, ENTERING
HUNDREDS OF IMAGES TO THE MATRICES
THE KINRAVALY HAD PROVIDED, TALKING TO
OTHER TWEENERS AND SOMETIMES TO THE
ADULTS, PLAYING EXUBERANT GAMES WITH
VIRGIN AND HER VOICES, FLINGING HIMSELF
AFTER HER THROUGH THE SEVERAL TRANSPORT
TUBES. HE SLOWED DOWN SOME AS THE
DAYS PASSED, SPENT MORE TIME READING,
BEGINNING TO UNDERSTAND WHAT THE ZEM-
TRALLEN HAD PASSED ON TO HIM FROM
THE ALIENS, THAT TRAVEL IN A STARSHIP WAS

A LOT LIKE SITTING FOR A LONG TIME IN A SMALL ROOM WITH NOTHING MUCH TO LOOK AT.

AFTER SIXTY-SEVEN DAYS HOPELESS BROUGHT THE TRANSPORT INTO REALSPACE AND SLID IT INTO ORBIT ABOUT A CINDER OF A WORLD.

PART VI: THROUGH THE GATE

Lipitero stood beside Zelzony watching a world turn in the screen, a dead cinder of a world moving past beneath them. "That was once Surranal, the Nagamar homeworld," she murmured. "It was a waterworld, green and wet and hot. Timka told me that in the Tanul Lumat, that's a university of sorts, a museum of sorts, a lot of things, anyway, in the Tanul Lumat they have ancient Naga carvings and tapestries showing Naga memories of Surranal. It was a lush, beautiful place before the Six Year War." She sighed. "Hopeless has had a message from Skeen. She's out and clear, she'll be here in two or three days. Kildun Aalda is five days on." She held up her hands. They were trembling. "Five days. Six maybe. And I'm home. And I'm home with Ykx to fill the Gathers."

Zelzony only half-listened to Lipitero. She was thinking more of Rallen and what the coming years would do to it. Nothing would be the same. Even when she got back from this useless trip, she couldn't be sure she'd find the world she left. The Kinravaly had rented Workhorse, paying for it with some of the Great Treasures in the Kinravaly's Horde, masterpieces collected over the millennia since the Ykx had been on Rallen. What good will treasures do us if we die, she said, it isn't as if they'll be destroyed. Very much on the contrary, so Skeen tells me. But they won't be ours, Zelzony said, they won't be

here. They are the heritage of our species, Zo. A part of
that heritage, Zeli. Only a part. Tell me, my love, tell me
if you can, what use are treasures to a nation of ghosts?
With that tug we can mine our asteroids, the aliens say
some of them are almost pure iron, our Seekers confirm
the possibility. We gain far more than we lose by this
trade, Zel Zeli. It's not exaggerating much to say we can
have space flight in ten years, my Zel, our own tugs. In
twenty, who knows where we'll be. Ah, Zo, Zelzony
thought, ah, Zo, she wanted to say, it isn't as easy as
that. You can't separate out a single strand of endeavor
and keep it pure. In ten years we might have our own
tugs, in ten years we might have war. Do you have any
notion how bad things are getting in Urolol, how explosive that situation is? Do you have any notion how far
the infection from there has spread through workers everywhere? Even Itekkillykx workers are restless and unhappy. They aren't content to be what they were born to
be, not any longer; they can turn ugly at the blink of an
eye. Do you remember telling me that honors mean
more than achievement to our managerials? You're going
to have your hands full of displaced managerials, Zo.
Once this space ranging gets started, they won't be about
to cope, they won't have the flexibility of mind, and I
might be one of those, saa saa, all this gives me a headache that won't go away. Yeasty times! tchah. So many
angry Ykx. We've always comforted ourselves with the
proved notion that Ykx may get angry and thump each
other now and then, but they don't kill, that Gurns and
Gurn-sets can argue and reach the point of explosion,
but they explode into boycotts and attacks against property, they don't fight wars. Where's that comfort now
when three Ykx have tortured and killed for the pleasure
in it? Are they sports thrown off the main line of development, sterile failures, at least none of them had any
children. No official children. Are there others out there
with that heritage and ignorant of it? Are Peeper, Eshkel
and Laroul harbingers of genetic change? Are there hundreds, perhaps thousands, among us with that capacity
for savagery who don't know it themselves because for
one reason or another it hasn't been triggered in them?
What's going to happen in Urolol? In Marallat? What

are we going to do about them? Borrentye thinks he's
getting somewhere in Marallat, that he's going to be able
to displace Sulleggen and her pets with a minimum of
distress, but he's got nothing to work with in Urolol. The
Consortium won't budge a hair's breadth and the workers have mocked his efforts, he has nightmares of a
bloodbath one day soon, there's too much hate, too
much fear, the place is too polarized. I suppose we'll
have to wait till it happens then do our best to patch
things together. Aliens, ayy All-Wise, look what happened when a few came down on us, there'll be more of
them now that we're found. This first bunch is friendly,
probably honest enough, though who can say that for
sure even now? but what will the next bunch be like?
What will they do to us? Ah, Zo, I'm supposed to handle
this, how can I? Hmmm. Bohalendas is riding this wind
easily enough, well, he's an easy-going sort, not much
interested in anything outside his field. Have to talk to
Selyays, get an angversen group ready to evaluate alien
artifacts, alien ways of thinking, we'll need one of those
translators, saa saa, Zel, scratch a reminder on your ear,
you don't like thinking about all the confusion out here,
but you won't be able to get away from it, so a translator for the Kinravaly Rallen and the Zem-trallen. What
are they going to do to us, my Zo? All these aliens. Ahh,
I was placating my guilts when I brought young Giulin
along. My undermind could be brighter than my intellect. He comes from Seekers and managerials, he's no
rebel or malcontent and has no intention of leaving Rallen,
but he's at ease here, with the colonists and the aliens
both, he's made friends with the weird one called Virgin,
he uses the shipways as if he'd been born to them. Might
be a useful thing to gather angversen groups of Tweeners.
Use Giulin to help with this, saa saa; if I'd been thinking, perhaps I could have talked the aliens into bringing a
dozen tweeners along for the ride. No use regretting
what can't be helped. Ay All-Wise, I dreamed of soaring
starflight, but that was controlled soaring, on our own
terms, at our own pace. A dream. A nightmare now.
Control? Saaa.

    She scowled at the world cinder turning below them

and shivered. We are Ykx. We ARE Ykx. We are YKX. That will not happen to us.

Picarefy came swimming round the sun and wiggled into orbit beside the transport, Skeen's face bloomed in the screen on the transport's bridge.

"Ta, Hopeless. How's things?"

"Ta, Skeen. Damn quiet. Virgin's enjoying herself, but me, I'm about to rot."

"Mmf. Things are going to get hectic soon enough. I came round by Kildun Aalda. Fuckin' Junks, they've cleared the planet all right, but they've left behind a snagship and a couple maulers, I don't know what for, that world is starting to smoke. Hooo, Hopeless, we're going to have to go in when the Gate's nightsided or we'll fry."

"Try for a sneak?"

Skeen grinned. "Nooo. Petro came up with some neat little tricks. By the way, tell her the Shear worked but it was rather hard on Pic and us. Anyway, give me a five-hour headstart and don't hurry a lot coming after me, Pic will squirt the specs over to get you there when the Gate is in the twilight zone. We don't want to hang around waiting for the world to turn. I should've knocked off that snagger by then and got the maulers out of action. I'll take the Lander down and mark the spot for you to set down. Um, you'd better get the Ykx ready to go; you're going to have to get them out in a little short of twelve hours."

"No problem. You know, I like them, these Ykx, they don't screw around messing up like most species I come across. Pass me the specs, this is some thing we're doing, Skeen, but believe me, I want it over with. Virgin and me, we've decided we're going to use the rest of the gelt endowing University with Xeno scholarships, then start looking about for something interesting to do."

"Keep a little for me, eh? I've got a shield for you like nobody's seen, fool all but the best and luckiest of the flow readers."

"Ah, well, that's different, but you know I have to talk to Virgin and the Abode before I get fancy."

"Right. Where you want to meet?"

"Sundari. Cidder won't stick his long nose in there. I assume you kicked him in the nuts again and he'll be steaming around hunting for a way to get his teeth in you."

"So I did and so he is, far as I know. What's the Eye say?"

"Sundari, that's all."

"Ready?"

"Shoot." A soft crackle of arriving data, a beep when the flow was done. "Got it. See you down on Aalda."

"Ta."

Five days later, Hopeless translated to realspace, located the crippled Honjiukum maulers and eased round them in a wide half-circle. She listened a moment to the messages they were exchanging, grimaced. "That's one crazy mad bunch of Junks, Virgin. How long before reinforcements arrive?" She listened a moment, nodded. "Good enough, we should be out by then." She listened again. "I know, but that's Skeen. You got to take her as she is or let her alone. I'd bet she did her quota and more getting clear of Cidder's lice and couldn't bring herself to plink another can." She listened. "Uh-huh, looks like that shield's worth at least half what she's going to sting us for it." She listened. "Yes. Got it. Here we go."

The beacon from the surface was getting louder and firmer every moment. Hopeless glanced nervously at the swollen unhealthy sun with its continual small flares. "Look at that mess, sheeeyah, Virgin, I wouldn't put down dayside on a bet." She listened. "Yeah, I know. It's going to be a little hell even at night." She began concentrating fiercely on the readouts, nodding an occasional acknowledgment as the Virgin trilled, mouthed, muttered and otherwise conveyed data and instruction to her.

Skeen left Picarefy in orbit with Tibo and a rebellious Rostico Burn aboard to watch for swarming Junks, and came down, battered by winds and lightning, to a landing more precarious than she liked, hitting ground harder than was good for the Lander. She started the beacon, sat rubbing at her ribs where the safety straps had caught her. "My hide is going to be a crazy quilt when these bruises have a chance to develop." The Gate was open, sending out its Call, reminding her of the dance it put her through the first time she jumped it running from a Junk hunting pack. "This will be over in a few more hours. Hoosh, I need some playtime."

"I suppose," Timka said absently. She'd done her shifts, got rid of her own small hurts and was Pallah again in pants, tunic, sandals. Her skin was rippling, the ripples matching the Gate Call's throb. That Call was painful, but no more so than the indecision that tugged her two ways at once. She stared blankly at the screen. A powerful wind blew outside, driving the silky dust before it, pale dust lit by the aurora's erratic dance and the lightning that punctuated the minutes as she and Skeen waited for the transport to arrive. She couldn't see the Gate and the nearest ruins were shrouded by the dust; more than dust shrouded the way she'd take from here, two tracks for her, dividing at the Gate. If she stayed this side, she'd have Skeen as sponsor, expediting her way through the universe of the Pits. Or the universe beyond the Pits, if she chose that route. She knew enough now to realize the value of the promise of help Skeen made her back when all this started. And she'd picked up several offers of employment from people she'd met in Sundari Pit. The possibilities were enormous and exciting. She wanted that life and she was going to have it. Sometime. Now? That was the question. If she jumped to Mistommerk, Lifefire solo knew when she could jump back and what she'd find on Aalda when she did. She had no doubt that the Ykx would open the Gate for her, she'd earned anything they chose to give her in the succeeding years and being Ykx they were good at paying debts. I've done it, she thought. I've made up my mind. When did it happen? How did I do it without realizing it? Going home. Going. Home. She'd come away before without really making a break from her roots, drifting, yes, that was it, letting events pull her along because she saw no viable alternative. Oh, yes, Min, wasn't that what you'd been doing all your life? Drift? You never cared enough about anything to fight for it, not even yourself. Habit

and circumstances. Yes. No more. It was time she took
possession of her past, her world, the place she ought to
have in both. Then she could turn her back on all that
and take possession of the promise here. Crossing to
Mistommerk might mean decades over there, however
long it took for Kildun Aalda to cool and the Junks to
retake and remake it, but she had time; some Min lived
for centuries and she meant to be one of those. Going
home. After all this time, after all that had happened,
after a hundred decisions made one way or another that
unmade themselves after a sleep or two, it was done, it
was finally done. She was mildly surprised to find herself
convinced she knew, irrevocably unquestionably, where
she was going, now that she was up against the edge and
had to play or back off. Going home. Facing Telka and
kicking her where it hurt, teaching her not to be stupid
any more. Well, no. Stupidity is an incurable disease,
isn't it? Djabo's feeble brain, as Skeen would say, this
agonizing over come or go wasn't worth the sweat it
wrung out of me. She sighed and put aside those fidgeting memories. All they'd give her was a pain in the gut
and wind in the head.

Repellers flaring, whipping the powdery white dust
into ever greater frenzies the transport drifted overhead
then sank with ponderous dignity to the valley floor, its
weight driving it down and down into the earth until the
lower third was buried. Free electricity danced dangerously around the metal flanks of the transport until Hopeless scraped them clear and spun the charge away, drawing
after it the pall of dust, temporarily clearing the air about
the ship.
On the bridge Lipitero was shivering. Even through all
that metal she could feel the Gate's Call throbbing in her
bones. Her jaws trembled. She couldn't speak.
Zelzony watched the screen (dark ghostly lines of wind-
driven dust intermittently lit by jags of lightning and
changing tints leached from the auroras whipping hugely
across the hidden sky), feeling awe and a touch of fear.
In a moment or two she would be setting foot on alien
soil, one of the first Rallykx to do so since the Landing
on Rallen; despite the scouring gale she wanted urgently

to be out there. Part of her restlessness was the Calling of the Gate, yet only a part. Zelzony rubbed thumb against fingers. Alien soil. No, don't think of it, think of the Gate. Lipitero had warned her about the Call, had warned all of them and Skeen had underlined what she said. It will net you like a fisher nets a school and pull you in and there's nothing you can do to fight it—don't waste your energy, go with the flow. It's all true, Zelzony thought, all these places and people I never quite believed in. In a few breaths, she'd see this Stranger's Gate, she'd step through it and look around so she could report to Zuistro on actualities rather than emotional certainties. She gazed at the screen and began dreaming again, dreaming of the time when Rallen would have other Gates, when Rallykx would go soaring in and out of them, free as the winds outside; she shivered, that simile wasn't exactly comforting when she looked at the scourbath of dust waiting for them, an Ykx caught in that would be driven by the wind's will, not her own. Ah, well, there was a green and pleasant world beyond that dust, and cousins waiting there for them. Improbable fantastic story, improbably fantastically true.

A courtesy beep sounded and Hopeless cleared a cell in the center of the dust storm, greeted Skeen and said, "I wouldn't like to repeat this landing when the weather's bad."

"Try it in a lander, you'll learn the real meaning of insecurity. Your passengers ready to move?"

"Soon's they get the signal. I'm going to break out some spare cable, otherwise who knows how many we'll lose to the wind. My gauges here say fifty km gusting to seventy. How close is that thing?"

"Any closer and you'd be sitting on it. Your forward lock is about twenty meters away. I've got the exact point plotted, when you give me the go, I'll shoot it over to you. Um, you're probably feeling the Call."

"Some. Virgin?" She listened. "Virgin says it makes her skin itch and the Eye has got the twitches. She wants to be one of those who crosses. You mind?"

"None of my business to say who goes and who don't. Listen, that cable of yours, have a couple remotes stretch it to the post and lintel arrangement that marks the Gate this side and anchor it, fix it so you can shoot pulses of current through it, something that will jolt but not crisp whoever catches hold of it. I was caught in that call and I couldn't break it even when it was scaring the shit out of me, and it wasn't a tenth that powerful then. Um. Let me know when the cable's up, I'm not moving till it's ready."

"I hear. Consider it done."

Breather mask on, muffled to the eyebrows to keep out as much dust as she could, Skeen let the Gate take her and lead her through the ruins; she stumbled into the cable, felt the mild shock and smiled when it temporarily muted the compulsion. After following the cable to the Gate, she plunged through and jerked off the mask. The glade hadn't changed in the past two years, though it was night now, not morning as it was when she and Timka left, a cool quiet spring night with a crescent moon just above the treetops. She wiped a hand across her face, stood slapping the mask against her sides, driving out spurts of powdery dust as Timka came lunging through, arms outstretched, eyes jammed shut behind the lenses of her mask. The little Min stripped, snapped into bird form and jumped clear of the cloud of dust she left behind. When she was Pallah again, she looked at her clothing, wrinkled her nose and grew a neat coat of silver-gray fur instead of getting dressed. She glanced at Skeen, but said nothing; she started prowling about the glade, her green eyes turning and turning, taking in the stiff silent trees, the white wall glistening off toward the west. Skeen saw her shiver as the Ever-Hunger reached for them both, she could feel it tugging at her and she knew Timka was more sensitive to it than she was, but the seductive compulsion had a tentative, rather lacka-daisical feel, the Hunger had gorged royally two years ago when Lipitero loosed it on Telka and her followers, growing immense and sated, then the Sydo Ykx spanked it and slapped it back behind that prison wall. As a result, the greed and need weren't quite what they were when Skeen jumped the Gate the first time. Timka reached up, touched a spray of leaves, rubbed a foot across the grass, an odd bemused look on her face. Finding out there's no going home, I suppose; I couldn't wear this world for six months, given my choice. "Any of your cousins hanging about?"

Timka started, twisted her head around, moonglow glistening on wide eyes. "None close enough to bother us."

"What about the Ykx? I thought they'd be swarming around here when the Gate opened."

"They are. They're watching us now. Waiting. Hoping. Afraid to hope too much."

Skeen fished in a pocket, pulled out a beeper. "Then I'd better signal Hopeless to send Lipitero and the Zemtrallen through. The sooner we get this organized the sooner we can get the fuck out of here."

Timka watched Skeen pull the mask on again, then lean through the Gate, her head and torso vanishing into the swirls of dust. The Ever-Hunger started whining at her again, flesh in the Gate seemed to stimulate it; she ignored its tug and began shaking out her clothing.

Skeen drew back into the glade. "Five minutes."

Timka nodded. She got rid of the fur and pulled on her trousers, ran her thumb along the closure, then pulled the tunic over her head. She dropped to the grass and sat cross-legged, gazing into the shifting darkness under the trees. All her certainties were gone, evaporated, that irrevocable decision made in the Lander proved as evanescent as all the other ones. Here she was, home. In her own Mountains. It didn't feel like home. Everything was familiar, yes, the smells, textures, the look of things, even the one thing she'd never thought to include in her list of sense impressions, the pull of Mistommerk on her body. (Do fish ever wonder about water? She didn't think so. She never thought about gravity. A silent tickling giggle. Not something for after dinner conversation. Gravity. It was just there, like water was there for a fish). Yet . . . she had a puzzled sense that everything about her had acquired a patina of strangeness. She seemed to have imported it with her. Yes. I'm what has changed; I don't see with the same eyes. She closed her eyes, tried to regain that unthinking acceptance of home that was hers not so long ago. Maybe I just need a little

time, maybe in a senn't or so I'll relax into inattention
again and the strangeness will be gone. She sighed. She'd
been so busy celebrating the way she'd grown, she hadn't
stopped to think what that might mean when she came
home.

Lipitero was the first through; Zelzony came after,
then Bohalendas dragging a trolley with his cases on it,
then Virgin and Giulin. Spitting and coughing, the Ykx
unwound improvised wrappings and slapped dust out of
their fur. The Hunger stirred, reached for them. Zelzony
looked up, startled, Lipitero ignored it, Bohalendas didn't
seem to notice it. Tongue clicking, eyes wide, her tiny
bitterbrown body naked and sleek, apparently the dust
had flowed around her without settling, Virgin ambled
about the glade, head tilted to inspect the silent unmov-
ing trees, then the clear night sky with its spray of stars
and ascending crescent moon. Her the Hunger ignored;
like the dust, it flowed around her without touching her.
She moved to the edge of the deeper night under the
trees, stood staring into the darkness and chattering in
tone ripples with her accompanying Invisibilities.
Eyes still watering, Giulin threw off his wrappings and
worked excitedly to clear his imager of the film sealed
about it. If he felt the touch of the Hunger, he brushed it
aside like a pesky gnat, too concentrated on his work to
have time for anything else. He rubbed at his eyes,
peered through the viewfinder, began entering images
onto the matrix, Skeen squatting stolidly beside the Gate,
stone patient, face unreadable, Timka beside her, leaning against one of the Gateposts, Virgin from the back,
like a small strange idol carved from a brown tight-
grained stone, silhouetted against a pale gray tree trunk,
Bohalendas unpacking his cases close to the Gate, working with meticulous care, his face intent, Zelzony with
head lifted looking wary and expectant, Lipitero waiting. . . .
Virgin laughed and ran across the glade to squat beside
Skeen.
Two Ykx stepped from the thick blackness under the
trees. A tall bronze and a shorter smoke. Lipitero moved
away from Zelzony, stopped. For a long moment she and
the newcomers stared at each other then the stiffness

broke in a whirl of flightskins, laughter, tears, shouted questions that never got answered.

"One thousand," Lipitero said. "Adults and children. Poets and farmers, med-techs and soardancers, more, so much more. Chosen by lot out of a throng ten times a thousand." She turned, beckoned to Zelzony and when the Zem-trallen reached them said, "Affery and Charda of Sydo Gather, know Zelzony Zem-trallen of Rallen, representative of the Kinravaly Rallen, here to be sure we're not slavers selling Rallykx on the block."

Affery extended his hand, fingertips curled up, claws retracted. "Be welcome and doubly welcome to Mistommerk, Zem-trallen. We hoped our sister would succeed, but O such a wild, long chance."

Zelzony inclined her head, moving stiffly. "You can thank the honesty of your ambassador; Kinravaly Rallen sponsored Lipitero because she was so transparently true." She glanced at the moon. "Time is pressing. The otherside will be unbearable come daylight and we have to unload a thousand Ykx plus their gear. How do you want to do this?"

First came a remote pulling a barge that carried enough collapsed wings and support packs for a hundred colonists, with spare wings for the locals, cases of seeds and ova, packs of rekkagourds with Rallykx history, literature and technologies. Groping along behind it, fastened to it by something like a slave coffle, though the loops were snap-linked to their harness rather than their necks, were a hundred Ykx. Another remote and barge, another hundred Ykx, and so it went. The storm outside had calmed a bit as the night latened, but the transfer from howling hell to pastoral serenity was still a shock and the local Ykx (with the help of Zelzony and Lipitero) had to prod the volunteers into clearing the Gate so those coming behind them could get through.

Working swiftly, troubled but not endangered by the rather bewildered old Ever-Hunger, the newcomers flipped on the lights in the wings, activated the bacteria, fed in the yeast that fueled them, stuffed infants and cubs into carrywebs, strapped down the support packs and other gear, snapped on their harnesses and were on their way in less than half an hour, guided by two of the locals fighting hard to control their euphoria in seeing at last so many of their kind.

On and on it went, a steady stream through the narrow Gate; the treads on the remotes and the barges chewed up the grass and took bark off when they were shunted aside once they were empty to make room for the next; the silence and the serenity of the glade was a bit moth-eaten also after hours of this. Skeen was terminally bored, but there was so much noise about, so much agitation and excitement polluting the air that she couldn't sleep; she watched Bohalendas doing his measurements, but she didn't have a clue to what they meant so that was as boring as the rest after a short while; she watched Giulin shift here and there, his young face intent, his energy unflagging as he got images of everyone coming through the Gate, got more images of them winging off, black silhouettes against the blue-violet sky and the thick spray of stars, the rising then setting crescent moon.

About four hours into the transfer, Timka stiffened, then stepped away from the Gatepost and stood staring into the trees. Shortly after that, two Min came round one of the barges near the Gate and stood by the flatbed, watching her, one generously built with gray-streaked brown hair, a round lined face, her large, shapely hands laced together over a solid expanse of stomach, the other small, a cowl drawn forward over the head, shadowing the face, the body hidden by a robe of heavy unbleached linen.

Virgin put her hand on Skeen's knee. An Invisibility whispered in Skeen's ear. "Home folk. Maybe trouble, maybe not."

Timka's back was rigid; her hands were behind her, closed into fists. She was staring (as far as Skeen could tell from the angle of her head) at the little one.

Skeen began digging at the film sealing her darter, cursing under her breath as a fingernail gave, bending back on itself, and bits of the film tore, leaving her with a fragment and the need to dig some more to find an edge she could get hold of and peel away. When the weapon was cleaned off and usable, she looked up.

The Min in the robe had pushed the cowl back, showing a mass of black curls and a strong facial resemblance
to Timka. For a fleeting instant Skeen thought it was
Telka come to challenge her twin, but a second look
convinced her it wasn't. Some relative, though. Her
mother? She never said her mother was dead, only that
she'd gone off somewhere and refused to have anything
to do with her and Telka. Hmm.

The elder Min woman was watching the steady stream
of Ykx coming through the Gate, expanding their wings
and springing into the sky, escorted by constantly re-
cycled guides. The younger (the longer Skeen watched
her the more certain she became this was Timka's mother)
visitor and Timka were engaged in something that looked
like a contest of wills, leaning slightly toward each other,
neither making a sound.

The Invisibility spoke into Skeen's ear. "They're feeling around each other; pair of strange cats, that's what
they are, looking for something to scratch."

Giulin came running around the Gate, intent on new
arrivals. He caught sight of the tableau and stumbled to a
stop. "What's that?"

"Timka's mother and her aunt Carema." A tenor Invisibility, with amusement in its voice. It'd been following Giulin about, enjoying itself offering suggestions and
occasionally being helpful, warning Giulin when he was
about to get himself run over by a remote or its barge,
when he was about to step on a cub or back into a busy
Ykx.

Skeen looked up. "Take a moment to breathe, Giul."

He grinned at her. "Do my breathing tomorrow." He
entered images of the visitors and trotted off.

The tension broke suddenly. Timka's mother laughed,
took a step forward, arms open. Timka laughed, ran into
them. Then they were hugging each other, babbling High-
Min (Skeen could only understand a word in ten, this
was the pure Min tongue, not the corrupt speech called
Trade-Min), weeping, swaying. A moment later they broke
apart, swept Carema into the celebration.

Voice in Skeen's ear. "Reconciliation. All very senti-
mental."

Timka broke the closure on her trousers, stripped them

off, kicked them away, tugged off her tunic and threw it
after the trousers. The other two cast aside their clothing, then the three of them shifted into eagles and in
minutes were dark shapes against the stars vanishing
southward.

The moon set. The night got darker and colder. Skeen
glanced at her ringchron, scowled at the last Ykx as they
came wearily through the Gate. The local Ykx acting as
guides were still smiling and content, but their fur was
roughed about the shoulders, they had reddened eyes
and moved slower. Zelzony stretched and groaned quietly as the last hundred came through and stood gaping
in the sudden coolness. She shook herself and began
unclipping the colonists from the line.

Skeen watched the Ykx wing north, Zelzony and Giulin
winging with them this time. Going to see the Gather,
she thought, one last check. Well, if it was my kin, I'd do
the same. She got to her feet, did a few bends and
stretches to work the kinks out of her body, then started
shuttling the remotes to the Gate. Once they were
otherside, the transport would reacquire them and bring
them home, but this side they were left with only a
minimal program to keep them from running into something. She slapped the first one through and went for the
next.

She was heading for the sixth when an eagle spiraled
down beside her and shifted to Pallah. Timka shivered,
grew a coat of fur. Skeen laced her fingers behind her
head, stretched, yawned. "I didn't know if you'd be
coming back."

"I'm not."

"Oh?"

"Just came to say fare you well, my friend. Lifefire
burn in you longer than the world gives most." Timka
scratched at her ribs. "I'm going to stay a while."

"That your mother?"

"Yes."

"Looked like you. Talking about looks, what's Telka
doing? If she's still around."

"Definitely around. Mintown kicked her out after she

got so many Min killed. So she gathered up what the Hunger left of her lot and took them North. Aunt Carema tells me she's set up a new Town, running it along the lines she wanted to push on Mintown. Remember what I told you about the zecolletros and the Tatt-Habor just before the Sea Min hit us? Well, she's trying to put together a new Tatt-Habor. I suspect she's kept her ties to the Sea Min and their gunja and will be stirring up more trouble for everyone." She spread her hands, sighed. "As long as she keeps clear of me, I don't much care what she does."

"This is it?"

"Don't know. I keep changing my mind every five minutes. Right now I'm staying, tomorrow. . . ."

"You've got quite a few tomorrows to wait before you can cross again. Aalda has to cool down some."

"That I do know. Save me some dithering, won't it. I expect I'll be ready before Aalda is. Ah, well, Mistommerk is a big place; if I get bored at home, I can go see what happened to the Aggitj boys, or ship out with Maggí Solitaire for a while, or visit the Gathers and see how the Ykx are settling in."

A short silence. "If you jump the Gate," Skeen said slowly, "come see me."

Timka chuckled, caught hold of Skeen's hand, squeezed it and dropped it. "Only to say hello, Skeen, only to say hello." She looked up. "Dawn's close. You'll be going soon." She took a step backward. "See you sometime, Skeen." She shifted to the eagle, went spiraling up until she cleared the treetops, then vanished southward.

Skeen scratched at her cheek, raised a brow, then went back to sending the remotes home.

Zelzony and Giulin came winging back, settling beside the last of the barges. Giulin was drooping with fatigue, the Zem-trallen moved with the excessive care of someone refusing to admit she was drunk. She unsnapped the wing harness, let the wing fall to the torn and trampled grass, walked slowly over to Bohalendas who was still working with his instruments. She put a hand on his shoulder, produced a harsh bark of laughter when he jumped. "Time to go."

Skeen looked at her ringchron. "More than time." She
looked around. "Virgin," she called. "Unless you want
to walk . . ."

Whistling bits of birdsong, Virgin came out of the
dark, climbed onto the remote and settled herself on the
bulge of its sensor drum. She ignored the rest of them,
sat there, still whistling, kicking bare heels against the
drum.

Working together, the Ykx and Skeen loaded Bohalendas' instrument cases onto the barge, wrapped themselves against the dust, climbed up beside the cases and
used the lead line to link themselves to the bed so they
could resist the Call. Virgin started the remote rolling,
headed it toward the Gate. Skeen took a last look at the
tranquil scene. She smiled with pleasure at the thought
she was done with Mistommerk, for the moment at least.
As the front end of the barge passed into the Gate, she
dragged on her breathing mask and wrapped her hands
tight about the line.

Tibo swung round. "You look peeled."

"Dusty down there. Let's get out of here."

"Where to?"

"Sundari first, then we'll work it out. Hear that, Pic?"
She pushed her shoulders back, stood yawning and scratching at her ribs as Picarefy flowed smoothly out of orbit.
"Ti-cat stayed below. Came across her mother, wanted
to get to know her again. Where's Ross?"

"Inspecting his take."

She ambled over to him, smoothed her hand over his
head, ran fingertips along the curves of his large pointed
ears. "Just one to go. We can drop him at Sundari.
Djabo, I wish we didn't have to hit back for Rallen, I
could use some R and R. Pic, how you feeling?"

"Worn. Food's low, you might have to go on basic for
a while."

"Fuck."

"I hear you. Transport's made it up, it's on our tail.
We'll be at the limit in five minutes, nothing to bother us
out there, the maulers are drifting, no reinforcements
visible in the flow, seems we've got a clean run for
once."

"We have enough water for a shower?"

"Enough to rinse you off, that's it."

"Then I'd better use the sonic."

"It's only three weeks to Sundari if we hurry."

"We hurry."

Tibo chuckled. He got out of the chair. "Come on. I like the sonic, it inspires me, luv."

"I'm too limp for inspiration right now."

"Well, we'll see."

At the doorway, Skeen twisted her head to look over her shoulder. "Pic, keep Ross off our back, will you, I don't feel like worrying about privacy."

"I hear. Limit one minute off, don't hit the sonic till we transfer."

Skeen waved a hand, yawned again and followed Tibo into the transport tube.

THAT'S IT. STORY'S OVER.

AN EPILOGUE OF SORTS, SKIP IF YOU FEEL LIKE IT.

Abel Cidder.

We leave him with his career balancing on the point of an if. He's fuming and humiliated, plotting new attacks on Skeen, knowing that one more failure might mean he'd be cut loose and left drifting on his own, his power gone.

Fafeyzar.

Not long after the colony transport leaves, he is swept into a spontaneous explosion of rebellion against the Consortium, an explosion triggered by the hope experienced in the rest of the world and denied in Urolol, the clandestine return of those escapees from the slave camps who didn't manage to get on the transport, and to some degree by the prodding of Fafeyzar and his associates. The coms and bugs and other small items Ross sold them help these to gradually gain a measure of control over the explosion and when things settle down, to establish rather precariously something like a participatory democracy where every individual had some say in what the government does, something the other Gurn-sets watch with unease and in one case outright hostility.

Zelzony.

She still doesn't like what's happening, but the Kinravaly keeps her too busy to brood, organizing controls on the new technolgies, setting up

301

oversight boards, drafting laws on the possible invasion of privacy enabled by the devices beginning to flow into Rallen society. The quiet stable society she'd known is changing drastically, but there are no more Burn-deaths; suicides in general have dropped off drastically. There are more killings, though not quite such horrendous ones and Zelzony's ortzala quickly run down and cage the killers, convict and send them down to University where they join the others undergoing study.

Timka.

She and her sister never do meet, Telka uses up her energies whipping her Town into shape and has none left to go after Timka. Timka settles into Mintown for a while, telling her adventures, getting to know her people again, serving as a center of restlessness and disruption until she gets bored as Skeen had predicted, takes off and begins wandering about the world, visiting people and places she'd touched on her hurried drive across the world and back.

Rostico Burn.

Dumped on Sundari, he converts his take to credit and goes off on a roon raid with Henry O.

Skeen and Tibo.

They fill their contracts with the Rallykx without interference from Cidder, retrieve Workhorse, collapse afterward at the Nymph's Navel for some much needed playtime. They are flush with credit and constrained only by the need to keep an eye open for Abel Cidder and his minions.

SO. THERE YOU ARE. CYCLE COMPLETE, A NEW CYCLE BEGINS.

DAW

DAW Presents
The Fantastic Realms of
JO CLAYTON